A LIFE UNINVITED

Praise for *A Life Uninvited*

There are some horrific experiences in life that cannot be softened without diminishing the lessons and values we take from them. Rudy Apodaca's historical novel, *A Life Uninvited*, is an illuminating and brutally honest rendition of the horror of war. Apodaca's account of the atrocities, indignities, indiscriminate deaths, human suffering and sheer terror experienced by his literary characters is overwhelming. The clear message from Apodaca's detailed account of the men who fought and were surrendered as prisoners of war at the battle of Bataan is that their story must be told just as it occurred if the commemoration of these courageous soldiers is to have a true and meaningful purpose. *A Life Uninvited* relates the story that its heroes were unable to express for themselves. God bless them, everyone!

—Arturo L. Jaramillo, author of *Conversations with Quijote* and other anthologies of poetry, published by Sunstone Press.

Rudy Apodaca has done readers (and history) a service by writing an unblinking, highly readable, and well-researched novel about an important and terrible moment in our history. By presenting his protagonist both before his participation in the Bataan Death March and long afterward, as he confronts with his family the inner trauma caused by years of brutal and inhumane treatment as a prisoner under primitive conditions, he greatly enriches our understanding. Through Apodaca's vivid prose, we share the thoughts of the protagonist and the other prisoners and understand the incredible perseverance and strength demanded of them. The novel's narrative will move general readers, and the wealth of accurate detail will satisfy the experts.

—Peter Goodman, newspaper columnist and author of *The Moonlit Path*.

In this marvelous novel, beginning with the account in the foreword of the Bataan Death March, Rudy Apodaca's exceptionally well-told story of a captured New Mexico national guardsman's struggle to survive the horrors of a Japanese prisoner of war camp in the Philippines, as well as the sinking of a torpedoed Japanese naval vessel by an American submarine during World War II, grips the reader early and refuses to let go until the end.

—Bert Goolsby, Author of *Sweet Potato Biscuits and Other Stories*, published by Adams Press.

Kelley Hestir's resin replica (2002) of her *Heroes of Bataan* sculpture unveiled at Veterans Park, Las Cruces, New Mexico on April 13, 2002.

Also by Rudy Apodaca:

The Waxen Image
Pursuit
A Rare Thing
When the Angels Came

A LIFE UNINVITED

A Novel Based on the Untold Story of Bataan in World War II

RUDY APODACA

SUNSTONE
PRESS

SANTA FE

Sunstone books may be purchased for educational, business, or sales promotional use.
For information please write: Special Markets Department, Sunstone Press,
P.O. Box 2321, Santa Fe, New Mexico 87504-2321.
Printed on acid-free paper
∞
eBook: 978-1-61139-780-2

Library of Congress Cataloging-in-Publication Data

Names: Apodaca, Rudy S. author
Title: A life uninvited : a novel based on the untold story of Bataan in
    World War II / Rudy Apodaca.
Description: Santa Fe : Sunstone Press, [2025] | Summary: "The story of a
    prisoner of war in the Philippines during World War II and of his
    struggle to survive events uninvited in his life"-- Provided by
    publisher.
Identifiers: LCCN 2025052854 | ISBN 9781632937810 paperback | ISBN
    9781632937827 hardcover | ISBN 9781611397802 epub
Subjects: LCSH: Bataan Death March, Philippines, 1942--Fiction | Prisoners
    of war--Philippines--Fiction | World War, 1939-1945--Prisoners and
    prisons, Japanese--Fiction | LCGFT: Novels | Historical fiction | War
    fiction
Classification: LCC PS3551.P5 L54 2025 | DDC 813.54--dc23/eng/20251210

LC record available at https://lccn.loc.gov/2025052854

WWW.SUNSTONEPRESS.COM
SUNSTONE PRESS / POST OFFICE BOX 2321 / SANTA FE, NM 87504-2321 /USA
(505) 988-4418

Dedicated in memory of the courageous men of the
200th Coast Artillery, New Mexico National Guard

FOREWORD

This is a work of fiction, but the events on which the story is based are not. They took place in the South Pacific during World War II, and this novel's historical facts are well documented in books and in many military and governmental references available to the public.

The 200th Coast Artillery, a regiment of the New Mexico National Guard, and of which most of the novel's characters in this story were members, was a real military unit existing in the early to mid-1940s.

The men of the 200th, along with thousands of Filipino troops and units from other American military groups, were surrendered to the Japanese on April 9, 1942, by their commanding officer only seven months after the 200th's arrival at the Bataan Peninsula in the Philippines, including four months of fighting. After being forced as prisoners of war to march their way to their camps of imprisonment in what was to become known as the infamous Bataan Death March, they were imprisoned as POWs for over two and one-half years. Many died during the march itself, having been subjected to much cruelty and inhumane treatment.

The march was actually a series of marches from various locations following an 85-mile journey to Camp O'Donnell, their first prison camp, lasting anywhere from five to nine days. The sun, dust, and the brutality of the guards took their toll on the starving, diseased, and thirst-crazed men. Some prisoners fell along the side of the road as sadistic guards hit and kicked them back into the columns.

Those who stumbled or faltered due to their weakness were beaten, shot, bayoneted, and some beheaded. Of the 73,000 POWs who began the march, consisting of 62,000 Filipinos and 11,000 Americans, only 42,000 Filipinos and 9,500 Americans survived to reach Camp O'Donnell. Of those, another 1,500 Americans died at the camp from various diseases, malnutrition, or their injuries. Their bodies were buried in mass, shallow graves.

The surrender of Bataan gave the state of New Mexico the tragic distinction of having the highest number of Americans (per capita, as a percentage of the state's total residents) captured by the Japanese during World War II.

Of the 1841 men of the 200th who began the Bataan Death March, almost half, 819, wouldn't survive imprisonment and return to their homes.

As noted earlier, the historical events related in this narrative are documented, including the Bataan Death March. Another true event was the sinking of the *Shinyo Maru.*

From time to time during the imprisonments, some of the prisoners were transported to labor camps in Japan on vessels known as Japan's "Hell Ships." One of these unmarked ships, the *Shinyo Maru*, carried 750 American POWs in its two cargo holds.

The stench of disease and human feces, as well as the lack of space and stifling heat in the holds, were deplorable, and the prisoners lacked oxygen, as well as food and water, which were lowered in buckets into the holds.

On September 7, 1944, soon after dropping anchor off the coast of Mindanao, an island in the Philippines south of Bataan, the unmarked ship was torpedoed by an American submarine, the *U.S.S Paddle*, believing it carried Japanese troops. Of the 750 prisoners on board, only 82 survived the sinking. One was the protagonist of this story.

As a part of my research for this book, I interviewed some of the ex-POWs who survived the march, the sinking of the *Shinyo Maru*, and the imprisonments in the POW camps. As this is a work of fiction, I haven't used their real names. I've also taken the liberty, for dramatic and creative effect and to move the story along its historical track, of creating dialogue and descriptive narrative that obviously didn't take place but exist only as a part of the creative process.

To move a story along, the writer needs only to imagine what was said or done by those involved in the events as they unfolded or what might have or could have been said or done by the characters as the story takes place. It follows that none of the dialogue or descriptions contained in the novel's narrative should be attributed to any living or deceased persons, ding those I interviewed, but only to my own imagination.

Each Spring, since 1989, the men of the 200th and other POWs who ficed their lives or survived the ordeals of Bataan are honored in an nt now known worldwide, the *Bataan Memorial Death March*, captured idly in this book's cover. The memorial is the setting where the opening pages of this historical novel begin. Thousands upon thousands each year have traveled from throughout the U. S. and other countries to participate in this event. Participants enter the memorial march to walk or jog either a 26.2-mile journey or a 14.2-mile trek, wearing field uniforms and packing equipment.

Each of the prisoners who survived the brutalities during their imprisonment was a living testimony to the human tenacity and the will to survive. This is the story of one of them and of his own struggle to survive events uninvited in his life.

It is a story of triumph over adversity. And it is a story of human frailty, strength, and forgiveness.

ACKNOWLEDGEMENTS

First off, I wish to thank the many individuals who've supported and encouraged me along my writing career, as well as the many readers who've told me they enjoyed the diverse stories and genres I chose to write about in my novels. It's always heartening when a writer, in the telling of a story, succeeds in evoking the emotions of his readers, which I've always believed is the task of the fiction writer.

I want to also thank the individuals who, at my request, read the manuscript of *A Life Uninvited* and provided me with their suggestions, criticisms, and incredible insight, which helped me immeasurably in tightening the plot, story, and theme. Some of them also volunteered to proofread the manuscript for errors and typos, which I found invaluable.

One of those individuals was my wife, Nancy, who has always been my No. 1 supporter, not only by way of encouragement when I needed it but in allowing me to set aside a part of our life as a couple to devote to my writing, which took away from moments of our togetherness for the 58 years of our marriage.

My heartfelt thanks and appreciation to my other manuscript readers, all of them dear friends or relatives: my daughter, Cindy Fox, my grandniece, Kristie Garcia, my *compadre*, Tito Medina, Betty Melragon, Ernest S. Alvarez, and Peter Goodman.

I'm especially grateful for the help I received from the POWs who survived the imprisonments described in the novel and whom I interviewed individually (and especially Mike Pulice, who was fortunate to survive the sinking of the *Shinyo Maru*, the Japanese vessel carrying 750 American POWs, of which only 82 survived the sinking). Mike was especially helpful to me in detailing the horrific events and sufferings during the sinking and the prisoners' desperate attempts to get to shore from the sinking vessel and miraculously escape being gunned down by Japanese soldiers seeking them out in the water. Mike is the only POW I interviewed whose name and character I "borrowed" as a composite in creating the character by a similar name, Jim Puglisi ("Pulga"/the flea), in the novel. The other ex-POWs I thank posthumously are Lorenzo Banegas and Ruben Flores, both lifetime family friends, and Tom Foy, Weldon C. Hamilton, David O. Tellez, Julio Barela, Michael Jovicevic, and David Chavez.

I wish to acknowledge the following references as extremely useful in my developing the storyline of the novel and the use of information, dates, events, and ideas in my accurately creating the plot, characters, and the story's theme and in acquiring an understanding of the events not only surrounding the treatment and imprisonment of the American and Filipino prisoners of war under captivity but during the battles against the Japanese forces before the surrender:

The Fall of the Philippines, part of a U.S. Army in World War II series by Louis Morton (1953), U. S. Army Center of Military History, Department of the Army;

General Wainwright's Story by General Jonathan Wainwright (1946), published by Doubleday & Company, New York, New York;

Shinyo Maru Survivors Reunion Booklet, containing the individual stories of the then-living survivors and compiled by the organizers of an annual reunion held in San Antonio, Texas on September 7, 1998, and attended by the survivors;

The most important reference I found, *Beyond Courage (One Regiment Against Japan, 1941–1945)* by Dorothy Cave. Published by Sunstone Press. Ms. Cave's detailed narrative was especially useful to me in understanding, and my compiling of, the timeline involving the battles described in the novel, as well as some of the events and descriptions of the imprisonments I used in creating the story.

PROLOGUE

WHITE SANDS MISSILE RANGE,
NEW MEXICO, MARCH 2012

Mick Duran, age 92, sat upright, almost stoically, on the front row, one of 16 elderly men sitting as a group on the dais of the Frontier Club. One inch short of reaching six feet, he wasn't especially tall, but, sitting there, he appeared taller than the others. He wasn't slouching, which the others appeared to be. The black hair he possessed as a younger man had now given way to a white/grayish tinge and it was thinner, although his heavy eyebrows had escaped the change in color and thinness. They were still black and full.

The 16 men, former prisoners of war in the Philippines during World War II, were honored guests of the commanding general at the U. S. Army post, a military testing area and firing range consisting of some 3,200 square miles in the desolate desert of southern New Mexico. It sprawled on a flat basin near the foothills of the purplish-blue Organ Mountains to the west and, much farther away, the Sacramento Mountains to the east.

Mick awaited his turn to speak to the large audience, a capacity crowd squeezed into the banquet hall of the club. The building housing the club, in its heyday, used to be the Officers Club, before it, along with all other Officers Clubs at military posts throughout the world, were phased out by the U. S. Army.

Earlier in the day, the honored guests participated in interviews with news media and other events, and at this moment, mid-afternoon, were speaking at the survivors' recognition ceremony. The ceremony was to honor Bataan veterans and their families and participants of the Bataan Memorial Death March, taking place today.

Mick spotted his daughter, Lilia, sitting on the second row of the audience. She smiled at him. He loved her smile. It was the same smile as her mother's, who couldn't smile without a twinkle in her eye. He smiled back for only a split second, shyly aware many eyes were on him. Her smile deepened as a result.

Lilia was 70 years of age, having been born on April 14, 1942, only a week after Mick was taken prisoner by the Japanese. Not until he set foot in the United States in November of 1944 two and a half years after his imprisonment as a POW did he learn his wife had given birth to a daughter.

Lilia also possessed the same dark brown eyes as her mother's. Almost black, they were so dark. She also had the soft, silky hair her mother, also named Lilia, possessed. But she had something her mother didn't—a singing voice. Her mother died seven years ago, in 2005, at age 85. Lilia was christened Carmen Lilia, but soon after entering her teens, she made it clear she wanted to be known as Lilia, despite any confusion it might cause having mother and daughter with the same name. Her parents, of course, obliged her.

The order of the speakers from the group of former POWs had been chosen at random, and Mick was scheduled as the last speaker.

At this moment, Mannie Campos, a resident of Las Cruces and a life-long friend of Mick's, was behind the podium, speaking to the audience.

"I remember the thirst that seemed never to go away," he said over the microphone. "And I was always hungry, and it, too, would never go away. And there was never enough food to go around, not only in the prison camp—Camp O'Donnell, but even before the surrender, when we were with our units, fighting the Japanese troops and trying to stay alive." He paused to catch his breath, then let out a long quivering whiff of air.

"It was no wonder, then, that we—all of us—found ourselves eating weeds, grass, then lizards, then snakes. Finally, even rats. Anything you could get your hands on. We were that desperate.

"There were many senseless beatings I, or the fellow next to me, got if a guard thought we weren't working hard enough in whatever they had ordered us to do. Some guards were that brutal, and those were the ones everyone knew to keep a distance from. Unfortunately, sometimes you couldn't avoid it. A guard suddenly appeared and there you were—unlucky you—taking a beating from his baton. Often, it seemed like you were beaten for no reason at all.

"There was a lot of hard work they would force upon us in the blistering sun, first in the rice paddies, the rice fields. We'd pray even a small cloud would appear, to keep the hot sun away from us, if only for a brief moment. Sometimes they put us to work in the jungle, cutting down bamboo and other greenery and wood they'd use around the camp. This turned out a blessing—a joy we yearned for because the jungles were so thick with trees and brush the sun rarely showed its face on the ground there.

"I remember the countless diseases going around no one could escape—malaria, scurvy, beriberi, diphtheria, and many others. And there was jungle rot, swelling of arms and legs, poor eyesight, teeth falling out, failing eyesight, and the horrible loss of weight. No one could escape that, with what little we were fed. I myself went from a hundred sixty-five pounds to eighty pounds.

"I, along with other prisoners, some who are here today and others I knew, were taken from our work in the camp and put on an old ship to be sent to Japan, where we would be put to work in the factories, farms or some prison camp there, doing hard labor."

He turned around to face the group, his eyes on Mick. "Mick Duran, Jim Puglisi, and Sixto Duarte, here with us today, were on the ship with me when it sank. The *Shinyo Maru*, the vessel was called.

"It was an old clunker the Japanese bought at an auction somewhere, I heard. The Japs put seven hundred and fifty of us in the ship's two cargo holds, where we were so cramped in we had to take turns sleeping on the floor.

"The crew of an American submarine, on seeing a Japanese vessel off the coast of the Philippines, not knowing the ship carried American POWs, sunk it with two torpedoes, and we had to scramble for our lives out of those holds. Of the seven hundred and fifty prisoners onboard, I was fortunate to be one of only eighty-two who escaped the sinking. But as we tried to grab on to a piece of wood or something, trying to swim to shore, the Japanese on small boats sought us out and gunned many who were trying to save themselves.

"To this day, I thank God for being with us during those dark days. I thank Him for allowing me to return to my wife of seventy-two years.

Without my memories of her, which I held onto every day back then, not only in my mind but in my heart, I don't think I would be here with you today. I thank God for our two children and six grandchildren we had upon my return home. Finally, I thank God for this beautiful country of ours and for the freedom we all enjoy living here."

After Campos finished his remarks, an Army staff officer approached the men to inform them another former prisoner might be joining them.

"I don't know if he couldn't make it at the last minute or what," he explained. "We'll just have to wait and see if he gets here."

Mick had no idea what the man was referring to and turned to Campos. "What's he talking about?"

Campos shrugged.

"Ask Pulga," Mick said, motioning to James Puglisi, who was sitting next to Campos. Puglisi was small in stature and was nicknamed Pulga as a child, meaning "flea" in Spanish. The nickname stuck.

Campos turned to Puglisi and spoke to him. Mick didn't hear what Puglisi replied but saw him shake his head.

Campos turned back around and shrugged. "He said he has no idea."

Mick nodded. He was tired, even though the recognition ceremony had begun at three o'clock and it was now only a few minutes before four. He'd be glad when this was over.

It had been a long day. Lilia had driven him on the thirty-minute drive from their home in Las Cruces to the west about twenty miles away and the two of them arrived at the post's command headquarters a few minutes before six am, the time he was instructed to report to register for the activities of the day. Their day was to begin with an opening ceremony at 6:35 in the morning entitled "Their Past, Their Glory, Our Thanks." During the ceremony, held at a soccer field, those who died at Bataan were to be remembered and the survivors honored through reveille, invocation, remarks, and a moving roll call.

On the way to the ceremony at the beginning of their long day, as they began climbing the steepness of U. S. Highways 83-70 East nearing San Augustin Pass at the crest of the Organ Mountains, Lilia was about to turn the car radio off because of static it had picked up, and her father stopped her.

"Hold it," Mick said, "those are The Andrew Sisters."

Lilia looked at him quizzically. "I don't remember the Andrew Sisters. Who are they?"

He grinned. "They were popular back in the day when your mom and I graduated from high school in thirty-eight." Mick enjoyed listening to a local station in Las Cruces that played pop hits from the thirties, forties, and fifties. He had turned the radio on as they left the house.

Lilia grinned. "You're such a sentimentalist, Dad. What about that song? Is it special to you?"

"No, but it was to your mom. It was popular when your mother and I were in school back then. Your mother liked it. It was one of her favorites the year we finished school."

"I can't understand the words, especially with the static. What language is it being sung in?"

"I think it's Yiddish. Or Germanic. The song's title is *Bei Mir Bist Do Shein*. The words mean something like 'To Me, You're Beautiful' or 'You're Grand To Me.' Your mom played it a lot back when we were dating. Had the record, too, playing it all the time."

"It doesn't sound romantic, like something I'd have thought Mom would have liked."

"Those she liked, too, and she had her favorites. Yes, your mother was a romantic, even back then." He turned the radio off, smiling sheepishly. "But you're right, we're picking up static as we near the pass." He switched off the radio.

As they began to travel over the pass, the sky above, without a cloud, was semi-dark this early in the morning, and still shined with seemingly millions of brilliant stars.

The Organ Mountains, so named by one account because its jagged peaks resembled the pipes of an organ in the musical instrument's early years, were the trailing edge of the Rockies, and San Augustin Pass was the name given to the point where the paved highway crossed over the mountains to the eastern side. Many often referred to the pass as "Organ Pass" because of its proximity to the small community of Organ and the name of the mountains.

From the pass, one could look down on the endless miles of barren desert land and rugged terrain on either side of the mountain range as far as the eye could see.

They crossed the pass to the eastern ridge where a strong wind from the northwest hit the car so hard that it shook it from side to side. From there, as they descended, to the right, they could clearly see the mountain range's jagged peaks and solid, purplish-blue rock and below them the lights and white buildings of White Sands Missile Range, set far below the foothills of the high and steep peaks.

"You used to work there, right, Dad," Lilia said, pointing to the base below, "during your early years as an engineer?"

"Yes, for four years, before my work with General Dynamics in California."

"I've hardly set foot on the base. I went there once when I was dating a soldier stationed there several years before getting married. Do you remember?"

Mick thought for a moment. "Yeah, vaguely. I'd forgotten."

"Anyway, I recall his telling me the post and the area in general bored him because there wasn't much to do. He was from back east and was used to the big cities and being around lots of people. He said he felt so isolated here."

"Yes, I'm well aware of people's impressions when they first move here. When I worked there, I'd hear a few of the engineers I worked with, as well as some of the officers and enlisted men stationed there, complain there was little to do on base or in the surrounding communities.

"But it'd often happen a few of them, mostly the career-types, found themselves returning several years later to retire either in Cruces or El Paso."

He smiled. "To me, Lilia, southern New Mexico is God's country. And your mother, by the way, felt this way about the area too."

"I recall her telling me more than once she loved Las Cruces' setting in the valley."

"I enjoy the view of Las Cruces coming by car on the highway from the west, as you hit the ridge of the west mesa, and you see the city below spread in the greenery of the valley and dwarfed by the peaks of the majestic Organ Mountains towering high up in the background."

"I love that view too. The Organs almost look as if painted there, don't they?" Her eyelashes fluttered slightly.

"They certainly do."

She smiled at him, then sighed. "I'm looking forward to these recognition ceremonies, Dad."

He smiled at her. "You are? I'm glad. I've been to so many of them, but every year, I seem to be ready for another one."

"Why haven't you asked me to drive you here before?"

"I've always had a ride with Mannie or someone else. Some relative of the other guys from Cruces usually brought us." He patted her on the shoulder. "But I'm glad you drove me here this time, Lilia. Thank you."

"I'm more than happy to do it, Dad."

It was chilly as Mick and Lilia got out of their car in front of the headquarters building. Each wore a light jacket as they approached the building's entrance. Mick could smell the strong scent of coral honeysuckle in the air as they were about to enter the building. Upon entering, they were ushered into a reception room, where Mick registered and received an identity badge, which Lilia hung around his neck.

Other guests had already arrived or were steadily arriving as Mick and Lilia entered the room. Campos and Puglisi were already there. Mick knew all of them, including Campos, with whom he had grown up since first grade. He knew Puglisi and the others from the Philippines or met them at prior memorial events at the post.

Mick offered to pour Lilia a cup of coffee, but she declined. He poured a cup for himself and took a doughnut from a table of assorted pastries. Lilia couldn't help smiling when he did so, for she knew well his sweet tooth as long as she could remember.

Mick introduced Lilia to the ones she hadn't met before, as they mingled through the crowd, awaiting instructions to board vans that would soon take them to the opening ceremonies at the soccer field.

Today marked the 70th anniversary of the fall of Bataan to the 4th Japanese Army in April of 1942. The march today, aptly named the Bataan Memorial Death March, was the 23rd annual memorial march since the event's inception. Today, a record number of participants, 6,786, from all over the world would be marching, beginning at precisely 7:05 this morning. The start of the march wasn't far from the opening ceremonies, at the intersections of Goddard and Aberdeen Avenues on the southern boundary of the post, near Martin Luther King, Jr. Boulevard, generally marking the southern border of the military post.

Mick hardly had time to finish his coffee and doughnut when everyone was asked to exit the building and enter one of several vans parked outside. Once everyone got in a van, it didn't take long for the ride to the soccer field. When the guests exited the vans, they were ushered to a VIP section of chairs behind a podium located in front of one of the two goals.

Already, the area was bustling with activity, as the march participants, who began arriving at the post as early as 5:00 am, gathered in rows extending as far as the eye could see along Martin Luther King, Jr. Boulevard and beyond.

The field was located alongside Building 1316, known as the Youth Services Teen Center or the Middle Teen Center. The Frontier Club, located on Martin Luther King, Jr. Boulevard, was only about 100 yards from where the opening ceremonies were taking place. The Club would later be used to feed the participants and guests of honor throughout the day.

The memorial march would proceed eastward along MLK, Jr. Boulevard for a few hundred yards, then turn northward along Wesson Street and follow a path past the missile range's main entrance on the north end of the post, which was just south of U. S. Highway 70-82, connecting Las Cruces on the west side of the Organ Mountains to Alamogordo several miles to the northeast, near the base of the Sacramento Mountains.

The march then would proceed several miles northwesterly, moving along a wide, circular path and eventually turning southerly to return to the starting point along a different route, a grueling 26.2-mile journey. The desert here was part of the Chihuahuan Desert, the largest desert in North America. The shrubbery found here were common plants, such as Mesquite, Ocotillo, Sagebrush, Desert Willow, Yucca, Prickly Pear Cactus and Barrel Cactus, and Agave, as well as a variety of grasses, such as black grama and blue grama.

Preparation for the memorial march was a monumental task planned each year under the direction of the Business and Recreation Division of the post's administration, with the coordination and assistance of other administrative personnel at the post.

Extensive plans were essential to prepare for the thousands of participants and spectators expected at today's event. Many spectators had arrived yesterday and would come here today, not only in motor vehicles, minivans, and buses, but also in motor homes and trailers. Post administration permitted these vehicles to enter and set up for camping overnight in a designated area along the western edge of the missile range.

This section of the post had in the past been filled with housing no longer necessary and long ago vacated. The outlines of the old streets and lots, overgrown with weeds, were barely visible. In recent years, the post had decreased considerably in size of its military personnel with the change of its mission, thus not requiring the housing once demanded by the military presence.

Preparatory plans were already in place for a variety of food and beverages to be made available at various locations for both participants and spectators. Food trucks and vans were permitted by the post authorities to be set up by private vendors at various prearranged locations throughout not only along the route of the march but elsewhere on the post for the crowds expected to attend.

For this year's event, planning was necessary to accommodate and allow for the following:

The 6,786 participants; 1,200 volunteers: 148 portable latrines; 10,000 cups for the participants; 100 cases of bananas; 156 cases of powdered Gatorade drink mix; 112 cases of oranges; 12 water points along the 26.2-mile course; 7 water points along the 14.2-mile course; 484 medical volunteers; 10,000 spectators; and 40 credentialed media who would cover the event.

The opening ceremony this crisp spring morning began precisely at the designated time, 6:30 am. There was no question in anyone's mind this was, after all, a military function, where events were expected to start on time. The program went smoothly and ended on time, a few minutes before 7:05 am, when the march was scheduled to begin.

The group was permitted to get up from their seats and visit with one another as they awaited the beginning of the march, before being transported a few minutes before 7:30 am, after the march was to begin, to the Frontier Club for a breakfast buffet awaiting them.

Lilia joined her father as the group stretched and visited again with one another. They visited for several minutes before the opening blast of a cannon alerted everyone the march was about to begin.

After the roar of the cannon, all conversation ceased and the group's attention, as well as the attention of the spectators and the participants, became focused on the beginning of the march.

The march was divided into what were called "flights," about 50 of them. The participants had long ago registered to participate in the march either as a member of a particular team or as individuals, whether they were civilians or members of the military. Today, they had come not only from every state in the United States but from other countries throughout the world. Each had received instructions on when they, as individuals or as a part of a team, were to begin the march, depending on the flight number assigned to them.

Already, from the time the first blast of the cannon was heard, there was a noisy jostling among the participants as they readied themselves for the march, maneuvering into a particular order.

First in line were a group named the Wounded Warriors, followed by Military and Team Heavy, designating the weight of the pack carried. Next followed the National Guard and ROTC Team Heavy, Military Coed Heavy, Military Individual Light, Military and ROTC Team Light, National Guard Team Light, JROTC Light, Military Coed Team Light, Civilian Team Heavy, Civilian Team Light, Civilian Individual Heavy, Civilian Individual Light, and finally, the Honorary Marchers, registered to march the 14.2-mile trek, not the 26.2-mile journey.

As the first flight began the march in rows of four to six participants, the announcer announced through the speaker system for the second flight to get ready. In that manner, three flights were called after a second and third blast of the cannon, before the ex-POWs and their families were asked to walk to the vans to be transported to the Frontier Club for the breakfast buffet.

After finishing their breakfast, the group was informed meals for them and members of their families accompanying them were to be made available throughout the day at the Club. Before disbanding, they were informed they were welcome to attend, and transportation would be provided for, various seminars at the Professional Development Center or the Post Theater, to be held later in the day before and after their attendance at the recognition ceremony in the afternoon.

After a five-minute break following Mannie Campos' remarks, the moderator asked Sixto Duarte, another ex-POW from Las Cruces, to say a few words. Duarte stood up and walked awkwardly up to the podium, where he adjusted the microphone to his height.

When Duarte started his comments, Mick began listening, then tuned him out as he reflected on what had brought him here—his decision to join the New Mexico National Guard, the activation of the 200th Coast

Artillery, a Guard regiment, as a unit of the United States Army, and its eventual deployment in the Philippines. Little would he know what awaited him there within a few months as a prisoner of war.

As he reflected on these memories, in flashes, he thought of his young life at home at the end of 1940, where and when it all began.

PART I

THE FATE IN LIFE

1
CHANGE

LAS CRUCES, NEW MEXICO—DECEMBER 1940

Ever since his engagement to his high school sweetheart, Lilia Contreras, Mick Duran was excited about his future, despite the possibility the country might soon be entering the war in Europe. Although he was now enrolled as a sophomore at the college in Las Cruces, New Mexico College of Agriculture and Mechanic Arts, better known as New Mexico A & M, he just joined the New Mexico National Guard. He was assigned to the 200th Coast Artillery.

What motivated him to join the Guard were rumors the draft law might be extended and students might not be exempt. And, because of the war in Europe, not only were tensions around the world building up, but pressures, too, here at home for this country to enter the war against Germany were mounting. Although a student, Mick wasn't sure his enrollment in college would protect him from the draft, and he heard joining the Guard might do so. He didn't want to interrupt his schooling.

He and Lilia were classmates at Las Cruces Union High School, graduating with the Class of 1938 in May of that year. For a year after graduation, he worked as a laborer for a private contractor constructing Williams Gymnasium on the college campus, before entering the college under scholarship in the Spring semester of 1939 and finishing his freshman year in May of 1940. He was now enrolled in the fall semester, which he hoped to complete in mid-January of the following year.

The 200th Coast Artillery used to be known as the 111th Cavalry, a regiment of horse soldiers. When in existence, the 111th drew the interest of young men, who joined for many reasons, including the chance to have a little extra money in their pockets.

Some youngsters joined mostly for fun or to have something to do and get paid for it. For others not so serious-minded, it was a way to learn to ride horses for free.

But all fun aside, the men of the 111th worked hard at their tasks. Even as late as the late 1930s, they'd report to Fort Bliss, in El Paso, Texas, a short distance from Las Cruces, for training. There, they weren't only trained as horse soldiers but competed with regular cavalry in the U. S. Army.

Historically, New Mexico cavalry units, known back in 1898 as the Territorial Militia, entered service that year for the United States as a squadron of the First United States Cavalry, known as the Rough Riders, to fight in the Spanish-American War. The unit, which gained its fame during that war, consisted of a diverse group, including miners, cowboys, law enforcement officials, and college athletes. The unit fought alongside Teddy Roosevelt in Cuba. For the most part, the New Mexicans fought as infantry men.

The Rough Riders participated in the Battle of Las Guasimas, where they drove back the Spanish forces as they struggled to gain control of crucial territory in the heights of Santiago, known as San Juan Hill. They also fought in the battle that followed, the Battle of San Juan Hill, a pivotal battle because it gained control of the heights overlooking Santiago after the Rough Riders had secured the hill.

Some historians believe the battle was one of the main reasons why the Spaniards surrendered two weeks later. It also played a crucial role in the subsequent treaty giving the U. S. control over Guam, Puerto Rico, and the Philippines.

The Rough Riders' actions in Cuba, mostly because of the victory at San Juan Hill, propelled Roosevelt as a national hero, which in turn helped him gain the presidency in 1904 and the award of the Medal of Honor posthumously in 2001 for his "conspicuous gallantry and intrepidity" during the charge up San Juan Hill.

But in time, changes soon became necessary for New Mexico's calvary units. Horses, most in the military believed, were going out of style. The 111th moved on with the times. In April of 1940, it became first, the 207th Coast Artillery. But soon after the change, it was learned the "207th" designation was already in existence. The 207th, within months, became the 200th Coast Artillery, much later to be nicknamed by its men, the "Old Two Hon'erd."

As the 200th would eventually grow to a strength of about 1,800 men, to some, its membership were referred to as an assortment of "Mexicans, Anglos, and Indians." It was true a few Native Americans made up a small part of the regiment and over half of the unit's 1,800 men were Mexican American. But such distinctions didn't matter to the men, for they considered themselves brothers.

The Mexican Americans in the unit referred to all of the members of the 200th as *compadres*, the Spanish word for friends, pals, or buddies. On the outside, they may have been college students, lawyers, athletes and even farmers or ranchers, but in the 200th, they were all *compadres*.

Having been trained in the past as horse soldiers, the men of the new regiment were soon sent to a three-month course at an artillery school in Virginia, to train as anti-aircraft artillery gunners.

World events also changed, ever since Japan had joined the Axis in August of 1940, and it appeared the war in Europe was not going to end soon.

In September, the 200th was federalized and called to active duty, the threat of war still growing. Before Christmas, soon after Mick joined the Guard, word was spreading the 200th was going to be activated as a unit in the United States Army. Sure enough, on January 6, 1941, the 200th was officially activated and became a part of the U. S. Army, and its two battalions, Battalion A and Battalion B, were ordered to Fort Bliss, Texas for training in artillery gunnery.

Mick got word of the regiment's activation the next day, a Monday, and he drove immediately to Lilia's parents' house to break the news to Lilia. She was in her bedroom, listening to one of her favorite records from the past year on her record player, Glenn Miller's *Moonlight Serenade*, when Mick knocked on her door. She left the music on as she opened the door.

"Mick!" she said, surprised. "What's wrong?" She could see the distraught look in his eyes.

Mick broke the news without closing the door. "The Guard's been activated. I'm in the U. S. Army now!"

"Here, sit down." She gestured to the bed. "It's not as if you hadn't heard it was happening."

"But it's different now. I mean, knowing it's happening. And what about our plans to get married, Lilia? And my schooling?"

This event would definitely change the lives of Mick and Lilia, who already were planning a wedding set for June of 1941, soon after Mick would have finished his second year at the college.

Within two weeks of breaking the news to Lilia, Mick found himself with his unit, training and living at Fort Bliss. Mick's plans to enroll for the spring semester at the college were disrupted because the day-to-day training at Fort Bliss wouldn't allow him to attend classes some 40 miles away in Las Cruces. Luckily, he was able to rearrange his final exams scheduled in January of 1941 and was permitted to make up for classes missed after he had to report to Fort Bliss the third week of January.

By the third week of training, strong rumors among the men of the 200th began to surface that after training, sometime before the end of the year, the 200th was to be assigned to duty overseas, destination unknown. During those three weeks, Mick hadn't found the time to travel to Las Cruces to be with Lilia. Instead, on the two weekends Mick found himself with a few hours, Lilia made the trips to Fort Bliss to spend time with him. On each Saturday of those two weekends, they dined at two restaurants in El Paso and were able to enjoy a movie afterward both times.

After the unit's first three months of training, the men were granted two weekend passes every month, including both Saturdays and Sundays. Although most of the men used the time to go home to visit their families, some stayed to visit their favorite hangouts for fun in Juarez, Mexico, just across the border from El Paso. There, a soldier, whose pay was low by civilian standards, could find drinks, entertainment, and food at restaurants a lot cheaper than in El Paso.

Mick took advantage of those free weekends to spend the time with Lilia at home. Because they knew in a few months, Mick would be gone, most likely, if the rumors turned out to be true, to an assignment overseas, they decided to get married sooner than planned. At first, they spoke of plans to elope without telling their parents, once they applied for a marriage license, but in the end, neither felt good not including their parents in the ceremony.

In the end, the two of them, together, broke the news to their parents, whom they had brought together at Mick's parents' house for such a purpose. They announced they wanted to get married as soon as possible.

When Mick suggested a small ceremony at home, conducted by a Justice of the Peace, a local magistrate authorized to perform marriages, neither Lilia's nor Mick's mother would hear of such a thing. Both families were Catholic.

"*No, mijita*, No, my child," Lilia's mother said, addressing both Mick and Lilia, "that will simply not do. You must get married in a church by a priest." She spoke loud enough to be heard over the music playing on the radio in the background, Artie Shaw's orchestra playing *Stardust*.

Mick walked over to the radio to turn down the volume.

"Just turn it *off*, *mijo*," Mick's mother said to Mick.

"It's okay, Mom," he said. "I turned it down."

She turned to Lilia. "For certain, Lilia, this is the only way," Mick's mother said.

"But that'll take too much time," Mick protested.

"And time, you have."

"I'll be at Bliss for several more months of training, *Mama. No se puede ser. No tengo tiempo*. It can't be done. I don't have time."

"*No, mijo, tiene que ser un casorio en la Iglesia Catolica*. No, son, it has to be a wedding in the Catholic Church."

"Lilia and we can do it," Lilia's mother volunteered. "We can meet with the priest and make all the arrangements. All you'll have to do is arrange to meet with the priest, you and Lilia together, a few times, which is required before the wedding vows are permitted."

Mick knew better than to argue with both mothers; their wedding plans were to be made according to their wishes.

Arrangements were made with Father Gregory McCarthy at St. Genevieve's Catholic Church for a small ceremony to which only the family members and a few close friends of both Lilia and Mick were invited. The day set was Tuesday, May 20.

When Mick's mother learned Lilia and Mick had picked a Tuesday to marry, Lilia's mother, although not superstitious, told Lilia her grandmother, Lilia's great grandmother, was extremely superstitious and had told her, just before Lilia's mother made her own wedding plans, not to marry on a Tuesday, admonishing her, "*En martes ni te cases ni embarques*," meaning in Spanish, "On Tuesday, neither get married nor embark."

Lilia had planned to be a June bride but would now have to settle for being a May bride. Both Mick's and Lilia's mothers made plans for a small reception at Mick's parents' house after the ceremony.

Both families pitched in for the newly married couple to enjoy a three-day honeymoon trip to Ruidoso during a weekend. Mick was surprised his commander obtained the necessary approval for a four-day leave, which gave him enough time for the trip to Ruidoso and back. The day following his return, he returned to his training at Fort Bliss.

Since Mick's training wouldn't be completed until the middle of August and it was estimated the 200th wouldn't be leaving for its overseas assignment until sometime in September, Mick and Lilia decided to accept Mick's parents' offer for them to live in their home. Mick's sister married the prior year and moved out of the house, leaving enough space for Mick and Lilia to live comfortably with Mick's parents. The arrangement was easier than trying to find a furnished apartment or house to rent for only a few months.

One day in the first week of August, Mick's time at home on a weekend was extended to three days because Monday was a holiday. On Saturday afternoon of the weekend, he and Lilia were sitting out in the gazebo in his parents' back yard. Mick's parents had gone shopping, and Mick and Lilia had the house all to themselves.

With his father's help, Mick had built the gazebo for his parents. He learned carpentry both in junior high and high school, having taken shop classes in both schools. He also got additional training working during the summers as an apprentice to a carpenter who worked for a local contractor building houses.

Carpentry wasn't his only creative talent. Even as a child, one would find him sketching or drawing in pencil. As a youngster, he'd find whatever piece of paper was available and begin to draw. He was good at drawing landscapes but was good at drawing people, too, especially portraits. Because drawing and sketching came natural to him, he took advantage of the art classes available in the schools, and he enrolled in them.

Sitting in the gazebo, Mick and Lilia enjoyed the cool breeze blowing through the mulberry trees from the northwest. A Jasmine shrub on the yard's corner in back of the gazebo was in full bloom, its flowers' strong and sweet fragrance filling the air. Just enjoying each other's company, neither had spoken for a minute after sitting down. Mick noticed earlier in the day Lilia was especially quiet throughout the morning.

Finally, he spoke. "I've noticed you've hardly said a word all day. Got something on your mind?"

She turned to him and smiled, pursing her lips. "Yes, I've been trying to find the right time to tell you when we were alone."

"Tell me what? Is something wrong?" He'd been resting against the back of his lounging chair and now sat erect, waiting for Lilia to reply.

"No, nothing's wrong." A slight frown appeared. "It's something important to us, but the timing may not be right." Her frown turned to a smile. "But I hope it'll make you happy."

Mick stood up and walked up to her. "What is it, Lilia? Don't keep me in suspense, please."

"I think I may be pregnant." She smiled again, faintly at first, then she grinned. "Is it okay to you if I am? It is to *me*."

He knelt down in front of her and took her two hands in his. He grinned. "Of course it's okay with me, silly girl. I'm ecstatic!"

Tears appeared in her eyes.

"How sure are you?" he said.

"Fairly sure. I missed my period last month."

"Have you been to a doctor?"

She wiped the tears running down her cheeks with a Kleenex she pulled out of a pocket. "No, not yet, but I've made an appointment. It's set for next week."

"I'll go with you. Is it okay?"

"Of course, silly. I'd want you to." She gave him a serious look. "But I wasn't sure this was good news because of everything else going on in our lives."

"No, no, Lilia. It's definitely good news. I'm thrilled, actually."

"I'm glad you are. I am, too, but was a bit worried with all that's happening. After all, you're going away soon."

"That'll be okay. It's a happy occasion to celebrate. He grinned and stood up, still holding her hands. "I heard Mom and Dad arrive a moment ago. Let's go break the news to them."

They entered the house and told Mick's parents their good news. As expected, they, too, were happy.

The visit to the doctor's office the following week didn't confirm the pregnancy, and the doctor thought it was too early to tell, based on Lilia's last menstrual period. But tests ordered later by the doctor following Lilia's visit confirmed her pregnancy. The doctor set the due date for April 14 of the following year.

Although Mick was happy he and Lilia were indeed going to have a baby, during his hours of training, he pondered the thought of leaving Lilia alone to have their child. He should be with her, he thought, now, more than ever. He suddenly resented the 200th's activation into the U.S. Army. As a result, he sensed an overwhelming anger come over him.

He was in a trap. And there didn't seem to be anything he could do to get out of it. They were both trapped, and he was responsible for bringing Lilia into it.

"Things just aren't going the way I thought they would when I signed up for the Guard," he said out loud to himself.

The more he explored his feelings, he suddenly realized a sense of guilt growing alongside his anger and resentment.

Wasn't he being disloyal? To the oath he had taken when enlisting in the Guard? To his country, which activated the 200th as a part of building up its armed forces in case the country entered the war?

2

ADAPTATION

The following weekend, back at home, Mick found the time to talk to Lilia about his feelings. Once again, they were sitting out in the gazebo on Sunday, enjoying a beautiful and sunny afternoon listening to music over a radio Mick's father installed in the gazebo. The sweet scent of the Jasmine wasn't as strong this afternoon, probably because a strong breeze was moving it away.

Mick would soon be leaving to return to Fort Bliss later in the day for his training first thing Monday morning.

"That's such a beautiful song," Lilia said. Tommy Dorsey's Orchestra was playing *I'll Never Smile Again*.

"It *is* beautiful," Mick agreed, "but *sad* also."

"Yes, it's that too." She frowned a bit. "Can you imagine what it'd be like, to feel you can't smile ever again."

"You'd have to be feeling truly sad to feel that way, for sure," Mick said with a wide grin.

She nudged him hard on his shoulder. "Be a romantic, for once in your life, *Mick Duran*."

"I thought I was one." He hugged her, then kissed her on the forehead.

They sat there without a word, listening until the song came to an end.

When the tune finished, Lilia asked Mick to tell her what his past week was like. To show her interest, she always made it a point to ask him about his training, and he enjoyed explaining to her what his group was doing in a particular week and how the training was coming along.

After telling her how his past week had gone, he thought he'd take the opportunity to tell her about the resentment and anger he'd been feeling for quite a while now. He finally realized he hadn't been fully aware of the resentment and anger building up within him until after he learned Lilia was going to have a child. He also told her about his guilt.

They were sitting on a loveseat, and she moved up close to him. A sudden breeze came through the yard, rustling the tree leaves above.

"But why feel guilty, Mick? I understand why you resent and even feel angry about having to leave home once we learned about the baby, but you shouldn't feel guilty about it."

"But I do!" He explained he felt he was being disloyal to the oath he took when he joined the Guard and now as a soldier in the U. S. Army.

"And you shouldn't. You're not being disloyal to your country. First of all, you were being loyal to your country when you joined the Guard. When called upon, you reported for training at Fort Bliss. You're fulfilling your duty and oath as a soldier. If that isn't loyalty, what is?"

He looked into her eyes, then displayed a slight grin. "I've never seen you get so emotional, babe."

She laughed, and Mick quickly joined in her laughter.

As soon as they stopped laughing, he said, "You've covered the guilt part. What about my resentment and anger?"

"That's what I meant when I said you shouldn't feel guilty. Your resentment and anger are perfectly justified. It's easy to understand your feelings under our circumstances. In a way, it's natural. But it doesn't mean those feelings are justified."

"That's what I've tried to tell myself, and it helps for a while, but then they resurface. Those damn negative feelings start all over again."

She took his hands and held them to her breast. "You know what, Mick, you know I'm going to be supportive as your wife, but possibly a little biased. Not too objective."

She paused in thought, then continued. "Why don't you pay a visit to Father McCarthy. You've gotten along with him since he was assigned as associate pastor at St. Genevieve's. I think you should go talk to him about this. He'll give you some wise advice. And it'd be objective."

Mick pondered the thought. He nodded. "You know, Lilia, that's a great idea. I'll do it. I'll give him a call later. Possibly, he's available this evening."

"Maybe you could go see him before you leave tonight."

He gave her a big hug. "I'm glad I mentioned this to you today. I thought you should know about it."

"I'm glad you brought it up. I would've been unhappy if you hadn't." She gave him a bright smile. "I love you, Mick, with all my heart."

He looked into her eyes. "And I love you too." He kissed her on her cheek, and she kissed him on his mouth.

Later in the day, after Mick and Lilia sat in the living room chatting with Mick's mom and dad, Mick excused himself and telephoned Father McCarthy. It relieved him to hear the priest say he could see him early in the evening. It'd give Mick plenty of time for his drive to Fort Bliss before having to report at his headquarters.

Father McCarthy was a little out of breath when he answered the phone and explained he'd just returned to the rectory from playing a short game of basketball at the outdoor basketball court next to the church. Mick wasn't surprised, for he himself had played one-on-one basketball with the priest on several occasions.

Later in the day, after having enjoyed Sunday dinner with Lilia and his parents, Mick took the short walk to St. Genevieve's. He was glad when Father McCarthy ushered him into the main rectory office for their visit, instead of his own, private office, which was rather small in comparison. Mick found the smaller office a bit cramped when he visited the priest there in the past.

After a few words of small talk, with each catching up with the other's life and laughing often, Father McCarthy cleared his throat and spoke.

"Tell me, Mick," he began in a serious tone, "what's going on with you that you think requires consulting your parish priest? I spoke to your mom this morning after mass, and she happened to break the news to me Lilia's expecting. I believe she said the expected due date is sometime next April. Is that what this is about?"

Mick displayed a wide grin. "Well, indirectly."

"Congratulations, by the way. And please congratulate Lilia. I wish both you well with her pregnancy and will pray for you all goes well and Lilia will give birth to a healthy baby."

"Thanks, Father. I'll pass on your congratulations to her."

The priest smiled. "I wish you'd address me as 'Jerome,' Mick. I've just turned 30, not much older than you are, and, after all, you and I play basketball with each other." He grinned.

"I know, I know. But I feel I owe you the respect your position as associate pastor deserves from all parishioners, including me, whether we know each other personally or not. I've always addressed priests that way. It's how I was taught."

Father McCarthy smiled. "I fully understand. Tell me, what gives?"

Mick went on to tell the priest the negative feelings he was experiencing, especially since he and Lilia learned of her pregnancy. He spoke of his anger and resentment, which he'd been feeling for even before he learned Lilia was pregnant, and finally, he explained the guilt he'd been experiencing, all of which were affecting his work at Fort Bliss and even his life at home with Lilia and his parents. He also related his talk with Lilia and what she had said to him.

The priest kept nodding as Mick spoke. When Mick finished, Father McCarthy broke into a smile. "Well, for openers, I agree with everything you told me Lilia said. I've always found most women, no matter their age, are wise in these matters of the heart."

Nodding, Mick replied, "I agree Lilia's bright. She's been wise since I knew her in high school. That's one of the qualities I found attracted me to her."

Father McCarthy grinned. "You're showing you're wise, yourself, Mick."

They both laughed.

"Thanks, Father. But to go on, although I felt Lilia made a lot of sense, she thought I should get your opinion." He paused in thought. "I understood all that Lilia was telling me, but it's one thing to comprehend the logic and rationale behind what's said but another to allow for the reasoning to affect or change one's feelings, especially when they're strong, as mine are."

"Specifically, you're speaking of the resentment and anger you've been feeling?"

"Yes, Father. And my guilt."

"Yes, of course, your guilt." He paused with a soft sigh. "I think Lilia was right on both counts. Your guilt is unjustified. You're being too hard on yourself in that regard. As I understand from what you've told me, your guilt is predicated on what you believe is your disloyalty to your country for feeling resentful and angry your commitment is taking you away from home and your family. That's especially true now that you feel Lilia will need you during her pregnancy and in raising a child you won't be here to help raise."

"Yes, I think that's a good way to put it. And I should add it makes me appear a bit selfish."

"That last part comes with the territory, I think. And I'll add one other thought I think enters into the mix of why you might be feeling some guilt in all this. I think your guilt might be caused by something else."

"Oh. What do you mean?"

"You might be feeling guilty because of the commitment you made when joining the National Guard. You're thinking of yourself as the cause of what's suddenly happening to you and Lilia."

"How so? I don't quite understand."

"I think you believe by committing to the National Guard, you set in motion a string of events, including your unit being made a part of the Army, which has brought you to this point in your life when you're having to leave Lilia at a bad time.

"It has to do with 'cause and effect,' I think. I want you carefully to think about this, not only now, but when you go home and think about your problem some more. It might be because you committed yourself to the National Guard, the commitment has brought about not only your unit being activated into the Army but the possibility you may be assigned to duty outside the country, taking you away from your family and Lilia, especially now that she's with child." He paused and gave Mick a serious look. "What do you think?"

Mick didn't say anything for a moment, trying to take in everything Father McCarthy was saying.

Finally, he said, "I think you might be right, Father." He nodded to himself. "I hadn't thought of it in that way. I'll think seriously about what you've said, for sure."

"And when you give the matter more thought, bear in mind, Mick, many of us are forever wrongly blaming ourselves for consequences in life we believe are caused by our actions. Often, our actions or words bring about certain events we may take responsibility for, even when there's no way we can predict or know what those consequences may be."

"But we should be held responsible for the consequences of our actions."

"Not necessarily, Mick. Think about it. As I suggested before, there are some things in life we can't foresee, we can't predict, even if we're the ones who set in motion the events causing those things to happen. It's not reasonable for us to be held responsible for everything happening on down the line."

"What you say makes a lot of sense, Father. I guess maybe I've been doing just what you said. It's something to think about."

"As an aside, Mick, in my studies for the priesthood, I learned a little something about the law. In the field of negligence law, I learned to hold someone responsible for, let us say, a car accident, the law of liability requires foreseeability as a factor before holding someone liable for the damages or injuries caused by a car collision. It's known as 'proximate cause.'"

He sighed, then smiled. "But I'm getting a little too technical. Just bear in mind what I said about your feeling guilty possibly because you believe you brought about what's happening to you and Lilia. I think, as Lilia obviously does, you're being much too hard on yourself."

"You've given me good advice, Father. I very much appreciate your time." He looked at his watch. "I've overstayed my welcome, I think." He stood up.

"Not at all, Mick. I hope I've been of some help to you in sorting things out." He stood up and walked around the desk.

"You've been a great help to me. I thank you." He held out his hand with a grin, and the two shook hands.

"And don't stay away too long. It's been a while since we played a game of one-on-one."

Mick laughed as he walked to the door. "Let's do it next time I come home some weekend from Bliss."

They walked out of the office and into the small hallway leading to the door to the outside courtyard. The sweet smell of flowers blooming in the garden filled the air as they exited the rectory.

"I'll be waiting to get a call from you," Father McCarthy said as they shook hands again outside the door. "And I'll take the time to sharpen my skills. I think you won the last time we played."

"Did I? I don't remember."

"I do. You won, fair and square. I'll be gunning for you."

They laughed, then Mick walked down the short steps from the porch onto the courtyard, as the priest closed the door.

There was considerable worldwide activity during the closing weeks of the 200th's training before the end of summer. In April, the Soviet Union and Japan signed a neutrality pact; in May, a German U-boat torpedoed the SS Robin Moor, a United States cargo steamship, even though the U. S. hadn't entered the war in Europe; in June, Germany invaded Russia. In July, Japanese troops landed in Indochina, and the day following, the U. S. froze all Japanese assets in this country, with Great Britain and the Netherlands soon following.

Still, rumors circulated about the 200th's first mission after training. Some were saying the regiment was bound for Samoa. Others said Alaska was its destination. There were some predicting they were going to the Philippines. But even the commanders of the Guard or the 200th weren't certain of the regiment's destination.

At the end of their training, the men of the 200th heard some good news. After traveling through the United States rating every antiaircraft unit in the country, a high-ranking group of U. S. Army officials named the 200th as the best anti-aircraft regiment in the United States Armed Forces in 1941. With that bit of good news, the men of the 200th were ready and eager to leave, no matter where its mission might be.

Because regular U. S. Army units rigorously worked hard to be the best of the best, some of them reacted negatively to the citation of the 200th being rated the best anti-aircraft unit in the country.

Trains would take the 200th to San Francisco, where they were to board a vessel to who knew where.

As for Mick, who disliked goodbyes, he readied himself nonetheless to say farewell to his beloved Lilia and his proud parents, his married sister and her family, and a multitude of aunts, uncles, and cousins. He paid a special visit to Father McCarthy and asked for his blessing. Because of Mick's work schedule, they hadn't gotten a chance to play basketball. Afterward, Mick and Lilia spent many hours together as the men of 200th awaited sailing orders.

Finally, on the second week of September, Mick's parents and Lilia accompanied Mick to the train depot in Las Cruces, where he was scheduled to embark for transport to the El Paso Train Station for the long trip to San Francisco. Mick's mother was in tears, as was Lilia, although hers were more subdued. Even Mick's father shed some tears. Witnessing such emotion, Mick couldn't help himself and got teary-eyed as he hugged his parents and Lilia several times before boarding the train.

On September 16, the 200th boarded the *USAT Willard A. Holbrook*, a converted passenger ship. Its former lounges were filled with double deck army cots for the regiment's men. On board, the men heard further rumors they were headed, first, to Alaska, then to Hawaii, then to some unknown island in the Pacific. It wasn't until the vessel arrived at Honolulu, Hawaii the men learned of their true destination—the Philippines, a place some of them, having been raised in small communities or farms, never heard of.

3
THE ARRIVAL

MANILLA BAY, THE PHILIPPINES, SEPTEMBER 1941

After logging over 6,000 miles across the Pacific from San Francisco, the *USAT Willard A. Holbrook* sailed through the Philippine Sea as it neared its destination. On September 26, ten days after its departure from San Francisco Bay, it was a bright sunny afternoon as the vessel entered the port at Manila Bay, in southern Luzon, the largest island of the Philippines.

The Japanese were known to be patrolling the Pacific for many months, ever since Japan joined the Axis, and, as a precaution, the vessel sailed most of the way in what was known as a "black out," and with an American cruiser escorting them out of Hawaii. Periodically, a reconnaissance plane from the escort ship scouted the skies and the seas from above.

Once the vessel passed the island of Mindoro, the southern tip of the Philippines, on the right, the ship's entry into the bay proved a unique experience for the men of the 200th. What first attracted them, even as some scanned what was to be their new home only from the limited view through the portholes, was the overwhelming greenery surrounding Manila Bay. As dwellers of the desert landscapes and flat terrains of New Mexico, never had they seen such vegetation as existed around the bay, except in the state's forests, which were mostly uninhabited.

Those observing the bay from the deck railings could see clearly the Bataan Peninsula to the west as the *Willard* approached the docking area. The numerous docking ports of the bay were packed with boats of all sizes, large and small, the big boats farther away. Surprisingly, the smaller boats were nearer to where the *Willard* was approaching the pier to dock.

A few sailboats were buoyed on the water away from the docks, leaving the other small boats powered by engines along the docks. Most of the smaller boats were fishing boats, with dozens of fishermen hurrying around them. The boats obviously had just returned with their catches, thus explaining the bustling activity visible throughout the docks, as the fishermen's hauls were moved into containers and then onto trucks to be transported to the markets.

The deep blue sky above them was filled with squawking sea gulls, attracted by the fish being hauled off the fishing boats.

Beyond the docks were the buildings in what was evidently a business or commercial district, with people on foot moving about through the streets and in and out of places of businesses and stores. Most were shoppers carrying bundles and packages of goods they had obviously just purchased. The men found the variety of colors everywhere fascinating, first on the fishing vessels and then on the buildings and the clothing of the persons moving about at a fast pace doing their business.

Their dress was richly colorful, especially of the women, who wore dresses and skirts of extremely bright colors worn leisurely. Even the men's shirts possessed an assortment of vivid shades. The stuccoed buildings, too, were of different colors and shades—yellows, greens, blues, and an occasional white or beige.

"Reminds me of Juarez," Charlie Atkins said to Mick, as the two men viewed the busy scenery from the upper deck railing. Mick had known Atkins from grade school.

"Yeah, you're right," Mick said, "except for all the water. And look at the narrow streets leading away from the docks. Just like in Juarez."

"What's not like Juarez, though," Pete Graciano added, "is this stifling air around us." He scowled. "It's humid as hell here." Graciano, standing along the rail on the other side of Atkins, was from Lordsburg, who Mick hardly knew.

"Yeah," Atkins added, "but I already knew it was muggy here. But the heat, along with the humidity, makes it more suffocating." He wiped the beads of moisture on his forehead with the back of his bare hand.

Within minutes of docking, some of the men, loaded with their duffel bags and whatever other gear they could carry, were already at the top of the gangplank, ready to go offboard. As soon as the gangplank was secured at the bottom, the first of the men, Mick included, were allowed to walk on down.

Even before the first soldier had set foot on the dock, Filipinos, who had gathered to watch the American soldiers disembark, began to shout, greeting them to their homeland. They were a noisy crowd, conversing with one another as they welcomed the Americans with rollicking cheers and loud applause.

"Hi, G. I Joe," one called out from the bunch.

"Welcome to Manila," another shouted.

"It's God's country!" someone else yelled.

"God's country, my ass," said Graciano. "With this goddamn moisture!"

There were many children, most of them in groups, among the large crowd. "Welcome, American soldiers!" one of them yelled.

As he stepped off the gangplank, Mick thought he heard an adult Filipino yell above the noise of the crowd, "You suckers!"

Mick wondered, was the yell an indication of what lay ahead of them or even a suggestion they've been deceived about some sort of paradise awaiting them.

The line of soldiers disembarking maneuvered through the throng, led by one of the staff sergeants who greeted the first group on deck and called out to the next group to follow. The sergeant led them away from the docking area along a narrow street leading them to a wider street. In this broader avenue, Army convoy trucks lined one side of the street for as far as one could see as the street curved to the left. The convoy would take them to Fort Stotsenberg, their new home, not too far from Manila.

The men who entered the broad street first, which included Mick, were instructed to board the first and second trucks. When the first truck was full, it took off for Stotsenberg, and other soldiers already began boarding the second and third trucks. The trucks continued to move at a tortoise's pace to the front, where others began boarding them. In that manner, all of the men of the 200th left Manilla to arrive at Stotsenberg, where they would both live and work.

Fort Stotsenberg was adjacent to Clark Field, an airfield, which the men of the 200th would soon learn was their mission to guard and protect against an enemy invasion.

As the men arrived at headquarters from their short trip, they were assigned to barracks. They were instructed to unpack their belongings and sit tight until they received further instructions for orientation and indoctrination into the camp environment.

The barracks the men would live and sleep in had been built within a semi-secluded area of the post to allow for some privacy. Some were constructed of plaster board and wood framing but most were made of Sawali, a type of bamboo grown in the Philippines. The structures stood on pilasters, a few feet off the ground, with windows shuttered to protect from the heavy rains sweeping through the region regularly, which the occupants would soon find out for themselves.

Once the soldiers settled down in their quarters, it didn't take long for them to find native Filipino youngsters, for a few pesos a month, could be hired as houseboys. These youths were eager to perform a multitude of tasks. They shined shoes, made beds, picked up the soldiers' dirty clothes, got them washed, and returned them starched and pressed.

Mostly the officers, who earned much more than the enlisted men, were the ones who could afford such luxuries. But once in a while, a corporal or private would find themselves with a little extra spending money to benefit from the cheap labor.

Carabaos, or water buffalos, animals resembling oxen, roamed in abundance in the Philippines. They wallowed in creeks and ponds, especially muddy pools. They had a peculiar smell they left in whatever they moved around in, especially in water. Most of the dirty clothes picked up by houseboys were washed in the creeks and streams, and when the clothes were returned starched and pressed, they carried with them the odor of Carabao, which the soldiers learned to get used to.

It didn't take long for the post's new residents to explore their surroundings, even places at some distance from the post. Climbing Mount Pinatubo was a feature soon to become popular for most of the soldiers. The steep mountain proved to be somewhat of a challenge to climb. At the top, if the men reached it, they could sign a notebook showing the date of their climb. The notebook was on top of a rock cairn piled high on up and protected from the elements by an encasement built with small rocks.

The officers of the 200th soon complained they found the Officers Club on post a bit highfalutin and overly restrictive. The club required members to change uniforms twice in a day, wearing whites in the evening, even to visit the bar/lounge, not the dining room. Members were also required to wear shorts for tennis. Aside from the dress code, the Guard officers felt the officers from the regular army looked down upon them because they were originally National Guard officers before being brought into the Army upon activation months before. As a result, the men of the 200th frequented the Army-Navy Club in Manila, which they found more welcoming and relaxing.

Within two weeks of the 200th's arrival at Fort Stotsenberg, a group of nurses arrived, some of them whom the men knew from Fort Bliss. They put up quarters at Fort McKinley, although they were assigned to work throughout the area, including the clinics and hospital at Fort Stotsenberg. Every chance they'd get, the enlisted men would rush to Fort McKinley to party with the nurses. Although invited by the men often to join them, Mick would decline and instead occupy himself with some chores or a movie, and often writing to Lilia, who wrote to him most every day.

Mick was surprised at the speed and efficiency with which the post office on the post handled both outgoing and incoming mail. The internal network in the mail system within his unit also apparently handled the mail without undue delay, it seemed to him.

He was especially happy Lilia wrote to him often, sometimes every day. He kept track in his head of dates or days when he mailed a letter to her and the date of her response. It seemed to him only a matter of a week or at most ten days went by between the day he sent her a letter and the day she received it. He calculated the same result with how long it took for a letter from her to reach him.

Telephone communication weren't especially great in the Philippines or even in Fort Stotsenberg, which relied on the telephone companies in Manila to provide service. For that reason, placing or getting a call to or from the United States was practically nonexistent. Mick relied on mail service to stay in contact with his small world back home.

And that's why he was glad to receive Lilia's letters. She and his parents were practically his only link to the outside world. Lilia was a great letter writer and would tell him bits and pieces of everything going on in Las Cruces, the state, and the country.

She knew he was interested in any news involving her pregnancy and her health as well as the baby's. She'd tell him whenever she went to see her doctor, what he said, but more importantly, how she was feeling. It was too early for the doctor to detect a heartbeat, but he told Lilia the tests he ordered showed she and the baby were doing fine and there was no sign of a problem. Soon, he'd order a Doppler to detect a heartbeat, he explained.

One weekend, Mick received a large package Lilia sent full of *bizcochitos*, Mexican sugar cookies, and apricot *empanadas* his mother baked. *Bizcochitos* were a tradition among Mexican Americans, especially at Christmas time. The *empanadas* were small half-moon-shaped fried or baked pies filled with cooked and sugared apricots. Mick shared them with his bunking buddies, who devoured the treats in no time.

What Mick enjoyed the most in receiving Lilia's letters was when she spoke about the future. Their future. She looked forward to the day when she gave birth to their baby. She was hoping for a girl, she explained to him, but would be happy for a baby of either sex, as long as he or she was healthy. Despite her pregnancy, she was taking courses in stenography, hoping to land a job as a secretary so when he came home, he could continue with his schooling with her financial support.

Her hopes and desires, which she described in detail in her letters, excited him, but with some hard felt impatience to return to his college courses in engineering, which he was concentrating on when his schooling was interrupted. He wrote to her about his excitement and stressed to her he, too, was looking forward to their lives together on his return.

Often, when Mick wasn't writing letters to Lilia, and he had time, he'd draw some pencil sketches of whatever he found interesting close by, including some of his friends as subjects. He had brought some drawing paper and a few sketching pencils with him. He never had to go scrounging around for material to sketch with. He wrote to Lilia he had taken up sketching again to occupy his time when he was bored, and he sent some of them to her. She was happy to hear he was continuing his drawing and to have received some of them, she wrote to him in one of her letters.

He knew she kept up with the news at home about the war in Europe but also of any threat to the American troops in the Pacific from Japan. She'd write to him about her concerns, prodding him to write about his feelings of an impending war with Japan. She told him she had taken a look at a world map in her family's encyclopedia and was reminded how close the Philippine Islands were to Japan.

He knew she was seeking the truth from him, as he perceived it as a military man stationed in the Philippines. She was fully aware of his training at Fort Bliss in antiaircraft artillery. And she knew full well the job he was sent to the Philippines to do.

For those reasons, when he'd write back to her, he'd confirm his concerns mirrored hers. He wouldn't lie to her, he explained, and wrote the possibilities of the United States entering the war in Europe and the possibilities of war against Japan were both real. He added the guys he visited with also felt the same way.

"The picture painted here for us is grim," he wrote. But because he didn't want to alarm her any more than she already was, he didn't tell her about the two big things worrying him ever since the ship landed in the Philippines.

First, he was concerned the 200th came here ill equipped. The ammunition shortages they experienced at Fort Bliss were plaguing them again here. But there were additional concerns. For example, they discovered a problem in setting up the necessary gun emplacements. During installation, they soon found out the sites necessary for the emplacements were on private land and not within the control of the army or post headquarters.

Many of the weapons were found defective if not obsolete. Some of the ammunition was the wrong size for the only weapons they had on hand. There were other problems encountered during the installation and placement of the gunnery adversely affecting their defense of Clark Field.

Second, General Douglas MacArthur, the Commander of the U. S. Forces in the Philippines, repeatedly requested badly needed reinforcements, as well as for more weapons, ammunition, food, and medical supplies. Evidently, his requests had fallen on deaf ears in Washington. These facts, known to the soldiers of the 200th, were proof to Mick Roosevelt was ignoring the American troops in the Pacific and concentrating his efforts instead to helping Britain and France in their war against Germany in Europe.

4
THE EVE OF BATTLE

Mick realized Lilia may have already heard, by keeping up with the news, Roosevelt felt helping Britain and France in their war in Europe was more important to him than the safety of the American troops in the Pacific, which weren't yet in a war. But divulging the first part of his concern to Lilia, he felt, was giving her proof what she heard about Roosevelt in the news was true. And Mick didn't think it important for him to reinforce what she had heard. It would only add to her worry.

Several times in her letters, Lilia would ask him about his anger and bitterness. Had he been able to overcome those feelings, she wanted to know. In responding, Mick admitted he hadn't yet been able to overcome those negative feelings but was keeping in mind his talks with her and Father McCarthy. He asked her not to worry, he'd eventually succeed in changing his attitude about being here and not with her.

In his own mind, he realized his negative feelings were working against him. They were affecting not only his loyalty to his country but his attitude on the job and toward those around him. But he also realized Father McCarthy was right. The only sensible option was for him to make the best of what was going on in his life, which was to put his whole being into his tasks so he could survive in case of an attack by the Japanese.

Unfortunately, the facts he kept from Lilia in his letters, his knowledge of the faulty equipment, lack of weapons and ammunition, and the president's refusal to provide them with reinforcements and needed supplies and food, were preventing him from improving his attitude toward the military.

But he was well aware his survival, in case of a Japanese attack, depended on his changing his attitude. He convinced himself a negative attitude would affect his ability to perform his tasks effectively and to do the best he could as a comrade to his fellow soldiers.

For those reasons, he vowed to himself he'd work on his determination to do what Lilia and the priest had asked him to do, not only because he wanted to feel he wasn't ignoring their wishes and suggestions but also for his own mental self-preservation and wellbeing. He didn't want to disappoint them or himself.

At times, in the evenings, instead of going out "with the guys," Mick would join a few of the men in his barracks who'd gather to listen to a local broadcaster on the radio, Ron Walters. Nick Sanchez, a fellow from Silver City, whom Mick had played high school basketball against, owned a homemade radio picking up even weak radio signals.

Walters had a radio news show on radio station KMLP, "News of the World." The men got to know him as an aloof loudmouth, whom they nicknamed "Big Mouth." In addition to providing the news in a biased fashion, he'd be found forever daring "the Japs to attack us," almost daily.

A few listening to the radio announcer often would join him. "Tojo and comrades," *Tomate* DelaO would often say, referring to the prime minister of Japan, "Com'n and get us, you mother fuckers!" DelaO was from Santa Fe, whom Mick hadn't known until he joined the Guard. His real first name was Frank, but he was nicknamed *Tomate*, the word for "tomato" in Spanish, because of his freckles and red hair, even though he was Mexican American. Genetic rarities existed, and *Tomate* was one of them.

There was much about their new environment that fascinated the men of the 200th, but they especially found intriguing the tribes of pygmy aborigines. These natives lived in the jungle surrounding Fort Stotsenberg and would run around half-naked. Some of them wore pants; others didn't. The soldiers found it especially funny the aborigines, at night, when they were done with whatever they were doing, would fall asleep on the ground, wherever they happened to be at the time.

The barefoot natives, with their bows and arrows, snuck onto the post and ran around at will. Barring them proved futile, and they succeeded in sneaking past the guards whenever they pleased. The troops named their leader "King Tut," who wore a top hat and dressed only in a loin cloth.

Carrying a cane, he was often the guest of the post's commanding general at formal reviews. He'd sit proudly and erect alongside the general, apparently having the time of his life.

Passes to Manila were easy to get. Mick believed the stifling heat had something to do with the liberal policy allowing the men to entertain themselves outside the post. In setting up the weapons, ammunition, and gun emplacements and other fortifications, the men would toil in the suffocating heat and humidity. They were worn out by the end of the day. In the evenings, after a long day of work, they were ready to get out and enjoy the sights and sounds of Manila. And the Army staff knew they worked hard and were entitled to have some fun.

Making it easy to get passes was definitely the answer, Mick thought.

In Manila, there were plenty of night clubs, entertainment, and movie houses. Ladies in colorful costumes and dresses pranced around downtown, having fun and visiting with American soldiers, hoping they'd be invited somewhere to dance the night away. Many men would frequent the dance halls in a community known as Angeles or a barrio known as Sapung Bato, but called "Sloppy Bottom" by the soldiers. There, they drank a popular beer, San Miguel beer.

Some enjoyed riding the Calesas around town, two-wheelers pulled by ponies or donkeys. Others liked to visit the countless barrios in Manila or in outlying areas surrounding the city. In the barrios, many children were found roaming the streets, enjoying fun and games with their comrades.

Mick once frequented one of the barrios after watching a movie with a few friends. One of the children, on seeing he was an American soldier, went up to him and, looking up at him with a quizzical look, said, "Fight Bad Japs?" Even the children, Mick thought, felt the tension in the air that fighting the Japanese would soon be a reality to reach them in their own homes.

Those who enjoyed the outdoors could board a narrow-gauge train through the dense country.

In concentrating his efforts on the war in Europe and not taking care of the American troops in the Philippines, President Franklin Roosevelt may not have realized Manila Bay was of strategic importance to the United States in the event of an attack by Japan. Because of its location, it was the only harbor west of Hawaii adequately serving the U. S. Naval fleet.

If the Japanese landed on Luzon, the Americans in Bataan and Corregidor could delay the enemy long enough to assure defense of the bay for possibly half a year, giving the Navy time to arrive with ground forces to assure the defense would hold and Americans would continue to control the bay. But more help was urgently needed.

Yet, President Roosevelt wouldn't budge. Although American tank battalions arrived soon after the 200th's arrival, thus adding to the American defense, MacArthur kept requesting more help, but his requests kept being ignored in the nation's capital. The President again continued his financial efforts to help Britain and France in Europe.

As matters now stood in the defense of the Philippines and in particular, Clark Field, every military man in the Pacific felt it wasn't enough. At present, in addition to the 200th's presence in Luzon, the 60th artillery regiment occupied Corregidor. This was the total of the antiaircraft artillery in the Philippines. The 200th's 75 officers and 1,825 enlisted men were set up to defend Clark Field and its 35 B-17 bombers with a battery of .50 caliber machine guns, 26 37-mm guns, and 15 three-inch guns. The arrival of the two tank battalions added considerable support but not enough.

Although the tension in the air was always felt by the men of the 200th and other units since their arrival in the Philippines, the alerts didn't begin until the third week of November.

A major alert came in late November. "Military personnel report immediately to your units!" was heard not only throughout Fort Stotsenberg but on loudspeakers in nightclubs and movie houses in Manila.

Dennis Gurley, a northern New Mexican from Taos Pueblo, and Andy Gluck, from Las Cruces, were together in a movie house when they heard the announcement. They immediately left the theater and returned to Fort Stotsenberg to find the 200th on full alert and already setting up in the field. This alert had been ordered by General MacArthur himself.

Gluck and Gurley got to work right away, helping their battery build dummy gun emplacements to mask the dearth in weapons from the enemy. When they finished with their task, they helped move the sensitive shells into underground shelters to prevent loss of the ammo or possible explosions on the ground in case of an air attack.

To the men of the 200th, there was no question war was coming for from that point onward the post was under complete blackout every night. American reconnaissance planes reported a gigantic Japanese buildup in Formosa, and a Japanese task force was spotted navigating down the coast of China.

Meanwhile, plans to avert war between Japan and the United States were ongoing and being discussed at length. Proposals were submitted back and forth between Tokyo and Washington. Unaware Japan's plan for war had already been completed, a high Japanese diplomat representing the Japanese Emperor, Hirohito, flew to Washington to assist the Japanese ambassador in attempts to reach an agreement for peace between the two nations. But delays and misunderstandings stood in the way of negotiations to prevent a war.

A final proposal presented by Japan to President Roosevelt contained unacceptable concessions, the president believed. An attack was imminent, the President thought, if an agreement wasn't reached. With both countries unable to reach an agreement in the first week of December, on December 6, Roosevelt made a final plea to Emperor Hirohito for a peace agreement to be reached, but the request wasn't acted upon.

Finally, on December 7, what would be remembered as a "day of infamy," and what should have been foreseen but wasn't, occurred.

Nick Sanchez, along with Mick, were working quietly in the wee hours of the morning at their duty stations. As they worked, they were listening to easy listening music on Sanchez' homemade radio. The last chords of the Glenn Miller Orchestra's rendition of *Chattanooga Choo Choo* was just finishing playing and the announcer had gone directly into the next song, the Spanish version of *Green Eyes—Aquellos Ojos Verdes*. He had played only the first two phrases of the song when the announcer stopped the music. Both Sanchez and Mick were singing off-key along with the music when the disc jockey made the announcement everyone had feared.

A nervous but yet excited Sanchez immediately went for the phone and dialed.

"Get off your ass and tell the lieutenant they bombed Pearl Harbor!" he shouted into the phone, as Mick, standing alongside him, listened. "Tell him they're attacking the American naval fleet in Hawaii!"

No one should have been surprised whom Sanchez meant by "they."

PART II

THE PAINS OF WAR

5

THE FIRST CONTACT

General Jonathan Wainwright, of World War II fame, was to say a few years later of the day after the bombing of Pearl Harbor:

On December [8], 1941, when the Japanese unexpectedly attacked the Philippine Islands, the first point bombed was Fort Stotsenberg. The 200th Coast Artillery (AA), assigned to defend this fort, was the first unit in the Philippines, under General of the Army Douglas MacArthur, to go into action and fire at the enemy, also the first one to go into action defending our flag in the Pacific.

When Japan planned its attack on Pearl Harbor, its plan included the simultaneous bombing of Clark Field in the Philippines. But in Formosa, where Japan maintained its war arsenal, the naval pilots of the bombers scheduled to fly to the Philippines to attack Clark Field were beset by a heavy fog. For that reason, the planned attack was scuttled until the fog lifted a few hours later.

As bombs hit Pearl Harbor, the Japanese naval pilots were still on the ground in Formosa. At midmorning, the fog lifted, and the Japanese pilots were given the go ahead to take off. Within minutes, the twin-engine bombers and the Japanese fighter strafers, Zeros, started their engines and soon were in the air, flying south to their targets in the Philippines.

Sometime after noon that day, without warning, the Japanese planes hit Clark Field with the twin-engine bombers. They were followed by numerous strafers in very low-level attack. By the time the attack was over, the enemy attacks would destroy many of the aircraft, including most of the B-17 bombers still on the ground.

A major slip up in communications led to major damage to the American aircraft that hadn't taken off and remained on the airfield. Pilots who landed their aircraft just that morning at Clark Field took a quick lunch as their planes were being filled up with fuel. At the same time, the first of the Japanese bombers and Zeros that had taken off from the airfield in Formosa earlier were flying over the northern coast of Luzon, just minutes away.

False reports had been issued and were heard in the communication radio networks Clark Field was under attack already. Communications from the 200th's command post weren't reaching Clark Field; they couldn't confirm whether the reports of the attack were true. In any event, warnings were being issued by the command post for all aircraft to get in the air, but for some reason, Clark Field didn't receive the message.

By noon, every fighter plane on Luzon was aloft with the exception of the aircraft at Clark Field. They became easy targets for the Japanese bombers and strafers.

Mick's battery was assigned to the outer edge of Fort Stotsenberg. By eleven o'clock that morning, they were set up and ready to engage. The battery had scored high in efficiency and accuracy at Fort Bliss. For those reasons, the unit was assigned by Mick's company commander to set up their weapon entrenchments in a key area of defense. From this vantage point, the unit would be the first of the artillerymen to intercept enemy bombers flying overhead and strafers flying in low and targeting the American bombers and small aircraft on the field.

It was about 12:30 pm when Mick first heard the roar of heavy aircraft flying above. The roar kept getting louder, and as Mick looked upward to the northwest, he spotted the aircraft, fifty-four bombers in two V-formations.

"Hey, it's the Navy," someone yelled to Mick. "Look at them. They're so high, you can't see the insignias."

Mick knew better. "Navy, hell!" he shouted. "They're fucking Japanese bombers!"

The bombs hit when several of the post's soldiers were in the mess hall, eating. There, mess flew off the table and dinnerware rattled as the bombs began to hit. Explosions rocked the ground as the men left their meals and the mess hall, running for cover toward their units.

Mannie Campos had just finished having lunch with Ron Patterson, a fellow from Deming he played football against in high school, when the bombing began. Patterson was Campos' crew member. They rushed from the mess hall to their entrenchment, where they had already set up their weapon. As they ran, a truck was crossing the field a hundred or so yards ahead of them when a bomb exploded in front of the vehicle. The explosion lifted the truck off the ground in a ball of flame and smoke. Campos and Patterson, and a few others, ran to the burning truck, but they found its two occupants inside burning.

In his entrenchment, Mick readied himself to fire his 37-mm weapon. He glanced up and saw the bombs hitting the runway one right after another as they moved away from him in a straight line down Clark Field. Minutes before, he had been firing at the bombers with his three-inch gun. But he soon discovered the powder-train fuses they were issued wouldn't allow the shells to reach the aircraft. The bombers flew beyond the maximum range of the fuses. The pilots must have known the limits of the fuses, for they kept flying above that altitude.

The strafers, Zeros, approaching aircraft on the ground nearby, on the other hand, would be better targets for the 37-mm gun, which Mick now was ready to fire. And Zeros swarmed all over the airfield. He spotted one coming toward him from the left. As he aimed, he easily spotted the "Rising Sun" emblem under the wings of the plane. It was a first time visual he'd never forget.

He began firing away, but the pilot spotted him and immediately streaked to the right, and Mick found himself missing his target on his first attempt. As the plane flew away low, Mick could see the pilot, who was grinning.

"I won't miss the next one," he whispered to himself.

He was about to get ready for the next Zero when he noticed six or seven pilots leaving the mess hall and racing to their P-40 Warhawks, the American fighter-bombers, to take off and join the battle in the air. As they ran, two Zero pilots saw them and immediately gunned two of them down. The others managed to escape and made it to their planes.

The runways were heavily cratered from the many bombs already dropped and those few pilots making it to their aircraft had to maneuver around to avoid the craters, but they managed to take off to join the P-40s already in the air.

Mick saw two P-40s lined up ready to takeoff, and then quickly glanced up and spotted a Zero sweeping the field low heading in the direction of the P-40s to the right, getting ready, Mick sensed, to mow them down. The Zero was moving sideways to him, a relatively easy target, he thought. Taking into account the target's speed, he quickly calculated his aim a few feet ahead of the Zero and released repeating blasts from his 37-mm gun.

"Gotcha, you bastard!" he yelled, as the Zero's fuel tanks exploded in a ball of fire. Luckily, the pilot hadn't fired, and the two P-40 pilots started on their take offs. The Zero, pilotless and already in flames, hit the ground with a loud crash and skidded toward a smoldering army truck, causing a second explosion as the plane's second fuel tank ignited upon impact.

The hit drew yells and cheers from those around Mick, including his own crew. Hopefully the first of many, he thought, then took a few seconds, which is all he could afford, to say a few words in prayer. Zeros were still sweeping across the runways, creating havoc when they succeeded in hitting their targets. Mick knew he couldn't relax and kept aiming and firing as the Zeros continued coming, seemingly out of nowhere. "And too many of them are finding their fucking targets!" Mick said and swore to himself.

He swore again when he saw an ambulance carrying away the wounded get hit by two, not one, approaching Zeros, as the vehicle neared the edge of the field. The ambulance exploded as the multiple hits ruptured its gas tank. Mick had momentarily fixed his gaze in the opposite direction on another approaching strafer and hadn't had time to react to the attack on the ambulance. "Bad timing or just plain ol' not being fast enough for the task," he said to himself.

One of his crew members heard him and said, "Don't be too hard on yourself, Mick. You can't cover everything you see."

"I'm pissed off for not seeing it to begin with." Having said that, he again turned to the Zero to his right. It seemed to be coming directly at him, and he began firing right away, focusing his aim on the cockpit, a lesser-sized target. Once again, he could clearly see the face of the pilot. He wasn't smiling but grimacing as he got ready to unload his weapon at Mick's position. But Mick beat him to it, firing several shells in succession at the smaller target. No matter, he thought, as he hit his mark.

"Bullseye, you asshole!" he shouted, as the airplane and dead pilot veered to the left and crashed without exploding, about a hundred yards from him.

"Attaboy, Mick!" yelled the two men alongside of him. "Another one!"

Mick was reloading when he saw an American pilot who had bailed out of his P-40 Warhawk parachuting down about a half mile away. His helper pointed him out to Mick as Mick was busy getting his gun reloaded. Suddenly, seemingly out of nowhere, a Zero appeared. He was headed toward the parachuter. Mick moved faster, still trying to reload his weapon. But before he could even ready his weapon in position, the Japanese pilot unloaded on the man under the parachute, mowing him down in the air still about fifty yards off the ground.

"Damn, the fuck!" Mick cried out.

Attacks by the Zero pilots continued for what seemed to Mick hours, but by two pm, the enemy bombers were gone, returning apparently unscathed to their landing field in Formosa, and only a few strafers remained, still easily finding their targets on the ground. The artillerymen in Mick's battery had gunned down fifteen enemy strafers. Mick had added one more downed Zero only a few minutes before the Zeros disappeared from the air.

He found himself still wired up mentally but at the same time, completely exhausted physically.

"That's a hellava weird experience," he said to himself as he pondered the contradiction.

He took in a deep breath, his first, he believed he had taken in the past few hours. He began to look around at the devastation left behind from the bombing and strafing.

What he saw shocked the hell out of him. He had been so occupied at his task of finding targets and firing his weapon that he now realized, as he witnessed the devastation for the first time, he hadn't been aware of anything else. Clark Field had been utterly destroyed.

All around him were pockmarked runways, where B-17 bombers and P-40 Warhawks still burned, clouds of black smoke rising from them into the air already filled with smoking debris, dust, and smoke, hiding the blue sky above. Nearly every plane on the ground had been damaged. Beyond the runways, twisted masses of metal, still smoldering, were all that was left of some hangers. Buildings behind the hangers were still ablaze.

He was so stunned in seeing the damage to the planes and buildings he had blocked out the sound of the loud activity around him. Only yards away, truck drivers were picking up bodies of dead soldiers off the ground, still burning, then dumping them onto ambulances. The ones on the ground still alive but badly injured were lifted onto stretchers and carried to ambulances quickly maneuvering around dead bodies, bomb craters, and debris to take them to the hospital.

And the carnage. Mick had never seen so many mangled bodies and was simply stupefied he was now witnessing what remained of all that had taken place during the many moments he concentrated on staying alive and firing at the enemy in the sky. Just seconds ago, a loud explosion went off only a few yards away from him. The blast was so strong it almost knocked him over. Other explosions soon followed as burning debris found its way to heat and explode stored shells somewhere nearby.

Mick heard the roar of a plane and looked up to where the sound came from. The plane was flying low, and a couple of men with rifles began shooting at it until they realized it was a damaged and smoking P-40 coming back for a landing from some place where the pilot had escaped death. The plane swayed as it neared the ground, maneuvering above the cratered runway until it found a clear spot and finally landed. In a minute, the pilot slowly managed to crawl out.

All around him, it appeared to Mick the men of the 200th were literally picking up the pieces after their first whiff of battle. His crew members at the entrenchment had already left, leaving Mick alone as he took another look at the devastation, again unable to believe his eyes. Having seen enough, he walked toward a group of his comrades milling around a food truck already serving sodas and water gratis to anyone needing to cool off.

There, he ran into Mannie Campos and Dennis Gurley. Mick got himself a soda and walked up to them.

"Well, Mick, we've found ourselves right in the middle of this war now, haven't we," Campos said.

"I was just telling Mannie," Gurley said, "this is just the beginning. And I think we may have underestimated the Japs."

"Yeah," Mannie added, "And I was saying to Dennis they must have good bombsights. We had been told they didn't and couldn't see well either."

"That's hogwash, obviously. Those pilots are seasoned fellows. They seem to have learned some things we weren't told about."

"Just look around you and see what they've done. What they're capable of. And we could have done better if we had more ammo and if the ammo we did have, as well as our guns, weren't defective or obsolete."

"That's a fact. I had those problems the whole time." Gurley turned to Mick. "Did you, Mick?"

Mick frowned and nodded. "You bet I did. Especially with the three-inch guns. Half the time, the fuses wouldn't reach the bombers. I concentrated on the strafers. And I had my hands full with them."

"I had the same problems," Mannie added.

"I was also telling Mannie, Mick," Gurley said, "I just got back from listening to Captain Bell talking to one of the other fellows. The guy had asked him, 'Why didn't our army build up the strength to defend against this kind of attack?' The captain replied, smirking, 'I'd guess we weren't as important to them as the ones in Europe.'"

Mick lowered his head, shaking it. "That about says it all," he said softly, then walked away.

Later in the day, Mick heard horror stories from some of the men talking about the hard lessons they quickly learned during the fighting.

Larry Garcia, known as "*Lencho*," the Spanish nickname for Lawrence, a neighbor of Mick's in Las Cruces, told him, "Hell, I learned a lesson about the 37-mm guns, which none of us had fired until today. That weapon's shells explode with any 'cut-off' of air.

"Any sort of debris in the air will make it explode. Whenever I fired at a low angle at the Zeros, if I struck a reed or tree branch, the shell would explode prematurely. To make sure the shells reached the planes, I had to adjust."

Santiago Montes, a resident of Portales, whom Mick got to know at A & M, said "We thought it a good idea to get our ammo out of sight, and so we built trenches to hide it. But the blast of the weapon shook the ground, caving in the trenches. And we found ourselves having to dig out all the ammo we'd buried, wasting time."

There were other bleak tales.

"When using the three-inch guns," Romulo Alvarez, known as "Roque," from Anthony, said "we found the shell cases heavily corroded. Before we fired a shot, we had to clean them out so they'd fit into the breech box."

"And we found some of the fuses not usable. They were frozen together with corrosion, and we had to break them apart with any tool we could find. Some of our modified ammo created too much pressure on the gun, resulting in muzzle bursts, which injured several of our men."

Javier Chavez, from Albuquerque, complained about the outmoded and obsolete weapons. "The machine gun ammo we were using," he said, "was old, man, made during World War I. We had to scrape off the corrosion with knives before they could be loaded and fired."

The night after the attack, the 200th was split. Up until now, Manila, where MacArthur's headquarters was located, didn't have any effective anti-aircraft protection. Army headquarters in Manila recognized, too late, the 200th, the only anti-aircraft unit in Luzon, was too small to defend Clark Field from further attack without badly needed reinforcements.

As a result, headquarters issued orders sending a third of the 200th to Manila to defend the city from air attack. The new, restructured unit relocated to the capital, known initially as the Provisional Artillery Regiment, together with other men assigned to the new regiment from other units, would later be christened the 515th, the U. S. Army's first unit organized during World War II.

Mick and Jim Puglisi were among the 587 men, 22 officers and 565 enlisted men, sent to Manila to man artillery entrenchments at various locations within Manila and in fortifications surrounding the city. They got their gear, boarded the trucks, and moved out during the dark of night, leaving their comrades, some teary-eyed, behind at Stotsenberg.

6
THE LOST HOPE

After the split of the 200th, resulting in two regiments, the 200th remained in Luzon at Fort Stotsenberg but with a weakened strength of the original 200th, having lost the almost 600 men sent to Manila. In addition, the 200th was ordered to send additional soldiers to man weapons elsewhere. Other losses came about when some of the ex-calvary officers in the 200th were transferred to the 26th Cavalry and to other units. As a result of all these transfers, the regiment total left at Clark Field was about 1,100 men.

The move to Manila proved to be painfully slow, for the 515th found the roads and bridges filled with countless Filipinos in wagons, carts, motor vehicles, or any other means of transportation they managed to get their hands on. They were escaping the city from the bombardments and strafing sure to come. Peck, the 515th's commander, moving on ahead of the new regiment, reached a place near the docks known as the Walled City, and then traveled through narrow streets to reach General MacArthur's headquarters not far away.

There, Peck met with the commander of the Coast Artillery Command and with him, made battery assignments for the men of the 515th, now enroute, and arranged for guides to meet the regiment at a place named Rizal Monument in the city, where they were to be guided to Port Arthur. Peck would later locate his headquarters just a block away from MacArthur's headquarters.

The 515th convoy, truck after truck, moved slowly and silently through the night on a debris-strewn road into Manila and sometimes was mistakenly shot at by American or Filipino sentries not informed of the regiment's arrival. The convoy found the monument and soon were guided into Port Arthur, their new home.

There, they found their new artillery, but the guns and ammo were still in crates. Again, they found themselves with the same outdated weapons they had left at Clark Field. The men discovered some of the weapons broken, with no parts to repair them. And they found themselves with no communication equipment. A few of the trucks transporting some of the equipment were delayed, they were told, and some of the batteries had to wait until the next day to get their weapons.

To prepare themselves to defend the city, the men worked hard on the docks to get their weapons cleaned before the next attack. Cleaning the guns proved to be a formidable task, for the weapons had been packed in a thick grease, taking hours to remove. To clean them, they heated water in drums, then swabbed the inside of the weapon barrels with soap and water, using whatever they could find to ram rags down the barrels. Some barrels, they were able to clean with gasoline.

They found themselves lacking searchlights. Charlie Atkins, put in charge of finding sources, could only find three searchlights with all the accessory equipment. He had to ask the ordnance officer for additional equipment. After several hours, Atkins arranged for the delivery of searchlight trucks, one searchlight generator, and the ordnance officer's promise more searchlight equipment would soon be delivered. He was able to persuade the officer to dispense with military protocol and technical niceties to get the equipment set up.

Upon his arrival at Port Arthur, Mick was assigned to Battery H at Nichols Field, not far from Manila. He and his battery were helping to fuel trucks and generators when the first Japanese planes flew over. Mick immediately stopped his work to rush over to his machine gun to return the strafers' fire. The larger artillery hadn't been readied and was still inoperable.

Some of the men were still cleaning the grease-like substance off their weapons when the planes hit. Mick learned when he and his battery were unpacking and cleaning the weapons the substance used to preserve the weapons was called Cosmoline. But a few of the machine guns, including Mick's, were ready to be fired without the cleaning. Mick and the others opened fire on the strafers flying low.

Those in the battery who weren't operating the machine guns used their rifles to fire at the strafers and even the bombers, if they were flying low enough. Even the Filipinos used what were called popguns to fire at the bombers. Mick, along with a few other members of his battery, took cover from strafer firing in a ditch near a road, as he fired his machine gun.

Battery F, to which James Puglisi had been assigned, got the select position of all the battery assignments, the Sea Wall, next to the Manila Hotel.

"We're in front of the Manila Hotel, buddy!" Puglisi said to Mick when he ran into him the day after their arrival. "And the kitchen is bringing us free food. Tons of it, it seems like!"

Mick grew envious on hearing this, for food was a shortage not only his battery but the other batteries had been fighting against. Mick heard plenty of the men complaining they were going to bed hungry at night and the morning rations weren't enough to take their hunger away.

Meanwhile, more bad news spread throughout the new regiment. They heard the U. S. Navy was pulling out of Manila Bay. The naval task force, which was present for naval support of the Army troops in case of attack, would be moving south to join the Dutch, who had requested the support.

Notwithstanding the bad tidings, the American troops were determined to do their best with what they had. After all, they were constantly reminded reinforcements were on their way. A convey, they had heard, made up of seven ships escorted by the heavy cruiser, *Pensacola*, was steaming to Manila, not only with artillery and ammunition but planes.

During the second week of December, however, without MacArthur being told, some military brass in Washington ordered the convoy to return to Hawaii. To make matters worse, four troopships headed for Manila Bay were ordered back to San Francisco. MacArthur wasn't told of these reversals, and again, was kept in the dark about a secret accord between Prime Minister Winston Churchill and Roosevelt to "Get Hitler First." Instead, General George Marshall, U. S. Army Chief of Staff, informed MacArthur to expect assistance. And the men of the 200th, already expecting the reinforcements and support of material, food, and medicine, were also not told of the change.

In mid-December, assault forces from Japan arrived on the north shore of Luzon, preparing for a major attack to hit Manila Bay and Nichols Field, with over fifty bombers and twice as many fighter aircraft.

Meanwhile, Mick's battery and the other batteries fortifying Manila and its immediate surroundings, including Nichols Field, where Mick's battery was stationed, were reeling under one of the bloodiest attacks of the war in the Pacific. What they had encountered at Clark Field seemed a poor second to the heavy bombardments they were experiencing since their arrival in Manila. The number of dead mounted.

The men found it hard to protect themselves from the low-flying strafers sweeping Nichols Field with dogged and pounding fire. For one thing, digging the soil for trenches and foxholes was difficult because of the high water table in the vicinity of Manila. It was like plowing through mud, a member of Mick's crew said repeatedly. Mick realized they should have predicted this problem because nearby, there was a cemetery built up above the natural terrain to avoid the buried bodies from being raised to ground level.

Here again, as at Clark Field, Mick and his crew found it difficult to hit any but the lower-flying bombers, for most of the Japanese pilots already knew the range limit of their shells/fuses and would try to fly above that altitude. The bombers appeared to be unstoppable as they pounded and devastated Cavite Naval Base nearby. In the third week of December, during a lull in the bombing, Mick watched across the bay as medical personnel, assisted by soldiers, hauled truckloads of the dead and wounded.

Somewhere in the distance, someone was playing Christmas music. *Hot and muggy weather, and Christmas will soon be here.* Mick got a tinge of homesickness when he heard the bass baritone voice of Bing Crosby crooning "White Christmas." After the onslaught, Mick heard headquarters estimated five hundred died from the onslaught throughout the heavy fighting during the past two days. That was a lot of dead Americans, Mick thought, during such a short period.

Lack of manpower became a big problem. Cooks were assigned to some of the gun crews. Officers were ordered to KP duties and to fill sandbags. To help with the need to fill needed positions, and as a sign of support, the Philippine Military Academy assigned cadets to assist in any way they could. Because they were too young and not experienced to fight, they were placed with the searchlight and other noncombat crews, to help with their operations and allow the regular crews to rest and sleep.

Supplies in the city, not being replaced, ran low. Businesses would only sell for cash. The mandated blackouts gave rise to looting. Fearing the worst and not able to rely on American sources for needed equipment, food, and supplies, the Army began to buy all available motor vehicles, as well as radio and telephone equipment, medical supplies, food, and clothing from private businesses.

With the navy gone, Manila was left unprotected as the Japanese bombers flew above the range of the artillery shells, continuing to pounce the city every day. The city was filled with sounds of bells and sirens, and horns blared everywhere, traffic almost coming to a standstill as citizens fled the city for the jungles and outlying country.

Admiral Hart, who had ordered the naval forces out of Manila earlier, remained in Manila with only a few minor surface craft and a few submarines. A heated exchange came about when Hart informed MacArthur that he was pulling out what remained of his command personnel. MacArthur complained to General Marshall of Hart's refusal to cooperate. Neither were aware at the time that ten days later, another British-American conference was due to take place, once again, with the thematical resumption of "Get Hitler First."

The Japanese air and ground forces continued their attacks. Into the fourth week of December, Japanese bombers hit Del Monte Airfield in Mindanao at about the same time Japanese ground troops landed at Davao. The Japanese troops landing earlier in Aparri and Vigan farther north joined forces with the enemy troops at Davao. Japan's 14th Army, commanded by General Homma, landed at Lingayen. Japan's invasion of the Philippines was now a reality and a real threat.

As evidence of the threat, the Japanese ground forces continued to push southward in northern Luzon. They captured Legaspi, southeast of Manila and seized both an airfield and a railway station located there. Due to the heavy losses of aircraft suffered by the American forces, American operations in the air were limited to reconnaissance or other non-combat missions, such as transport. The Americans had only a few bombers capable of flying offensive missions.

There were only a few P-35s, P-26s, and P-40 Warhawks remaining, too insignificant in number for the effective combat needed to fight Japan's arsenal. The losses of planes suffered at Clark Field during Japan's initial attack would come to haunt the Americans, who could make good use of such aircraft against the Japanese's aggressive buildup of troops on the ground and in the air.

MacArthur's eventual plan was to control the beaches so most of the American troops could retreat to the Bataan Peninsula. His thoughts were that he could protect and control Manila Bay from Corregidor and Bataan until the reinforcements he expected arrived. In anticipation of the retreat into Bataan of all troops, the troops stationed in Manila and the outlying areas were ordered to gather their gear and weapons to begin their trek to the peninsula.

Jim Puglisi's battery, still located at the Sea Wall, on Christmas Eve, pulled out to join the retreat. The new instructions for the men in his battery were to set up positions at the two bridges at Calumpit crossing the Pampanaga River, a key entry into Bataan from Luzon. The bridges were important, for without them the American forces would be unable to cross into Bataan to set up the defenses against the Japanese attack at Manila Bay.

Once the remaining units of the American forces in Southern Luzon crossed over the bridges, the plan was to blow up the bridges with dynamite put in place by the engineers, to prevent the Japanese from gaining access to the peninsula by land.

With the exception of a few, all of the other batteries of the 515th, including Mick's, moved out of Manila to join the retreat into the peninsula. They, too, were assigned to guard the bridge at Calumpit until all of the American troops crossed over into Bataan. The few units remaining in Manila were to guard the city until the American troops in Corregidor and Bataan were in place to defend the city and the bay.

Near dawn, at Fort McKinley, the remaining batteries packed up their equipment and loaded it into trucks, as the bombs continued to fall, not only at the post but throughout the burning city. When they were gone, only a few badly wounded soldiers remained in the city. The plan was eventually to evacuate them from the Philippines.

Even as the last of the troops crossed into Bataan, the morale of the men was high, having a good feeling they'd be victorious. After all, they still believed reinforcements were on their way. On New Year's Day, 1942, the order was given to blow up the bridges. Soon thereafter, Puglisi's battery and others were assigned to set up positions at Cabcaben Airfield in Bataan, and the units quickly packed their gear and weapons and were on the road to the airfield to set up their positions.

Once all the troops were settled in Bataan, the men began their work in the new environment. They dug foxholes and trenches, planted mines, and hung barbwire. They set up their gun emplacements and constructed their own roads where there were none.

The American troops in Bataan numbered 80,000. Because of time restraints and the limited passage into Bataan, a large amount of food was left at Fort Stotsenberg, Clark Field, and Manila.

For that reason, the order was given to place the soldiers on half rations. But food wasn't the only problem. The men were still lacking ammunition, medicine and other supplies, such as mosquito netting. Although there weren't enough vehicles or gasoline, morale still remained high, for their retreat had been successful.

When General Homma and his forces entered Manila, he believed he would capture MacArthur and the American forces. But by then, the American troops were safe on Bataan. And the general was forced to accept failure.

To relieve his men of their shortages, at one time, MacArthur requested a submarine blockade so that badly needed food and ammunition could be brought into the peninsula. Although Admiral Hart was ordered to assist in making the submarines available and setting up the blockade, he failed to do so. Again, MacArthur pled. This time, General Marshall in Washington finally lent an ear to MacArthur's request.

Marshall was able to find a few vessels, old but usable, in Australia. Somehow, some of those vessels made it through the seas swarming with Japanese ships and got the much-needed food and ammunition to the troops.

The Battle of Bataan, as known in the annals of military history, began in mid-January of 1942, with a massive Japanese artillery attack on the west coast of the Bataan Peninsula, near the coastal city of Abucay. Aided by the artillery attack, one of General Homma's infantry divisions pushed down the east coast, while another of his infantry divisions attacked from the west coast on the other side of the peninsula and through Mount Natib, a dormant volcano, hoping to encircle the Americans.

But the Japanese suffered major casualties, primarily because the Japanese infantry division attacking from the west couldn't penetrate the difficult terrains and jungles of Mount Natib. Three times, Homma's troops assaulted the American line at Abucay. And three times, the Americans pushed them back. This initial encounter in Bataan was an early victory for the Americans.

But it was short-lived, for constant night attacks and continuous heavy bombing against the Americans proved too much for them. They were tired, lacking sleep, and fighting all kinds of diseases. Malaria, dengue fever, and dysentery weakened the men the most. And the lack of food weakened them further, giving way to scurvy and beriberi, and tropical ulcers.

Fighting these diseases, many of the men believed, was as bad as fighting the Japanese. Aside from the diseases, the men had to contend with the straddle trenches, where the swarming flies fed on the feces, then spread the diseases elsewhere. Dead bodies in the streams polluted the water, making it undrinkable. And permeating the air everywhere was the stench of dead Japanese left in the surrounding jungles from previous battles.

The men grew much weaker, not only from the wide spread of diseases but from having been living on half-rations for a long time.

And they were running out of ammunition again.

To the west, the coastal towns gave way to Japanese forces overtaking the Americans at Subic Bay, Olongapo, and Grand Island. American counterattacks at these points failed, mostly due to the lack of ammo and the weakening of the men brought on by lack of nourishment and the spreading diseases.

7
THE EVE OF DEFEAT

The latter part of January, General MacArthur, realizing he couldn't push his men any further, had no option but to order his troops to withdraw.

Despite the loss of ground in these initial encounters in Bataan, throughout the battles in these encounters and from this point forward, the Native Americans in the 200th proved of value to the American troops in one particular area—communications. Often, the Navajos would use their own language as a sort of code in conveying messages by radio and other electronic transmissions.

The Japanese tapping into the American lines tried to break the unknown code without success. The successful use of the Native American's language as a code led to wider use later developed during World War II by the Marines and other American units, known as the American Indian Code Talkers, which encompassed other Indian Nations, including the Choctaws.

Believing the Americans had shown their vulnerability early on, Homma was eager to end the war in the Philippines soon. To do this, during the first week of February, he planned another attack on the west coast. Some of his troops would attack the port of Bagac on the western shores from the south, while other units moved in from the north, and then his troops would continue south to seize the port of Mariveles on the southern tip of the Bataan Peninsula.

In so doing, he hoped to cut off supplies from Corregidor into Bataan. This plan of General Homma was the first of five Japanese landings that were to be known as the Battle of the Points.

Anticipating Homma's initial plan, General Wainwright moved his forces, smaller than Homma's, to new positions in preparation for the planned attacks. The 200th and 515th were a part of Wainwright's defense. But the men of both regiments were again running out of ammo and food.

As part of his plan, Homma sent a large convoy of barges carrying infantry soldiers down Bataan's western coastline toward Quinauan Point, one of the points in the Battle of the Points. From the air, P-40s attacked the vessels, while from the ground, American torpedo boats and artillery along the shore fired on them. The coordinated attacks worked, sinking several of the barges. Those remaining after the American attacks, some still on fire or otherwise unable to reach their destination, retreated. The men of the 200th and 515th, which were manning the artillery, let out cheers of joy as they saw the enemy turn back.

In the second week of February, the Americans trapped the Japanese forces at Silaiim Point and then fought back a counterattack by the Japanese, eventually taking control of an important piece of terrain. Thus ended the Battle of the Points, with about 600 American casualties and 1900 Japanese soldiers dead. It was another clear victory for the Americans. But Homma had considerably more troops and arsenal and was ready to exert pressure on General Wainwright's units elsewhere.

In the meantime, by mid-February, the American troops had held back the Japanese forces in the Battle of the Points and caused significant losses. Of the almost 4,000 Japanese soldiers who fought at the battle, only about 400 survived. Of the 2,881 men in the Japanese's 20th Infantry, only about 650 survived.

But Homma remained confident, despite his losses in the battle. He was far from being beaten, even though he had failed to take control of important terrain, if he was going to win in Bataan. His bombers continued the heavy bombing, which was keeping the American forces from penetrating farther into enemy lines. The Japanese general also was aware Wainwright's men were weakening from lack of food and were running out of ammunition and medical supplies.

General MacArthur had long ago sent a message to Roosevelt that Philippine President Quezon was upset, accusing the United States of abandonment. Roosevelt had broken his promises, Quezon protested. Through mid-February, MacArthur had been assuring his troops that Roosevelt said help was on its way, with thousands of troops and hundreds of planes.

But in the third week of February, Roosevelt broadcast by radio that thousands of planes were being sent to Europe. The broadcast angered Quezon, who then informed MacArthur he'd request of the President immediate freedom from U. S. control, then surrender, disband his army, and neutralize the Philippines. MacArthur had long ago disagreed with the President's "Europe First" policy and therefore sympathized with Quezon.

He hoped that in relaying Quezon's threat to Roosevelt, the president would have a change of heart. But although the president again promised immediate relief to the American forces in the Philippines, he demanded Quezon stay on course and further ordered MacArthur not to surrender, "as long as there remains any possibility of resistance." MacArthur, taken aback, answered the President he had no intention of surrendering.

Occasionally, enemy planes would fly over Bataan, dropping leaflets, which the men got a kick out of. Mick, too, found much humor in the leaflets. One contained pictures of naked women and read, "Hey, Americans, come see what we have waiting for you! Come on over to our side." Some of the men, initially keeping the leaflets to chuckle, later sold them as souvenirs.

Some of the men listened to the Voice of Freedom, but a few thought the "Jap" station at Manila had better music, although the station repeatedly played "Waiting for Ships that Never Come In." Afterwards, the Japanese disc jockey would say, "Hey, G. I. Joe, show your white flag, give us your rifle, and surrender. We'll treat you well with food and girls!"

The heavy bombing and the strafing continued through the month of March. But there would be moments when they had a reprieve from the shelling and fighting. Such moments, the men treasured, as if life for them had once again become normal. In such moments, they forgot about the stenches in the air and the hollow emptiness in their stomachs and instead enjoyed the calmness, even if only temporary, from the loud shelling and bombing that had become very much a part of their day.

If they were fortunate, they ate twice a day. Otherwise, they scrounged around for extra food. Half rations soon became quarter rations, and the two meals a day became one meal a day. Some of the men were starving and getting weaker by the day.

They began eating worms and grasshoppers. A few thought monkeys, if you could catch them, were tasty. Charlie Atkins found the practice unacceptable, cringing every time he'd pass by a skinned monkey being boiled in water, saying it looked as if they were boiling a young child, and Mannie Campos complained in a humorous tone he wouldn't eat them because they looked too much like one of his uncles, the ugliest member of his family.

Mick got his first taste of horsemeat when the few units with horses started to kill their mounts for food. As he saw the men around him weaken from starvation and sickness, Mick listened to an American broadcast through a short-wave radio, announcing something to the effect that, "as far as the eye can see in every direction, there are ships and planes filled with food and weapons bound for the Philippines to help the brave soldiers fighting in the Bataan Peninsula."

"Fucking lies," Mick said out loud to himself. "They're feeding us fucking lies!"

He was so angry, so disenchanted by what he considered a betrayal by the United States and its president that he took out his sketching pad and pencils and drew a caricature of Uncle Sam in his red, white, and blue top hat, jacket and pants, looking sternly into the eyes of a group of soldiers, and saying to them, "I am sending you more medicine, more weapons, more food, and more reinforcements so you can continue to fight for your country in Bataan."

He first showed the sketch to his friends and members of his battery, then would post it from time to time on the side of a large mess tent during meal times.

Some of the men lived off the land, so to speak, having been raised in the prairies and deserts of New Mexico. They found plenty of edible and nutritious jungle plants. The inside of a palm tree tasted like cabbage, they discovered. The men caught small fresh-water shrimp in the creeks. They caught and killed wild hogs and carabaos in the wilds. Grenades were used to kill groups of fish in the ponds.

Whenever there was strafing and bombing, some of the men would climb up mango trees for protection. Often, after the strafing and bombing, they'd stay up there, collecting the mangoes to eat later.

A few men would often wander into the jungle in search of anything edible. At times, they'd come upon a Filipino or American soldier dangling from ropes, their hands tied behind them. They were either dead or dying, their bodies scarred with burns or bayonet injuries. Many were mutilated, their penises torn or cut from their bodies and shoved into their mouths.

Aside from the shortages of food, ammunition, and medicine, there were other shortages depressing the men. A whole cigarette was hard to find. Uniforms became ragged, shoes were worn with no heels and worn soles, and some men wore torn underwear or no underwear at all. In addition to those personal items, tents, mosquito netting, and bedding were in short supply.

By this time, it was common knowledge amongst the troops they had been forgotten or ignored by the American president. During a so-called "fireside chat" from Roosevelt, the men of Bataan listened for some presidential reassurance and hope. The president reminded his listeners "this was a global war" and "the Pacific was vast, the distance long," as well as the "capacities of the democracies were strained. And we must realize the great sacrifices that must be made...."

When the men in Bataan heard those words, they knew only too well they were the sacrifice.

Sergeant McKenzie became more demoralized by what was happening when he heard the Voice of Freedom keep telling them on the radio to "Hold out for a few more days. Help is coming."

"They could have told us the truth," McKenzie said, "and we would have accepted it. They didn't have to lie."

"We're the battling bastards of Bataan," some of the men of the 200th began to shout. When that statement caught the eyes of the press, a journalist said it well:

We're the battling bastards of Bataan;
No mama, no papa, no Uncle Sam;
No aunts, no uncles, no cousins, no nieces,
No pills, no planes, no artillery pieces.
And nobody gives a damn.
Nobody gives a damn.

When Mick first heard the reference to the battling bastards of Bataan, he remembered when stationed at Fort Bliss having heard of a comment attributed to a member of the regular units when the 200th was cited as the best artillery unit in the country. It was something to the effect that, "If they're so damn good, why don't you send those bastards to the Philippines where they can show it!" He wondered if the men who started the chant were remembering the comment at Fort Bliss months ago.

On the same day President Roosevelt gave his "chat," he ordered General MacArthur to assume command of the Southern Pacific in Australia. Upon departing the Philippines, he gave his famous speech from Australia, promising, "...and I shall return." General Wainwright assumed command of the U. S. Forces in the Philippines when MacArthur departed for Australia.

The Japanese boasted that without MacArthur the Americans were now leaderless and much more vulnerable to defeat. There were many signs of Japanese buildups throughout the Pacific, especially in the Philippines. Strategically, the Japanese attempted to mask the buildups by increasing the bombing and front-line activity.

There were more sniper attacks and skirmishes between Japanese and American patrols throughout. There were deafening barrages. Soon, the American soldiers found themselves jumping from one foxhole and into another to avoid the barrages. The Japanese dropped incendiary bombs causing fires the Americans had to constantly put out, taking them away from other tasks.

Daily, the men grew more emaciated, their eyes more caved in, as Tokyo Rose, in Japanese propaganda broadcasts, urged the Americans to give up, offering steaks and sex. "Tokyo Rose" was the nickname given by the soldiers to all female English-speaking broadcasters working for the Japanese. Meanwhile, the Voice of Freedom kept insisting "help is on the way" and encouraged them to "hold out a little longer."

Mick heard from a radio broadcast in Los Angeles that Wainwright's forces were gaining stronger positions while Lencho Garcia, standing next to Mick listening, said, "'stronger positions' hell, the Japs are running our fuckin' ass off our positions."

On Good Friday, April 3, General Homma began his greatest artillery barrage of his campaign in the Pacific. Howitzers and mortars pounded

Wainwright's troops, and heavy bombers began eliminating the American defense positions throughout Bataan. Japanese infantry advanced easily, and tanks pushed through an opening gap in the eastside of the island. By evening, the enemy was ready to take control of Mount Samat, a strategic land mass, and by the next day were at the foot of the mountain.

At Cabcaben Airfield, near Mariveles, where an exhausted and hungry Jim Puglisi continued to man his artillery gunnery, he watched as battle fatigue gnawed at the men in his battery. Shelled daily, they had been under combat conditions twenty-four hours a day. These weren't the front lines, where the soldiers periodically would be rotated to the rear. Here, Puglisi knew, there was no rear for a soldier to take a badly needed rest. Instead, the fighting was ongoing 24/7.

Just two days ago, while Puglisi was taking a breather, the battery crew next to Puglisi's, about seventy-five yards away, was countering enemy fire with their 3-inch gun. Puglisi watched as a faulty fuse of World War I vintage caused a round to detonate, known as a muzzle burst, only a few feet from the crew. Several Filipino scouts and the two fire direction officers were hit hard by the exploding shell's fragments.

Puglisi and his crew immediately left their artillery weapon and rushed to their neighboring crew to see if any of the crew were still alive and needed medical help. They found all of them dead. The weapon was out of service until early the next morning, when another crew began manning the emplacement. Puglisi was relieved the position was once again in operation because it took the load off of his crew's position from the enemy attacks daily.

It was on Easter Sunday, near the end of the day, that Puglisi met death face to face. For the past month, there was an enemy reconnaissance plane coming around every day at the same time. "You could set your watch by it," Puglisi told one of his crew members. The Americans called the pilot "Photo Joe" because he'd take pictures of the area every time. Although it was a reconnaissance plane, the pilot always dropped a bomb at the end of his taking photos. As usual, on Easter Sunday, Puglisi watched as the plane dropped its bomb.

The pilot never dropped the bomb on a particular target; he just dropped it wherever he happened to be just before leaving the area. Without warning, this one hit just outside the edge of Puglisi's crew's deep foxhole. Puglisi was the closest to where the bomb hit, and the explosion blew him and three of his crew through the air some forty feet from the foxhole.

Within minutes, when an ambulance arrived, the medics found Puglisi alive and conscious but paralyzed from the waist down. The blast killed another of his crew and caused minor injuries to the other two. Aside from his paralysis, he was covered with wounds all over his body from shrapnel, especially his legs. He was rushed to Base Hospital 2, conscious and glad to be alive.

A few days after Homma had captured control of Mount Samat, on April 6, Wainwright ordered a counterattack to take back the mountain. He had grave misgivings about his attack, for his men were starving, sick, and exhausted. Homma, whose forces were fresh and stronger, blocked Wainwright's assault, both from the east and west, and came out of the battle having gained more ground.

By the end of the day, only a short line along the San Vicente River stood between the Japanese and Manila Bay. As a result, the Americans couldn't hold out much longer and prevent the eventual takeover of Manila Bay.

After the win by Homma at Mount Samat, the Japanese advanced elsewhere, tightening the hold of several key positions on Bataan. The starving and weakening Americans were unable to fight back. The situation was critical, General King, the commander in Bataan, messaged Wainwright. Surrender might be his only choice, he said, even though Roosevelt had forbidden surrender "as long as there remains any possibility of resistance." King believed there wasn't much resistance now, if any.

Meanwhile, the Japanese advanced unimpeded toward Mariveles. General King ordered all antiaircraft equipment that couldn't be moved or used by the infantry destroyed.

At 11:30 am on April 8. King made his decision, after concluding there was no way of stopping the Japanese from reaching Mariveles, a key location. He refused to sacrifice any more of his men for what he determined was a hopeless cause, even though he knew he might face a court martial if he surrendered his troops.

At 6:00 am the next day, he officially surrendered. He insisted it was his own decision and Wainwright wasn't to be informed. He wanted to take full responsibility and didn't want General Wainwright, as commander of the U. S. forces in the Philippines, held responsible for the surrender.

"A terrible silence settled over Bataan about noon on April 9. It deepened with the coming of the night... Bataan was something dead that lay up there two miles across the dark water.

If there is anything worse than a battlefield that shakes with explosions and the cries of men it is one that becomes mute and dead and just sprawls there dead and broken and exhausted.

That was Bataan on the night of April 9, 1942."

General Jonathan M. Wainwright
General Wainwright's Story
Doubleday & Company, 1946

PART III

SURRENDER AND REPENTANCE

8

THE SURRENDER

"Wake up, Mick!" someone shouted at Mick as he lay asleep on his bedroll he had set up just outside his small tent. It was only five in the morning, still dark.

He opened his eyes and managed to see Mannie Campos's darkened face only a few inches away from his.

"All hell's broken loose," Campos began to explain as Mick got out of his bedroll and sat on the grass near its edge. "King's surrendered us!"

By now, Campos's loudness had awakened the others around the grounds who were fast asleep.

Mick was still groggy-eyed and not quite wide awake. "To the Japanese?"

"Who else, man! Who the hell have we been fighting all this time, *ese?*"

"Mannie, I'm half asleep, *bato*. Give me a break and let me wake the hell up." He stood up and yawned.

"I just saw a jeep going around, flying a white flag. "The officer riding with the driver was shouting, 'Do not engage with the enemy. Our camp commander has ordered a cease fire.'"

A bit more alert now, Mick finally understood the reality, but the thought of an actual surrender nauseated him, although inwardly, he wasn't surprised. For a few days now, there were rumors of a possible surrender, and he and others felt the men in their unit had weakened to the point of not being able to function around the camp, much less to fight the Japanese. *The signs of defeat appeared everywhere, yet could it be true.*

But now Campos had told him there was an actual surrender, it didn't seem real. *To live as a captive; what would it be like? Nothing in training prepared us for this.* He was repelled by the thought of living in captivity. Under the Japanese, no less.

"You actually saw the jeep with a white flag?" Mick walked up to Campos. "I'm still finding it hard to believe, Mannie. This is terrible."

"I know, man." A deep frown formed on Campos's forehead. "To answer your question, 'yes,' I actually saw the flag. It's happening, *bato*, whether we like it..."

Just then, Captain Bell, their company commander, appeared. "General King has surrendered us to the Japanese!" he shouted so everyone in the vicinity could hear.

He walked quickly to the center of the group that had gathered. "The orders have come down from regiment headquarters. You are to turn in or destroy any and all weapons in your possession. Turn in all ammo to Ordnance at once! And pass it along!" He turned around without waiting for a salute and walked away.

Mick began putting on the rest of his fatigues as Campos told him he had to go and hurriedly walked away.

Mick walked out to a clearing a few yards away and looked around. It was beginning to dawn, and the streaks of light through the trees made it easy to see the activity around their camping area so early in the day. He sensed gloom all around him. Even the birds appeared not to be chirping as loudly this early morning as he had grown accustomed to hear them at daybreak. It was almost as if they, too, sensed a change in the air and in what was to come in the silence of surrender.

He heard the roar of tanks nearby. *The enemy's or ours.* He could hear distant blasts of shelling and rifle fire. *Who's firing? Did somebody not get the word?*

A half hour later, as he was eating his morning ration, he heard a few units of the Japanese tank battalion and some of their infantry men hadn't gotten word of the cease fire and were still engaging the American troops. That explained the firing he heard earlier, he thought. But even an hour or so later, Japanese bombs dropped in the distance away from their encampment, obviously still not having gotten the word of the cease fire. *Or were those coming from Corregidor?*

The rest of the morning was unreal, it was so silent. It actually wasn't quiet, for there was much noisy activity in the camp vicinity, with nervous and anxious soldiers hurrying around, in and out of their tents and visiting with one another. But the silence in Mick's mind was the total absence of the shelling and bombing that had been a constant reality continuously day in and day out for months. Now, the shelling and blasts were completely gone. It seemed surreal to him. An eerie silence.

Again, he began dreading about what was to come, and the dread lingered in his mind all morning. There were no rations handed out for the noon meal, which didn't surprise him. He hadn't even been thinking of his hunger, of the deep emptiness in the pit of his stomach. And it would worsen in captivity, he surmised, for it was common knowledge among the troops the Japanese soldiers, too, were starving. If so, how much food could they possibly provide to their captives? Thousands of them.

Meanwhile, it was reported General King met with Homma's operations officer, Colonel Nakayama, to discuss terms of the surrender. At the time, fighting continued in Corregidor, which hadn't yet surrendered. Nakayama denied various requests made by King and insisted the unconditional surrender of *all* Philippine forces, not just those in Bataan. But would the American troops be treated as prisoners of war under the Geneva Convention parameters, King wanted to know. Nakayama assured him they would.

As it turned out, however, much later Japan persisted that until such time as the United States surrendered not only Corregidor but the other Philippine islands, the American soldiers weren't to be treated as prisoners of war but mere captives. As such, the Japanese claimed, they wouldn't be afforded the protections under the Geneva Convention. The American forces outside the Bataan Peninsula eventually were surrendered, but even then, Japan insisted the prisoners wouldn't be entitled to be treated as prisoners of war under the Geneva Convention protections because Japan claimed it had never signed the Convention agreements.

At the time of the surrender, Jim Puglisi still lay paralyzed at Base Hospital 2. The hospital was only an assortment of tents in the middle of the jungle, where it was unbearably humid. It rained there every day for at least half an hour every evening, beginning at around five o'clock. Puglisi learned of the surrender when some of the fellows he knew came by to visit and told him, "King threw up the white flag last night and surrendered us."

Later in the afternoon, Mick had gone into a clearing with Javier

Chavez for some peace and quiet, away from the crowds of soldiers gathering soon after a long briefing of the members of the three batteries encamped in the vicinity.

At the briefing, the men had been told what they might expect to happen to them as POWs once the actual surrender took place. The men were loaded with questions the officers who called the gathering couldn't answer, although they were able to answer a few.

"What about mail?" someone shouted. "Will we still be able to write and receive letters. All of us have families we stay in touch with."

"I've been waiting for that question," the first officer, a lieutenant, replied. "We're attempting to get clarification on this issue, but I'm sorry to have to tell you our preliminary reports are none of us will be allowed to write home or to receive mail from anyone, whether family or not."

Even as the lieutenant was in the middle of answering the question, loud murmurs and then shouting could be heard in the large crowd of listeners. When he stopped talking, a loud roar of disapproval and disappointment came from the audience.

"Fucking assholes!" someone shouted. "Who do they think they are?"

"Mother fuckers!" another shouted.

"That's just the pits, man!" another yelled. "The goddamn, fucking pits!"

The lieutenant held both of his hands up, palms down, gesturing the audience to calm down.

"Listen, please," he said loudly into the microphone. "We hear you loud and clear. All of us agree the mail policy sucks. But as I said, we're trying to get clarification, to make sure we understand it as a total prohibition. We'll let you know as soon as we get some more words on the subject."

"We've answered some of the questions you asked," the second officer said, "because we knew the answers. But we ourselves don't know most of what we should expect until the ones higher up provide us with some answers.

"As I speak, General King and others are meeting with their Japanese counterparts, ironing out some details of the handling of prisoners and possibly, getting some ideas of what their plans are and how they intend to handle the imprisonments. The mail issue is one of those matters they'll discuss. And I assure you we'll have a final answer to you on something we know is important to you."

"Remember," another officer announced, "this is something new to the Japanese too. It's not every day a military army is prepared to handle the intricacies of a prisoner of war encampment. There are a lot of logistics coming into play. A lot of planning."

"Like how they'll be treating us!" someone yelled out.

The first officer broke in. "Listen, men, I'm sure we'll have some answers for you soon. We expect some Japanese officials to move into the area, sometime later today I've been told, and we hope they'll provide some answers to your questions. Let's wait until then, shall we."

With that comment, the briefing was adjourned.

9
ACCEPTANCE

Mick and Javier Chavez sat down at the secluded clearing and immediately began to talk about the surrender and what lay ahead of them under captivity.

"After hearing what was said at the briefing, I'm worried about not getting mail from home," Mick began. "Lilia's expecting our child. It's due sometime the middle of this month. Fuck, that's just a few days away. Last time I heard from her, she was fine. And the baby's doing well, according to the doctor. But now, if we don't get to receive any mail, I won't know a damn thing in another week or so. I'm pissed."

"I hate to hear that, Mick," Chavez said. "It's terrible. I'm sorry for you." He sighed. "This thing scares the hell out of me too." He picked up a thick blade of grass, which he put in his mouth and began chewing it.

Mick was amused by the quickness with which Chavez bit on the blade. "I can see you're nervous, Javier." He smiled for a quick moment.

"You bet your ass I am. Aren't you?"

Mick smiled again and nodded. "Of course. But I don't chomp on grass like you're doing to show it."

The comment made them both laugh.

"I wasn't even thinking when I picked it up. It just seemed natural to stick it in my mouth."

"Go to it, man. Do whatever you need to do. I didn't mean anything by my remark, other than it was a bit funny to me."

"It's good to show some humor at such a bleak time. Maybe it'll help us get through the day."

Mick nodded. "I think so, and..."

Mick heard a rustling sound and looked up. Malco Ventura approached, followed by Jaime Soltero, Andy Gluck, and Rabbit Carbajal.

"You guys planning an escape?" Ventura asked.

"If you are, let us in on it," Soltero said.

"Naw," Chavez said, "we just needed to get away. Mick and I were just saying we're both scared like hell being prisoners of the Japanese."

The four newcomers sat down in front of Mick and Chavez.

"That's all we've been hearing from others," Ventura said. "They're afraid too."

"Fear in this situation is natural, fellows." It was Sergeant McKenzie who spoke. He was walking up to the group, followed by Pete Graciano.

Graciano sat down to join the group. McKenzie remained standing.

"Have you fellows turned in your weapons and all ammo on your person?" McKenzie said.

Javier Chavez nodded. "First thing this morning. Hated doing it, though."

"Yeah, me too," Graciano said.

The others nodded.

"There must be someone who hasn't," Gluck said. "I still keep hearing shots being fired close by. Even this morning."

Graciano nodded. "Yeah, me too."

"I think all the men in my platoon have," Mick said.

"You guys been following us?" Ventura asked, looking up at McKenzie.

Sergeant McKenzie grinned. "Pete and I saw you guys going into the trees and just wondered where you were headed." He found a spot next to Mick and sat down cross legged. "We're in a hellava mess, aren't we, gentlemen?"

"The anticipation of what to expect is killing us," Mick jumped in. "I hope we find out soon."

"I heard a group of Japanese officers will arrive by the end of the day. Our commander will be splitting us up into groups at some point so as not to create too much chaos."

"The Japanese will be talking to all of us directly?" Chavez asked.

"No, my understanding is they'll meet with the higher-ups first, then they'll in turn round us up and explain the details of what's going to happen. I've heard they plan to imprison us at Camp O'Donnell."

"That's miles away," Mick said. "How'll we all end of up there?"

"I don't have the answers yet, Mick. I suppose we'll be transported there by trucks, or possibly, the train. There are trains running up through O'Donnell and past it, I think." He paused to clear his throat. "We'll find out soon enough, I suppose."

"And what about this mail thing, man?" Chavez said. "They're not allowing us to write or receive fucking letters."

"That's not a 'for sure' thing, Javier," McKenzie replied. "The lieutenant at the briefing said as much. They're checking it out, but to be honest, I think it's going to turn out to be true—no mail, I'm afraid." He let out a big sigh. "But listen, all of your family—your loved ones, your friends—will be notified through Army channels we've become prisoners of war. They've already heard it on the news. At least some of them have, or will soon."

"Well, it still sucks, sergeant."

"It sure does, Javier," said Andy Gluck. "Meanwhile, we've got nothing better to do than sit here and wait." He shook his head. "If only the help we'd been promised all along had arrived, we wouldn't be in this pickle."

"Yeah, not only reinforcements but ammo, more weapons," added Rabbit Carbajal, "and the medicine to deal with all these fucking diseases that's worse than fighting the Japs."

"And what about food," Gluck said. "We've been starving for months on one-quarter rations. I'd have settled for food, if nothing else."

"And now, we've got the humiliation of a surrender," Carbajal said. "It's a black day for us, guys. I can't believe we were so low to give up. I was willing to keep on fighting."

"And so were the rest of us, Rabbit," McKenzie said. "Remember, we didn't surrender. General King did. We had no choice in the matter. I remember an uncle of mine telling me before I left home, 'Whatever you do, Mike, don't dishonor your country. Be a proud soldier.' And I honestly don't feel I've let him down."

He paused in thought. "You're right, Andy, we do find ourselves in a pickle. And there's no sense trying to second guess King. I heard it broke his heart to surrender, but he just wasn't willing to sacrifice any more lives. He was thinking of us when he did it."

He sighed. "He made his decision, and now you fellows and I have to live with it. Let's tighten our grip and deal with what comes, as much afraid as we may be."

"Good words of advice, Sergeant," Mick broke in. "Thanks for saying them."

The others followed. "Yeah, yeah." "Amen to that." "Right on, Sergeant."

McKenzie nodded and smiled at the group but didn't say anything else.

"If you're right, Sergeant, about King's thinking when he surrendered," Ventura said after a pause in the discussion, "it's terrible he felt forced to surrender. But the way I see it, it was inevitable, as terrible and humiliating as a surrender is.

"But without food, no ammo, with Japs running at us everywhere, and we sick as hell with all kinds of diseases. Maybe it was the only sensible thing he could do. That way, some of us may get home eventually."

"You're right, Malco," Soltero added. "There's only so long a person can go without eating. If we had the food and the ammo, maybe we'd have managed without a surrender. Despite the fear I see in all of us, I can't help thinking I see a lot of brave and tough guys amongst us.

Soltero took a deep breath. "I, too, am scared. But humiliated at the same time. I feel let down. It's such a helpless feeling. Degrading, even."

Javier Chavez appeared in deep thought—almost mesmerized—as he listened to Soltero, who was sitting next to him. Soon, tears appeared, rolling down his cheeks as Soltero continued.

"After using our rifles to fight the enemy every day for months and months, it seems, and then to have to lay down our arms. It's enough to break one's heart." He noticed Chavez's tears.

He put a hand on Chavez' shoulder. "Nothing prepared us to be prisoners. But even though we don't know what to expect as captives, we mustn't lose our morale—our spirit. And we can be friends to one another. We can help each other. Let's continue to buddy up."

When Soltero finished, he looked over at Chavez, who was still shedding tears. He leaned over and hugged him. That's all it took—Chavez broke down and sobbed on Soltero's shoulder.

No one stirred for a long moment, allowing Chavez to cry. Soltero patted Chavez on his back, lending him his shoulder to cry on.

Chavez, becoming aware of the stillness in the group, stopped crying and raised his head up.

"I'm sorry, you guys," he said softly, taking a handkerchief from his back pocket to wipe his tears away. "I don't know why I did that. Jaime's words just got to me."

"Don't think anything of it, Javier," McKenzie said. "It's a tough time for all of us."

"Yeah, Javier, don't give it a thought," Mick said. "We're there with you."

"Hey, did you guys hear about Sergeant Follett?" Malco Ventura asked.

"What about him?" Carbajal said.

"I heard he and eight others in his unit, rather than surrendering, decided to run into the hills in the jungle."

"You've got to be kidding!"

"I'm not kidding. They took all of the food, weapons, ammo, and food they could carry and ran off into the jungle."

"What were they thinking?" Pete Graciano asked. "That's kind of daring. Even dangerous."

"Yeah, but I'd think Follett was aware of that. Not only because the jungles are full of Japs, but there's the Moros to contend with."

The Moros were natives of the surrounding area and were known to dislike the Filipinos and the Americans. And they'd kill anyone to get hold of a rifle.

"What do they intend to do there?" Sergeant McKenzie said.

"I believe their thinking is to join the guerillas and keep on fighting the Japanese. I understand they were strongly against surrendering."

"I knew Follett well. He's got a level head on his shoulders and not a fly-by-night sort of fellow." He let out a big sigh and stood up. "I wish him well and Godspeed. He'll need it to overcome what they've got going against them in the jungle. And I don't mean just the Moros."

With that comment, the group disbanded. Mick walked out with the group. Once out of the secluded area, he wanted to be alone and told the group he was going to take a long walk. The others walked toward the command post to find out the latest. Off in the far distance, they could hear rifle fire and occasionally, the blast from the 3.5 guns, probably coming from Corregidor, where they knew fighting was still going on.

Mick walked down a foot path along the edge of the trees bordering the jungle he had taken before. He was going nowhere in particular—just walking. His thoughts were on what he heard the others say back there in the clearing. He agreed with everything said. Yet, he hadn't spoken up. He didn't share his feelings and didn't comment at all.

As he trudged along, he began to gather an idea in his mixed up thoughts why he may have remained silent. He now realized the comments from the others appeared to border on lack of loyalty. But were they being disloyal when speaking of the lack of food and medicine and the reinforcements we were told time and time again were coming and never came? No, they weren't, it finally dawned on him. They were only speaking the truth.

They were let down. They were saying what he himself had felt before. He had thought those things, time and again. They were being deceived help was on the way when all the time those in power in Washington were concentrating their efforts in helping the British and French in Europe.

As he processed these thoughts, it came to him he hadn't spoken up at the gathering precisely because he felt he'd show disloyalty to his country in expressing his feelings he himself felt deceived. But believing a deception took place, was that disloyalty or was it just an acknowledgement of facts existing right before your eyes?

"No," he said out loud to himself, "I'm not being disloyal. I've just opened my eyes to the truth, that's all." And the guys back there weren't being disloyal either. They were only speaking the truth about how they felt of their situation. For the past six or so months he lived and fought in this island, he began to realize, the men around him hadn't waivered in their loyalty to their regiment, to their country. Not one bit.

Expressing one's complaints about what was happening around them wasn't necessarily disloyalty at all. It was only our perception of what we believe as reality. We could complain all we wanted to about our country and still be loyal to it. It was no contradiction. Our country provided us the freedom to complain. To have our grudges. *To bitch. It is a right our country gives us.*

His thoughts reminded him of his talks with Lilia and Father McCarthy about his bitterness and anger in believing he was in a situation for which he himself was to blame. It now became clear to him he hadn't quite absorbed the true meaning of what they had been telling him when he was feeling down on himself for believing he was disloyal to his country and blamed himself for his predicament. But now, it was clear.

He thought of the irony of it. The surrender to the Japanese was what afforded him the clarity to view his dilemma much differently. It suddenly occurred to him he could make use of this entire line of thinking by adjusting to the captivity to come under the Japanese for as long as it lasted. *My time on this island, especially imprisoned, doesn't have to be a total waste of my life. I can make use of it to shape me under captivity, to mold me in a beneficial way, not only now but in the near future.*

After all, wasn't a person who or what he was due to what he's been through in life, good or bad. Even unpleasantness or tragedy in the past might eventually prove beneficial and a sign of growth and maturity in the long term. In an individual's future.

Can I view the situation I now find myself in in that light? So what if my life has been thrown off balance in the past or even now with a turn of events not of my own choosing. I can try to overcome it whatever way I can.

If he was to survive what was yet to come under captivity, he must take such a path. Equally important, he owed it to Lilia, to his child, and to his family, no matter how difficult life might be under the hands of the Japanese. He became determined to hold on tight to that attitude.

10
THE FIRST SIGN OF CRUELTY

The next day, midmorning, Mick watched as the enemy tanks rolled in. They were led by an enclosed military vehicle. Many soldiers crowded around the command post. It was a blistering, sunny day, without a cloud in the sky. There was again a wet mugginess in the air seeming to stick to one's skin, not unlike any ordinary day in the Philippines. Despite the dampness, there was a sweetness in the air, brought on by the breezes sweeping through the wildflower fields nearby.

Earlier in the morning, at a briefing, Mick learned the definitive answer to the mail policy question. The answer—All prisoners, as captives not entitled to protection as prisoners of war under the Geneva Convention, would not be entitled to send or receive letters or packages through the mail. All families of prisoners would receive notification through Army channels of their imprisonment, as well as the Japanese mail policy prohibiting mail to and from prisoners.

Mick left the briefing as soon as it was over, walked into the jungle, and wept. He wouldn't be in touch with his beloved Lilia, he pondered for a long time, and wouldn't even learn of the birth of his child, much less the condition of Lilia or his child for months to come. *Now, another form of punishment. Of cruelty. How much can one bear?*

Ten of the tanks, as if to show Japanese mightiness, came to a loud grinding halt in front of the command post. A Japanese sergeant's head stuck out of the hull's opening of each tank, all of them displaying somber faces. Three or four enlisted men carrying rifles sat along the top of the tanks.

The engines of the tanks stopped, almost simultaneously, and their loudness was replaced by a sudden quietness, as two Japanese officials exited the vehicle in front of the tanks. The two Japanese officers were guided into the regiment commander's large tent. One of them appeared to be a general, but Mick wasn't certain.

The area now became more flooded with the camp's curious soldiers, now prisoners, watching in silence, in spite of an occasional murmur, cough, or clearing of throat amongst them. The armed Japanese soldiers sitting on the tanks remained motionless, no expression on their faces, but the growing crowd didn't appear intimidated by them.

The prior day, each battery of the 200th had issued the last of the rations to be distributed to its men before the arrival of the Japanese officials this morning. What food remained, the regiment's commander reasoned, would be distributed to the men, rather than turned over to the Japanese officials along with all the weapons and ammunition in the regiment's arsenal not destroyed.

When Mick's battery commander had given the final order for all men to turn in their weapons, he heard some of the men complain in anger.

"I'm not going to hand in my rifle to the Japs," one of them said. "I need it to defend myself."

"Don't act like a fool," another said, "you're a prisoner now. Get it through your head, man. We're fucking prisoners."

"Well, I'm gonna hide it, then. That's what'll I do."

As Mick gathered his rifle and what ammo he had in his person to turn it in to Ordnance, he heard others say they were going to dig a hole in the jungle to hide their rifle and ammo. He understood they were acting out of fear. To be weaponless, without the ability to defend oneself, might not be a good feeling in a battle. But they were prisoners now, and under orders from their superiors, whether they liked it or not. And besides, what could one man do against an armed enemy. It was senseless to resist turning one's weapon over to the enemy.

Yet, as Mick now stood in the midst of the enemy, without a weapon by his side, glancing at the armed Japanese soldiers on the tanks, he felt vulnerable, and he guessed the other men did too. If one of the Japanese soldiers, or worse, several of them, got off the tanks and began walking through the throng of Americans, all of them would feel helpless, for they couldn't fight back, even as victims of a cruel and senseless attack, should one of the soldiers decide to club someone with his rifle.

The soldiers, still remaining there stoically, without moving, didn't appear as if they were ready to make any threats. *But what if they got off the tanks and began making those threats? We'd be at their mercy.* Mick quickly erased the vision from his mind.

The talks inside the command post lasted over and hour. When they ended, the two Japanese officers were accompanied by two of the command post's officers to their vehicle. There, the officers saluted each other, the two Japanese officials entered their car, and the vehicle, followed by the loud tanks, left.

What Mick envisioned could happen did happen the following day, when three truckloads of Japanese soldiers arrived midmorning. These soldiers immediately dismounted the trucks and quickly got in formation by platoons, made up of three or four squads, each squad with a sergeant as squad leader. A company commander began issuing loud orders to the four platoons in formation. He spit out his words fast in Japanese, without a pause.

After about five minutes of issuing orders, he shouted what apparently was to be his final order, after which the platoon leaders gave the platoons orders of dismissal. Each platoon broke up, but each of the squads remained with their squad leader, who began leading his squad, armed with rifles, into the crowd of American soldiers. The company commander and the platoon leaders quickly disappeared, and Mick never saw them again.

As each squad moved extremely slowly through the groups of soldiers, the soldiers began parting, making room for the squads as they passed through. The squad leaders set the pace. No words were exchanged. Only curiosity seemed to fill everyone's minds. Many of the Americans, apparently feeling a bit awkward, began to disperse to get away from the Japanese soldiers, who had by now taken over the grounds once occupied by the Americans.

One of the Japanese squad leaders surprisingly stopped in front of a soldier who wore eyeglasses. The soldier was possibly six feet tall, and the sergeant was short and pudgy and had to look up high at the soldier's face.

Without saying a word, the sergeant reached up and grabbed the eyeglasses off the soldier's head. Laughing and saying something in Japanese, he put on the glasses, smiling. Instead of returning them, he put them in his shirt pocket. He next took the soldier's hands and examined them, apparently looking to see if he was wearing a ring. The soldier's hands were ringless, and the sergeant, obviously disappointed, grunted something unintelligibly and moved on.

Next, the sergeant pulled out a pair of pliers in front of another soldier. He then forced the stunned soldier to open his mouth. The soldier complied, and the sergeant began examining his teeth. Finding a gold filling, he brought up the pliers to the soldier's mouth, took hold of the gold filling, and pulled it out without warning. The soldier pulled back in pain as well as from the shock of the intrusion. Satisfied and smiling, the sergeant stuck the filling in the same pocket and then continued along his way.

Elsewhere on the grounds, the other squad leaders were doing the same thing, again, seemingly at random. If they spotted a wristwatch or ring, even cigarettes or any U. S. currency, on a soldier, they'd take it. They'd grab any piece of jewelry they found on the neck, hands, or wrists. It was the same with any gold fillings they found in someone's mouth. They didn't hesitate to bring out a pair of pliers and yank the fillings out, however many there were.

If one of the soldiers who underwent examination had nothing on him, occasionally, the sergeant would kick him and throw him on the ground to show his anger at not finding anything of value on him. Not one of the Americans resisted, out of fear they'd be shot if they did. For who was there to stop them. Other Americans who possessed nothing of value weren't able to escape the sergeant's anger with just a kick. Instead, they were clubbed painfully on the face or head by the cruel and angry squad leader, not having provided their newcomer with a "gift."

Mick and some of his friends, who were standing as a group, quickly realized they should stay clear of the squad leaders as squads moved unimpaired through the clearing on the edge of the command center, brutalizing and stealing along the way. Keeping their distance from one of the roving squads wasn't easy to do, as there were four of the sergeants, all who, it appeared, were equally aggressive in their illicit tasks. Mick's group decided to split up, thinking it'd be easier to move through the clusters of their comrades. This worked, for they succeeded in avoiding the abuses.

These examinations and brutalities went on for hours throughout the day. When most of the Americans had dispersed to avoid the violations, assaults, and thefts, the squad leaders led their armed squads to seek them out wherever they could be found, even in the jungle, to where some had retreated to stay out of sight.

These and even worse atrocities were to continue on for days.

After a week of this behavior, when the abuses worsened, Mick saw one of the squad leaders slapping one of the members of his squad, evidently for some minor disobedience or infraction. In seconds, the hard slapping turned into a beating of the soldier's head and face with a baton, as he fell to the ground from the beating, trying as best he could to fend off the blows with his hands and arms, as he crawled into a fetal position.

Mick thought to himself as he witnessed the brutality, if they attacked their own with such viciousness, what could be expected from them in dealing with our own by way of punishment for some perceived violation of conduct or some sign of disrespect of their authority, no matter how minor?

Mick received the answer the following day, when the Japanese decided to transport some of the Americans with major wounds for treatment at one of the Japanese field hospitals set up by the Japanese nearby. When the last truck used for transport was about to leave for the hospital, a wounded American reached his hand to a fellow soldier to be pulled up into the moving truck. No sooner had the newly boarded soldier sat down at the edge of the bench when the Japanese sergeant onboard the truck hollered instructions to the driver to halt the truck.

When the truck came to a stop, the sergeant began beating the American soldier on his head repeatedly, causing him to slip from the edge of his seat and eventually fall out of the truck onto the ground from the force of the trauma. The sergeant jumped off, relentlessly continuing to beat the poor soldier on the head as hard as he could until he left him there, bloody and unconscious. The sergeant jumped back into the truck, shouted in Japanese to the driver, and the driver drove the truck away, leaving the battered body on the ground.

When a few Americans rushed to the unconscious soldier to render aid, several Japanese soldiers with bayonets attempted to keep them away.

The American closest to the man lying on the ground, hovering over him to see if he was alive, got jabbed on the side by one of the Japanese soldiers, who screamed something in Japanese.

When the soldier rendering aid turned around to face the Japanese soldier threatening him with the bayonet, Mick recognized him. It was his buddy, Charlie Atkins.

"At least let us move him away from the roadway where he might get run over," Atkins pleaded with the Japanese soldier. "He's breathing. He's alive."

Without waiting for a response from an uncomprehending enemy soldier, Atkins hurriedly motioned to the other two American soldiers standing nearby to help him. The Japanese soldier made no threatening movement at all as Atkins and the other two lifted the American off the ground and lay him down a few feet away from the side of the road.

Someone had already reported the incident to the command post, and within minutes, an ambulance arrived and transported the injured soldier to the closest Japanese hospital. Mick learned later he survived the beating.

After witnessing what happened during the long day, Mick quickly rushed to the edge of the jungle a few yards away and threw up. He remained there vomiting for several minutes. When he finished, he walked a few feet farther into the jungle and sat down leaning against the trunk of a tree, stunned, where he stayed without moving for what he later guessed was at least an hour.

He would have stayed there longer, but his solitude was ended unexpectedly when a Japanese soldier scanning the area discovered him. He kept shouting at Mick while jabbing the bayonet attached to his rifle just inches away from his face.

Mick didn't have to understand their language to know what the soldier wanted him to do. The angry look on his face and his body language said it all. He quickly stood up, and as the soldier continued to threaten him with the bayonet, he moved out of the trees and walked away into the clearing, the Japanese soldier, still relentless, following closely behind.

The following day was no different. Throughout it, the Americans spread the word to their comrades and superiors of the atrocities they witnessed committed against their comrades by their captors. Day by day, the Japanese guarding the area appeared to have grown angrier and more vicious in their senseless attacks and obvious disrespect of the protections afforded prisoners of war under the terms of the Geneva Convention.

The Americans had already been warned time and time again the

Japanese government, supposedly not having signed the convention agreement, were not bound by it and were free to treat their "captives" in whatever manner they pleased or found necessary.

The incident on the back of the truck he witnessed that one day was enough for Mick. It sickened him throughout the night and for days to come. Afterward, he tried to stay away as far as he could from any of the Japanese wandering around the American encampment. But he couldn't help overhearing others report the senseless and brutal killings taking place right before their eyes.

Some of Mick's friends were picked at random as part of a group of about 50 prisoners for some work detail, such as clearing a field or building bridges over creeks. While doing this work, they witnessed on several occasions their fellow workers being beaten unconscious for not following supposed orders issued to them in a language they didn't understand.

The lack of communication, caused by the failure of captor and captive to understand each other's language, Mick thought, was a problem he hadn't foreseen, although it was a possible situation clearly staring anyone in the face, if any thought was given to it beforehand. He heard there were language interpreters in the area to assist communications between the two sides.

Such interpreters, however, must be few and far between, he thought, for he hadn't come across even one since the Japanese arrived at their location. He surmised what few there were assisted at higher levels of command, not among the enlisted men of both the American and Japanese troops, where he felt they were needed most because of the brutalities taking place mostly due to communication barriers.

Or was he kidding himself, he wondered. Maybe it wasn't just a lack of communication skills in this instance causing the brutalities and senseless killings. He had heard several American soldiers tell in tears of their witnessing what they described as murders in cold blood of several American soldiers committed by angry Japanese sergeants, reacting to the misperceived disobedience of orders in a language the victims never understood.

On three occasions, Mick himself witnessed guards putting their bayonets to use by slicing into a wounded soldier or even the body of a dead soldier, to further mutilate the body, as if to satisfy their hunger for cruelty and the maiming of others unable to help themselves.

Were these killings caused by simply the lack of communication or by the more complex lack of humanness and morality on the part of aggressive and meanspirited Japanese sergeants? The noncommissioned officers obviously had no one to answer to, for they continued their brutality without provocation and without warning repeatedly.

Mick also heard of several instances of what evidently turned out to be "faked" firing squads. According to several sources, whose word spread around the encampment, several squad leaders, while patrolling among the throngs of prisoners, randomly lined up eight to ten blindfolded prisoners. With other prisoners watching the gruesome spectacle, the particular sergeant would then instruct his squad to aim their rifles at the line of terrified prisoners, then lift up his saber, as if to order the firing of his men's rifles, only to continue holding his saber up for a prolonged period, and finally bursting out laughing, saying something unintelligible to himself, as if satisfied he had done a fine job of putting fear into the minds of his helpless captives.

11

THE EVE OF THE MARCH

After their first week in captivity, the prisoners hadn't heard any word of their move to Camp O'Donnell. Mick inquired of his platoon leader, Lieutenant Bill Forsyth, several times about the planned transport of prisoners, but he hadn't heard when the move would take place.

Meanwhile, at about the same time, word got around quickly the American troops in Corregidor had surrendered. Unless reinforcements from elsewhere arrived at this late date, Mick was thinking, the rescue chances of the prisoners now held in Bataan were gone. Up to the moment he heard of the Corregidor troops' surrender, he hadn't realized his personal hope of rescue was a mere fantasy, but he now realized the strength of the American troops on Corregidor wasn't enough to overturn the tide in their favor in Bataan. Yet, it depressed him to think first, Bataan, now, Corregidor, had been lost to the enemy.

A few days after the sinking news hit the encampment Corregidor had fallen, Mick, along with 20 other men in his battery were randomly selected by a roly-poly Japanese sergeant to be a part of 50 American soldiers to build a bridge over a wide stream a mile away preventing use of a road crossing the stream when the flow of the water got too high.

Mick looked forward to the work for two reasons. First, it gave him something to do. He had grown tired of sitting around in captivity with nothing to keep him occupied. Staying busy doing something he saw as productive, even if it only benefitted the Japanese, would make the day pass quicker. Second, good drinking water was scarce at their encampment, and this particular stream had fairly clean water passing as drinkable.

And there were no limits to the quantity one could drink. But even if it turned out not to be potable, the wading in the cold water they would be required to do in constructing the bridge would be refreshing— rejuvenating—in the heat of the day.

This work detail lasted a little over a week. The workers put the final touches on the bridge nine days after starting their work. There was one drawback to the work during those nine days, the constant and painful hits with the baton on the backs, heads, or shoulders of the prisoners. This would happen whenever the Japanese soldier supervising the assigned tasks believed one of the workers wasn't putting out enough effort into his work.

Every time a guard clobbered someone with his baton, he'd do it with a wide grin on his face, causing Mick to believe he really had no legitimate complaint a worker wasn't putting his whole effort into his work but only used the force to satisfy his need to cause pain to others.

Meanwhile, in the jungle, just after his fellow Americans had experienced their gruesome first week of captivity, Bob Follett and the other soldiers who escaped with him were busy building huts to live in. When they first arrived there, they discovered a tribe of indigenous natives who they found friendly and hospitable and decided to settle not too far away from the natives' own abodes.

The day after Follett and his fellow soldiers settled in, two of them decided they'd go hunting. Wild hogs, boars, and caribou roamed the jungle and were relatively easy prey. The two men never returned. Follett sent out search parties, fully armed, to see if they could find them, either alive or injured; or possibly dead. But no trace was ever found of them, giving rise to the fear the Moros had killed them for their rifles.

Sergeant Follett and his men, as a rule, took special care to go out fully armed and in pairs whenever the group was in need of food. The group questioned the natives about Filipino guerrilla forces in the area. Were there any, the group wanted to know. The tribe leader explained a hunting party of his tribe had come across guerilla soldiers about ten miles farther into the jungle, but none had shown themselves near his tribe.

The sergeant had grown somewhat bored, even though there was much activity in maintaining watch to defend against any Moros learning of their presence and deciding to attack without warning, day or night. Daily chores, such as searching for food or maintaining and improving their camp ground, kept them busy, but Follett and his men wanted to continue fighting the Japanese troops. He believed the best way to do that was to join the guerillas. He decided to give some thought to uprooting their location and moving farther inward to find the Filipino forces.

One day, his men were either busy building some furniture out of bamboo or out in the jungle hunting, and Follett, feeling edgy, decided to venture into the jungle alone. Realizing the danger, he felt he'd take extra precautions and carried with him several grenades, as well as his rifle and a pistol he had stolen before escaping the camp prior to the Japanese takeover. Aside from the natives who were neighbors and the Moros, who could appear anywhere, he had never seen anyone within the immediate area. But he'd have to be extremely cautious of unexpected danger as he ventured farther into unknown territory.

In his walk, he came across a narrow stream and, curious where it led, began following it. He walked several yards until he came to a place where the stream changed directions to the left. There, crouching at the edge of the stream, drinking the clear water from it, he spotted a small, Asian man with a cap and uniform. Follett immediately recognized the Japanese army uniform and pulled out his pistol, approaching cautiously from the soldier's rear. The man didn't appear to possess a weapon, even a knife, but Follett wasn't going to take any chances.

He thought of announcing himself to the man, who was still hunched over drinking water, but he decided against it, instead continuing to creep along. When he got to within ten feet away, his boot broke a limb on the ground, and the soldier quickly turned and saw Follett with his pistol pointing at him.

The soldier stood up hurriedly and, trembling, quickly raised both arms in the air. He spoke fast and loud in Japanese, his eyes glued to Follett's pistol. The look on his face wasn't only one of surprise but of fright. He was so frightened he was still shuddering, and he wouldn't stop jabbering, obviously fearing Follett would use his gun any moment.

Follett began to feel sorry for him, which surprised him. "Don't worry, don't worry," he said in a calm voice, putting up his flat hand out, gesturing he wasn't going to shoot if he wasn't threatened.

He moved closer and motioned for the man to put down his hands. "I'm not going to hurt you." He gestured toward a small boulder nearby on the edge of the creek. "Here, sit down. Sit down!"

The man appeared to understand and walked over to the rock and sat. His trembling had subsided by now, but his face clearly showed apprehension.

Follett put away his gun and walked up to the man. He appeared tiny, sitting there. "I'm going to search you," Follett said, motioning the best he could with his hands he wanted to search him. "I don't speak Japanese, and I'm assuming you don't speak English, and we're going to have to do our best to communicate with one another." He immediately thought it strange to utter words of meaning, at least to himself, to a person who didn't have the slightest idea what you were saying. It was a weird and unique sensation for him.

For the first time, the soldier smiled and nodded his head, which Follett took to mean he would allow the search. Follett conducted a thorough search and found no knife and no firearm.

The two would have to communicate the best they could with body language, Follett decided as he led the soldier to a large tree, where he gestured for the man to sit against the trunk of the tree. Follett sat down on the grass a few feet away from the soldier, who by now was considerably more relaxed. Follett was glad for that.

For about an hour, by a gesturing of their hands, Follett finally was able to piece together the soldier had gone AWOL from his unit only a few days ago. He had walked for miles, lost in the jungle for three, possibly four days. He couldn't remember exactly, for he had lost track of time. The soldier knew a few words in English. Follett, none in Japanese. The soldier knew the meaning of "walk," "soldier," "food," "water," and "escape." It was the latter that allowed Follett to conclude the man had gone AWOL.

At one point, the soldier used the words "escape" and "no good" several times close to each other, which Follett concluded meant the man was regretting having gone AWOL and now felt at a loss what he should do.

At one point in their "conversation," the man gestured with his hands, bringing one to his lips, as if puffing, conveying to Follett he was asking if Follett had any cigarettes. As it happened, Follett, a smoker, had stolen a couple of cartons of Camels from the hodge-podge "commissary" a Filipino eager to make a few bucks had set up in their encampment a few weeks before the surrender. He still had a few packs left back at the camp and was carrying one in his shirt pocket.

He took the package out and offered a cigarette to the soldier, who took it with a smile and obvious appreciation. Follett took one out for himself, lit the man's, then his.

In the hand/body "conversation" that followed, Follett believed the man wasn't aware of the surrender and possibly free to return to his unit without having to undergo sanctions or a court martial. Follett thought the man understood but wasn't sure. Having giving him the advice, Follett felt a little guilty suggesting no sanctions for the man if he returned, for he didn't know the strictness with which a returning and repentant AWOL soldier would be treated by the Japanese.

Before they parted, Follett shook the soldier's hand, and in a final gesture of friendship, gave him what cigarettes were left in the pack in his pocket. The man gladly accepted the gift and continued grinning and waving as Follett walked away from what he considered an extraordinary encounter. Whether the man was grinning from his joy of still being alive or from the gift of cigarettes, Follett would never know.

Up until the fall of Corregidor to the Japanese troops, Base Hospital 2, where Jim Puglisi was still hospitalized, had suffered a few heavy blows from artillery shelling hitting there from time to time. But these weren't attacks from Japanese guns. They were accidental shells from American artillery in Corregidor falling short of their target.

The Japanese had strategically placed an encampment and their artillery just beyond the hospital, whether by design or coincidence, no one knew. But the effect of such placement was that the hospital, and necessarily its patients, were used as a shield protecting the Japanese troops from the shelling by the American artillery in Corregidor. Unfortunately, there were occasions when the artillery rounds from the Americans fell short of their target and at times came close to, if not actually falling on the hospital, still causing collateral damage and injuries.

Usually, the Americans would only fire at the Japanese artillery near the hospital only when the Japanese themselves were actively firing their artillery. Because of such Japanese activity nearby, the hospital usually would have some warning of the shelling to come and could therefore try to protect its patients and staff by having them take cover before the barrage began. Luckily for the patients up until now, the damage had been minimal, allowing the hospital to continue with the care of its patients.

On the day before the surrender of Corregidor, Puglisi was still in a body cast from his chest to just below the knees. Within seconds of the hospital's alarm going off, alerting the staff and patients to take cover from expected shelling, a hefty Filipino ward boy showed up at the side of Puglisi's bed. He was assigned to Puglisi, and every time there was an alert, the boy was instructed to help Puglisi off his bed and place him and himself under the bed to protect them from any explosions and flying shrapnel.

The day the alarm went off, the boy hurriedly lifted Puglisi off the bed, and as he was getting ready to drop down to place Puglisi under the bed, his grip slipped and Puglisi fell from the boy's arms to the floor flat on his back. After Puglisi fell, the boy quickly shoved him under the bed and he himself squeezed in next to Puglisi. A shell came down on the hospital in another room, killing a nurse and a patient not far from where Puglisi and the Filipino boy were huddled under the bed.

A day later, just after he heard of Corregidor's surrender, Puglisi began to recover feeling in his legs. The feeling was subtle at first, but then it became stronger. In an hour or so, the feeling was one of hurt, and as the hours went by, he was in great pain. His doctor was summoned by Puglisi's nurse when Puglisi could no longer stand the pain. He described it to the doctor as a heavy tingling, stinging sensation throughout both legs, which were still covered by the cast.

"It's like being eaten by ants!" he shouted at the doctor. "Please do something!"

The bewildered doctor was at a loss what to do, having no idea whatsoever what was happening to his patient.

"Tell me what you've been doing that may have caused this?" the doctor asked.

"Nothing," Puglisi answered in great pain. "I've just been lying here." Then he recalled his being dropped by the ward boy and told the doctor what had happened the day before.

The doctor kept nodding as Puglisi was explaining. "Let's get you to X-Ray."

Within minutes, a moaning Puglisi was carried on a gurney to get an X-ray of his back. While waiting for the results, the doctor gave Puglisi a shot in both legs, which quickly began working, easing Puglisi's pain.

On examining the X-rays, the doctor explained the accidental fall "has cured you, my friend." He went on to explain Puglisi's vertebra had been pinching a nerve, and the pressure on the nerve was causing the paralysis to his legs.

"Is it like a miracle, doctor?" Puglisi asked.

"Well, you may call it that, if you wish. Another way to put it, your fall, in some magical way, straightened your back, relieving the pressure on the nerve. We'll take off your cast tomorrow, and let's see what happens, okay? Your fractures have had sufficient time to heal."

The next day, the doctor removed the cast, and within two days, Puglisi was walking, with considerable weakness at first, but with some physical therapy to strengthen his leg muscles, he was walking all over the hospital in a few days.

A few days later, the Japanese arranged to have Puglisi and the other patients in the hospital, whom of course were prisoners under the surrender, moved to Bilibid Prison as patients, located in Cabcaben on Bataan. Puglisi was "cured" but still a prisoner.

When Mick returned from helping to build the bridge the Japanese had ordered, he learned all the prisoners in the encampment were to be taken the following day to Camp O'Donnell for their imprisonment as captives, not prisoners of war.

He wasn't surprised about the trip, for everyone knew by now Camp O'Donnell would be where most of them would be imprisoned as POWs and the trek there would be taking place soon. Mick had learned a week or so ago a group of about 300 prisoners had been chosen by the Japanese to travel to Camp O'Donnell by train and trucks to help ready the camp for the thousands of prisoners to be imprisoned there.

What was surprising—shocking, really—was that, despite the Japanese had plenty of trucks and a train rail ran practically all the way to Camp O'Donnell, they had instead chosen to force the prisoners to walk the entire distance to their imprisonment.

The horrid examples of mistreatment by the Japanese for the few short weeks of their imprisonment so far would be no match for the gruesome and brutal treatment they were to receive in the eight-day trip to Camp O'Donnell some 85 miles away.

Whether they'd be better off knowing what was in store for them during the trek or not knowing was a question without an answer. Some might argue neither option would prepare them for what lay ahead. Others might say that for at least some of the prisoners, knowing would dampen their morale, thus hindering their efforts to survive the ordeal, and for the other prisoners, the knowledge would better prepare them to survive by strengthening their determination and mental and physical energy to instinctively embrace the will to live, surmounting any challenges standing in the way to survival.

But either way, it wouldn't be only a question of whether they were weak or strong individuals, mentally or physically, for either kind could be unfortunate enough to come in contact with a brutal Japanese guard at the wrong place and at the wrong time during the trek, an occurrence possibly ending their lives. Sadly, it might be this misfortune determining their fate, not their strength or weakness to survive.

PART IV

THE ROAD TO HELL

12
THE BEGINNING OF THE MARCH

Dennis Gurley, Mick's Native-American friend from Taos Pueblo in New Mexico, had been among the approximately 300 prisoners chosen to travel the distance to Camp O'Donnell to ready the camp for the imprisonment to come. In being chosen at random, these prisoners were fortunate to have escaped the march on foot to the camp.

Gurley's group began the trip by being loaded onto trucks, which took them to San Fernando, where they spent the night. There, they were squeezed into a small corral, where they were forced to sleep in the manure. And because it had rained hard the day before, the corral was muddy, and they slept in the moistened and odorous manure and deep mud too. They went to sleep tired, weak, and hungry, for they hadn't eaten for two or three days.

The next morning, they were packed tightly into boxcars, where everyone had to stand because there was no room for anyone to sit or lay down. The box cars, having been used to transport cattle, were full of manure, wreaking a stifling stench, which, with the heat of the day, overcame some prisoners to unconsciousness.

Not having any water for several days didn't help their already extreme dehydration, and some died standing up. The train only took them to a place called Capas, where they were unloaded and made to walk the remaining eight to ten miles to Camp O'Donnell. The men who had died within the boxcars during the transport were unloaded by prisoners under orders of the guards and placed on the ground away from the rail tracks.

"At least let us bury them," Gurley said to the guard when he had placed the last dead prisoner on the ground. "It won't take long."

The guard, Gurley had found out at the beginning of the trip, knew a little English.

"No, no time," the guard said. "Got no time. Move! Move!"

"We can't just leave them there, for God's sake!" Gurley protested.

"No! No! No time, no time." The guard prodded Gurley with the tip of his bayonet to join the others on the walk.

Once they arrived at Camp O'Donnell, Gurley and the other members of the 200th in the group separated from the others to bunk together as a group in the barracks. Before entering the barracks, they were searched, even though they had already been searched before being transported to the camp. Whatever meager possessions they still had on their person were taken away. They weren't given any food at the beginning of their stay. Later, they were served rice and even seaweed, which was tasteless, but they hoped was at least nutritious.

During their first week, they were made to work twelve hours a day, from sunup to sunset, readying what was once a Philippine Army training camp for their imprisonment and the imprisonment of the POWs who were to arrive in a few days. In the blistering heat of the day, they repaired broken sewer, gas, and water pipes, build kitchens from scratch, build fences, both wooden and wire, and erected guard towers throughout the camp.

After Mick learned of the forced walk to Camp O'Donnell on his return from working on the bridge, upon waking up the next day, he was immediately herded into a group of men from the 200th who were soon to begin their journey to their destination about eighty miles away. Evidently, for better control and security, the Japanese made plans to gather the marchers in groups of about 200 each, assigning two or three guards to each group.

The first groups to begin the march were made up of about 1,000 Filipino soldiers who were found scattered throughout Bataan during the shelling of the last battle before the surrender. Here again, they were broken into groups of 200 prisoners, traveling in rows of three to four men abreast.

Mick's group had a distance of 82 miles in front of them, while other groups who were made up of soldiers from other units, Filipino and American, not belonging to the 200th, had less miles to travel, depending on where along the route they had been held captive. The men of the 200th sought each other out before the march, determined to march together as soldiers who had sworn a bond to each other to survive any mistreatment laying ahead of them.

In truth, then, what was to be later known in the annals of military history as the Bataan Death March was not one, but several marches from different parts of Bataan. Each of the several marches consisted of a multitude of thousands of soldiers converging into one line from many sectors, depending on the location where the prisoners were collected to begin the march or from where in the jungles they had become prisoners.

Mick began the march with a large group of men from his battery, desiring to be with his friends and soldiers whom he knew well enough to feel he belonged. When he first started on the journey, he wasn't feeling well and had a fever. He had suffered in the past from many different diseases and ailments but recently, was feeling as strong as one could be despite feeling the pangs of hunger in one's belly. It wasn't until the day after he returned to their encampment from the bridge-building project when he began feeling the effects of malaria resurfacing. The fever was one of the first signs and the high fever still persisted during the first day of the march.

But his spirits were strong, nonetheless, which he attributed ironically to having witnessed the malevolent treatment of his fellow prisoners during those initial two weeks of captivity, which he had luckily escaped. The cruel treatment during those weeks had somehow reinforced his determination— his desire—to overcome the Japanese's unparalleled sadistic behavior. *Go figure such logic.*

Still suffering from the fever late in the day on the second day of the march, he suddenly became weaker and began shuddering. He decided to risk the wrath of the guards and, when the guard closest to him was on the other side of the columns of prisoners, he quickly dropped to the side of the road. He guessed it was now about the time shortly before they'd be stopped to sleep for the night along the side of the road, which he based on when they had been stopped the first day. He was just taking his break a few minutes earlier, he reasoned. He hoped if he was unnoticed by a guard until the march ended for the day, he'd be only one of thousands of prisoners resting on the ground alongside the road for the night.

Lying there resting near the edge of the road for only a moment, still weakened by the fever and his body tremors, he suddenly lost consciousness.

He remembered nothing at all until just before dawn on the following day, when he'd been awakened by a hard kick to the head. He opened his eyes and saw a Japanese guard shining a flashlight clamped to his bayonet pointed right in front of his eyes. Fearing the guard would use his bayonet on him, he stood up the best he could, despite his grogginess. The first thing he noticed was his fever was gone. It must have broken during the night while he slept, he thought.

Hurriedly, trying not to give the guard a chance of reacting to his perceived misconduct, he rushed into the columns of prisoners who were already marching, and lost himself somewhere in the middle of the rows of prisoners. Even the day before, he learned the way to stay out of the reach of the guards' mistreatment during the march, if only from a poke of a bayonet, which the guards seemed to take joy in doing repeatedly, was to stay away from marching on the outside of the columns.

Realizing he had lost consciousness soon after dropping out of the march to the side of the road, he was grateful he escaped being pierced by the guard's bayonet. He was lucky to be alive, and he thanked God for that. He had lost his place amongst his buddies, but that was the least of his worries. He'd soon find them, he thought, and he did later in the day.

The bayonets prodded them along the third day, and they were stopped again at noon to receive a meager bowl of rice. Water trucks stopped on that day where they were being served their one meal of the day, and the prisoners were allowed to fill their canteen with fresh water.

Mick hadn't filled his canteen since the start of the march three days before. The first two days, even when the march was halted to allow the prisoners and guards time to rest, the prisoners weren't allowed to go to nearby creeks or ponds as the marchers passed them. Many believed the water from that source was potable and would have taken advantage of the opportunity to either drink or fill their canteens. Mick would rather risk dehydration than become deadly sick from contaminated water. He vowed to himself he wouldn't be tempted to drink from any creek or pond along the way, even if he had been permitted to do so.

The guards of each group of marchers set the pace. The prisoners would have to keep up or slow down, depending on the guard's gait. At times during the day, the walking guards were replaced by guards riding a bicycle, and because the prisoners were required to keep pace, they had to walk at a faster pace, thus creating difficulties for most of them, especially those who were limping from some ailment or injury. The blistering sun, aided by lack of food and less than enough water, took their toll on the POWs, who were already weakened by disease and hunger.

Mick saw a few of his buddies suffer throughout the fourth day. That, to him, had been one of the drawbacks of having found them again, after dropping out on the second day.

Tommy Van Heflin and Pete Graciano were two of them. Van Heflin looked extremely pale and walked as if he would keel over any second. But Mick could tell by the grimace in his face he was determined to stick it out as long as his legs held out.

What Mick didn't know motivated Van Heflin to stay upright and continue walking was that on two separate occasions, he had witnessed two prisoners a few yards ahead of him fall down, and before they could get up, a guard quickly ran his bayonet through them, not once but twice, leaving them dead or bleeding to death on the side of the road. When another prisoner knelt down to help, the same guard threatened him with the bayonet. To Van Heflin, the travesties he was witnessing all seemed so unreal that he questioned if he was hallucinating.

Pete Graciano faced a different problem. His stomach was cramping as he walked, the horrendous pain causing him to hunch over so much he kept losing his balance. He, too, had seen the same two fallen soldiers bayonetted and left helpless or dead on the side of the road. The thought of his being the guard's next victim motivated him to straighten up as he walked, despite the pain.

He tried with all his might to continue walking, but the pain got so great he stumbled to the side of the road. There, holding both his hands to his abdomen, he knelt down from his weakness. He immediately spotted the guard ahead, who saw him and hurried toward him. Graciano quickly forced himself to stand up and, without waiting to explain to the approaching guard, moved quickly into the columns of marchers, hoping to get lost on the other side.

For whatever the reason, the guard decided not to go after him. Having escaped a thrust of a bayonet, he considered himself fortunate. The relief he felt kept his mind off his painful stomach cramps, and he managed to continue on until the pain suddenly disappeared.

For Mick, he'd rather go thirsty than risk trying to quench his thirst from water sources along the route. He found his canteen empty on the fourth day and was tortured when he spotted water wells or spouts with dripping water. But he had already seen what would happen if a prisoner tried to fill his canteen with water unless it was during a rest stop. And even then, he'd be taking a risk. You'd get shot, bayonetted, or get your head busted with the butt of a rifle, he believed, if an overzealous guard overreacted to stop the effort.

The temptation to drink from the ponds and streams along the way was much greater when the marchers were allowed a rest break. It was then a few of the prisoners, their faces showing their hysteria and their mouths swollen from lack of water, made the mistake of rushing to a stream or worse, a ditch, and drinking from it. Those water sources were extremely polluted with carabao dung, dead bodies, refuse, and sewage from native tribes.

Roque Alvarez and Nick Sanchez had grown up together and were life-long friends, and they were walking the march alongside one another since it began. Together, during the rest stops, they had seen the prisoners, delirious for water, race to the polluted water holes and ditches, only to pay for it afterward with painful stomach cramps and bouts of diarrhea, having to continue their trek in soiled underwear and clothing.

During one rest stop, Alvarez came very close to following the hysterical soldiers to a water hole. As Alvarez took a few steps toward the water, Sanchez stood up and pulled him by the arm.

"All right, go drink and die, for all I care, you fucking son of a bitch!" Sanchez yelled at him inches from Alvarez's face. "Go on, die, why don't you!"

Sanchez' passion worked. Reluctantly, Alvarez pulled back and abandoned the futile attempt to quench his thirst.

13

THE CRUELTIES

How inhumane can a fellow human being be, Mick thought as he saw the men constantly driven from getting a drink of water with a butt of a rifle to the head or worse, a slash of a bayonet to the body. *What is driving the Japanese to such treatment?* It was difficult to comprehend.

Several times during the day, trucks would pull up on the side of the road, with new guards on board who'd relieve the guards who had been at their task for several hours. All of the prisoners came to hate it when that happened, for they knew the new guards would walk at a faster pace, forcing the prisoners to increase their gait to keep up with the refreshed guards.

The next day, the fifth day of the march, was no different from the one before. The days, for all of the prisoners, were beginning to blur together, the atrocities repeating themselves time and time again, with no end in sight.

The heat on this day was especially hard on Andy Gluck, who had been suffering from malaria for several days, even before he began the march. He realized in the middle of the afternoon he had apparently lost consciousness while walking. It started raining, and when the rain began to hit him in the face, he suddenly became aware he had been walking in his sleep or a state of unconsciousness, although he couldn't understand how it could be possible. He couldn't remember exactly when he had lost consciousness. And he couldn't believe he lost track of time and remembered absolutely nothing of the past two hours or so even though he continued walking.

Jaime Soltero, the Native American from Acoma, got bayoneted in his upper leg near his buttocks for aiding his buddy, Ron Patterson, who suddenly suffered a cramp on his leg and knelt down on the side of the road to try to rub the cramp away. Soltero risked the wrath of the guard in their group, who had shown before he wouldn't hesitate to use his bayonet or the butt of his rifle in such instances. Luckily, the bayonet struck Soltero's femur, which stopped it from going straight through. Surprisingly, the guard gave him enough time to wrap his handkerchief around his leg to control the bleeding. Soltero couldn't believe such generosity from someone cruel enough to have caused the injury in the first place.

For whatever reason Mick at first couldn't figure out, the men in the 200th were warned soon after the surrender to burn or destroy any Japanese currency they had on their person. There was some concern if caught with the currency during the searches to be conducted by the Japanese they might suffer severe consequences.

Later, Mick asked his platoon leader, Lieutenant Forsyth, why the Japanese felt so strongly against the possession of Japanese currency by any American soldier. The lieutenant explained what he had been told, namely the Japanese assumed any soldier who carried such currency had taken it off a dead Japanese soldier after either killing him or finding his body in the field of battle. That made sense to Mick, although he didn't agree with the extent of the punishment the Japanese believed the theft warranted, even assuming the theft had occurred.

When two prisoners not in the 200th were found with Japanese currency during an extended rest period of the march, Mick was surprised, reasoning the warning had been given throughout the American forces to get rid of the currency. Why these two soldiers had the money in their possession, having been given the warning and with no possible way to use it, Mick couldn't understand.

The "severe consequences" Mick had been warned about soon came about before his eyes. The two men found with the Japanese money were stripped of all their clothes, forced to stand naked, holding the currency in both hands in front of them, and shot by four Japanese soldiers lined up as some kind of firing squad. But that wasn't the end of the brutality. With their bayonets, two guards sliced off the two men's penises and shoved them in their mouths.

The guards then shoved two shovels into the hands of two prisoners nearby and ordered them to dig a grave for the two dead soldiers. The men with shovels were only partly finished digging a hole when the signal was given to resume the march. The two diggers were ordered to stop digging and to leave the mutilated bodies on the ground, not even half covered with dirt.

Mick was sickened by the incredible scene he had just witnessed and continuously dry-heaved onto the side of the road, not having anything in his belly to vomit.

Over and over again, Mick witnessed other similar brutalities, too many for him to keep count of. Some of the guards appeared to enjoy inflicting pain on prisoners without killing them. Instead, they'd leave them to suffer and eventually die from the pain if not the wound.

A prisoner was better off being shot to death with one bullet, then bayoneted or shot only to be left there with pain until he died. Such were the thoughts going through Mick's mind as he walked past beheaded American soldiers and the countless headless Filipinos on the side of the road. Aside from such cruelty, he saw his fellow soldiers stagger for hours before falling unconscious to the ground, where they would remain until . . . "God knows when," Mick said to himself in disgust.

Not all about the march was of man's inhumanity to man. There were signs of benevolence, kindness, decency, and other positive signals coming not from the guards but from others.

Such signals came across to the marchers as they passed through the barrios, where natives were eager to come to their aid, if but for a brief moment and with a simple gesture. There weren't enough guards to prevent a native from passing a bottle of water to a moving prisoner from time to time, or giving another a cone of brown sugar or rice wrapped up in a banana leaf. Such acts of benevolence took place at each barrio the march passed through.

In one barrio, a little girl tossed Charlie Atkins a big, red, juicy tomato, and Tomate DeLaO got a small packet of fish and rice from a small boy. Both the boy and the girl, as they passed along their gifts, kept a watchful eye for guards who might be ready to swing their rifle or thrust their bayonet against any of the natives willing to help the prisoners. A small boy gave Mick a New York Yankees baseball cap. Some natives stood there weeping, even the Filipino men, when they saw the marchers' plight and suffering as they staggered by them.

Unfortunately, some natives who got caught red handed giving the smallest of gifts to the Americans paid dire consequences and some even paid for such acts of kindness with their lives.

One old Filipino woman hurriedly passed a paper cup of water to a prisoner, and when she saw the anger in the guard who had caught her doing it, hurried back into her small abode. The angry guard ran into the woman's dwelling and dragged her out by her hair, cut both her ears off and, as if that weren't enough to make his point, sliced off her breasts. He picked up the sliced-off ears and breasts in both hands and threw them into the columns of marchers.

Another woman, possibly six to eight months pregnant, was caught handing a piece of cake over to a prisoner. The guard who saw her "infraction" immediately ran up to her, screaming at the top of his lungs. He grabbed her hand, held her up, and pierced her in the abdomen with his bayonet. He let go of her, and she fell to the ground in agony. As if he hadn't yet finished making her an example to the other natives, the guard bayoneted her again, this time near her heart, as she lay helpless on the ground. He then cut her belly open, pulled out the unborn child, and laughed loudly as he held the fetus up in the air, a proud look on his face.

On the sixth day, not during a rest stop but as the prisoners were moving, Malco Ventura suddenly pulled away from his column and dashed toward an artesian well he spotted a few yards from the road. He had been walking a couple of rows ahead of Mick, and Mick saw clearly as the guard close by aimed at the running Ventura and fired. The bullet hit him in the upper back and went through his body, exiting at his right chest. But he had fallen on the wall of the well, and he got his drink of water.

Incredibly, he was able to walk back, holding a handkerchief to the bleeding wound on his chest. The guard who had wounded him prodded him with his bayonet back to the columns of marchers, where Ventura, still pressing his wound, continued marching, apparently not weak enough from his injury to prevent him from walking.

During the next stop, Mick collected enough water in his canteen from a running spout alongside the road, which he shared with Ventura, who by now was growing weaker from his chest wound. Mick stayed with him as they sat resting. When they started off again, Mick helped Ventura get up but realized as he was pulling him off the ground Ventura was hardly able to lift himself to stand up. Mick helped him to the columns and, as they began walking, helped to hold him up by having Ventura put one arm around Mick's neck and holding him by his wrist to keep him upright.

Mick wasn't surprised when only half an hour later, still bleeding, Ventura grew weaker. But they continued their pace.

"Please, Mick," Ventura whispered as they trudged down the road. "Leave me here. Let me die here alongside the road."

"No, Malco," Mick whispered back, "we'll get you some help for that wound soon." As he mouthed the words, he knew they weren't true. He just didn't want to believe what seemed inevitable was going to happen, and Ventura knew that.

"There's no help for me, Mick, and you know it." He took a deep breath. "Just leave me here to die in peace."

Mick shook his head but didn't answer.

They continued on.

Several times, Ventura again pled with Mick to leave him. Mick refused, urging him to continue walking. In his own mind, Mick wasn't sure Ventura would make it through the day. But he didn't want to give up trying to help a friend, although he questioned his own strength to continue helping.

At the next rest stop, Mick helped Ventura sit down with his back against a large boulder on the side of the road. He left him there, holding his bloody handkerchief to the wound, and went off in search for more water.

A few minutes later, he returned empty handed. As he neared where he had left Ventura, he immediately noticed several POWs and a guard surrounding the boulder, looking down. He found Ventura, still perched against the boulder, covered in blood. He was dead. In his hand was a piece of broken glass. He must have found the glass on the ground next to him and used it to slit his carotid artery on the side of his neck.

For Mick, the rest of that day was just a blur. He found himself demoralized. Ventura's death, to him, epitomized all of what he saw wrong at the moment. In this senseless march. In the unbelievable brutalities. In the absurdities of war, even. The next day, too, was a blur, as he fell into a deep depression caused by the death of Ventura. But by the end of the day, he convinced himself that, if he was going to survive this ordeal, he must find a way to pull out of his depression. If he didn't, he was certain he was going to die.

He thought of Lilia, of his parents, and of his and Lilia's child, who, if the doctor had calculated correctly, had been born about a week after the surrender. He had to survive. For them. To do that, he'd have to pull out of his demoralized state.

Experiencing Ventura's death was horrible, but he knew he'd have to get beyond it's impact on his mental state and not dwell on its horror. As terrible as it was, he had to move on to the next day, and the next after that. If he was to survive the coming months so he could return safely to Lilia, to his child, he'd have to surmount the grim reality of this march and Ventura's death.

By the end of the day, he grew in his resolve to do exactly that. He said a special prayer to God, thanking Him for having gotten through another day. And he promised himself to continue his resolve the following day and the next.

Believing he had regained his self-confidence to move on ahead, he couldn't help wondering what would happen after this march was over. What then? What lay in store for them when they reached their destination? The same brutalities? Would the suffering be endless? Mick prayed it wouldn't. And he prayed for strength to persevere whatever lay ahead. No matter what it might be, he vowed he'd never again let anything sway him from his determination to live so he might return to Lilia and his family. Of that, he became certain.

14
THE END OF THE MARCH

The march's eighth and final day ended in the municipality of San Fernando. Apart from the deaths occurring during the march, the prisoners witnessed many of their comrades who were sane before the march become deranged by the time they arrived at the rail station at San Fernando. From there, all of them would be transported in boxcars, which would take them most of the remaining approximately eight miles to Camp O'Donnell.

For Mick, his arrival at San Fernando was a godsend. Several times during the march, he was ready to give up hope he'd make it all the way. When it suddenly came to him he'd succeeded doing that upon arriving at the city, heavy tears came to his eyes as he bowed his head and thanked God for his having lived through the incredulous ordeal. His survival, he believed, would provide him with the strength to endure the rest of his imprisonment with the hope of one day seeing and being with his beloved family again.

Many thousands perished during the unbelievably onerous ordeal the American and Filipino prisoners underwent in the final days before imprisonment at Camp O'Donnell, not the least being the gruesome brutalities during the march that took many lives.

No one would ever be able to pinpoint the exact number of lost lives, but if one took into account the approximate number of American and Filipino soldiers who took to the hills soon after the surrender and those who were patients in hospitals, a fair estimate would be that 62,000 Filipinos and 11,000 Americans, a total of 73,000 soldiers, participated in the march.

It was also estimated, through examination of the military records kept on the number of Filipino and American soldiers assigned to units in the Philippines during the time of the march, about 51,500 prisoners survived the march and made it to Camp O'Donnell. Of this number, about 9,500 were American soldiers. One could conclude from these numbers that about 21,500 prisoners who participated in the march died during the march, of which about 1,500 were American soldiers and 20,000 were Filipino soldiers.

Although it'd be difficult to compute the numbers, due to the many deaths occurring at Camp O'Donnell and elsewhere during the imprisonment of the POWs, there were additional deaths at the camp easily attributable to injuries or complications arising from the prisoners' treatment during the march.

Before they were to board the boxcars, the prisoners were kept in a large corral at the rail station used for cattle while awaiting transport to slaughter by rail. There were no trenches or holes dug out in the ground for human excrement, much less latrines or toilets. There were no sinks or wash basins to clean or bath in. Only two spigots at each end of the corral were available for water, and the water pressure was extremely low. Two long lines formed at each faucet for splashing or drinking, and the lines were to continue throughout the night spent in the corral.

The corral itself had never been cleaned from animal excrement, and piles of not only manure but both animal and human feces covered the ground. The men who suffered from dysentery couldn't escape the diarrhea caused by the disease and, without control of their bowel movement, soiled not only their clothes but left droplets of contaminated body fluid and feces mixed in with the manure and animal excrement already on the ground. The combined stench, mixed with the heat and humidity in the air, made their stay in the corral unbearable and caused many to vomit or pass out.

Not long after the prisoners were herded into the corral, much like cattle, a curious small boy wandered into the yard, seemingly dazed by the spectacle of the prisoners' arrival to his hometown. He was friendly with the prisoners and appeared happy to be in their presence. As soon as Mick spotted the friendly boy, he recognized him as the same youngster who had surprised him a few days earlier in the barrio with the gift of the New York Yankees baseball cap. The boy recognized him as well, and the two of them began meandering through the crowded corral toward each other.

Mick and the boy exchanged a few words of greeting and visited with each other, the boy in broken English, for only a brief moment lest a guard get overzealous with his bayonet or baton and hurt the youngster. Or Mick, for that matter.

Before they parted, Mick took his cap off. "Here," he said to the boy, offering for him to take the cap. "It helped me keep the sun off my head, and I won't be needing it anymore."

The youngster hesitated, shaking his head. "No, no," he said with a frown. "It gift."

"Yes, yes, I insist." Mick forced the boy to take the cap, who quickly put it on and grinned up at Mick.

That evening, the boy returned and sought Mick out in the corral. Finding him, he reached into the inside of his shirt and brought out a couple of peaches he had smuggled in.

With a big grin, he offered the peaches to Mick. "Here. For you from my mother." He glanced around to make sure he hadn't been spotted by a guard.

Mick took the peaches with a smile. "Thanks. And please thank your mom." Even with the stench in the air, Mick could smell the peaches' freshness.

The boy nodded and went on his way out of the corral. Mick was never to see him again, but he was certain he'd never forget the boy's generosity. This coincidental incident, Mick believed, together with his arrival at the end of his arduous journey, was remarkably important to, and symbolic of, his will to live long enough to get home, whenever it might be.

"No more negativity," he whispered to himself. "Only positive thoughts of seeing my family again no matter what might lay in store for us at Camp O'Donnell or elsewhere in this war." *That thought alone, and only the thought, will be what will help me get through all this ugliness and get back to my beloved Lilia and child, so help me, God.*

It was in the filth and stench of the corral where the prisoners were forced to spend the night, most falling exhausted to sleep on top of the manure and excrement. Several didn't awaken early in the morning when the prisoners were herded into the boxcars at the train depot a few yards away. They were dead.

At the depot, 110 men were shoved into each boxcar, where they were crammed in like sardines, and the trapped heat and odor proved to be more unbearable than in the open air of the corral. By the time the train started its journey, the weakened prisoners couldn't get enough air, and some, especially the sick and weakened, began to suffocate. Eventually, the prisoners discovered the doors hadn't been locked, and they were able to open them almost halfway, to allow some air in. That alone saved some lives.

Because of the partly open boxcars, as the train slowed down through small towns, the prisoners found groups of natives who, knowing the prisoners were passing through, threw food at them in containers through the open doorways. Some threw water bottles. Others, raw eggs and fruit. Several threw baked sweet potatoes.

They were signs of goodwill, for a change, that wouldn't be sanctioned as they had been when Japanese guards were around to prevent what they considered punishable infractions and disrespect to authority. Here, in these rural communities, where the natives showed such generosity, there was no one to put a halt to their benevolence.

Most of the weakened and sick didn't survive the trip through the night, and in the morning the prisoners, when unloading at Capas, a tiny community, placed the corpses in piles a few yards from the track. The American commander of the prisoners, General Sage, was assured by the Japanese officers monitoring the transportation of the prisoners in Capas a proper burial of the dead prisoners piled high along the rail track would take place soon. General Sage had to take them at their word, not knowing if they would keep it.

From Capas, the prisoners were marched the remaining ten or so miles to Camp O'Donnell. Before entering the camp, all of the prisoners went through a thorough search, one of several they'd undergone since the beginning of their captivity. Once again, the prisoners were quietly reminded by their leaders before the search to rid themselves of Japanese currency or any item of whatever kind possibly of Japanese origin. By now, the men had learned, as Mick had long before, the reason why it was important not to possess anything Japanese.

At Bilibid Prison, Jim Puglisi was still confined as a prisoner of war but as a patient also, recovering from his injuries. Prisoners held there, as other prisoners of the Japanese elsewhere, were fed mostly rice daily. But

Puglisi learned soon after his first day there a Filipino came around almost every day selling fried bananas, fruit, and other food items not otherwise available at the prison.

Those confined at the prison were allowed to buy from the Filipino any food item as an alternative to the rice served every day, assuming they had the money to pay for it. Because patients under Japanese captivity were allowed to possess American currency, which was legal tender in the Philippines, Puglisi was allowed to keep his money when the Japanese made the patients of Base Hospital 2 their prisoners. Because he could afford it, Puglisi became a good customer of the vendor.

It so happened Puglisi knew the Filipino vendor from his days spent as a patient at Base Hospital 2, where they had become friends. He knew him as Edgar Guzman. And Guzman knew Puglisi as Pulga, his nickname. Guzman spoke and understood English quite well.

One day, after making a purchase from Guzman, Puglisi came up with an idea.

"Edgar, what kind of ID card do you need to get in and out of here to sell your stuff?" Puglisi asked.

"The same one other vendors possess," Guzman answered.

"Would you please show it to me?"

Guzman nodded and took out a card with his photo on it. "Here, take a look." He handed the card to Puglisi, who examined it. It was in Japanese, and Puglisi recognized nothing but the photo.

"I have a proposal to make and a favor to ask of you, Edgar. You and I have known each other for quite a while, and you know you can trust me. I'll make this worth your while."

"What you got in mind, Pulga?"

"What would you say to the idea of you and I switching places. You can stay here in my place as a patient just for a couple of days. The nurses won't care and will treat you well, and the Japanese guards don't even come around to check on us except in a great while. We could do it. They don't give a shit. What do you say?"

"Why you want to do that?"

"It's just that I've been confined for so long as a patient, and I get antsy. I'd like to see the outside world for a change, like you do every day. Please do it as a favor to me, Edgar."

Guzman smiled. "I consider you friend, Pulga, but I don't want to get in trouble if you caught. What happen to me then?"

"We won't get caught, I tell you. And we can arrange some payment to you in return. I've got some money. And you'd be doing a favor to a friend."

"But photo. They know you not me."

"I've seen how the guards operate here. They won't give a shit, I tell you. They'll never look at the photo. We can make it happen, I assure you, and it's worth a try. And more money in your pocket."

Guzman grinned, then displayed a serious face. "Where you go if I say 'yes?'"

"Well, I hadn't thought of that. I'd have to think about it. You have any ideas?"

Guzman laughed. "Gee, I don't know." He paused in thought. "Maybe you can stay my parents. I live with them."

"You don't think they'd object?"

"Naw, don't think so. I tell them about you from the hospital. They know already we friends."

They spoke some more and came to an agreement on compensation. Guzman agreed to speak to his parents but assured Puglisi there'd be no problem. They'd go along, he said. But he was worried about the guards.

"They won't be a problem, believe me," Puglisi assured him.

Puglisi was right. The first time he went out the gate, carrying the same bundled containers of food Guzman carried, he acted nonchalant, added a smile, and just flashed the ID card to the guard, who was occupied doing some task and just waved him off without looking up.

In this manner, Puglisi stayed with Guzman's parents, who he found exceedingly friendly. They lived on a houseboat on the Pasig River. As Edgar's friend, they, too, considered him a friend and insisted that when he wasn't away, he'd eat with them. The scheme Puglisi concocted worked better than he had imagined, and he got to enjoy Guzman's mother's home cooking as a bonus, which he hadn't bargained for.

He got away doing this many times, and it went smoothly each time. On several occasions, Guzman's father helped Puglisi buy sulfa powders, which were good as antiseptics, and quinine, which the soldiers took for the treatment of malaria, bouts from which they suffered constantly. Every time Puglisi returned to the prison, he carried with him a basket filled with fried bananas, some of which he shared with the guards and nurses. Hidden beneath the cloth covering the fried bananas were the medicines he was bringing for the patients.

Several times, he realized he could simply take off and not return to the prison. But two things always kept him from thinking about an escape for too long. First, he really had no place to go where the Japanese wouldn't eventually find him, and he didn't know anyone else. If he were to be found, he was sure he'd be shot. Second, and more importantly, he didn't want to do anything that would cause Guzman any problems, and he reasoned that doing it a few times temporarily wouldn't get Guzman in trouble but staying away permanently would.

"That was something I'd never do and couldn't live with," he said out loud to himself.

PART V

THE STRUGGLE FOR SURVIVAL

15
THE BEGINNING AT O'DONNELL

Captain Yoshio Tsuneyoshi, a short and chubby reserve officer in the Japanese Army, was the commander at the prison camp at Camp O'Donnell. A pompous man, he possessed skinny legs, which he displayed every day because he wore shorts, and this combination accentuated the size of his belly, protruding quite visibly. Despite his distorted stature, he might have been considered a good-looking man, but for his visibly scared, pockmarked face, which gave him a somewhat grotesque appearance.

He possessed a high-pitched and cracking voice forever shouting threatening and cruel words, grossly unsympathetic to the plight of "his" captives, not prisoners of war.

He'd relish shouting to the Americans through an interpreter, "You are *my* captives!". Occasionally, he'd refer to them as "the Emperor's captives."

Because of his shortness, he'd always use a small wooden box about a foot high whenever he spoke to the prisoners.

He first spoke to the men in the prison camp two days after they were assigned to their measly living quarters, referred to as barracks but were really elevated huts made of straw, not the structure of barracks in the traditional, military sense.

"You are *my* captives," he shouted, "not entitled to protection under the Geneva Convention. Any disrespect to me or to my men will be considered insulting and disrespectful to the Emperor and *will not* be tolerated. If you disrespect any orders given to you, you will be punished severely."

The prisoners soon learned not to stand too close to him when he mounted his box to begin shouting at them because his spittle could be seen traveling several feet into the air due to the force of his piercing, annoying shouts.

"I dislike non-Asians," he said the first time he spoke to the Americans through an interpreter, "especially Americans. You are evil and because you are, you will be subject to our control once we win this war. You are worse than infidels. To me, you are nonentities and because I believe you are, I don't care whether you live or die. Any violation of our rules *will not* be tolerated and may cause *instant death* for any of you who disobey our rules."

Although he said he disliked non-Asians, the tone of his words showed clearly to the men though he might *dislike* all Caucasians, he *especially hated* Americans. With a venom, it seemed.

"And in summation," he erupted in closing his remarks, "I order you to be good captives and behave according to our rules, for otherwise you will suffer the consequences, which, I promise you, you will *not* enjoy." He displayed a big grin, which lasted a long time.

"Show your loyalty to the Emperor by obeying our rules. You are his guests here. Only his mercy permits you to live." He cleared his throat.

"One final word of warning. You will be put to death if you should try to escape." He let out a big sigh, his face showing his pride in himself. "That is all for now! You are dismissed!"

The Americans dispersed from the "welcoming speech," which had gone on and on, knowing the commander succeeded in making his point. He made sure they clearly understood their imprisonment under him would be a living hell. His threats resonated with them that if they wanted to survive, they should always obey the commands of the guards, otherwise suffer serious injury or even death. His menacing threats were made plain.

Despite their fear of Commander Tsuneyoshi's hate and ramblings, the men soon began to refer to him as Baggy Pants because he had no buttocks to speak of to fill out his pants, and, adding his skinny legs to the equation, he appeared as a laughable caricature from a comic strip. But no matter their injecting humor into their predicament, and their constant laughing amongst themselves about the distorted image of their commander, they wouldn't dare even come close to mocking the man in his or any of the guards' presence, for fear they'd suffer severe consequences.

Not long after everyone in the camp began referring to their camp commander as Baggy Pants, Mick took out his sketch pad and sketching pencils and, once again, put his magic—his drawing skills—to work in sketching a caricature of Baggy Pants. Mick drew him in full uniform, with his swagger stick and skinny legs, standing on his small, wooden box. And to complete the image as true, he added droplets of his spit propelled into the air as he mouthed off, "I am Captain Yoshio Tsuneyoshi, your supreme camp commander, and you are my captives!"

The sketch, when completed, went from prisoner to prisoner all over the camp and in a few days, there wasn't a prisoner who hadn't seen and laughed over it. It was passed around over and over again for several weeks, until finally one of the alert guards confiscated it from one of the prisoners. The sketch eventually found its way into the hands of Baggy Pants, who became infuriated when he saw it and even more so when it was explained to him what the English words he was mouthing off in the drawing meant.

For several weeks, after Baggy Pants announced to the entire camp the "infidel and culprit" who showed such disrespect to him and the Emperor would be found and punished severely, several prisoners were questioned. The interrogations went on and on, with the hope that sooner or later, through intimidation, one of the prisoners would reveal the "infidel" who drew the caricature. Not one of them broke, insisting untruthfully they knew nothing about the drawing, and the matter was finally laid to rest without finding the artist, much to the chagrin of Baggy Pants. Mick was safe.

By this time, General King had already designated General Sage commander of the American contingent at the prison camp.

The camp was split by Tsuneyoshi to separate the American soldiers from the Filipino prisoners. Although the units of the regiment were separated, as more prisoners came into the camp from other units, the living quarters structure became somewhat disorganized.

And despite a new organization later ordered by the Japanese commander, in an attempt to prevent units from organizing or segregating living quarters for certain groups, fearing strength in numbers, the men of the 200th became determined to stay close to one another; they sought each other out to make sure they stayed together as best they could.

The camp was served by three artesian wells, but initially, when the camp was first occupied, the pipes leading from the wells weren't the proper size to serve the single tap from which drinking water was made available. Through the constant insistence of General Sage, who badgered

Tsuneyoshi daily, the camp commander finally agreed to the addition of two more taps, which helped decrease the long lines of men standing to get the water from the spigots. At times, whether for repairs or just out of spite or meanness, the water supply was cut off, leaving the camp without water for hours at a time.

The outcome of the limited supply of water led some of the men to drink water from unsafe and polluted water sources. On one occasion, a group of prisoners were on a work detail outside the encampment near a stream into which, unbeknownst to the prisoners, several latrines from the encampment were emptied periodically.

The water from the stream was too tempting for two of the prisoners who were severely dehydrated for several days and, when they saw their chance, believing the guards weren't paying attention, drank to their hearts delight from the stream. Two days later, back at the camp, after vomiting throughout the night, they died from contaminants in the water.

Through the repeated intercessions of General Sage, Tsuneyoshi finally approved the Red Cross to come into the camp to set up a small clinic at the camp, which the Red Cross would supply with bandages and medicine, and a nurse, who came in weekly, to treat minor injuries and ailments. A few prisoners had medical training in civilian life and volunteered to assist at the clinic, as "medics," although they hadn't received training as such.

Eventually, bedding was made available for what the prisoners came to refer to as the camp's "hospital," even though it wasn't large enough or equipped to be a true hospital. The mattresses and bedding would allow some of the more critically injured patients to stay overnight, but the treatment was rather limited. Even so, it was an improvement to the health care of the prisoners.

Lencho Garcia and Andy Gluck volunteered to assist as "medics" at the hospital. To help keep the place as sanitary as they could, with limited resources, Garcia conceived of a way to "sanitize" the hospital patients by bathing them before they entered the hospital. To do so, they cut the end of a 60-gallon drum to fill with water from a nearby stream supplying fairly clean water. Although not potable, it sufficed for bathing.

Through the intercession once again of General Sage, Garcia and Gluck got permission to carry water from the stream, using whatever size cans they could find. The two men found volunteers to help them fill the cans from the stream. In such a manner, they'd fill the drum with water just outside the hospital periodically, and the patients would bathe there just before entering the hospital.

Because of the heat, high humidity and the closeness of the jungles, it was difficult to control the green flies in the camp. These flies carried numerous diseases. Most of the prisoners suffered from malaria, diphtheria, or amoebic dysentery, and these men were the ones most susceptible to becoming infected by the flies, who swarmed on open wounds or body cavities freely.

High fevers, caused by these new diseases, and compounded with the malaria and dysentery, resulted in the men crawling out of their bunks to seek refuge underneath the buildings in the camp. There, they would wallow in the coolness of the mud, seeking relief.

The ones who didn't survive such illnesses and may have died from them sometime during the night would be taken out of their bunks the next morning and piled outside the barracks with other bodies.

Initially, volunteers would take the dead bodies nearby to be buried in individual graves. But the practice didn't work because the holes weren't deep enough and the torrent rains daily would cause the bodies to float up to the surface. Aside from the rains, scavenging dogs and other animals digging up the graves proved to be a constant problem.

Eventually, with more and more prisoners dying every day, the pile of bodies grew higher, maybe as much as two or three feet high before they were taken away in truckloads to be buried in a common grave somewhere far away so the stench from the decaying bodies couldn't reach the camp.

At first, the mass graves were dug by volunteer prisoners using shovels, digging as deep as they could. Later, though, when the task of digging deep enough became overwhelming, General Sage persuaded Tsuneyoshi that keeping the mass graves deep enough to prevent wild animals from digging up the dead bodies would help safeguard his own soldiers from contracting diseases.

In time, Tsuneyoshi agreed to bring in backhoes, bulldozers, and other equipment to dig deeper and larger holes to prevent scavenging dogs and other animals from digging up the corpses from the graves. At first, an effort was made to keep written records for the common burial sites, but in time, the number of the dead made it impossible to keep track of the names of the soldiers buried.

Although dysentery and malaria were considered the "big killers," Mick saw men die of plain thirst and starvation, when the dehydration and lack of proper nourishment were too much for the body to bear. Mick learned from a "medic" at the hospital a soldier might survive either malaria or dysentery if they were contracted at different times. But if a person suffered from them at the same time, together they were more than the body could endure and would most likely cause death.

It was no wonder, Mick thought, there was so much dysentery and malaria going around. There was stench and filth everywhere. Every place a person stepped, there was feces in many places from uncontrolled diarrhea or from soldiers stepping on human feces somewhere else. Many men were walking without shoes. If they suffered a cut on their feet, they were susceptible to becoming infected with one disease or another, Mick reasoned.

Mick eventually volunteered to work at the hospital, where he saw a man suffering from cerebral malaria, which was the worst disease of the bunch, Mick was told. Without the proper medication, Mick helped the medics tie the man down at his wrists and ankles, after which, the patient kicked and screamed as he squirmed endlessly from the pain until he lost consciousness. When he'd awaken, he'd repeat his kicking and squirming until he became unconscious again. And the cycle repeated itself through the night until he died early morning of the next day.

Mick continued to volunteer part time as a medical assistant, helping the nurses and medics at the hospital, although no doctors from the outside had ever set foot in the place to treat patients. But nurses from the Red Cross kept coming weekly to treat patients there one or two days a week.

Every prisoner was often assigned by one or two of the sergeant guards to pools of workers called "work teams." Each team was put to work performing various duties in the camp or somewhere outside of it, ranging from minor duties such as picking up trash and debris, to more arduous tasks.

Those consisted of clearing fields, tilling rice fields, digging holes and trenches for latrines or larger ones to use as landfills, clearing wooded areas to use for planting, and construction of buildings and bridges. A few of the prisoners who had experience in operating large equipment such as bulldozers and backhoes were assigned to bigger projects.

Mick would have liked to spend more time helping at the hospital, but several of the guards were already assigning him to a mixture of work teams, preventing him from working with the medical personnel at the hospital. He enjoyed staying occupied and never complained of whatever work detail his work teams might be assigned to do, but he'd much rather help the medics, assisting with the patients at the hospital. When he did find himself with free time, he continued volunteering to help the nurses and medics.

One day the latter part of May, about a month after the prisoners' move into Camp O'Donnell, Mick was assigned to a work team to clean vast areas of the camp overgrown with large weeds and had accumulated large quantities of trash and debris. Because Mick was a corporal, he was usually placed in charge of the work teams, consisting of about ten workers each. For this particular project, no tools were provided, only gloves.

The team was told to use their hands to do the work the best they could. Having been shown beforehand the area that needed to be cleaned and cleared of trash, debris, and weeds, Mick estimated it'd take at least a week to finish the work.

After the first day of work in the blistering sun, Mick realized without the proper tools it would take much longer than a week to finish the job, possibly even two weeks. He also complained to the sergeant guard in charge when he forbid the workers from picking up the piles of manure and feces on the ground.

Only a few of the sergeants spoke limited English. This one did.

"Just trash, I say!" he blurted loudly. "You understand, stupid?"

Mick knew better than to start an argument with the man. Yet, he thought the piles created an unsanitary environment not only for the prisoners but for the guards. Not to mention the awful stench in the air persisting day after day for everyone.

When Mick reported the following morning to the team's work detail, he noticed for the first time a young-looking Japanese officer, a captain, walking around the encampment near where the team would begin their day's work. After about an hour went by, he noticed the Japanese captain was still in the vicinity, walking around and occasionally conversing with several guards assigned to a few other work teams doing other projects in the area.

Curious, Mick decided to query one of his team members, Javier Chavez.

"Who's that Japanese officer walking around?" he asked Chavez.

"I really don't know," Chavez replied. "I was wondering myself."

"I've never seen him before. In fact, I've never laid eyes on a Japanese officer before except for Baggy Pants and his staff of lieutenants, who consistently allow the harsh treatment by the sergeants and guards."

"One of the fellows thinks he's overseeing the guards' work in this section of the camp," Chavez replied. "I've never noticed him before either. Maybe he's been sent here from higher up. They might be checking up on Baggy Pants."

"If he comes near here, I'm going to ask him a few questions."

"Like what?"

"About a couple of things. We need hoes and shovels, for one thing, if we're going to do a good job with all these weeds. Digging them by hand is the pits." He paused and looked around. "And for another, that asshole of a guard yesterday wouldn't let us pick up the goddamn shit all over the place. I'm sick of the smell. It stinks to high heaven all over the fucking camp."

"You don't need to tell me, man. I can smell too."

16

A NEW FRIEND

About an hour later, Mick looked up and saw the captain nearby, headed toward his crew. Good, he thought, now was his chance, although he didn't relish the thought the sergeant guard was only a few feet away, watching the men working with an eagle's eye. Mick was concerned the sergeant wouldn't look favorably on his addressing the Japanese officer. *The hell with him. I'll take my chances.*

The captain was only a few feet away now. Mick only knew a few words in Japanese, but not enough to converse. Maybe, he thought, the captain spoke and understood some English, at least.

It was worth a try, Mick thought. Seemingly possessed of courage that appeared out of nowhere, he arose from where he was kneeling, pulling weeds.

"Pardon me, captain, but may I please speak to you for a couple of minutes." *I said a mouthful, but maybe he'll understand.*

The captain stopped abruptly but said nothing, just staring at Mick in surprise. The sergeant, his anger showing clearly in his pockmarked face, rushed up to Mick and raised his baton, ready to strike him.

Without uttering a word, the captain quickly put his hand out and held the sergeant's arm, stopping him from bringing the baton down on Mick's head. The captain, with a serious face, spoke sternly to the sergeant in Japanese, and the guard retreated. His anger was still plain on his face, despite the captain's presence.

The officer walked up to the sergeant, and the two of them exchanged words in whispers. The sergeant then bowed respectfully to the captain and said something in a tone sounding to Mick much like an apology. The sergeant walked away as if he was humiliated, not in his usual aggressive manner.

The captain approached Mick. "You wished to say something to me, corporal," he said in perfect English. "Please do."

Mick was at first shocked to hear the officer speak English so well. His face probably showed it, too, he thought. "You speak English well. It took me by surprise."

The captain, his face still serious, showed the glint of a smile. But he just stood there, not uttering a word. Mick quickly realized he was waiting for Mick to speak.

"Sorry, captain," he finally said. "I'll try not to take too much of your time." He then explained the task of the work team and to do a proper job, they'd need shovels and hoes. He also told the officer about the mounds of manure and dried human waste forming from the diarrhea of the prisoners caking with the manure and soil, but which the guard hadn't permitted the team to remove the day before.

He spoke of the stench and spread of disease. The men were glad to do the work, he explained further, but with a proper set of tools and being allowed to pick up the manure and feces, they'd do a much better job.

The captain was a little shorter than Mick, who stood just shy of six-feet tall. Until now, the only Japanese Mick had come across were much smaller in stature. Much shorter.

The officer had dark, almost black, piercing eyes and a well-shaped face. He appeared to be studying Mick. Again, he gave Mick a quick smile.

"I understand fully your wanting to clear the area of body waste," the captain said in a firm voice, but his tone had softened. He took a deep breath, as if to exaggerate his smell of the odious odor in the air.

"I'll have to check into that," he added. "Let me find out about the camp commander's policy, and I'll let you know, possibly by tomorrow if not later today."

He took a few steps back. "As for the hoes and shovels, you'll have them by tomorrow. How many do you need?"

"You may have heard the expression in English, 'Beggars can't be choosers.' As many as you can spare. There's ten of us."

"All right. I'll get you as many as I can. We'll see."

Mick saw the name tag on the officer. It read "Takahashi."

"Thank you, Captain Takahashi. I appreciate your concern and your time. Please have a good day. Now, I'll get back to my work."

The Japanese officer only nodded with a smile and didn't offer his hand. He walked away with a bit of elegance in his gait but not arrogance.

Mick didn't see him the rest of the day.

The next morning, when Mick reported to the sergeant guard with the rest of his team, the sergeant, disgruntled, instructed them to pick up their tools at the warehouse, a small building where the camp kept work implements and equipment. There, they found ten new hoes and five new shovels waiting for them, which they were required to sign off for and were instructed to return the implements at the end of the day.

All through the day, Mick looked for Captain Takahashi to thank him, but he was nowhere to be seen. The sergeant guard who had shown his anger toward Mick the day before never came close to him during the day. He stayed away from Mick, whether because the captain had told him to or because he was still angry with Mick and wanted nothing to do with him, it didn't matter to Mick. They got the tools they needed.

He soon learned from one of the team members the sergeant had said earlier they were permitted to pick up all the manure and body waste and dump it in the large trash bin along with the weeds, trash, and debris they collected throughout the day.

Meanwhile, whenever he felt strong enough and had some extra time and energy, Mick continued to spend time helping out at the hospital. Because they weren't equipped otherwise, the medics and nurses there only treated prisoners with minor wounds or ailments. Infected sores were cleaned and sanitized, small cuts were sutured, and all sorts of skin fungi were treated. A few medications were occasionally dispensed for healing the wounds or to treat minor ailments.

But those inflicted with severe depression or other mental conditions driven by starvation or hopelessness were turned away, as well as those who suffered from diseases still running rampant around the camp. Yellow jaundice and dengue fever were new diseases finding their way into the lives of the prisoners. Some prisoners suffering from eye problems, such as tunnel vision or partial blindness, were referred to General Sage, as commander of the prisoners, with requests hospitalization be sought for such major illnesses.

Mick disliked treating sores infected under the skin, and which gave out a putrid smell causing him to gag. He found out some of the prisoners who sought treatment for infected sores had urinated on them, having heard from others such treatment had worked on them. Mick doubted urine would cure an infection, believing the opposite was most likely true, it'd further enhance or prolong the infection. He came away from the experience with the impression a person would try anything to end their suffering when either desperation or fear took hold of them.

He was also surprised to discover while working at the hospital many prisoners who sought help there had worms somewhere in their body, most often in their esophagus and even in their stomach and intestines. One of the patients, when he came in, first gagged, then threw up a worm several inches long. Mick wouldn't have believed it if he hadn't seen it with his own eyes. He was disheartened to learn afterward from a nurse most of the prisoners likely had worms in their digestive systems, including him, but she believed most of them were essentially harmless.

"They only live there," the nurse explained, "just gorging on food and bacteria swallowed into the system by its host."

Mick cringed at the thought. "Isn't there anything we can do to prevent it?" He squirmed as he pictured his intestines full of worms.

"Not here, I'm afraid." She paused in thought, then grinned. "And don't go try pouring iodine down your throat like one fellow who came in here the other day did. That'll poison your system if it doesn't kill you first. He was lucky we were able to get him to regurgitate all the poison out of him, but he was still in great pain after dry heaving for another hour or so."

Outside the hospital, prisoners continued to weaken from a combination of their starvation and dehydration. Some were so weakened they might pass out three to six times a day, often when they were at a chow line, waiting for a cup of rice. Quite often, when a prisoner became deadly ill, for whatever the reason, their "roommates" carried him to the shade underneath the camp's buildings, to die if for nothing else.

Jimmy Montes, his body full of unexplainable infected sores, was moved underneath his barrack on two occasions, but he didn't die either time. He claimed while he spent the time down there for two days, maggots got into his sores and cleaned them out of bacteria. He swore that was why he lived to tell the story.

Only rarely, the prisoners were treated to a sample of other foods by their Japanese hosts, but the main dish of the day was always a saltless paste of rice, which was never enough to stave off the men's hunger, much less to satisfy it. Most of the time, weevils and worms, as well as maggots, were a delicacy coming along with the rice, but the men ate the dish happily, reasoning it added nutrition they'd never get elsewhere.

The amount of the daily rations of rice was calculated in advance, using the number of prisoners to be fed. For this reason, the prisoners passed the word around not to report nor reveal those who had died around them during the day so as not to reduce the amount of rice served. As a consequence, corpses lay around in the barracks for days before they were taken out and disposed of in the burial pits.

The prisoners used their ingenuity to figure out methods to supplement their daily ration of rice, even though those ways were often risky. When prisoners went out of the camp with a work team tasked with a project that might last several days, they found ways to smuggle into the camp not only food but medicine as well. They did it by sneaking off the work site, ransacking farms or homes nearby the project, and coming away with whatever food or medicine they could find.

Pete Graciano, who was on one of those extended work projects and was on the way back to camp from there, was able to escape the guards momentarily as the workers passed the barracks where the Japanese guards lived. There, in the guard's kitchen, he found squash and cantaloupe, which he managed to carry in a tote bag he made with his shirt, and snuck into the camp with his goodies undetected.

It wasn't until a week later Mick spotted Captain Takahashi again. Once again, he was walking slowly around the wide encampment grounds at a distance, apparently overseeing the actions of the guards as they supervised the work teams doing various tasks around the prison grounds. Mick and his work team had already finished with their clean up duties.

After having picked up the human waste, at least there wasn't as much of it for prisoners to walk through on their bare feet, spreading the diseases bred on the grounds into their barracks. And although the pungent odor in the air was still present, it wasn't as prevalent and revolting as it had once been. The crew's work certainly improved the conditions on the camp.

Mick thought Javier Chavez could have been right in suggesting the captain might be there to oversee the guards' treatments of the prisoners during their work. In the past week, Mick had seen much less use of the guards' batons to beat prisoners and they appeared more accepting of the teams' work. If not actually accepting, possibly at least less displeased with the work.

Mick hoped the captain would show up nearby and possibly come near where he and his crew were building some shelving outside the mess hall. The shelving was to supplement the shelving already existing in the hall's kitchen. He kept an eye out for him as he worked.

After an hour passed, he finally spotted the captain, trotting along Mick's side of the prison grounds and heading his way. When he was only a few feet away, Mick walked up to him, despite the fact the same guard he had circumvented before was only a few yards away.

"It's good to see you again, Captain Takahashi," Mick said, displaying a bright smile. A little nervous, he shifted his stance. "I've been hoping I'd see you again to thank you for your help in providing tools for us to work with."

Takahashi smiled. "Thank you." He made a slight bow. "I'm glad I could help."

"As you can see, the grounds look a lot better." He gestured with his arm extended toward the clearing. "Clean of weeds, and we got rid of at least some of the bad smell."

The captain grinned. "Yes, I noticed the minute I stepped onto the grounds. I expected no less, after observing your crew's work ethic."

"Thanks. We don't often get such appreciation from your sergeants and their men."

"My apologies for that."

Mick thought the man was indeed a gentleman with few words, for he was short of long answers. Thinking the captain might be getting impatient, he decided to break it off. "I apologize for taking too much of your time." He smiled. "Again, thank you."

The captain returned the smile. "No, no, not at all." He motioned to a spot on the grass behind him. "Take a break from your work and sit here with me. I don't mind us visiting for a while." He took a few steps and sat down. He gestured at the ground in front of him. "Please, sit with me."

Mick put the hand saw in his hand down. The others on the crew had overheard the conversation.

"Talk to the captain, Mick," Javier Garcia said. "We'll continue on, if what's his face doesn't mind." He gestured toward the guard.

Mick walked over to the officer and sat down in front of him. "I'll appreciate the rest. Thanks, captain." When Takahashi didn't say anything, he felt a bit awkward.

He decided to break the ice. "I was curious about you—about your background—where did you learn to speak English, if you don't mind my asking? You're quite fluent."

The captain laughed. "I spent a couple of years in your country. I studied at Stanford my last two years of college. Graduated with an electrical engineering degree a few years back."

"I thought you might have spent some time in the United States. Your English was too good to have learned it any other way."

"Very intuitive of you. I don't know your name. Would you mind?"

No, of course not. Mick Duran. I'm from a little place called 'Las Cruces' in New Mexico."

"I thought you might have some Mexican blood in you. I've actually heard of Las Cruces. Near El Paso, Texas, isn't it?"

Mick found his mouth opening a little in surprise, and he couldn't help grinning. "I didn't think my hometown was known by anybody outside the state."

While in the States, I made it a point to learn as much as I could about your country. I studied your geography during my time at Stanford, especially your Southwest." He must have noticed Mick's quizzical look. "You know, cowboys and Indians." He smiled. "I was determined to learn more than engineering while I was in your country."

"I find that impressive. I don't know your full name either."

"My given name is 'Hinata.' It is associated with the sunflower, a symbol of radiance and positivity."

"That's interesting. Do all Japanese names of persons have some meaning behind them?"

"Yes, most of them. My surname, 'Takahashi,' for example, means 'high bridge,' a common name in Japan, especially in the Gunma area in the Kanto region, where my family's from, located in the southern part of our country. It's just north of Tokyo." He eyed Mick with a questioning expression. "I was correct you're of Mexican origin, right?"

"Yes, of course. Full-bloodied on both sides. Most of the 1800 men in my regiment, the 200th Coast Artillery, are Mexican American or Native American."

"With a few cowboys and 'gringos' sprinkled here and there." He said 'gringos' with a broad smile.

Mick couldn't help laughing and grinned. "Yes, you have it right."

He glanced over at the guard, who was holding his distance but eyeing the two men sitting there visiting with a disapproving eye.

The captain noticed Mick's glance. "Don't mind him." He paused. "Just stay as far away from him as you can. And the others as well, when you don't have to be near them because of your work."

"I usually try to. It's common practice amongst the prisoners. But often they inject themselves in your space, and it can't be helped to find yourself at the end of a rifle butt or a baton."

"Yes, I know." He said the words with a grimace.

Mick felt comfortable getting bold. "Is that why you're here?"

Takahashi looked him in the eye somberly and waited to speak. "Partly," he finally said. "But now isn't the time to get into that."

Feeling awkward, Mick decided to change the subject. "How long were you in the States after graduating from Stanford?"

I left soon after getting my degree and returned to Japan. My fiancée awaited me. We got married just before being ordered to report to duty in the Emperor's Imperial Army." He sighed. "And now I find myself here, where I'm happy to have met you." He stood up and wiped off the blades of grass stuck to the seat of his pants.

He extended his hand to Mick, who had stood up too. Mick shook hands with him, and both men smiled at each other as they let go.

"I'm sure we'll be talking some more, Mick. May I address you by your first name? That's a nickname, isn't it?"

"Yes, yes. I was christened 'Michael' but the nickname stuck when I was just a child." He looked Captain Takahashi in the eye. "But I'll continue to address you as 'Captain Takahashi,' out of respect."

"No, no, I will insist you address me by my given name, too, 'Hinata.' Please, I insist."

They shook hands again, then parted, and Mick picked up his saw and went back to work as Takahashi resumed his slow walk. The captain passed by the sergeant guard and exchanged a few words with him as he glanced back at Mick before walking away.

17
THE MOVE TO CABANATUAN

From the onset, the Japanese soon became aware Camp O'Donnell, for several reasons, wasn't suitable for the imprisonment of the great number of prisoners imprisoned there. They had miscalculated their plans and decision since the surrender.

Aside from encountering difficulties in the terrain and the vegetation within the camp, the crowded conditions in the camp created difficulties for the Japanese to maintain discipline and security among its own ranks and finding efficient and secure ways of feeding and controlling the prisoners. They had experienced several escapes that were successful because of the terrain and abundant vegetation and trees in the nearby jungles, which they felt they could prevent elsewhere.

But it took them about three months to decide that to alleviate the problems they were encountering, the prisoners must be moved to another location.

In the first week of August, they decided on Cabanatuan, located in the central part of Luzon, in the Province of Nueva Ecija. The prison camp at Cabanatuan already housed prisoners captured when Corregidor fell, but there was plenty of space there to accommodate the many more prisoners held at O'Donnell.

But, putting security and control concerns aside, conditions for the prisoners at Cabanatuan weren't any better, where, in a camp of about 8,000 prisoners from Corregidor, four to 40 prisoners died every day, not only from malnutrition due to the poor diets, but from the usual diseases—beriberi, scurvy, and pellagra, a new disease increasing quickly, as well as the other diseases killing prisoners elsewhere.

By the first week of September, Camp O'Donnell was completely vacated. Statistics would show that of the some 9,000 American prisoners imprisoned at O'Donnell, more than 1,500 died in the three months the camp was used for their imprisonment. Of the approximately 50,000 Filipinos held in the separate encampment assigned to them at O'Donnell during the same period, about 21,000 of them would die there.

The prisoners were marched from O'Donnell to Capas, a town in the Province of Tarlac. Although the march was only a few hours long, the conditions and treatment were no different than what the prisoners had undergone during the Bataan Death March. It rained during part of the march, which offered the men some relief from the heat of the day.

As they were used to doing at O'Donnell, the prisoners took their shirts off during the rain and allowed it to cleanse, and be absorbed by, their pores. They had quickly learned this common practice, even before their imprisonment. At Capas, once again, like cattle, they were led and stuffed into hot and stifling boxcars for the remainder of the trip to Cabanatuan.

The trek from Camp O'Donnell to the prison camp at Cabanatuan, Mick was surprised, made him melancholy and added to his hopelessness. He had been doing well in keeping his spirits up until then. He thought the change might have been caused because he was reminded of the 80-mile march to Camp O'Donnell just three months before, where he had been conscious of little but death before he finally got a grip on what he had to do to survive.

But his depression didn't last long this time around, for, just as he had done when he became depressed upon learning Corregidor had fallen or when he learned he wouldn't be able to send letters to his family or receive letters from back home, he reminded himself of his commitment to survive so he could return to Lilia and his family.

His short-lived despondency during the trip to Capas also reminded him on his early months in captivity, before the Death March, when he had grown both emotionally and physically weaker. A numb feeling, which he believed at the time was a feeling of peace, had come over him then. It gave him the feeling he wasn't tired anymore, and he interpreted the sensation as a sign he had given up. And if that was true, he would be dying. A slow death, maybe, but a death, nonetheless. As soon as he had resolved to live, his exhaustion came back and he never lost it because he realized it was a good sign he was fighting for his spiritual survival.

It was then he had begun to discover new ways of thinking about his life and about the cards fate had dealt to him. He had thought of Father McCarthy's words to him. He also found his old kind of thinking had stopped working for him. Yes, he had hit a new bottom in his life when he considered his circumstances and his physical surroundings, here in a strange land away from Lilia and his family. All of this was beyond his ability to control but only for a moment.

He had discovered a way to see all of the gloom as a good thing, for he alone had the option to reject it for something better. Spiritually, he had vowed to himself then to reject the feeling of unhappiness and look at his life in a glorious way with Lilia, his child to come, and his family in it—as a part of his life.

My mind was always teetering through a narrow path of misfortunes and inconsistences meandering along an infinite gloom in my head lasting forever unless I myself put an end to it. And that's what I think I've managed to accomplish.

He was fortunate to have seen the light beyond his darkness, and the vision allowed him to overcome his depression and, to regain his will to live.

Back at the prison in Bilibid, Puglisi and the other prisoners, too, packed up their belongings for the move to Cabanatuan, where most American prisoners would be held for now, with the exception of several hundreds of others held at the Davao Penal Colony. About 500 additional prisoners would later be transferred to the Colony, to help build an airfield.

At Cabanatuan, Mick soon learned the move didn't make treatment of the prisoners any better. If anything, it may have even worsened, as hard as that might have been for him to imagine when he left Camp O'Donnell.

Despite this unwelcomed news, he was happy to learn that even though Captain Yoshio Tsuneyoshi, the Camp Commander at O'Donnell, better known to the prisoners as Baggy Pants, along with his entourage of lieutenants, would follow them to Cabanatuan, Captain Hinata Takahashi would also be joining the prisoners at the new prison camp.

Mick considered meeting him at O'Donnell a happy experience and wouldn't mind getting to know him better. It offered him an opportunity to lessen his perceived ugliness of Japanese culture and ethnicity he had gotten to know only through the unprincipled treatment the prisoners received at the hands of the horrifically brutal guards at Camp O'Donnell.

The barracks here were, as at O'Donnell, merely huts made of straw or thatch with four tiered compartments for the prisoners to sleep on. The top ones were high, and in a weakened state from malnutrition, it would sap a prisoner's strength to gain access to them. Yet, if one chose a bottom or near bottom cot, they'd have to risk watered feces from men suffering from dysentery dripping through the slats from above. Either choice had its negative consequences.

Three separate camps existed at Cabanatuan. The Japanese occupied the one in the middle, designated Camp 2. The prisoners from Corregidor occupied the barracks of Camp 1, a larger camp where most of the American prisoners from O'Donnell moved into. The remainder of the Americans occupied the barracks at Camp 3 on the other side. As at O'Donnell, only one water pipe served each camp with only one spigot. Eventually, the American commanders, General Sage of the 200th being one of them, managed to obtain approval to install additional piping and faucets to service all three camps, if not quite adequately, at least with some improvement.

Not long after arriving at the new camp, Mick and the others from the 200th were surprised to run into Bob Follett. They thought of him still in the jungles if not dead. He explained he and his group had finally joined the guerillas and had fought alongside them until they were captured by the Japanese after a surprise attack on a guerilla encampment, which he was fortunate to have survived.

After his capture, Follett and the others who had fled into the jungle with him were taken to where a group of American prisoners from Corregidor were being held. From there, he and the other POWs were transported to Cabanatuan, just a few days before the group from O'Donnell arrived. Those in the 200th were happy to see him alive and well.

The first warning Mick got the prisoners were having to face some of the same dismal treatment here as they did at Camp O'Donnell was the existence of what became known as the "blood brother" groups of prisoners. The Japanese, to deter the prisoners from even thinking of escaping, divided the Americans into groups of 10 prisoners. If one either escaped or made any attempt to escape, the other nine would be shot, whether or not the escapee succeeded.

To avoid this dire consequence, the Americans set up their own, assigned guards within the prison fences, to stop any prisoner from trying to escape. This was necessary because many prisoners suffering from malaria went through crazy spells, not allowing them to see things clearly or rationally. Thus, they were easily compelled to seek escape. Often, the Japanese guards outside the fence would put food out just beyond the reach of the fence to tempt the malaria-stricken prisoners. If a prisoner sought to crawl under the barbed wired fence, the guards didn't hesitate to plunge a bayonet into him.

Often, the sergeant guards would put on a show with music for the Americans, to emphasize their intolerance of escape attempts or any other prohibited act. This was done usually at or near the front gate. To the sound of marching music, a group of guards would march through the gate carrying the bloodied head of a dead Filipino hanging from a bamboo branch they carried to clearly display the gruesome result of rule infractions. This display was repeated anytime the sergeant guard believed a reminder of sanctions to the prisoners was necessary.

There were other forms of punishment confronting the prisoners, even for the slightest of "offenses" decided by the guards to have been committed, even when there was little evidence of the perceived infraction. One such punishment was known as the "sun treatment." It either consisted of a prisoner being stripped naked, with his hands tied behind his back, and forced to stand there all day or possibly two days facing the baking sun.

Depending on the severity of the offense, a crueler version of this treatment was sometimes employed, in which the prisoner was hung by his wrists, tied behind him, from a tree branch or a large piece of timber.

Suspended in such a manner, with the weight of the prisoner pulling down on the wrists, it took little time for both shoulders to become dislocated. Often, with the body suspended, guards passed by, smoking cigarettes, and either put out their burning cigarettes on the prisoner's belly or back or simply held them gently against the flesh to cause burns and pain. If this punishment continued for two or three days, it was unusual if the prisoner survived.

Another "sun treatment" consisted of nailing the prisoner into a small box cut to the length of his body, and, with the body crammed in there, drilling small holes to allow a small amount of air to go through. The box was then left in the hot sun for several days. During this time, the prisoner must breathe in the fumes and odor from his own urine and feces, as well as contend with the heat of the day and the low volume of oxygen in the box. After such treatment, it was a miracle if the prisoner survived the ordeal.

It wasn't unusual to force the American prisoners to watch Filipino prisoners already clubbed to death for some infraction hung by their necks while a firing squad standing in front of the dead bodies "executed" the Filipino prisoners. Mick was forced to watch such executions on three occasions. Each time, he went away from the gruesome scene to vomit alone anywhere he could find seclusion.

After spending over a week being forced to witness many of these forms of punishment, Mick wondered what had become of Captain Takahashi, whom, for lack of a better title, he now considered a true "friend." He hadn't denied to himself since he last saw the captain at Camp O'Donnell he missed not having seen him again.

Then one day after he had been thinking of his friend, he spotted him strolling along, slowly, as usual, on the other side of an open field set aside as a recreational area, where prisoners occasionally would be found playing touch football. The field was a wide open space of flat terrain between Camp 1 and 2. The "football" was a carved piece of hard, solid walnut sewn over with the discarded skin of a dead dog or other animal someone had scraped up.

For the players who enjoyed the game, it worked quite well. It wasn't often, however, that the sergeant guards would allow them to play such a "foolish" American game. But play they did when they got the chance, which was rarely because the Japanese frowned on the game, believing it to be silly and a waste of time.

Immediately upon seeing the Japanese officer, Mick crossed the field. As he approached, he noticed Takahashi was looking at him, and he waved. The captain waved back, without a smile this time.

"I've been wondering when you'd show up," Mick said with a smile.

Takahashi smiled back. "I've been away elsewhere and just returned." He held out his hand to shake Mick's hand. "How have you been?"

"What can I say? For the luxuries of a prison camp, I'm doing as well as could be expected." Mick grinned at his attempt to inject humor into his circumstances.

The captain gave him what Mick perceived as a sympathetic stare. "I understand." He gestured toward a group of large boulders at the edge of the field, only a few yards away. "Let's go down there to sit."

18
TWO FRIENDSHIPS

As they walked over to the boulders, the Captain continued. "I, too, have thought of you since we last visited, wondering how you were doing in the 'luxuries' of your forced confinement, as you referred to them." He sat down on one of the boulders.

Both of them laughed. Mick sat down on the boulder next to Takahashi.

"Were you away on leave?" Mick asked. "Went back home on vacation?"

"No, no, nothing luxurious." He offered a brief smile for his attempt at humor. "Just went elsewhere on military business, which I'm not at liberty to discuss. Sorry about that."

"No, no, please don't be. I understand."

"Tell me, Mick, how are you finding things at Cabanatuan? I've got time to sit and chat. Go ahead. Tell me."

"As I said, as well as could be expected under these circumstances. If there's any difference between here and O'Donnell, it might be that our treatment here is worse, I'm sad to say."

"I'm sorry to hear that. But I can't say I'm surprised. Camp Commander Tsuneyoshi has that reputation. But he'll soon be replaced."

"Oh? How come?"

"No particular reason. Just a routine transfer, I believe." He paused in thought as he gazed to the other side of the field, then returned his attention to Mick. "Let me explain. Under my own circumstances, out of my loyalty—allegiance—to our Emperor and to my superiors, as well as my oath as a military officer, there's little I can say to you in addressing your imprisonment. I wish I could."

"I totally understand, Captain Takahashi."

"'Hinata,' please. We agreed on that much last time. "You're 'Mick' to me. And I am 'Hinata' to you." He smiled.

Mick returned the smile. "Of course. I'd forgotten." He cleared his throat. "Anyway, I don't expect you to let our brief relationship of sorts jeopardize or adversely affect your loyalties or even your duties here in this encampment. Those I understand to be important to you, and for that reason, I don't want to do or say anything to interfere with that. Or with what I consider as the friendship developing between us."

"I'm glad you understand." He sighed. "And I agree with you that, however brief, we've certainly developed a friendship. In the short time we've spent together, I've grown to like you. I can tell you're a decent and good person."

"Thanks for saying that. And I, too, believe you to be a decent person. And a fine gentleman and loyal Japanese officer, to boot." He couldn't help grinning when he added the slang at the end, which Takahashi might not recognize.

"Thank you, Mick. I appreciate your kind thoughts." He paused, as if in deep thought. He didn't speak for what Mick felt was a long minute but not an awkward moment until he spoke again.

"I've often thought back to when we first met and realized you and I find ourselves in a unique situation here, having met as we did, you, as a prisoner, I, as your..." He stopped briefly, then continued, "I was going to say, 'your captor,' but thought it a bit inaccurate, considering the obvious fact you and I have grown to like each other, despite the circumstances we both find ourselves entangled in."

Mick laughed. "I couldn't have said it any better." He took in a short breath. "I, too, have thought about the unusual nature of our relationship. Of how we met, and how civilly we approached each other when we did."

"One might say our meeting was much like a breath of fresh air, wasn't it?"

"Yes, yes, that's a good way to put it. We're both caught up in a reality of being from different worlds—different cultures—and then we find ourselves on opposite sides of a war, which neither of us asked for."

Mick paused to ponder the thought. "Yes, you're exactly right. We certainly managed to find ourselves in a unique—very unique—situation."

"And consider, too, Mick, our different ranks. You, a corporal in your army. I, a captain in mine. As I'm certain is the case in your military, officers and enlisted men don't socialize or fraternize, much less become friends. For good reasons, I'm sure, both our militaries traditionally have frowned upon such socializing for many years, and, as far as I can tell, it will always be the case."

He took a short breath and smiled. "But here you and I are, fraternizing simply because there are no rules in either army keeping us apart. You and I are free to be friends, if we wish to. And I'm glad."

"So am I. I've wondered if you could get in trouble for it."

"Not at all. Please don't let it worry you." He glanced at his watch. "And with that, I see that it's time for me to end our interesting conversation about the situation you and I find ourselves in."

"Despite everything else, I consider it to be a good and pleasant situation we find ourselves in."

"I couldn't have said it any better, Mick." Takahashi stood up, offering his hand to Mick.

Mick stood up, and the two of them shook hands vigorously.

"Until next time, Mick," the captain said with a brief and casual saluting gesture of his hand.

"Maybe we'll meet again sooner than later."

"Let's hope that, all right?" the captain said as he walked away.

"Yes, let's hope that we see each other soon." Mick stood there, transfixed at the figure of the Japanese officer walking away. *I feel comfortable talking to my new friend, despite his formal manner. In fact, that's what to me makes our conversations more enjoyable.*

Constantly, Mick continued to have death on his mind. For him, as well as for the other prisoners, each day required a firm decision not to give up because of the drudgeries day to day of dealing with his captors. Ever since the news of Corregidor's fall, which demoralized the prisoners on Bataan, he realized his morale was vulnerable. He did all he could to help the prisoners from Corregidor he met at Cabanatuan keep their spirits high.

He found most of them had turned to religion for faith. Often, everywhere he turned to, he saw prisoners praying and the Catholics saying their rosaries, whether kneeling, sitting, or standing. Mick would always encourage his friends who didn't appear to have a religion to seek refuge in prayer nonetheless, or if nothing else spend a moment meditating in private, for he realized how much his own faith helped him to garner the strength to resist giving up.

He realized his parents never had considered him an exceptionally devout Catholic, and he himself didn't think he was a good one even now. But he had much faith instilled in him by his parents, he was certain, and his faith, together with hopes of seeing Lilia and his family someday, would be what would keep him alive.

Mick befriended a prisoner from Natchez, Mississippi about a month after being transferred to Cabanatuan, a home-spun farm country native named Bubba McEntyre who was born in a farm into a large family. He possessed a southern accent so strong it clearly showed he was from the South. Although his family was raised by parents who were Southern Baptist, McEntyre never had shown much interest in religion.

When Mick first met him, his new friend inquired of Mick about his fellow New Mexicans imprisoned with him at Cabanatuan. He told Mick he admired the camaraderie and faith the men of the 200th possessed.

"And I think you're just like them," McEntyre explained slowly in his southern drawl. "I envy your faith. And I admire your positive attitude. If you don't mind my asking, did your attitude come from your being a Catholic? From having a strong faith?"

"Thanks, Bubba, for your kind words. I hate to admit I almost lost my faith a few months back, but I find myself hanging on to my faith now because I'm afraid without it, I wouldn't have the attitude you mentioned. I believe in a God now more than ever, and I ask for guidance every day."

"And I've found that hard to do here, which to me is a living hell. I admire you and your buddies from New Mexico keeping your faith through all we have to put up with."

"Believe me, it's a living hell to all of us, me included."

"Tell me, Mick, I've noticed the small silver cross you carry in your wallet. I'd guess it's something special to you, huh?"

"My mother gave it to me just before I left. It's actually a crucifix, not just a cross."

"May I see it?"

"Sure." Mick dipped into his back pants pocket and pulled out his wallet. He took out the sterling silver crucifix and handed it to McEntyre.

McEntyre examined it, to which was attached a sterling silver chain.

"Why you got it hidden in your wallet? Don't most Catholics wear it around their necks?"

"Yes, usually they do. I, too, used to, but with all the activity and fighting, I was afraid of the chain breaking and my losing it somewhere." He smiled as he took back the crucifix from McEntyre. "I decided to keep it in my wallet for safe keeping."

"Smart move." He took in a breath and wrinkled his brow as he looked Mick in the eye. "You know, Mick, I'd give anything to have the strong faith you do. Maybe I'll consider becoming a Catholic. You got any thoughts on that?"

Mick grinned. "It makes me happy to hear you say that, Bubba. I attend Sunday mass every week, given by Father Bartholomew at the little chapel we've built on the prison grounds. You can join me next Sunday, and I'll introduce you to him. You can ask him any questions you may have."

"I'd like that, Mick. Thanks. And thanks for your friendship. It's meant a lot to me."

"And to me too." Mick still held the crucifix and chain in his hand and offered it to McEntyre. "Here, Bubba, you can have this."

McEntyre grinned and gestured "no" with his hand. "Naw, Mick, I wouldn't want you to do that. Your mother gave it to you, to keep. You just go on and do that."

Mick took McEntyre's hand, palm up, placed the crucifix in it, and closed the hand into a fist. "My mom would have wanted me to give it to you, if she knew how you felt about having a stronger faith."

McEntyre displayed a big grin, took the crucifix and chain from his hands, and placed them around his neck. "I don't know what to say, Mick, except I'm grateful for your generosity." He touched the crucifix with the palm of his hand. "I promise I'll wear it with me always and promise you I'll take good care of it and not lose it. I won't let it out of my sight." He patted Mick on the shoulder. "This means the world to me, Mick. Thank you, thank you, thank you!'

Mick smiled. "I'm happy you accepted my gift. "Believe me, I'm glad I'm able to help in some small way."

"Mick, you've helped me in a big way, man," McEntyre replied, smiling. "Thank you, my friend."

From that day forward, whenever Mick crossed paths with McEntyre, his friend would always be wearing the crucifix. A mutual friend would mention to Mick occasionally one wouldn't find McEntyre without the crucifix around his neck. And, the friend said, McEntyre's demeanor and morale had significantly improved. It made Mick happy to hear that.

The Sunday following Mick and McEntyre's visit, McEntyre accompanied Mick to mass, where he introduced him to Father Bartholomew. Although Mick hadn't seen McEntyre at mass later, he had gotten word from the priest he and McEntyre were getting together for weekly sessions and the southerner was learning a lot not only about the Catholic faith but about himself and the spiritual life possible for him if he chose to find it.

From time to time afterward, whenever he ran into McEntyre around the encampment, they'd often sit down together and chat. His friend from the south always seemed in good spirits during those times, which made Mick happy.

In mid-October, a young Filipino youngster, delirious, wandered onto the grounds of the prison camp. Mick encountered the boy, who was moaning, obviously in great pain, and he examined him. The youth was suffering from a high fever, had chills, and seemed to have difficulty swallowing. His nose was runny, and he was coughing a lot. Mick decided to take him to the hospital, where a nurse happened to be on duty.

All the nurse had to do was to take one look to yell at Mick, "Get him out of here, away from the others!"

She gestured to the building's exit. "He's got diphtheria, which is highly contagious! Leave him segregated outside where someone can guarantee he won't leave, then quickly summon someone at General Sage's quarters to arrange for him to be admitted to a hospital equipped to treat him."

Mick did as he was instructed, but by the time the boy was taken away to a nearby hospital, through his brief contact with some of the prisoners, the disease spread and soon, an epidemic existed in the camp. Doctors at the hospital, which had admitted some of the prisoners at the encampment who had been infected, pled with Lt. Col. Shigeji Mori, known to the prisoners as Captain Mori, the camp commander who replaced Baggy Pants, to allow serum to be transported and used for treatment. The commander had first refused, stating the serum supplies in stock would be used only for any Japanese who contracted the disease.

As Captain Mori continued to refuse help, by the end of October, prisoners began choking to death. Finally, through the Catholic bishop in Manila, a few quantities of serum were found and brought to the hospital. By then, however, there were too many sick men, and there wasn't enough serum for all of them; the desperately ill had to draw straws to see who would be administered the medicine. Without enough antitoxin, the doctors had to perform tracheotomies to allow the choking patients to breathe.

For many, it proved too late, and they died. At the end of the month, Mori finally gave in and allowed some amounts of serum to be administered. Eventually, the deaths from the epidemic lessened until ultimately, the disease was eliminated.

Mick became friends with several prisoners from Corregidor, and by early November, he and one of them, James Rawlings, known by "Skip," a buck sergeant from an outfit out of South Carolina, became extremely close friends. Skip Rawlings was one of the prisoners who had become infected with diphtheria during the epidemic and had survived the disease while under treatment at the "real" hospital outside the camp. While a patient there, he was cared for by a young Filipino nurse in her mid-twenties, with whom he struck up a romantic relationship that eventually grew, and Rawlings proposed to her.

The woman, whom Mick had met and knew by the name of *Almita*, a nickname meaning "little" soul, was a native of a little village a few miles north of Manila. She was a petite woman, fairly attractive, with a small oval face Rawlings said he "fell in love with" the moment he met her. Almita's given name was Alma, meaning "soul" in Spanish. Alma de La Cruz was her birthname, but she had been known as Almita since she was a child because she was petite.

Almita, too, was madly in love with Rawlings and wanted to marry him. But there was one hitch—she was a devout Catholic and very religious. And she wanted to have children who were raised Catholic. She would marry Rawlings, she promised him, but he would have to convert to Catholicism.

Rawlings' family was Presbyterian, but he had never been too religious. Changing religions to him wasn't an issue. His feelings for Almita were strong enough he agreed to convert wholeheartedly. Knowing Mick was Catholic, Rawlings asked him not only to be his best man but to help him become a member of his church.

Mick was happy to help. He introduced him to Father Bartholomew, who soon began the process with the required catechism lessons and all the other necessary steps to eventually be baptized a Catholic. When Rawlings was baptized, Mick became his *padrino*—godfather. About a month later, after the required notices were published in the Church's literature, Rawlings and Almita were married.

As a wedding present, Mick drew a facial portrait of Rawlings and his new bride, side by side. He did it in charcoal. It turned out an incredible likeness of both of them, and Rawlings and Almita loved the sketch and told Mick they'd cherish it for the rest of their lives.

19
A SAD GOODBYE

At Cabanatuan, the Japanese continued the firing squad executions so common at Camp O'Donnell. Mick deplored the idea of prisoners being executed in such a way for the slightest of perceived offenses. But he was as sickened, if not more so, by the insistence of the sergeant guards the executions be witnessed by as many prisoners as they could gather for the event.

He struggled with the question of what motivated any human being to partake in such cruelty. To him, it was as if the Japanese relished the idea of inflicting pain, not only to the prisoner to be executed but to other prisoners, who were forced to watch helplessly.

If several executions were to take place, they were scheduled so the entire camp would be forced to witness. But often, an unscheduled execution would take place at any time, and the guards hurriedly gathered whatever number of witnessing prisoners they could round up at the moment.

On one occasion of such a hurried execution, Mick was unfortunate to be in the area where the guards were gathering prisoners to be witnesses. Whether the five members of the firing squad were poor marksmen or their rifles weren't working properly, it took three volleys for the prisoner to fall to the ground. He was on his knees, still alive but moaning in great pain.

The firing squad just stood there, as if transfixed and unable to act.

"For heaven's sake, shoot the man!" someone shouted. "Can't you see he's not dead?"

The sergeant guard hurried to the prisoner, still kneeling, and thrust his bayonet in his heart. The man let out a loud gasp and fell forward.

The blood brother executions were still being carried out. One day in late November, Roque Alvarez, along with eight others of his blood brother group, were lined up and ordered to reveal where a missing prisoner was hiding. It was their last chance to save themselves from being executed, they were told.

The blood brother group stood there in terror, but Alvarez was especially terrified, and he tried to stand apart from the others, not wanting them to notice how much he was trembling. He felt ashamed, for he didn't think the other prisoners were as scared as he was. But he was wrong—they were as much afraid of dying as Alvarez was.

Finally, just before the group was spread in a line to be executed, the missing prisoner was found and dragged in front of his blood brothers. The guards decided to punish him by giving him what was known as the "water cure." They dragged him to a faucet, forced him to open his mouth, and began filling him with water until it became obvious his belly was bloated with water. The guards then jumped on his belly until the water came out of his mouth. They repeated the process several times until finally, the man was dead. Alvarez didn't know the dead man well, but he was sickened by the event he'd never forget.

The water cure was a punishment often done by placing a water hose up a man's rectum and once again, filling the man's abdomen and intestinal tract until the water stopped flowing, and then pouncing on his belly repeatedly until the man died.

Even in the midst of these cruelties, the prisoners never lost their sense of humor. They'd often make fun of the guards, even as mean and brutal as they were, and enjoyed giving them comical nicknames, so as not to be forced to pronounce their hard-to-pronounce names. Names such as Greasepaint, Balloon Lips, Sliver Eyes, and Donald Duck soon stuck and were used by everyone when referring to a particular guard who had earned the nickname.

As expected, the names were related to a particular trait of the guard in question. The guard nicknamed Donald Duck, for example, when he'd shout obscenities or issue an order in a high-pitched, raspy voice, sounded very much like the Disney character made famous in animated cartoons.

When the guard nicknamed Donald Duck learned of the nickname given to him by the prisoners, it was jokingly explained to him the character for which he was named was a good-looking and famous actor in Hollywood. His having taken the explanation to heart, one would often find him traipsing around the camp, showy and arrogantly.

One day, unfortunately for the prisoners, when movies from the United States were scheduled to be shown, the Japanese guards packed the movie house to enjoy watching American-made films.

As one would expect, cartoons were a part of the entertainment, and when the "real" Donald Duck appeared in his special cartoon feature, the angered Japanese guard named for him stomped out of the theater with vengeance in his eyes.

He later took it out on any prisoner he crossed paths with in the camp, hitting them with his baton on their shoulders, back, or legs, cussing them out in Japanese but still sounding very much like Donald Duck. No one again called him by his nickname to his face ever again.

Starvation and hunger continued to be big killers, weakening the prisoners to desperately seek extreme ways of finding something to eat. Dogs were a favorite to hunt and kill, even among the Japanese guards, who weren't immune to the hunger and famine throughout the camps. It wasn't unusual for prisoners to sneak into the Japanese section of the camp, scrounging in the waste cans for dog bones still containing pieces or even slivers of meat.

If a stray cat found itself roaming the camp, it wasn't there for long, instead being boiled or fried over a fire by a group of prisoners lucky enough to have found a good source of protein.

All prisoners who were assigned to work as cook assistants in the Japanese kitchens, at one time or another, managed to steal and hide food thrown in trash bins, such as the heads of fish or entrails of dead animals the Japanese cooks had cooked for the guards. No body part of an animal was discarded by the thieves.

One time, a lost horse happened to wander onto the camp. It didn't take long for a group of prisoners to capture the animal outside the view of the guards and kill it by beating his head with rocks. The prisoners then cut the entire horse into pieces and carried them behind the barracks, where they fried the pieces over a large fire. One of the prisoners even removed the horse's eyeballs and ate them raw.

At times, ingenious ways were found to provide extra food for the American prisoners. Captain Vince Bell, Mick's old company commander in the 200th, convinced the guards to allow his men to purchase food items from the Filipino natives. They'd buy two cans of fruit, for example, eat one, then sell the second one at a profit.

Eventually, since few prisoners possessed currency, they'd barter whatever item they possessed to purchase food stuffs. Tobacco and cigarettes, for example, became a medium of exchange. Others used rice or a non-food item in high demand to barter. The bartering system worked so well it became widely used, not only limited to Captain Bell's group.

Jaime Soltero, the Native American from Acoma, was half Mexican from his father's side and had learned to play classical guitar with nylon strings from his paternal grandfather, who was a fine musician. But he never brought his guitar to the Philippines and didn't know of anyone in the camp who had ever had one. He missed playing the guitar and singing Mexican corridos. With the help of others who did fine craftsmanship with wood, he built his own guitar out of mahogany, a hard and sturdy wood, using carabao guts for strings.

It was difficult to keep the guitar Soltero made in tune, but that didn't deter him. He even managed to compose a corrido with words paying tribute to the men of the 200th. Although the Japanese usually didn't allow the prisoners to sing, Soltero and his companions sang corridos anyway, and eventually, the guards became lax with the rules and let him and the others sing and play.

He'd often sing the popular Mexican tune, *El Rancho Grande*, which everyone seemed to know, even the Japanese. When he would play the tune, Soltero especially got a kick out of the guards, who'd tap along with their boots to the beat of the song.

Two separate instances of tragedy marred Mick's life at Cabanatuan the latter part of November. The first involved his godson, Skip Rawlings, and the second, his good friend from Mississippi, Bubba McEntyre.

Mick and Rawlings would see each other often, usually at Sunday mass. He had learned long ago Rawlings was happy the Japanese guards had relaxed the rules allowing non-prisoners to visit family on camp grounds. For that reason, he was able to see his new wife, Almita, more often than he had at first thought possible.

On the last Monday of November, Mick was struck with a bout of malaria that brought on a dangerously high fever. He had been battling many bouts of malaria for a long time and had won the battle several times, but occasionally, it would flair up. This time he got hit with it, he was slipping in and out of consciousness.

Because of his illness, he was unable to go on a work detail with his work team outside the camp, and Rawlings offered to get the guards off his back, who were insisting Mick join his team at the work site despite his illness. Rawlings wanted to substitute for Mick on the team. After several arguments, the sergeant guard finally permitted Rawlings to take Mick's place, and the work team left for the job site.

A few days later, when Mick had fully recovered from his bout of malaria and his fever, he learned Rawlings and the entire work team were slaughtered by two overly eager and trigger-happy guards.

When Mick first learned the work team hadn't returned to the camp, he tried to find out from a few of the sergeant guards if they knew why they weren't back from the project. He got nowhere with his inquiries, except to learn there had been "an accident." He finally contacted General Sage's staff, who told him of the massacre. Mick went into shock.

He found out later when he had recovered what had occurred. Apparently, the two guards supervising the work project, one armed with a machine gun and the other with a rifle, were disciplining some of the workers, who they didn't think were working hard enough. As they were chewing out the workers, one of the prisoners attempted to escape.

When the guard with the rifle fired at the fleeing prisoner, the other prisoners pleaded with him to stop shooting. When he didn't, two of the prisoners jumped on him, trying to take the rifle away.

The guard with the machine gun panicked and began shooting at not just the two prisoners trying to take control of the rifle but the others standing close by. He didn't stop until he mowed all of them down.

Afterward, the two guards moved the bodies into one big pile, and for whatever reason they couldn't explain, they poured gasoline on the pile of dead bodies and set it on fire. They left the charred bodies there and returned to camp, where they reluctantly reported the incident to their superiors.

Captain Mori's office later reported to General Sage his staff forced confessions from the two guards that they had been drinking homemade brew, which made them lose control.

Mori assured Sage the guards would be severely punished, but the American commander never was able to get a definitive answer to his query whether the punishment had been carried out. The burnt bodies were returned by the Japanese authorities to camp and were soon turned over to General Sage's staff, who were given permission by Japanese authorities to hold services for and bury the unrecognizable bodies.

For days after the mass burial and the one service held for all ten prisoners, Mick was still in a state of shock. He also went through a phase of survivor's guilt. He felt guilty because he reasoned Rawlings would be alive if he hadn't gone with the work team in his place. It added to his guilt when he realized in the days to come he had no way of getting in touch with Almita. *She probably isn't even aware of Skip's death. I must get word to her.*

But he hadn't a clue how to begin looking for her, and finally, he hoped in time, she'd try to get hold of him. To lessen his guilt, Mick requested of Father Bartholomew a mass be said for the soul of his godson. That provided him with some consolation, but he was to be tormented for a long time by the thought he was responsible for the death.

Mick and Bubba McEntyre, ever since Mick had made a gift of his crucifix to him, had shared some fine moments conversing about their separate futures. McEntyre, he had told Mick, was planning to return to his home state of Mississippi and ask the girlfriend he had left there before joining the Army to marry him, if she'd still have him.

But it wasn't meant to be. One Sunday, after mass, McEntyre informed Mick he had decided to take the steps necessary to become a Catholic. Mick had been surprised to see McEntyre at mass when he first spotted him there.

The following day, Mick learned McEntyre had been admitted to the hospital off the camp barely able to breathe with a bad case of typhoid. Unfortunately, while being treated, he developed pneumonia, and the next day, he died. Mick wasn't permitted to see his friend at the hospital but a few days afterward, Mick attended a mass burial service at which McEntyre's body was buried along with other prisoners who had died within the past week.

A few days after the services, Mick was summoned to General Sage's quarters, where one of his staff officers led him into his office. There, the officer presented him with a small manila envelope.

Mick looked at the lieutenant with an inquiring eye. "What is this?"

"Your friend, Bubba," the lieutenant said, "the morning after he died in his sleep, was found clutching the object in that envelope tightly to his chest with both hands. I was told they found it hard to pry it from him." He pointed to the envelope. "Open it."

Mick opened the small envelope and emptied it from one hand to the palm of his other. It was the crucifix Mick had given McEntyre. Mick put down the envelope and picked up the crucifix attached to the chain. "But why are you giving it to me? It should have been buried with him."

"We understand he spoke to one of the orderlies at the hospital the night before he died, gave the orderly your name, and explained the crucifix belonged to you, and he wanted it returned to you if something should happen to him." The officer sighed. "I'd guess he sensed he was dying. And so we're just following his last wishes."

Mick's eyes became moist with tears. Feeling awkward, he put the chain and crucifix around his neck. "I'm sorry, sir," he whispered, wiping the wetness from his cheeks. "Will that be all?"

"Yes, corporal. I'm sorry too."

Mick saluted, turned around, and quickly left the officer's tent. He never stopped wearing the crucifix around his neck.

Mick often thought of Captain Takahashi. They had run into each other several times during the past two months or so, but their visits then had been brief, with only enough time to say a quick "hello" and "How are you?" and not enough time to sit down and visit as they had before.

But in mid-December, Mick learned the prisoners, or some of them, would be moved the latter part of December to Dapecol in Mindanao, where the Davao Penal Colony was located. American prisoners were already being held there for several months. Mick wondered if he'd get the opportunity to see and visit with his Japanese friend before he was moved away.

Most of Mick's friends either knew directly or had heard through other prisoners, of Mick's relationship with the captain. They knew directly because they had either observed the two of them talking at one time or another or Mick had discussed the friendship with them. Not one of them spoke against it, but every one of them felt free to make some comment in passing or even jokingly.

"Don't you feel a bit weird, *bato*?" Javier Chavez asked him once.

Mick had laughed. "A little, sometimes," he answered. "I myself have said that to myself when I think of how the relationship has grown."

Mannie Campos, his closest friend, said a few times, "Don't worry about it, Mick. Do what you want and don't give it another thought. It's no one else's business."

One day, when the end of the month was only a few days away, Mick was walking casually in the open field where he and the captain had enjoyed some of their talks. By then, Mick had giving up hope he'd ever see Takahashi again. As he walked, he heard the heavy shuffling of boots a few yards behind him.

"Wait up, Mick," a deep voice said. "I've been trying to catch up to you."

Mick immediately recognized the voice. He stopped walking and turned around. He saw Takahashi standing there, grinning.

Mick walked up to him, and they shook hands. "I was just thinking about you, deciding I wouldn't be seeing you again. I heard we're being moved."

"Yes, to Davao. I know."

"Will you be headed there too?"

"No, I've been called back to Japan. I should be receiving my orders about the time you and the other prisoners will be moving to the penal colony." He looked around for a place to sit but didn't see anything. "We'll have some time to visit now, probably for the last time."

"We can walk back to the boulders where we sat last time." Mick gestured. "They're just a couple of hundred yards away."

"Yes, let's do it. We can visit on the way there."

They spoke as they walked, catching up on each other's lives. They walked at a fast gait and both were a little out of breath when they sat down on the two boulders.

"I've meant to ask you before," Takahashi said when they were both settled, "what's new for you from home. Heard anything?"

Mick gave him a curious look. "I've assumed all along you know we're not allowed to write or receive letters."

"Yes, yes, of course I know. It's not a policy I agree with, but I know the rule in place. What I meant by my question is whether you've heard anything through your army's channels, which would still be open to hearing word about your family."

Mick nodded. "Oh, I see." He paused for a quick second. "Yes, we've been told should there be a sickness or death in our family, we'd be informed officially by the army." Mick smiled at the captain. "You were wondering if I'd heard any bad news from back home."

"Yes." He returned the smile but seemed a bit awkward. "I didn't quite know how to inquire of such a delicate matter."

Mick nodded to indicate he understood. "No, thank God I've received no such notice. And so I can assume all is well." He hesitated. "I wish I could let them know I'm okay. It'd help both my family and me to be able to do that much."

"Yes, I agree. And for you to receive letters from them. You told me before your wife was with child when you left the States last year."

"Yes, and by now, I'm hoping she's given birth to a healthy baby. She would have delivered by now. I've been gone for a little over a year, and she was about two months along when I left."

"I don't want to give you any false hopes, but I think in time, the policy may change and you'll be able to at least send, if not also receive, letters." He sighed. "But if there's a change, possibly it may happen in another year or so. Just keep your fingers crossed, Mick. I hope it happens for you. It'll be something to look forward to. Try to look at it that way."

"Thanks for saying that." He looked Takahashi in the eye. "But based on what I know so far about our treatment here, I'm not going to hold my breath."

"I actually don't blame you."

The discussion about the mail policy took them to broad discussions about human relations in a world made up of different cultures and ethnicities and the difficulties coming about when differences of opinion rise to the level of conflicts and disputes amongst the human race. They then spoke about the "ugliness" of war and its effects not only on the soldiers fighting it but on their loved ones back home.

"I realize, for example," Mick said at one point, "despite the cruel treatment I've witnessed here by your own soldiers, there must be good and decent people in your country who've had no say on how we're treated. And may even be shocked."

"And believe me, Mick," Takahashi added, "those people do indeed exist in my country. That's what makes war so horrid, causing us to focus on our differences instead of looking to see all we have in common."

"Apart from civilians in both of our countries, I know there must be officers like you and soldiers in the Japanese army who are decent and normal human beings but have been thrust into, let us say, the winds of war, no more and no less than the countless Americans on our side."

"That's a fine way of putting it, Mick. I agree wholeheartedly with your sentiments." He paused in thought for a moment. "I was just thinking about what you now said. I believe this growing awareness we've been talking about and you and I share, may be a kind of epiphany or revelation for both of us."

"I agree with your summing up our discussions in such a way. For me, it may even help me overcome my bitterness toward my own fate as a prisoner of war. I've already come a long way in overcoming it, but I need to work on it some more."

"As I've said to you before, I think you possess a positive attitude in viewing your predicament here as a prisoner." He glanced at his watch. He grinned. "Will you believe we've been sitting here talking for over an hour." He stood up. "I've got to go."

Mick got up and extended his hand to the captain. "Once again, Hinata, it's been a very positive experience talking to you today. I've enjoyed our talks."

"We shall not see each other again, my friend, I suppose. But as you Americans always say, 'Never say never.' We may sometime in the distant future."

"Maybe. Who knows? I'll say it, too, 'Never say never.'"

The two men shook hands. Mick was tempted to embrace his friend—to give him a Mexican *abrazo*—a big hug—but he wasn't at all familiar with whether Japanese culture allowed or frowned upon anything other than a formal bow. And so a handshake would have to do.

But when they had released their grip on each other's hand, before he parted, Captain Takahashi stood, almost at attention, and bowed to Mick. Mick returned the bow.

20
FROM ONE CAMP TO ANOTHER

In late December 1942, Mick and the other prisoners left Cabanatuan by boat to the Davao Penal Colony in Dapecol, about 600 miles away. Among the prisoners arriving at the penal colony with Mick were Sergeant Mike McKenzie, Sergeant Bob Follette, Mannie Campos, Jim "Pulga" Puglisi, Dennis Gurley, Pete Graciano, Sixto Duarte, Tommy Van Heflin, and Andy Gluck.

During the four months of imprisonment at Cabanatuan, 2,500 Americans died. That great number during such a short period was a sign of the sad but real, long-term effects of the Death March, along with the shortages of food and medical supplies continuing to hamper the prisoners' efforts to retain their will to live. This new encampment in the island of Mindanao was to be Mick's home as a prisoner for the next one and a half years.

They arrived at the colony on January 5 as 100-pound skeletons. The colony, isolated deep in the southern jungles of the island, had once been an extremely large penal farm for hardened Filipino prisoners. The penal farm was well developed with extensive rice fields several miles east of the main compound. Vegetable gardens were cultivated nearby the barbed wire enclosure surrounding the camp. A short distance away was a fruit orchard. The vegetables and fruit were grown for Japanese consumption, not for feeding of the prisoners.

When the men first arrived at the colony, they found about 1,000 American prisoners already imprisoned there who had surrendered on the island of Mindanao or elsewhere. They found living conditions much improved from Cabanatuan, and they slept in wooden barracks, an improvement from the smaller and much more crowded straw huts they inhabited at Cabanatuan and O'Donnell.

There was plenty of work in the colony to keep the prisoners extremely busy. The main work consisted of preparing the rice fields for tilling and planting and finally, harvesting the rice near the end of the harvest season. Prisoners also worked in the vegetable gardens and fruit orchards, which included not only irrigating the crops but cultivating the soil and pulling out by hand the sharp blades of coogan grass growing wild and in abundance throughout the farm, especially along the irrigation ditches. In addition, much of the prisoners' work was devoted to road and bridge repair in the surrounding areas.

No matter where you worked outside the encampment, there were strict rules against work crews bringing any kind of food back into the camp, whether rice, vegetables, or fruit. These rules didn't keep the prisoners from sneaking away some vegetable or fruit from time to time, but they could count on being beaten with batons or rifle butts if they got caught.

There were plenty of oranges on the trees, for example, but when the guards caught prisoners taking some off the trees, they would line up the entire work detail, two rows facing each other. The guards would then order them to hit each other with their fists, not their open hands. The guards would laugh as the two lines of men went at each other, hitting as softly as they could.

The prisoners would "telegraph" their punches to the ones they hit so the "victim" taking the hit would roll with the blow. The guards would go up and down the lines, and if they thought the prisoners weren't hitting hard enough, they'd wallop them with a baton or even stick them with a bayonet.

The rice work details traveled to the rice fields on flat railroad cars pulled by an American-made diesel locomotive. Mick was a member of one of the rice work details. A detail typically consisted of somewhere between 300 to 500 men and left camp around six thirty in the morning. Ordinarily, the detail would return at five o'clock in the afternoon. This was a daily routine.

One day, because of some mechanical problems that developed, the locomotive arrived late for the return of the work detail back to the compound. It was raining, and the guards were somewhat nervous and unusually cranky. The return to the camp was uphill all the way, and, because of the constant rain, the wheels of the locomotive kept slipping. Not able to get the necessary traction to move the railroad cars along at a good pace, the guards ordered all of the workers to get off the flat cars and motioned with their hands for them to push the locomotive.

Because they were exhausted from the day's work and they were walking barefoot on splintered wooden railroad ties, the men didn't make much of an effort to push hard. But they knew how to put on an act to fool the guards into believing they were pushing really hard when they actually weren't.

About two miles from the compound, someone in the large group of men suggested the group start singing *God Bless America*. Gradually, the singing caught on and grew louder as more men joined in. The prisoners back at the camp heard the singing a mile away and began converging at the gate entrance to the camp, curious. As the locomotive approached the gate, the rested, able-bodied prisoners at the camp began cheering wildly at the singing men.

The guards, bewildered, looked on and didn't raise hell because of the singing. One American prisoner in the cheering crowd had snuck an American flag into the camp sometime earlier. He ran back to his barracks, pulled out the flag, and carried it to the cheering crowd at the gate, where he held the waving flag up high for the returning prisoners to see. Mick, who had been thrilled during the singing, got emotional when he spotted the flag, and tears quickly welled up in his eyes.

At Davao, unlike the other prisoner encampments Mick had been confined in, the strict rules in place, including the prohibition of bringing any food collected elsewhere back to camp, were never lifted nor modified to "fit the punishment to the crime." The Japanese guards here also had a reputation for severe beatings and would make use of that tradition if they found any prisoner or prisoners violating the rules, even for minor infractions.

To show the prisoners they meant to enforce the rules strictly, no matter how small the infraction, the Japanese officers would beat their own non-commissioned officers in front of the prisoners, knock them down to the ground, and whack them with the flat of their saber.

Such display of force would then follow down the line. Non-coms would beat privates; three-star privates would beat the two-star privates, and the two-star privates would beat the one-star privates. That left the one-star privates to beat either a prisoner or a civilian because there wasn't a lower rank.

On one occasion, about a month after Mick and several of his friends from the 200th had moved to their new surroundings, there was an incident causing him to fear one of the guards he had angered might come close to killing him. Often, when a prisoner finished an assigned task early, the guards would give him something else to do. They frowned upon seeing a prisoner with nothing to do.

One day, Mick finished his job early, and the guards put him and other prisoners to work in a six-foot wide irrigation ditch filled with coogan grass. If the grass were left to grow wild, the water wouldn't flow freely down the canals. The grass was sometimes referred to as razor grass because of its sharp edges, which could easily cut the prisoners' feet and legs if left unprotected.

Because the blades of grass were large, thick, and heavy, the guards provided the workers with a short shovel to clean out the grass out of the waterways. On this particular day, as the guards were rounding up the prisoners to return to camp, Mick accidently dropped his shovel in a ditch. When he reached down into the ditch to retrieve it, an angry guard began yelling at him at the top of his lungs, evidently under the impression Mick was attempting to hide something from him. If it was one thing Mick had learned about the guards, it was that they became infuriated when they suspected a prisoner was attempting to deceive them.

Although he didn't mouth off at the angry guard, Mick got annoyed and made the mistake of mumbling something to himself. After he picked up the shovel and was getting out of the ditch, the guard began repeatedly smacking Mick's back hard with the butt of his rifle. As a result of the constant and hard blows, Mick thought the guard was going to bludgeon him to death. But the guard finally stopped, and, miraculously, Mick only came out of the unfortunate incident with only three cracked ribs and many bruises.

Another time, on a Sunday morning, three men in a work detail in the coffee field working without guards disappeared from the field and didn't return to camp at the end of the day. Remembering what the escape punishment had been at Cabanatuan, the blood brother rule—nine prisoners killed for each "brother" who escaped—Mick had just cause for concern. Two of the prisoners who escaped were from Mick's barrack.

For two days, fear and uncertainty occupied Mick's mind. Finally, Mick and the other prisoners in the same barrack were moved elsewhere. Once there, they weren't assigned any work detail for a week, and their food ration was cut down to one light meal a day during the week. They felt reprieved, for the dreaded punishment didn't come to them. Mick found out later the three missing prisoners had returned after he and the other prisoners had been moved from their barrack.

Occasionally, during some work details, non-Japanese men from Korea and Formosa were assigned by the Japanese to guard the prisoners. Always eager to attach nicknames to the guards because of the inability to pronounce their names, the prisoners nicknamed one of the guards from Korea "Pisspoor." Mick never learned the reason behind the nickname, but he guessed that whenever he took a leak while on the job, the Korean was a poor pisser because his aim was erratic and might piss all over someone nearby.

One day, while guarding the prisoners, Pisspoor sat on a pile of debris, of all things, cradling in his arms an unloaded rifle surrendered by the Americans when taken prisoners. This particular weapon was a relic with a lever or bolt to insert a shell into the chamber. As he was fiddling around with the rifle, he accidently pulled the bolt out. With this kind of bolt action, when one pulled the bolt out, unless you simultaneously pressed a certain button, the bolt would get stuck halfway in and halfway out. The Korean sat there for several minutes, trying to move the bolt back and forth and to figure out how to remove it completely.

Humored, Mannie Campos and Mick, sitting nearby, watched the Korean becoming more and more frustrated with his unsuccessful efforts.

"Maybe we should knock him over the head," Campos said in jest. "I mean, since he's weaponless. What do you think, Mick?"

"And where would we go?" Mick replied, smiling. "We'd end up getting killed or be severely punished."

"I was only kidding, *amigo*. Besides, with wearing only our G-strings, we'd stand out anywhere we went." The prisoners occasionally wore only their G-Strings to beat the heat.

Mick smiled as he continued watching the Korean struggle with the bolt action. "Look at him, I think he's almost got it figured out."

Campos watched. "No, not really." He reached over to the Korean and gestured for him to let go of the rifle.

A frustrated Pisspoor gave him the rifle.

Campos pointed to the release button. "See here," he said, pushing the button. "All you do is push this down, then pull on the bolt lever. It releases right away." He gave the rifle back to Pisspoor. "Here, you try it."

Pisspoor took the rifle, slowly pressed the button and pulled. The lever came off, and Pisspoor, a wide grin on his face, turned to Campos and said something in Korean, obviously pleased he was able to remove the bolt from the rifle.

As they returned to camp, Mick said to Campos, "I guess we'll have to put off our possible escape for another day, Mannie."

Campos laughed. "I imagine so."

In the latter part of January 1944, Mick learned through the grapevine of intelligence in the camp the Japanese had begun to allow prisoners to receive mail from home. It excited him upon hearing the news informally, but he couldn't confirm whether it was accurate or not. Even if true, Mick heard the Japanese authorities were withholding much of the mail prisoners received and releasing only a few daily, notwithstanding the new policy.

Even up to his last month at Davao, Mick was yet to receive any mail from Lilia or his parents. He still didn't know if Lilia had undergone a successful delivery, the sex or name of their baby, or Lilia's or the child's condition. He tried not thinking about the issue too much because he didn't want to go through the anger resulting from dealing with it.

He also heard although prisoners couldn't send letters home, they were allowed to send a preprinted postcard to their families, filling out information, such as name, nationality, Prison Camp ID, and the addressee. In the back, the prisoner could circle an answer regarding status of health, any injuries, improvement status, and a very short message to family. Knowing the post cards were censored before being sent out, most prisoners who filled the cards out seldom marked the responses accurately, fearing they wouldn't be mailed out.

Mick requested the card, filled it out, and submitted it, hoping it would reach Lilia. Wanting Lilia to get the card, he lied about his condition. He knew if she received it, she'd pass on the information to his and her extended family.

Mick and the others from the 200th were kept so busy at Davao that the one and a half years they spent there went by relatively quickly, when one considered the slow passage of time they had suffered through at Camp O'Donnell and Cabanatuan, due to the harsher treatment of prisoners there. In comparison, as Mick reflected on the 18 months he had spent at Davao, the mistreatment here was at least more tolerable and less brutal than what he and the others had experienced at O'Donnell and Cabanatuan. As a result, despite some of the strict treatments and punishments that injured prisoners, in percentages, much fewer Americans ended up dying at Davao Penal Colony.

In the few days before Mick's departure in the early part of July 1944, he began hearing second and third-hand tales—rumors, really—that victory was in the air for the Americans. First, from Europe, there were stories the allied forces were winning more and more battles and Hitler's army was growing with disenchantment and mutiny. The prisoners had no way to confirm or disprove the rumors.

Dennis Gurley came up to Mick one day. "I hear General Douglas MacArthur may be coming back," he said with a smile. "You think it's true, Mick?"

Mick shrugged. "Who knows? There's all kind of rumors floating around." Then he smiled. "He *did* say he'd return, didn't he? But I think that long-ago statement might be what's feeding the rumor."

"We feed on hope, don't we? Maybe that's all it is—just hope and rumor."

"It's easy to deceive ourselves, Dennis. We'll believe anything if it helps keep us alive. That's one way to get through this living hell. And that's all right, I think."

"And we have to laugh, don't we? No matter how bad things get."

"Well, we've got to admit, as bad as things are even here at Davao, they're a hellava lot better than at Cabanatuan and O'Donnell."

"They were the fucking pits there, weren't they?"

Mick thought back on those bleak days but didn't answer.

Gurley waited for Mick to say something but then realized he was in deep thought. "Well," he finally said, "I have to believe a day of freedom from all this will come true some fucking day."

Mick thought he saw tears welling up in Gurley's eyes, but his Native American friend turned away.

"All of us have to believe in something, Dennis." He paused, then shrugged. "For us, it's freedom." He patted Gurley on the shoulder. "And that's okay to believe in."

"Yeah, I think I'll hang my hat on that," Gurley said as he walked away.

Mick went away from that conversation realizing he didn't want to rely on false hope. He had heard those in the 200th who fed on rumors repeat cute sayings going around from mouth to mouth since the beginning of the year, "Frisco shore in '44!"; "Frisco dive in '45!" His favorite was, "Christmas turkey in Albuquerque!"

There was one thing Mick thought was true. These sayings, which the Japanese guards heard repeated time and again, were getting on the guards' nerves. *Could it be the guards were somehow hearing some things of their own that might be worrying them?* Was it only his imagination or had he detected the guards appeared more irascible and mean recently? Was it only a case of his trying to gauge the winds of war by the temper of his capturers? *Or maybe* defeat *was in the air for them, just like* freedom *was in the air for us.* Or was he merely doing his own part of "wishing and hoping?"

In July of 1944, Mick and the other men of the 200th were moved with a group of 650 other prisoners to Lasang, a few miles south. The men were told they'd be at this new location a few months helping in the construction of a Japanese airfield.

The trip to Lasang was in trucks covered with canvas, leaving a small opening in the back. The prisoners sat on the floor of the truck's bed, with a guard standing at the back opening of the truck. For a few days prior to the trip, the prisoners had been enjoying an abundance of food provided by the Red Cross. As a result, they were full and satisfied in their stomachs, a rarity. But the extra food helped the buildup of gas in their gastrointestinal systems, causing them to "break wind" frequently.

Obviously, the guard standing in the back got the full effect, and his facial expressions periodically showed he was extremely unhappy with his situation. But although displeased, the guard couldn't blame anyone in particular. Mick himself farted several times, and when he did, he said to a prisoner alongside, "For once, I can make things unpleasant for a guard and not get blamed nor punished for it." He couldn't help laughing to himself.

The various construction jobs at the airfield were hard labor, which the prisoners worked on eight to ten hours a day, using picks, shovels, and wheelbarrows. There was nothing mechanical in their tasks beyond their hand, arms, and legs—simple hard labor. The only positive side to their new work details was that their living quarters were better and the food was more plentiful and tastier. At least compared to what they had experienced before. Their barracks, too, were roomier and more comfortable.

One morning, after awakening, Mick looked outside his barrack and at first, he thought it was snowing. The air was full of what appeared to him to be hundreds of snowflakes, but they were fluttering around. Instead, what he was witnessing were dense swarms of grasshoppers, seemingly thousands of them, flying everywhere. Not only were they in the air but were on the rooftops, the walls, blades of grass, trees, and bushes. Even the ground was covered with them. It was an unbelievable sight.

In the afternoon, after returning from his work detail at the airfield, Mick noticed several prisoners outside all of the barracks running across the grounds with mosquito nets. They were catching the grasshoppers. He walked up to where several of them were sitting down, doing something with their hands. The men collecting the grasshoppers were periodically bringing their collection over to the others sitting there, where they were pulling the wings and heads off the grasshoppers and discarding them. The bodies of the grasshoppers, they collected in their mess kits, roasted them in a fire to a golden brown, and ate them as if they were eating roasted peanuts.

At meal time, they mixed the roasted grasshoppers with their issue of rice and ate the assorted meal to their heart's delight. At first, Mick and the others frowned upon their fellow prisoners who delighted with their newly found delicacies. But the following day and the day after, the other prisoners joined in, and it soon appeared as if everybody was out there catching grasshoppers. Mick, too, found the roasted grasshoppers quite tasty. The incident reminded him of the biblical story when John the Baptist, hungry for food and to survive, lived on locusts and honey. The prisoners were now living on grasshoppers and rice.

Work on the airfield, a monumental project, was completed the latter part of August.

PART VI

THE SINKING OF THE SHINYO MARU

21

THE HELL SHIPS

On August 20, 1944, Mick's group of prisoners, 650 of them, were marched two and one-half miles to a port, where they were to embark on an old Japanese freighter, the *Erie Maru*. Mick, Mannie Campos, and Sergeant McKenzie got separated from the others of the 200th, Sergeant Follett, Puglisi, Gurley, Graciano, Duarte, Van Heflin, and Gluck, who ended up at the back of the group. Mick, Campos, and McKenzie were ordered to the front of the group, which was divided into ranks or files of five men each.

The guards looped a half-inch manila rope through the pants' belt loops of the men on the outside of the column. If a man had no pants and was only wearing a G-string, the rope was looped around the wrists. If a wrist was ulcerated, the guards looped the rope around the prisoner's neck. The road was wide enough so the men could spread and be comfortable on the march, but the guards often pulled the rope tight to squeeze the prisoners up against one another. Three of the prisoners behind Mick had apparently gone insane sometime in the past, for they kept shouting gibberish caused by their hallucinations.

At the port on the Davao Gulf, several days later, 750 prisoners were loaded into the hold of the *Erie Maru*. Among them were Mick and the others from the 200th who had been with him at both Cabanatuan and Davao. It was another hot and humid day, and, inside the hold, the heat was stifling. The prisoners were squeezed into the hold like sardines, and there was no room to stand. Shortly after the 750 prisoners boarded the vessel, a U. S. bomber made a pass at the ship and dropped four large bombs, none of which hit the vessel.

The ship was enroute to Zamboanga, where a convoy of several ships was to be formed. Enroute, there were several alerts, causing the guards to cover the hold with the hatch cover. No mechanical ventilation existed in older vessels such as the *Erie Maru*. The aged ships used the large openings such as hatches and ports to allow natural airflow to circulate through the ship. In addition, natural draft was created by the force of wind and the ship's movement through the water into and out of different areas of the ship. But holds were the exception. There were no openings to allow air into the hold other than the hatch cover. If the cover was closed, any ventilation ceased, as limited as it was.

Because of the crammed conditions and lack of air, the hold was "hell warmed over," and some of the prisoners began to panic. But within minutes, the others first restrained them and then slowly managed to calm them down. On especially hot days, such as existed in the Philippines, the prisoners continued to swelter with their perspiration in the hold, with little relief at night. Considering the unbearable conditions during the trip to Zamboanga, Mick thought the discipline of the men was truly remarkable.

Although the trip was to take only seven days, the men were kept in the hold of the freighter for nine days. Fist fights took place over a mere spoonful of rice on the first day. Many of the prisoners, with their diseases still raging within them, couldn't control their bowels, and the resulting stench became deplorable.

During the first hours of the trip, a young prisoner next to Mick was suffering from malaria and had a temperature of 108 degrees. He was burning up. Mick, who had struggled with recurring bouts of malaria at least thirty times during his imprisonment since the Bataan Death March, considered himself an expert on the disease.

Believing the young man would be able to tolerate his high temperature better lying down, Mick suggested to the other prisoners around him they make room and allow the sick prisoner to lie down. Pushing and shoving, the prisoners were finally able to make enough room for the youthful soldier, who managed to squeeze himself onto the floor in between ankles and bare feet.

Within hours, the prisoners in the hold managed to work out a good system benefiting all of them. Someone suggested all the prisoners take turns lying down for one hour during the day and one hour during the night. After the hour passed, the prisoner would then either sit or squat on the floor, whichever he believed made him more comfortable than standing up. Or, he could just keep standing until his next turn at laying down on the floor. This system seemed to work and was used during the duration of the trip.

Day by day, the morale of the prisoners reached new lows. Even the nights were unbearable, as rats came out from hiding and swept over the prisoners' near-naked bodies. The whole experience, day and night, filled McKenzie with revulsion, and what little food he had managed to eat was lost.

Mick, who wasn't next or near to McKenzie, nonetheless saw him throw up against the wall of the hold. Mick managed to inch his way toward him until he got right next to him.

"Are you doing okay, Sergeant?" Mick asked. "I saw you throwing up." He was standing behind McKenzie.

McKenzie turned slowly to face Mick. "Yes, Mick, I'm doing fine, considering." He wiped his mouth with the sleeve of his shirt. "For a second, I couldn't help reacting to what I was seeing and couldn't help myself. Had to express my revulsion somehow."

"This is beyond belief, isn't it. I hope they don't close the hatch cover again. We need the air."

"I just don't see how some of these guys will make it until we dock. They're half-dead already, Mick."

"And even the ones who aren't half-dead, they're passing out because of the heat and lack of air."

"How are the others from the 200th doing? You spotted any of them?"

Mick shook his head. "Not since we got separated when we first climbed down here. I saw Mannie and Andy Gluck together. Last I saw, Pete Graciano was with Sergeant Follett."

"We've got a strong bunch, Mick. They'll make it through this."

"I hope so." Mick frowned. "I just left a kid with malaria. 108-degree temperature. I'm not sure he's going to make it. He's maybe 18 years old. Barely starting out in life, but he's made it this far. I'm going to try to get back to him. See if he's still with us." He began moving away from McKenzie.

"I hope he makes it, Mick." He raised his hand and half waved. "See you soon, I hope."

Mick nodded as he continued to push himself through the maze of bodies.

Confined in the hold throughout the trip, the prisoners soon learned the routines of their day. They used buckets as latrines, which were pulled up by ropes twice daily for emptying. Their daily and limited portion of food, which consisted of steamed rice, and their drinking water, were also lowered in buckets.

But they lacked a sufficient amount of food and water, as well as lacking sufficient oxygen. They finally were successful in beseeching the Japanese sergeant in charge of the ship's crew to permit prisoners to rotate on deck, allowing them to breathe fresh air. Only once during these rotating trips were the prisoners allowed on deck in small groups, where they would be hosed down with salt water pumped from the sea.

Mick lucked out when he got his turn to climb up the ladder to the deck with a group. In the group, he was happy to see Dennis Gurley and Pete Graciano, whom he hadn't seen since a few days before they were taken into the hold.

And they were as happy to see him. Both Gurley and Graciano gave Mick a big *abrazo* as they were beginning to be hosed down, which all three found refreshing.

"It's great to finally see you, man!" Graciano shouted to Mick as they were hosed down. "Dennis and I both were wondering about you. You doing okay in that hell hole?"

"Enjoying every minute of it, Pete. As much as the two of you are, I'm sure."

All three of them laughed, not only at their own version of humor into their oppressive environment, but from the joy of feeling the cold water on their skins. They had no idea how long the crew hosed them down, but to them, it wasn't long enough.

"Hang in there, Mick," Gurley said as they were being led back to the hold. "Only a few more days in there."

"You do the same," Mick replied, forcing a smile. He patted both Gurley and Graciano on the shoulder. "I'll let the others know, if I see them down there, I saw both of you and you're doing well."

Graciano and Gurley nodded with a smile.

The ship arrived at Zamboanga on the ninth day, making better time than expected. On September 4, the vessel was moved from where it was docked alongside the *Shinyo Maru*, a much larger ship but a more ancient one. This vessel had two holds, not just one, one in the bow and the other in the stern. Under cover of a drenching rain, which the prisoners obviously enjoyed, they were transferred to the *Shinyo Maru*, as Japanese soldiers from the *Shinyo Maru* boarded the *Erie Maru*. Although the prisoners weren't aware of the reason for the transfer, it was undertaken by the Japanese to confuse the Americans, who were receiving intelligence on Japanese activities from the guerilla underground, which was still active after the surrender.

During the transfer, Mick sought out Campos and the others he hadn't yet seen on the trip, Follett, Puglisi, Duarte, Van Heflin, and Gluck, but he only managed to bump into and chat briefly with Duarte and Puglisi as the prisoners climbed onto their new vessel.

"Good to see you, Mick," Puglisi said when he saw Mick. "Sixto and I were wondering if you were even in the hold, since we hadn't seen you."

"As if you could find anyone in there," Mick replied with a frown. "We were one of 750 sardines in there, Pulga."

"Is that how many prisoners there were in there?"

"Yeah, and it might be worse in the freighter they're transferring us to, I hear." Mick glanced at the vessel's name, printed in white on the port bow. "*Shinyo Maru*" he said out loud as he read the ship's name. "We were in the hold of the *Erie Maru*. What the hell does '*Maru*' mean?"

"That's the first thing I asked when we boarded it," Duarte answered. "Someone told me it means 'circle' or 'round' in Japanese, but for some reason, it's traditionally used at the end of a ship's name."

"Interesting."

After climbing aboard the *Shinyo Maru*, before entering the hold on the bow, they began to become separated.

"Maybe we'll have more room in this one, since it has two holds," Duarte said as he began climbing down the ladder into the hold, "and we'll be able to visit. Have you seen the others, Mick?"

"Yeah, I got to chat briefly with Mannie Campos, Sergeants McKenzie and Follett, as well as Puglisi, Gurley, Graciano, Duarte, Van Heflin, and Gluck. They're around somewhere. Some of them might end up in the other hold in the stern."

As Mick finished his comment, a guard, armed with a rifle, shouted angrily at Mick as he raised the butt of his weapon. Mick quickly got the message. "Shut your mouth and stop talking," the guard's action was cautioning him.

With that, the brief visit ended as Mick disappeared into the hold.

As more and more prisoners climbed down, it became apparent the hold wasn't large enough to hold too many more prisoners. Already, the men in the hold sat on the floor with their knees up to their chins. It was then the crew led the remainder of the prisoners to the stern, where they instructed them to begin climbing down the hold there.

When the crew finally estimated the prisoners were about evenly divided between the two holds, at least half of the prisoners in each hold were able to lie down while the other half was forced to stand. There just wasn't enough room. Because of the closeness of the ones lying down, if one of them turned over, all of them in the same row had to turn over, unless they wanted their faces right up against each other, one or two inches away.

The rest of them were forced to stand, possibly all night, while the others slept, until a prisoner standing up was lucky enough to switch places with one who had been sleeping for a couple of hours or so. It took considerable cooperation, which they managed to attain, with only a few exceptions creating tension and arguments. Even with this arrangement, prisoners who were standing couldn't even fall down, for there wasn't a place to fall down onto, unless it was on top of a prisoner lying down.

As in the *Erie Maru*, the prisoners were forced to tolerate the unbearable heat and to go without water until provided in buckets by the crew whenever the crew chose to do so. Often, some of the prisoners would find their throats too swollen to swallow when water and food were made available.

Once the prisoners were in the two holds, the long ladders were pulled up and the hold covers closed. It soon became apparent to the prisoners they were to be kept in total darkness in the horribly suffocating heat.

Fortunately, there was an interpreter onboard, who would occasionally shout down orders or warnings in English through the hold openings when the covers were pulled open. The first warning he shouted down was stinging.

"We must warn you," the interpreter shouted into a bullhorn the day before the ship left the dock, "in the event our ship is hit by an American aircraft or a submarine, the guards have standing orders to annihilate all prisoners with hand grenades thrown into the ship's holds!"

The *Shinyo Maru* was to be part of a convoy with an escort ship alongside, which would head north, hugging the western coastline.

On September 5, the vessel left the Zamboanga port on its journey. Fortunately, in the two days following, although the ship underwent sporadic bomber attacks, no bombs fell on or near the vessel. The bombings, however, could be heard by the prisoners in the two holds, and they waited in fearful anticipation the hold covers would any second be opened and grenades would be hurled down at them. But the only times the covers were opened were to lower buckets down with food, water, or for use as latrines for the prisoners' human waste, as had been the practice in the *Erie Maru*.

Once again, as in the *Erie Maru*, the prisoners were fed twice a day. Again, lowered in buckets by rope, the two meals consisted of steamed rice and about four ounces of thin soup for each prisoner. The Japanese cooks boiled sweet potato, known as *camotes*, and made the soup by boiling the peelings in water. Water was a prized commodity and therefore rationed. Each prisoner was provided only two thirds of a cup of water each day. Initially, when the ship began its voyage along the coast, the crew would leave one board off on each side to provide light and air. But later, the guards would seal the hatches entirely, and once again, it became pitch black, with the prisoners having to struggle for oxygen. They panted, not unlike winded dogs running a long trek.

Again, the prisoners improvised to try to get the most comfort they could find. One of the ways was to have a prisoner sit between the legs of another, then the prisoner would in turn open his own legs for the next prisoner seated in front of him, and so on down the line of prisoners.

Another method they used to lessen their discomfort was to place as many of the buckets used as latrines together instead of separated throughout the floor of the hold. The thinking here was all the fumes from the urine and feces would be concentrated in one area, rather than spread throughout the hold. Whether this method actually worked, the prisoners weren't certain, but they were willing to try anything at all to minimize their suffering.

The prisoners, even before their imprisonment, when they were fighting battles against the Japanese, had grown accustomed to fighting battles against another enemy, the seemingly countless diseases continuously plaguing them in the islands throughout the four months of fighting before the surrender. Those same diseases had followed the men of the 200th through first, the Bataan Death March, then imprisonment at Camp O'Donnell, then at Cabanatuan, followed by Davao and Lasang.

Now, the same life-threatening diseases confronted them in the hell ship, the *Shinyo Maru*. It wasn't surprising, therefore, the diseases wouldn't only threaten them with death but would take the lives of those too weakened and sick to survive them. Every morning, upon waking up, each prisoner grew accustomed to feeling the prisoner next to him to see if he was still alive. If he wasn't, the first action taken was to strip the dead prisoner of his shirt, pants, and shoes or boots, assuming he had any.

Someone, usually the man taking the dead prisoner's belongings, would holler topside, "Get this prisoner out of here! He's dead."

The practice, which became routine, was followed several times a day, not just in the morning on waking up. The heat and suffering took its toll every day. Each day, in addition to providing the prisoners with their ration of drinking water, the crew would lower buckets of sea water for those who wanted to bathe or at least throw water on their skin to cool themselves off a little.

On two occasions, Mick saw three men drink sea water left in the bucket. The next day, they went insane, leaping around like animals. As they did so, they'd often belch, each time eerily emitting a blue phosphorescence. Mick wouldn't have believed this occurrence if he hadn't seen it for himself. If someone else had told him he had witnessed it happening, Mick wouldn't have believed the story. Mick didn't see the event happen, but later learned two or three courageous prisoners, driven by mercy, ended the three men's suffering by beating them to death.

The two-thirds of a cup of water rationed to each prisoner daily was definitely not enough to maintain the functioning of the human body. And so it shouldn't have come as a surprise to anyone the human mind oftentimes might trick a prisoner into believing extreme or bizarre actions were necessary for survival during dire times when they might crave any fluid containing water. And so the inevitable eventually happened on the *Shinyo Maru*.

On the day in question, a prisoner happened to find a small piece of wire on the floor near one corner of the hold. This occurred at a time when he was almost delirious for a drink of water. His need to satisfy his thirst was so great he took the wire he had found and slashed his wrist to drink his own blood. He succeeded in cutting his artery and began to suck at the wound to guzzle—not swallow, but guzzle—the blood spewing from his deep cut. As he drank from his wound, another prisoner, equally if not more desperate to quench his thirst, picked up the piece of wire off the floor and immediately slashed his own wrist to follow the desperate measure just taken by his comrade. He, too, began to suck up the blood gushing from his wound.

Witnessing the flow of blood from each of the wounds, a prisoner nearby cried for help.

"Someone up there pull these two prisoners out of here!" he shouted at the top of his lungs. "These men are going to die if they don't get help to stop the bleeding."

After the two men had satisfied their urge, several prisoners tore their sleeves off their shirts and tried to bandage up the two wounds. But the cloth merely absorbed the blood, almost instantly turning red.

The hatch cover finally opened and ropes were thrown down to pull up the two bleeding prisoners. But it was too late, and they lost consciousness even before they were pulled up. The Japanese medic onboard could do nothing to stop the heavy flow of blood, and the two men were pronounced dead within minutes of being carried out of the hold.

22
TORPEDOES HIT THE SHINYO MARU

The filth everywhere on the *Shinyo Maru* was deplorable, but especially in the ship's two holds, where the sick and weak prisoners lost control of their bodies, leaving urine and feces covering the floors all over. To help alleviate the problem, the guards, who saw the issue as a risk and danger even to themselves and the ship's crew, began to allow the sick and weakened prisoners to go topside, where they had set out bottomless wooden crates tied down with ropes and lashed to the sides of the ship, where the prisoners could defecate into the ocean.

But time on the deck was limited because of the small size of the crew and the number of guards needed to secure and safeguard the prisoners while on deck. A few of them had to be tied down to the crate to prevent them from falling down into the water. Some prisoners were too weak to crawl up the ladders, and during bad weather, the wooden crates proved to be hazardous.

As a last resort, through the interpreter, the prisoners finally convinced the captain of the ship to permit several prisoners at a time to stay on the deck for extended periods. This left enough space in the holds to allow the able prisoners, with buckets of soap, water, and a few mops, to try to mop up the urine and feces off the floors in both holds.

No sooner had the prisoners been allowed back in the holds, after the mopping up, when another deranged prisoner, evidently prompted by the slashing of the wrists of the two prisoners just hours before, attacked another prisoner, attempting to bite into his throat to suck the blood from the carotid artery.

Fortunately for the victim of the attack, the man was stopped before he was able to grip the man's jugular with his teeth. The prisoner failed in his attempt, but again, the prisoners prevailed on the captain to remove the deranged man from the hold and confine and isolate him topside where he couldn't endanger himself or the crew.

To Mick, it was hard to believe only a few prisoners became deranged, considering the many mental obstacles on the ship making it impossible to maintain one's sanity. Even he at times thought he might be losing his mind, and he wouldn't have been surprised if he woke up one morning to find he had. Mick believed the prisoners clung to sanity only through incredible courage. Some of the prisoners occasionally suffered from severe claustrophobia or terrible bouts of cerebral malaria. The claustrophobia was transient and could therefore be controlled. But the cerebral malaria affected the brain permanently to the point of lunacy clinging to the victims until someone had the courage to put them out of their misery.

Madness also occurred, Mick was convinced, not only from lack of oxygen to the brain but also the overdose of carbon monoxide from engine fumes spreading into the holds where it was trapped with no other place to go, consequently inhaled into the body with every breath a prisoner took. The deranged mind, whether caused by the cerebral malaria, carbon monoxide fumes, lack of oxygen or whatever, made the men affected howl like wild animals. It was tortuous to hear their howls while begging for mercy at the same time.

Mick believed the Hell Ships to be an assault on humanity, worse than even the Death March. But like the march, he wondered if such assaults resulted from a deliberate and planned policy of the Japanese hierarchy. The prisoners who were forced to walk the distance to Camp O'Donnell could have been transported there by trucks and rail, but the Japanese chose not to do so. Were they banking on losing thousands of prisoners on the march simply to get rid of them? *They'd have fewer prisoners to feed if they died along the way.*

Ostensibly, the *Shinyo Maru* was enroute to Formosa or Japan, transporting the prisoners there to work doing hard labor in the factories and farms. But if sunk by an American bomber or by a torpedo from a submarine, it was a way of getting rid of prisoners. The idea was farfetched, Mick knew, but he still wondered if it was the mindset of the Japanese.

Late in the afternoon of September 7, when the convoy was astride the wide mouth of the Sindangan River, the *Shinyo Maru* dropped anchor. The docking was short-lived, for soon afterward, a torpedo from an American submarine struck another, smaller ship in the convoy, creating chaotic reaction for the captain and crew.

In another minute, the *Shinyo Maru* quickly pulled up its anchor and began heading with its escort out to sea. The prisoners in the holds had just received their meager ration of rice and water for the day when a Japanese bugler began blowing an alert. He managed to get out only two or three weak notes, then the sound of the horn trailed off, as if the bugler had become windless with fear.

As soon as the short blasts from the bugle sounded, Mick looked up to the hatch, which was open, and saw an automatic rifle sticking down through the opening. As the man behind the rifle opened fire on the Americans below, like shooting rats in a barrel, another guard dropped a grenade. It was easy for the rifleman not to miss, and several prisoners were wounded or killed by the blasts of rifle fire. As for the grenade, it dropped next to Mick's foot, ticking.

With little time to think, he quickly reacted and managed to kick the grenade under some boards in the corner of the hold, where Mick thought it would do less harm. It went off there. The grenade's fragments injured three prisoners, including Mick. Nine small pieces of the grenade went into his left leg, four into his right leg, and three into his arm. Fortunately, the injuries caused to Mick and the two other prisoners were minimal, considering the blast could have killed someone.

Mick was still nursing his wounds when just seconds later, the *U.S.S. Paddle*, an American submarine off Sindangan Point, fired two torpedoes at the *Shinyo Maru*, believing it to be a Japanese troopship carrying Japanese soldiers. Within seconds, there was considerably more chaos topside— crew members yelling and running around aimlessly upon seeing the two torpedoes headed their way.

The commotion was followed by a loud clatter of machine gun and automatic weapon fire. None of the shells were coming into the hold, and so Mick surmised the gunners were firing their weapons at something off in the distance, possibly torpedoes coming toward the vessel from a submarine nearby.

A few seconds later, there were two loud explosions, separated by only a few seconds, as the two torpedoes tore into the side of the freighter's hull. A terrifying loudness and earsplitting shrieks filled the air, and Mick immediately felt the ship's vibration from the double impact, and then the strong shudder running through the ship immediately after. He then heard the roar of what he thought might be depth charges. He wasn't certain.

Suddenly, the steel plates holding the steel beams up above buckled and then loosened wildly, and the beams, along with the steel plates, fell loudly to the floor of the hold. The wreckage pinned several prisoners to the floor. Those who weren't injured by the wreckage began scrambling for the hatch. As the prisoners climbed the ladder and emerged onto the deck, Mick heard the machine guns open fire on them, and they dropped like flies onto others trying to climb out.

Despite his wounds, Mick managed to get up off the floor and move just beyond the hatch opening, just in case the guards decided to drop more grenades or began firing their rifles again. As soon as he situated himself at his new location, his body was shaken by another loud explosion so powerful it knocked him hard against the side of the hold. His forehead hit against a bolt protruding from a steel plate, and he was felled to the floor unconscious. Uncannily, as he lost consciousness, he had visions of diving off a high diving board into a front flip. Just then, a second explosion propelled him into what he envisioned as a back flip.

When he regained consciousness, he couldn't hear clearly. All sounds he could hear were muffled. He immediately noticed the ship was listing a little. Dead bodies were strewn all over the floor. He quickly guessed an engine room erupting nearby must have caused the two explosions knocking him out and killing or wounding several others.

He soon discovered he had lost his bearings and couldn't find any of his friends or even the group he was with just before the explosions. He was also bleeding from the shrapnel wounds he suffered when the grenade exploded a few feet away from him.

Although Sergeant Bob Follett felt the torpedoes sudden jarring of the *Shinyo Maru* when they rammed into the vessel, he was surprised the large bang of the explosions, as others around him described the shuddering sound, were to his ears, considerably muffled. He attributed the partial deafness to an ear infection that had done a good job of plugging up both of his ears. But even though the sounds of the explosions were toned down, the tremendous blasts knocked him unconscious for several minutes. When he regained consciousness, everyone in the hold, it seemed to him, had been tossed from one end of the hold to the other. No one was where they had been just before he blacked out. Bodies were scattered everywhere, and debris and fallen beams lay crushing prisoners who were trying desperately to get up. Others helped them.

When the torpedoes hit and sent vibrations and explosions throughout the ship, the wooden hatch cover right over Puglisi gave way and tumbled down on top of him, shattering Puglisi's right leg. He managed to crawl out from under the pile of debris to the ladder, but suddenly, there was a third explosion, and the hold was soon engulfed in water. Miraculously, through about 20 feet of water, he could see the light coming from the hold opening above. He swam toward it and reached the surface, climbed the ladder, and crawled out onto the deck. He saw in the distance Japanese soldiers gunning down the prisoners running on the decks.

Almost immediately, he ran into Dr. Cooper, a physician who treated him at Base Hospital No. 2. The doctor was fighting his way through the pandemonium Puglisi saw everywhere on deck, trying to treat the wounded.

Puglisi tried pulling Dr. Cooper back from where he appeared to be headed.

"Doc, they're shooting everybody up there," he barked. "Stay here! In a few minutes, we'll try for the shoreline."

But the doctor ignored him. "I've got to treat the injured. That's my job here." He moved on, and Puglisi went in the opposite direction, away from the gunfire.

After managing to find his bearings again, Mick noticed a few more steel beams and other parts of the decking had collapsed into the hold while he had been unconscious. He suddenly realized he'd better get topside before more beams came toppling down on him or the compartment suddenly capsized. He immediately spotted the iron ladder, still dangling from a gaping rent in the deck.

Mannie Campos blacked out from the impact of being thrown against the steel-plated wall of the hold by the explosions of the two torpedoes. He was unconscious for about a minute. When he came to, disoriented, it was pitch black, and he couldn't see a thing, although he heard the yells and rustling of the prisoners around him. Thinking he was underwater, he didn't dare breathe. After a few seconds, he realized he could feel his eyelids covering his eyes. He opened his eyes and discovered he wasn't underwater at all.

The stark blackness must have been caused by his keeping his eyes closed tight out of fear, he thought. The ladder was full of prisoners attempting to get out of the hold before it became inundated with water. It didn't take him long to decide he'd join them in the climb.

Soon after the torpedoes hit the ship, Pete Graciano was momentarily shocked to see water almost waist deep rushing toward him in the hold. What went through his mind was the explosions had knocked a hole in the hold, allowing the water to rush in from the breach. He rushed as fast as he could through the water and maze of dead prisoners floating and on the floor to get to the ladder. But he was suddenly overtaken by the rushing water, which was building. He finally decided to swim to the ladder, bumping into dead, floating bodies or prisoners also swimming to get to the ladder.

When he reached the lower deck, it was under water, almost but not quite to the top deck. As Graciano gulped for air above the water, the vessel rolled sideways, and the rolling water carried him under again. He thought he was about to drown.

Struggling and stumbling over bodies to get to the ladder, Mick soon reached it and began to pull himself up to reach the deck. He managed to climb a third of the way up when some object he couldn't identify came tumbling down on him from the open hatch and knocked him to the bottom. He tried again, and when he got halfway up the ladder, a big gush of water shot up from somewhere below and washed him upward onto the deck.

The wall of the hold must have cracked, he thought, from the pressure of water gushing into the ship from some hole below. The powerful gush of water saved his life, but it might have also drowned anybody below him who might not have been able to swim to safety.

After regaining consciousness, Sergeant Follett joined the other prisoners who were climbing up the ladder to get out of the hold. As soon as he exited through the hatch, he observed the blasts had blown off a part of the superstructure to the rear. He could see daylight through the gaping holes torn into its walls. He felt the ship listing, and immediately, decided there was no time to spare.

A prisoner he didn't recognize was standing next to him. Follett approached the rail and yelled at the prisoner, "Let's get the hell off this ship and go over the side!" As he got to the edge, near the railing, he could see the shore a few miles away. He crossed over the railing and without hesitating, dove into the sea.

On reaching the hatch opening, Campos stuck his head out of the hold slowly, trying to avoid gunfire. Immediately, his eyes came upon a Japanese soldier with a .25 caliber machine gun shooting every prisoner in sight. Two bullets only grazed Campos. Fortunately, one just skimmed the right side of his head and the other only grazed him just under his chin. *I'm lucky to have escaped a direct hit, otherwise I'd be a goner.* The wounds gouged not only deep creases on his skin, but the force he used to avoid being hit knocked him backward on top of others climbing below him and then onto the hold's floor.

23
THE STRUGGLE AT SEA

After the gush of water propelled him upward onto the deck, Mick picked himself up and surveyed his surroundings. He was surprised to find most of the superstructure gone. Dead guards were sprawled all over the deck, which was about two feet under water, with countless bodies floating in it. A Japanese guard suddenly appeared from out of nowhere and walloped him on the jaw, but the guard lost his balance and tumbled backward onto the deck.

Mick hurriedly placed his foot on the soldier's neck, attempting to yank off his life preserver. But he didn't get a chance to do so, for Japanese soldiers were shooting at him from what was left of the vessel's superstructure. He hurriedly pressed himself flat underneath to get out of the soldiers' line of fire until he decided what to do next.

Campos, floundering on the floor in a mesh of broken bones and torn flesh after having been thrown off the ladder, hurriedly scampered through the floor of dead bodies and, with other prisoners still climbing, managed to get on deck. He spotted another Japanese soldier shooting at fleeing Americans, and so he decided to slide prone along the deck to hide from the soldier behind a boom. From there, he surveyed the deck. Dead Americans and Japanese soldiers were everywhere, their heads bobbing in one or two feet of water covering the deck.

He saw the beach about three miles away. "That's a long swim," he whispered to himself, "and I better get my ass going." He took off his two pieces of clothing, his T-shirt and G-string and jumped into the ocean stark naked. As he was about to hit the water, he noticed for the first time he couldn't move his right arm. He had been hit in the arm by two small fragments from shattered plates after the torpedoes hit and hadn't realized they were still imbedded in his shoulder and upper arm.

From where he was laying down on the deck, Mick heard a noise coming from behind him. He turned his head and saw Javier Chavez. He was standing away from the open hatch cover, his back to Mick, throwing pieces of wooden boards over the side for the prisoners already in the water to use as life preservers.

Mick shouted loudly. "Duck, Javier! They're shooting this way and are bound to hit you!"

But his warning was too late. The board Chavez was holding flew up into the air as a bullet hit him in what appeared to Mick to be near his lower neck. He spun around from the impact and began to fall onto the deck. As he fell, Mick could tell he had spotted Mick down on the deck, for he was staring right at him with fear in his eyes, as if he knew at the exact moment he was dying. Mick crawled over to him and began groping under the water for the body, but the water, sloshing every which way on the deck with the sway of the ship, had already washed him away.

As Graciano struggled not to drown while under water, the ship began listing considerably, allowing the deck to drain slowly and permitting Graciano to stand up on the deck over about a foot of water. He spotted Rabbit Carbajal 40 or so feet up ahead toward the boat's stern.

He struggled through the water to get to where Carbajal, fear in his eyes, was holding tight to a rail alongside the superstructure.

"Good to see you, Rabbit," Graciano yelled at Carbajal as he got nearer to him.

"It's good to see someone I know," Carbajal answered in a halting voice.

"You're going to jump, right?" He saw clearly the hesitation and fear in Carbajal's face. "Let's jump from this fucking hell hole, Rabbit." He began moving toward the stern and looked back. "C'mon, buddy. Hustle, man."

Reluctantly, Carbajal followed him. His expression hadn't changed.

When they got to the rail along the stern, Graciano climbed over to the other side. "C'mon!" he shouted to Carbajal, who was now standing next to him, trembling.

"There's no fucking way I'm jumping all the way down into the water, Pete!" Carbajal shouted back. I can barely swim!

"Oh, yes, you are! Just do what I tell you to." Without waiting for a reply, he grabbed Carbajal with all his might and pulled him over the rail, taking him with him as he jumped.

When both surfaced, Carbajal, who had swallowed plenty of water upon hitting the surface, was coughing and struggling to breathe. He was dog paddling, doing a poor job of it. Fortunately, they had come up for air at a spot where they found a wooden ladder floating. They both grabbed on to it for their lives.

After Mick gave up trying to find Chavez in the water, his hands and knees still planted on the deck, he heard a noise behind him and turned around quickly, to find a dazed guard standing over him, like some wild-eyed demon. His rifle was pointed at Mick's chest, and for a split second, Mick thought he would soon be joining Chavez. He raised himself off the deck and slowly backed away from the guard. The vessel was now listing, and the water on the deck disappeared. Mick, surprised the soldier hadn't fired, continued to move to the high side of the listing ship. Instead, as if confused, the guard turned and galloped awkwardly in the opposite direction toward the bow, which had lowered because of the listing.

Mick, attempting to avoid any rifle fire from the Japanese soldiers who had opened fire at him and Chavez only moments before, scrambled to what was left of the vessel's stern. There, he ran into Sixto Duarte. No words were exchanged. Instead, they looked into each other's eyes, as if glad to see a companion in a time of need. The two of them saw the steel stringers running the length of the ship were exposed to the rear. All the steel decking behind the stringers had been blown away.

"Let's grab onto them to guide us toward the stern!" Duarte said. "We can then dive off the stern away from the gunfire."

"Great idea, Sixto," Mick said as he grabbed at the stringer on the starboard side. "You grab the one on the other side."

Duarte nodded and moved to the portside, where he grabbed onto the steel stringer there. In unison, each holding on to a stringer, they quickly moved upward toward the stern, which was now noticeably listing more. Having reached the end of the line, they glanced at each other immediately after looking down into the water below.

There was no hesitation for Duarte. He went over first. Mick, on the starboard side, waited too long as the stern moved higher. He started to jump but suddenly got cold feet and stopped. Just then, he heard the cracking noise of the ship beginning to break with a loud noise as the bow went into the water and the stress to the ship's hull heightened.

He took one last look at the water below, now farther away. He build up enough courage. "It's now or never!" he shouted at himself and jumped. He barely cleared the ship as he tumbled into a flip in the air.

After grabbing on to the ladder he and Carbajal found, Graciano, an experienced swimmer, instructed Carbajal, a poor swimmer, to get to the other end of the ladder and kick his legs while he did the same thing at the other end. In that way, the two of them quickly maneuvered away from the ship. After swimming a few minutes, from a greater distance, Graciano looked back and saw the *Shinyo Maru*, its stern now high up in the air, as the vessel, split apart and slowly slid down into the water.

After Puglisi separated from Dr. Cooper, who disappeared behind the superstructure in the opposite direction, the ship began to list faster, and Puglisi thought, even with his injured leg, he should jump overboard soon, before it was too late. With this in mind, he approached the railing on the starboard side of the ship. Without giving it any thought, he went over the railing and jumped.

He was lucky, for he found a large floating piece of what had once been a hatch cover. He examined it and saw it had considerable air space underneath, and so he went under the water and came up to the air space, which was large enough for him to breathe, even through his mouth.

As Mick fell after jumping, he spotted a wooden raft crowded with Japanese soldiers. They were armed. Mick appeared to be in the raft's path, and he sensed he might fall on top of them. The soldiers, too, Mick guessed, thought he would fall on their raft, and their scrambling for cover must have kept them from firing their weapons at him.

Luckily, Mick ended up splashing into the water several feet clear of the raft. The impact plunged him several feet under, and he swam as deep as his momentum would take him, while swimming underwater away from the raft as far as he could hold his breath. Although he couldn't see well, he tried to guess where the vessel would be so the suction from the sinking wouldn't take him down with the ship.

It seemed an eternity he was underwater but the need to surface as far away from the raft motivated him to keep moving until, finally, his lungs felt as if they would burst. He knew then it was time to surface. When he finally reached air, he immediately looked to see if the raft was anywhere in sight. It wasn't.

But he was among many prisoners, either swimming or dog paddling to stay afloat. Some were holding on to pieces of debris they had found floating, and some were in obvious distress because of disabling injuries or ailments. Without a life jacket or anything to hang onto, Mick thought, none of them, including himself, would survive.

He kept looking around as he dog paddled to see if he recognized any of the prisoners nearer to him. He finally spotted Tommy Van Heflin, the fellow from "little Texas" in the southeastern part of the state. He didn't appear to have any visible injuries.

Mick swam toward him. "Are you hurt?" he asked when he reached him.

Van Heflin shook his head as he spit out some water. "Not at all. Feel lucky to have gotten out of that ship alive, with all the shooting and all." He patted a flotsam, a large piece of timber he had discovered soon after jumping overboard. "And I was lucky to find this! Here, Mick, hang on to it while I get this other fellow over here. It's big enough for a bunch of us."

Mick held on to the flotsam as Van Heflin swam toward a prisoner who appeared disabled. He soon was back with the prisoner, who soon was holding on to the board for dear life.

"Have you seen Sixto Duarte?" Mick asked.

Van Heflin shook his head. "No, I haven't. But I've seen no one I know since I've been in the water. Been busy trying to help these guys who are ailing or hurt and can't stay afloat. Already, I've seen several go under from exhaustion." He spit out some water again. "Why do you ask about Sixto?"

"He's nowhere in sight. He and I were together and jumped into the water about the same time. But he was on the port side. He's probably on the other side of the ship."

"Well, we'll soon be able to see over there when the ship sinks completely."

"I hope so. But I've got a gut feeling he didn't make it. That he didn't come up. Just an instinct I have."

"Well, maybe you're wrong. Let's hope he came up."

As Van Heflin swam away from the flotsam to help others, Mick reflected on what had happened so quickly after the two torpedoes struck the *Shinyo Maru*. He had forgotten all about an incident possibly accounting to why he was now threading water in the ocean and not dead. Shortly before the torpedoes hit the vessel, a U. S. Army Air Corp captain asked Mick if he'd trade places with him so he, the air corpsman, could cool off. The man had been resting against the steel plates making up the ship's sides. Mick obliged the captain, and the two men moved to trade places.

As the air corpsman passed Mick, he asked Mick, "What do you think the small arms fire we just heard above us was all about?"

"I have no idea," Mick answered at the time. But later, he thought back on the captain's question and became sure the rifle firing was the sound of the Japanese soldiers firing at the torpedoes barreling down on the *Shinyo Maru*.

It was soon after the captain and Mick made the switch the guard had thrown the grenade landing at Mick's feet. Seconds after the grenade exploded, the torpedoes hit the ship. The resulting explosions occurred to Mick's right, bending the steel side around him, and he suddenly found himself covered with dead bodies or stunned prisoners all around him. He recalled when he glanced over at the spot where the captain had sat down to enjoy the cooler air he thought the hold would provide there, he lay lifeless, pinned under a steel beam and steel plate blown off by the explosions.

The question Mick was to ponder now and most likely, would still haunt him in the years to come, assuming he survived, was, *What would have happened if he and the captain hadn't traded places?* Surely, the switch saved his life, he thought now as he held on to the flotsam, and at the same time, caused the captain's death.

24
THE ESCAPE TO SHORE

Follett hadn't moved far from the floundering ship when he came upon two weakened Japanese soldiers. Both had life jackets on. He swam to the first soldier and attempted to take off his life vest. The soldier fought back. While he was struggling with the soldier to take the preserver from him, he noticed a motorized boat approaching with what appeared to be armed Japanese soldiers. He decided to end his struggle with the soldier and go after the other soldier's life jacket. But he, too, fought his attempt. Finally, seeing the boat was getting too close for comfort, he decided to abandon his attempt to get a life jacket. He quickly dove under and began swimming underwater as fast as he could to get away from the approaching soldiers, whose obvious intent was to pick up the two weakened soldiers in the water. He'd have to do without a life preserver, he thought, at least for the moment.

After helping Van Heflin get another prisoner to the flotsam, Mick heard a loud grinding and gushing noise coming from the *Shinyo Maru*. He turned his head and, with some fascination, watched as the torpedoed ship was swallowed up by the sea.

The stern, the only part of the ship above water, was crowded with prisoners who, like ants, were trying desperately to maintain a position on the vessel to stay afloat once they hit the water. As what remained of the stern disappeared into the water, the suction created by the sinking ship took with it some of the prisoners clinging to the stern for their lives.

Mick turned to Van Heflin, who was helping the last prisoner onto the flotsam. "Listen, Tommy, I'm going to swim down there to see if I can find Sixto. You've got your hands full here, and I need to try to find him, if he's still alive."

"How will you stay afloat, my friend? You're welcome to stay here. We've got a place for you here, brother."

"I know, but I'd rather try finding Sixto. Don't worry, I'll find something to hang onto. Besides, I'm a good swimmer and will manage okay."

"I noticed those shrapnel wounds on your arm. You gonna have someone take the shrapnel out sometime soon?"

"Yeah, I know, first chance I get. Got to get out of this water first, though."

"Yeah, for sure. Good luck finding Sixto, Mick."

"I hope I do."

He turned and began swimming to where the ship had sunk, hoping to see some sign of Duarte. As he swam, he saw a wooden raft to his left appearing to be carrying Japanese soldiers, probably the same ones he almost fell on top of when he jumped off the sinking vessel. He decided to swim underwater for a while so he wouldn't be spotted by them. He was surprised when he found himself swimming underwater for what to him seemed a long time, longer than what he thought he could stand without coming up for air. He finally decided to go up for air.

When he resurfaced, he found himself alongside several Japanese soldiers who were weaponless, like him, trying to stay afloat and alive. They appeared frightened. He didn't consider them a threat, unlike the soldiers on the raft, who were armed. Physically, even though he had lost many pounds while imprisoned, he was much bigger than any of them and could defend himself, even in the water. One of them was holding on to a small life preserver, which Mick had heard were called "doughnuts."

Mick, thinking the preserver might save his life, without hesitation grabbed at the doughnut and began pouncing the soldier on the head until he released his grasp of the life preserver. Pushing the soldier away, who was now dog paddling with panic and fear in his eyes, Mick left him there and continued toward the shore with the help of the life preserver, which he was certain would do just that, preserve his life.

Looking for Duarte, he dog paddled toward the shore, which he estimated was over two miles away. He soon came upon three prisoners holding on to a wide wooden plank. They were towing another prisoner lying down on the plank, obviously injured. Getting closer to the Americans, he recognized the prisoner lying on the plank. It was Javier Chavez, who had been washed off the deck after being gunned down by rifle fire. Mick was ecstatic to see he was alive after thinking he died on deck when Mick was last with him.

Mick swam closer and examined Chavez' wound. The bullet had torn through the shoulder, not the neck near the carotid artery, which Mick first thought when he saw Chavez go down into the two feet of water on the deck. It was still bleeding. A bad sign.

"You act as if you know him," one of the prisoners said to Mick. "Do you?"

Mick nodded. "Yes, he's a friend and a member of my unit. I was with him when he got shot by riflemen on the ship. He was washed away, and I thought he was dead." He was addressing the one who asked the question, but he now took the time to look at the other two. He didn't know any of the three.

"We spotted him floating in the water on his back. Lucky for him, we had this plank, which was heavy enough to hold his weight."

"We've tried several times to stop the bleeding," the second prisoner explained, "but we couldn't. He needs a special kind of tourniquet, considering where the bullet went in."

"We don't think it hit an artery," the first prisoner said, "or else he'd be bleeding at lot worse."

"We were hoping to get him to shore, but it's a long ways away."

"Seems to me you guys have done all you can to keep him alive," Mick said. "As his friend, I thank you. Has he ever regained consciousness since you came across him?"

"No, not while we've . . ."

Chavez suddenly drew in a deep breath, and his body jerked, as if reacting to a certain pain within. He was gone, Mick thought.

He felt for a pulse on the wrist. There wasn't one. He then checked the carotid artery on the left side of his neck. There wasn't one there either.

"He's dead, I'm afraid." He turned his head to address the three Samaritans. "Thanks again, fellows, for picking him up and being with him in his last moments."

"Don't mention it," the first prisoner said. "You want us to leave him on the plank?"

"What are you guys going to do? You could probably use the plank for yourselves."

"Actually, we had just talked about splitting up. We thought we'd fare better if we did that. We're going to try to get to shore as quickly as we can."

"If we manage to escape being gunned down," the third prisoner said. "We heard the Japanese might send their patrol boats around to kill as many prisoners as they can, trying to keep them from getting to shore."

"Why doesn't that surprise me?" Mick said with a scoff. "It's not anything we're not used to." He patted Chavez on the shoulder. "Goodbye, *mi amigo*," he whispered. "*Vaya con Dios*, my friend." He turned to the prisoners. "Good luck to you, fellows."

"And to you."

Mick left them there as he dog paddled toward the shore with the help of the doughnut, hoping to spot Duarte on the way.

Looking eastward from the water, Graciano could see mountainous land about two to three miles away, he estimated. Using the long ladder, he and Carbajal began paddling in that direction. After half an hour, they picked up two other prisoners who were wounded and were just about to go under. They happily grabbed onto the ladder. As the four of them continued moving toward the beach, a Japanese plane approached from a distance and as it drew closer, began to strafe the water toward them. To avoid the bullets, they ducked under, still hanging on to the ladder. Graciano was hit in the leg.

The four men continued on and eventually, came upon three prisoners hanging on to pieces of debris, just large enough to keep them afloat but barely. There was plenty of room left along the ladder, and so the three men joined them to try getting ashore. They came upon some floating boards and other debris and decided to use the boards and the ladder to build a makeshift raft to better reach the shore.

Along the way, they gathered other items they believed would be useful when they got to the coast. They found a Japanese medical kit, two canteens filled with water, a wooden ammunition box containing 14 cans of pork and beans, and several bars of what appeared to be homemade soap.

Puglisi was under the cover for a good half hour when a Japanese soldier approached the cover to use it as a flotsam. On discovering Puglisi underneath, the soldier tried to stab him, who, despite his small stature, was stronger than the Japanese soldier. In the struggle, Puglisi was able to force the weakened man to release the knife, while Puglisi held him underwater until he drowned. He noticed the soldier carried a canteen filled with water. He took it, drank a couple of swigs, and held on to the canteen to drink from later.

Within minutes, he decided to move farther away from the shore and moved out to sea to stay away from the motor launches he spotted a mile or so away toward the shore. The launches carried Japanese soldiers gunning down prisoners trying to swim to the beach. A half hour later, he was saddened when he came upon the bullet-ridden body of Dr. Cooper floating adrift on a wide board. *Doc would be alive right now if he had listened to me.*

Campos came out of the water gasping for air. As he dog paddled in place, he was surprised not only could he feel sensation on his injured arm but he was able to move it. He wondered if the cold water had anything to do with the change. He was on the side of the ship closest to the shore. The vessel was sinking fast, and he thought he'd better start swimming away from it so he wouldn't be sucked under. He began swimming toward the distant beach.

As he swam, he noticed spurts of water around him. He spotted an American hanging on to a plank just ahead and he began to swim toward him. The spurts of water now moved rapidly toward the prisoner quicker than Campos was swimming. Suddenly, when the spurts reached the plank, the prisoner's arms stiffened and went up in the air, then the prisoner sank out of sight.

Campos couldn't figure out what was causing the spurts of water until he headed toward a small group of other Americans treading water up ahead. Again, he saw the spurts of water headed toward the prisoners treading water. They, too, within seconds, threw up their hands in the air and went under, as they were hit by a barrage of bullets. It was then Campos came to realize the spurts of water he had seen all along were coming from a group of Japanese soldiers firing machine guns from a boat not far away. Up until then, busy with swimming, he hadn't spotted them. And, fortunately, they hadn't seen him.

He quickly took a deep breath and went under. He swam toward the shore and away from the boat full of Japanese soldiers. He swam and held his breath as long as he could and finally surfaced. He scanned all around him, but the boat was nowhere in sight. He continued his swim. Much later, as he threaded water in place to rest a minute or two, he spotted a whaleboat up ahead, headed to his left to another group of Americans treading water about half a mile away.

A Japanese officer stood at the rear of the whaleboat, a saber in his hand, shouting orders to the Japanese soldiers, who were armed with machine guns. They didn't fire their weapons at the Americans in the water, but instead, the boat slowed down near the group, and the officer began striking the helpless prisoners with his saber, over and over again until the last one disappeared into the water. Beyond, Campos saw other whaleboats and the glint of sunlight on the distant sabers as they, too, struck at the water there at the hands of the officers guiding those boats to helpless prisoners trying to reach shore.

Campos continued swimming away from the horrid sight to keep a safe distance from the whaleboats, even though he was swimming away from the coast. As he quickly moved away, the thought occurred to him the brutalities of the Japanese didn't end at the boundaries of their POW camps but followed them onto the sea, where they were intent on ridding themselves of prisoners struggling to reach the shore to survive.

He swam for a considerable distance from the shore until he came upon a Japanese soldier in a life vest, his eyes betraying his fright. Even though his injured shoulder and arm weakened him, Campos managed to gain the strength to take the life preserver away from the frightened soldier, who didn't even fight him, apparently frozen in fear.

When Follett resurfaced, after his close call in attempting to take a life preserver from the two Japanese soldiers, he got a last glimpse of the *Shinyo Maru* as the stern rose high in the air, and the ship gave one last gasp as it sunk almost vertically into the sea.

He then turned to see what or who he might find to help him get to shore without having to swim all the way. He suddenly became frightened, thinking the very worst. He now wished he had tried a little harder to get one of those life preservers. It might have saved his life, he thought. If nothing else, he'd have to try to get closer to shore, hoping some miracle would occur.

Thinking those positive thoughts, he began swimming toward the shore once again. When he tired, he'd stop and thread water for a while, then turn on his back and float for a few minutes. After he rested for several minutes, he'd began swimming toward the beach again.

He did that for what he thought might be an hour. When he realized he was getting too tired and the situation for him wouldn't get any better, he saw off in the distance, toward shore, what appeared to be a small vessel. He started swimming toward it. As he got closer, he realized it wasn't a boat at all. It appeared to be crates or wooden boxes of some kind floating in the water. He then thought for a moment he had seen movement to the sides of the object, which by now he determined definitely wasn't a boat.

He approached the object with considerable caution. He finally decided the movement he thought he had seen was in fact of persons holding on to what indeed were wooden crates floating on the water. When he finally concluded prisoners were hanging on to the crates, he began swimming as fast as he could to them.

When he got to within shouting distance, he hollered, "Hey, you guys, I'm American. I'm coming your way." He swam the rest of the way.

When Follett grabbed one of the ropes hanging from the crates, he introduced himself and got acquainted with the four prisoners, whom he'd never met. He found out the empty crates had evidently been onboard the *Shinyo Maru*, stored on its deck. Dangling ropes had been found with the crates, which were floating apart, and the four prisoners had brought them together and tied them to one another to use as a vessel to get them ashore.

But no sooner had they tied the crates together, they explained to Follett, they decided the size of the crates might make them easy to spot and sitting ducks for the Japanese whaleboats, which were searching for survivors throughout. Already, they reported, hundreds of prisoners had been machine gunned down by the armed Japanese soldiers seeking them out.

"We were about to dismantle our crates when you came," said one of the prisoners. He stopped when he heard the sound of a vessel in the distance.

All of them, including Follett, looked up and, off to the right, they saw what appeared to be a small Japanese destroyer coming towards them. They had no place to go without being seen. One of them suggested the only chance they had to stay alive was to make out as if they were dead already. There wasn't any other option. They hurriedly draped themselves below the ropes and against the edges of the crates, remained still, and pretended to be dead.

Follet, having no other choice, went along, praying as he lay still the plan would work. If it didn't, they'd all be gunned down.

As it got closer to the flotsam, the vessel slowed down and turned its forward guns, as if to fire, on the makeshift vessel. It circled the large flotsam twice without firing. When it came around the second time, Follett was certain the destroyer would open fire with its small forward guns. He let out a sigh of relief when the vessel increased its throttle and went off without firing a shot.

After the group of prisoners dismantled the crates, once again, Follett was on his own, having taken for himself a broad piece of wood he could use as a wide surfboard. With that, for what seemed hours into the dark of night, struggling inch by inch, foot by foot, yard by yard, he was shocked but relieved when he found himself, in the almost moonless ocean, only about a hundred yards or so from the coastline.

PART VII

DELIVERANCE, GRACE, AND RESCUE

25

SETTING FOOT ON SHORE

Hanging on to the doughnut, Mick continued dog paddling toward the shore. His breaths came quickly now, and he was suddenly surprised to find himself panting. For some reason he found hard to understand, the beach appeared farther to him than when he had left the three prisoners and the corpse of Javier Chavez floating on the plank. Working in tandem with his mind, his eyes had obviously played tricks on him, he assumed, making it appear earlier as if the shore were closer than it was, thus explaining the difference in perception. Yet, he hadn't ever thought of himself as being good at estimating distances, especially over water, and so his poor estimates could explain the difference.

He looked all around him as he paddled toward the shore, hoping he'd spot another living soul, but he saw no one. He was hoping he'd run into Tommy Van Heflin and the other prisoners on the flotsam. After another half hour, his legs were tiring from the paddling, and he stopped to rest them. As he stayed afloat with the help of the doughnut, he saw off in the distance someone who appeared to be hanging on to a flotsam and started to dog paddle toward the person, hoping he was American.

As he got closer to the flotsam, he couldn't believe his eyes. It was Tommy Van Heflin. Mick shouted at him.

Van Heflin yelled back. "Hey, Mick, fancy meeting you again, of all people."

"Yeah," Mick said as he reached Van Heflin. "What are the odds on that, I wonder."

"Whatever they are, I'm glad to see you."

"Me too. What happened to the others with you? You have the same flotsam, I see."

"I lost them. One of the whaleboats filled with armed soldier was passing by about a half a mile away, and they spotted us. When I realized they had turned and were headed our way, I dove underwater and began swimming below the surface as far as my legs and arms would take me."

Van Heflin paused to take a deep breath. "I never thought I could hold my breath that long, but it's a wonder what the human body can do when you're trying to get away from someone who's trying to kill you."

"And you got away. What about the others?"

"When I finally came back up for air, I looked for them but didn't see any sign of them. I spotted the plank, but neither the others nor the boat were anywhere in sight. I think they were gunned down, but some may have gotten away like I did. I swam back to the plank, figuring I wouldn't be lucky to find another flotsam."

"Well, I'm happy you got away. You think we'll be okay if we stick together?"

"I don't see why not. One person on this thing can be spotted as easily as two can." He turned around. Come on, let's head for shore, hoping the coast will be clear. But be on the lookout for those whaleboats. We won't stand a chance if they spot us."

"I was thinking it might be a good idea to wait here until night time. I don't think they'll be searching in the dark."

"You might be right, but let's head on out for a while. I'd feel better being closer to shore."

"Okay, let's do it."

Both of them got behind the plank and began paddling. As they moved slowly, they spotted someone hanging on to a life preserver, threading water. They got close enough and saw the man's shirt was soaked with blood and the man appeared to be barely hanging on to the preserver. As they got closer, Mick recognized the prisoner.

"It's Andy Gluck, Tommy!"

They paddled faster.

"Andy!" Mick shouted when they reached Gluck.

"Hey, Mick," Gluck said, almost in a whisper. His voice was weak and raspy. "Hi, Tommy. Good to see you, fellows."

"How badly are you hurt?" Van Heflin asked.

"Pretty bad, I'm afraid. A fragment entered through the back and exited from my right shoulder, leaving a gaping hole." He gasped for air.

"I'm so weak I can barely hang on." He was barely hanging on to the preserver with both hands and awkwardly managed to set his feet and part of his lower legs on a piece of wreckage from the ship.

Every time Gluck's shoulder came out of the water, blood spurted from his wound. Both Mick and Van Heflin examined the wound. They looked at each other with sad eyes but said nothing.

"Wish we had shirts to tear and bandage you up, Andy," Van Heflin said." He shook his head. "I feel so helpless. Can we do anything for you, aside from trying to get you ashore?"

Gluck tried to smile but instead managed a grimace. "Naw, face it, fellows. I'm not going to make it. And if you two keep trying to help me, you won't either. Thanks, but get the fuck out of here before some Japs spot all three of us and kill us all!"

"Let us keep you company for a while," Mick said.

"I'm dying, guys. Just do me the favor of getting the hell out of here before it's too late. I've already made my peace with this thing. I'm just waiting for the Lord to take me. I've been wondering what's taking him so long." This time, he displayed a real smile.

Both Van Heflin and Mick returned the smile.

"C'mon, get going," Gluck said weakly. "Thanks for stopping by. It's been a good visit while it lasted. Now, git!"

Reluctantly, Van Heflin and Mick continued on their way toward the shore without Gluck. Not too far away, they ran into Sixto Duarte, whom Mick had been keeping an eye out forever since they both jumped from the ship. He was holding on to a life jacket. Mick was happy to see he was alive and showed it by giving him a big hug.

"I've been looking for you all over, you rascal!" Mick said.

"And I've been looking everywhere for you too," Duarte replied. "Great to see you made it, Mick."

"At least up until now. Why aren't you wearing the life jacket?"

"I haven't had time to put it on since I took it off a Jap I came across a few minutes ago." He handed the jacket to Mick. "Here, help me with it."

Mick assisted Duarte put on the vest.

"It's good to see you, too, Tommy," Duarte said.

"Me too," Van Heflin said. "The first thing out of Mick's mouth when we first saw each other was whether I had seen you."

"Yeah, and like I said, I've been wondering where he was and hoping

I'd find him." Duarte smiled. "Now, here we are, having a sort of reunion, one might say."

"And now we're together, let's stay together," Mick said. "Let's continue to the shore."

The three of them held on to the flotsam and dog paddled to land. Before going far, they spotted several Japanese gunboats up ahead, picking up Japanese survivors. To their horror, they soon identified machine gun tracers to their right coming from soldiers in another gunboat behind them, aiming their weapons at a group of prisoners holding on to a large piece of wooden plank.

Caught in the middle of the gunboats up ahead and the sudden appearance of the gunboat behind them, the three men made a quick decision to split up, thinking they'd be a more difficult and smaller target if they did so. And so Mick struck out on his own, using his doughnut, and Van Heflin kept the flotsam and Duarte went off with his life jacket on.

Realizing the gunboat with armed Japanese soldiers would again circle the prisoners behind him, Mick decided to follow the tide out to sea, using a lazy sidestroke, rather than continuing on toward the shore. Because the water between his location and the shore was apparently swarming with gunboats, he decided it'd make sense to wait until after sundown to face the problem of making it to shore.

As Graciano, Carbajal, and the other five prisoners made some progress getting closer to shore, they heard rifle shots behind them in the distance. They immediately spotted two Japanese motorized lifeboats picking up Japanese survivors and shooting at a few Americans in the water. It was then they decided to split up and go their separate ways, so as to attract less attention. After they took bits and pieces of the makeshift raft to use as flotsams, they went off on their own, even Graciano and a reluctant Carbajal, who's ability to swim to shore was a big question at this point, and he knew it. But he understood the need to split up from Graciano and accepted the decision.

Graciano let another prisoner keep the ladder to himself. All he took was a small board, which he later realized wasn't enough to keep him afloat for too long a time. And so he struggled as he moved along, doing the best he could. When he left the ship, he wore only a pair of blue denim shorts, and he now discovered somewhere along the way, he had lost those and was now completely naked. He swam dog fashion, which was not only slow but strenuous for him.

The sun was now about to set, and Graciano was exhausted. He then heard the cries of a wounded Japanese soldier who apparently needed help. As Graciano drew near him, he immediately noticed the man was wearing a life preserver. Graciano immediately grabbed a long string tied to the preserver and eased up behind the soldier, who, because injured, wasn't able to defend himself. Without hesitating, Graciano dunked the soldier underwater until he drowned, took the jacket off of him, and continued on his way, with renewed hope and determination to reach land.

After paddling for several hard minutes, Mick stopped to take a breather, simply floating in place holding on to the doughnut. He took time to examine his wounds on his arm from the grenade shrapnel. He was surprised to find the pieces of shrapnel were gone. They must have worked themselves out with his body motion in the water. He recalled someone saying they could do that, and he certainly had hoped they would, dreading the thought of an infection, which would cause further problems.

Despite his injuries and the living nightmare he had witnessed in the water since the *Shinyo Maru* was torn apart by the torpedoes, he began to experience an exhilarating euphoria, feeling as if his body was bathed in refreshing cool water and his nostrils were sucking deliciously fresh air. He closed his eyes to fully enjoy the peace of the moment.

He was soon snapped back into reality, however, by a sharp, stinging on his right shoulder. A gunboat had found him. Fortunately, the bullet merely grazed him. Quickly, he submerged, leaving the doughnut on the surface. He swam underwater for a considerable distance toward the open sea, then came up for air for only a second or two, went underwater again, then came up again, and went under again. Every time he'd come up for air, he didn't take the time to look for the gunboat, instead continuing on until he was exhausted.

When he came up the last time and thought he couldn't continue because he was too tired, he scanned the ocean quickly. He saw whaleboats in the distance toward the shore, but they appeared to be concentrating on prisoners near the shore, leaving the spaces farther away alone.

As he was threading water in place, he found a long piece of board. How lucky can he be, he thought as he grabbed the board and hung on to it. He used it to float in place without swimming or even dog paddling. For the first time, he began wondering about sharks. So far, he hadn't seen any evidence the ship had gone down in shark waters. Yet, the thought scared him, and he decided he'd stay put and not go farther away from the shore.

When night came several hours later, Puglisi managed to sleep for a couple of hours on top of the hatch cover. He thought he was the luckiest prisoner ever for having come across the cover.

Night came quickly for Mick. In the dark, intermittently, the tracers from the gunboats in the distance continued, pointing the way to the shoreline. Soon, he was able to make out the surf along the coastline from the phosphorescence created by the wave action. The sight was uncanny. He remained there for what he guessed was another hour, when he decided it was time for him to try paddling again to the shore. He wouldn't be able to stay here the entire night without sleeping. *If only I had a wide enough board I could lie on top of and fall asleep.* But even that would be dangerous, he realized, for he might roll over unconsciously into the water and drown.

He began paddling vigorously this time, using the phosphorescence along the surfs of the waves hitting the coastline to guide him. From time to time, he'd stop to rest, then go on again. He *must* survive this ordeal, he kept repeating in his thoughts, over and over again. *I have to live through this hell to tell of it!* For hours, he hadn't given his wounds any thought, but now, he was feeling their stinging pain in his arm and shoulder, even though the shrapnel apparently had come out. In the water, he couldn't check if the shrapnel had come out of his legs, but he hoped they had.

But he was so, so tired. Yet, he had to get to shore, he kept telling himself, and so he continued on, even though he knew he was getting weaker with every stroke of his legs. Even his breathing was painful now. But he could see the phosphorescent surf getting closer and closer, which motivated him not to give up. Finally, the coast seemed so close he could reach out and touch it.

But when he reached the coastline, cruel fate appeared to have created another obstacle for him, for the surf was pounding on jagged coral reefs, something he hadn't even considered a possibility. He quickly discovered he was above the reefs when he cut the tip of his finger as he paddled forward. Instead of finding an inviting shore, it appeared he was required to cross this new hurdle. He swam out a bit and tested other places in this area, but the coral was all over.

When he finally decided he was forced to tackle his way through it, he realized he needed his hands to help him in the reefs. To prevent his naked body from contacting the razor-sharp coral, he used his hands to feel for the coral. In his effort to do that, he sliced his palms in several places. He came up with an idea. He still had the plank, which he placed against the small of his back, turned over, and tried floating on his back. He believed floating on his back might provide him the least amount of contact with the coral's edges. He found it helped, but soon, his shoulders, upper back, and his calves got cut even with the plank underneath him.

"God help me through this," he said out loud. *Is this a test of my faith, of my belief, in Him?* It took him by surprise when suddenly an image of his friend, Hinata Takahashi, came to his mind.

"You've got what it takes to get through this, Mick," Takahashi was telling him. "I knew your strength from the moment I laid my eyes on you. Do it!"

Mick couldn't help smiling at the thought of his Japanese friend appearing in his mind. He suddenly thought of Lilia and his daughter. It was a girl—he was sure of it. Lilia had given birth to a daughter. And he had to get back to them. It saddened him he didn't even know her name. *But I will soon.* He was so close to his freedom now and mustn't give up with his effort. And so he continued his slow movement through the coral.

Finally, after what seemed like hours he fought through the maze, he found himself lying on his back on a narrow strip of sand. The sparkling stars in a barely moonlit sky, which he hadn't paid attention to during his long swim and as he maneuvered above the coral, shown brilliantly in the sky. There were seemingly millions of them.

As he lay there, he enjoyed the soothing breeze as it moved across his face and abdomen. He turned on his stomach and just lay there, naked, resting. He sensed he was too weak to stand up, and besides, he wanted to make sure he was out of danger and no Japanese soldiers were nearby. He even fell asleep, woke up briefly, then went back to sleep. When he woke up, it was still dark, without the slightest hint of dawn in the sky and only the stars and the Milky Way above.

After reaching the shore, Sergeant McKenzie spent the night on a ledge of coral. He was surprised he hadn't come across a coral reef on the way to the beach he heard could slice your fingers off if a person wasn't careful. He spent the night in a secluded area a few feet from the edge of the jungle, where the coast and the sea were plainly visible.

The next morning, before heading inland, he watched as Japanese soldiers in lifeboats threw pieces of what appeared to be white paper or flowers into the water where the *Shinyo Maru* had gone down. He assumed it was some kind of symbolic Japanese ritual.

Although darkness had fallen, with what little light the starlit sky provided, from where he now stood beyond the beach, Graciano could see the outline of trees a hundred or so yards from the shore and behind him, he could hear the waves hitting against the rocky shoreline he had passed. He soon spotted a high coral rock cliff, from which large boulders had fallen into the sea. About 100 feet from shore, he came upon a boulder and used it to sit and rest. He had no idea if he was in Japanese-occupied territory.

Suddenly, he heard someone whistle. He froze with fear. As he began looking closer at the high cliff, and below it, he could barely see the outline of a cave, just above ground level. Then came another whistle.

Finally, someone inside the cave yelled, "C'mon in!"

Graciano moved slowly around the boulders until he reached the entrance to the cave. He cautiously walked inside and was greeted by four survivors. One of them was Rabbit Carbajal.

"You made it, Rabbit!" Graciano yelled out. "You rascal!"

Graciano and Carbajal embraced. They were all smiles. Graciano didn't know the others in the cave and introduced himself.

"You guys are from the 200th," one of the prisoners said, addressing both Graciano and Carbajal.

"Yeah, we are," Graciano answered. "We had to split up a few hours ago, but we've found each other now."

"You fellows from the 200th are a tight bunch. Closely knit, I've heard."

"We've tried to be. All of us consider ourselves good buddies."

All five of them were exhausted, but they spoke for almost a half hour, each telling stories of their escape, before falling asleep in the comfort of the cave.

After taking the life preserver from the frightened Japanese soldier, it took Campos two hours to reach the beach. Fortunately, he didn't encounter any problems on the way. In the distance toward the sea, as he set his feet on the beach's sand, he spotted the feared whaleboats gunning down prisoners, but none came close enough to him to be a threat.

As he moved inland from the beach, with every step, he felt thankful he was on solid ground. To him, it seemed like days, not hours, he had been in the water. Not long after moving farther inland, he was shocked when two or three Filipino guerillas suddenly rose out of the grass. From the field where he ran into the guerillas, he was high enough to actually see a coastline to his left, and he was surprised after traveling so far into the jungle, he was so close to the coastline on that side of the island.

Before any words were exchanged, one of the guerillas took off his pants and offered them to Campos. Campos, who was naked, without even a G-strap, thanked him and put the pants on. After Campos put on the pants, the guerilla who had given them to him pointed to the visible shore on the left.

"Look," he said, pointing. Campos looked to where the man pointed. A Japanese ship, apparently torpedoed, had run aground on the beach. The Japanese soldiers on the ship were shooting prisoners in the water trying to swim toward the beach. There was no end to their obsessive killing, Campos thought as he viewed the scene.

Two of the guerillas led Campos to a trail along the edge of the jungle, gave him directions where to find additional help, and then left to attempt to find and help other prisoners who were fortunate enough to reach shore. Campos continued on his own. He was following the path the guerillas had shown him, but he felt he was moving aimlessly through the jungle, and at one point felt as if he had lapsed into a delirium due to his injuries, for he couldn't remember how long he'd been walking. It had happened to him before.

As he walked farther inland in a stupor, he came upon a small nipa shack. He entered and found the remains of corn cobs with some edible corn still on them. They were hard to eat because Campos's teeth were loose due to some vitamin deficiency. From there, he continued walking without seeing other guerillas, and he thought possibly he had taken a wrong turn somewhere.

26

THE TREK INLAND

Minutes after Mick's futile attempt to avoid being cut by the coral, as he lay exhausted on the beach, a heavy but refreshing rain began to fall. He was still on his back, and he opened his mouth to allow the heavy drops of rain to enter his dry mouth, enjoying their wetness. It gave him the energy he needed to begin crawling toward the tree line a few yards beyond the beach. The wounds on his legs, back, and arms from the coral's sharp edges were so painful he still couldn't stand, much less walk.

His progress crawling to reach the trees was a slow process, but he finally got there. Suddenly he heard the sound of rifle blasts coming from an area on the beach about 200 yards north of where he had fought the jagged edges of the coral reef.

Turning around, half sitting on the soft sand, he saw Japanese soldiers aboard a beached boat open fire on some prisoners swimming for shore near the coastline. It surprised him that the Japanese were still hunting down prisoners trying to reach land, even in the drenching rain.

He had been wrong earlier when he thought they had stopped searching for the Americans after dark. It showed to him how obsessed and relentless the Japanese were in eliminating all of what was left of the escapees, and he thanked God he hadn't encountered them when he was near the shore. Instead, he had confronted the coral reef, a different danger that didn't end his life, as the soldiers would have. *I'd chose the reef over the gun-happy soldiers any day.*

Afraid he might be spotted, he quickly turned and continued his crawl into the jungle. As he entered the denseness, the rain stopped suddenly. He crawled, his movement quick as his mind struggled to catch up. He continued for several minutes until he came upon a fallen hallowed tree trunk partly filled with collected rain water. Although the droplets of rain he had swallowed while resting on the beach revived him, it hadn't quenched his thirst, and he now dug into the tree trunk with his hands and drank every drop of water he could bring up to his mouth.

After resting at the fallen tree trunk for several minutes, he thought he had regained some of his strength and thought he'd be able to stand and start walking with the help of a makeshift walking stick. He began searching for a long and narrow, good-sized branch he could use as a walking stick. A few yards away, he spotted one appearing sturdy enough to support his weight. But he struggled for several minutes to get up on his feet. Using the stick for support, he just stood there for several more minutes before trying to walk using his makeshift walking stick.

Slowly, he began hobbling along in painful steps, but he was moving, he thought, which was the important thing. In such a slow manner, he penetrated farther into the jungle. He wanted to find a hide-a-way where he could sleep for the night. But within minutes, he was enveloped in a cloud of stinging mosquitoes. As fast he could manage, he reeled through the jungle until, finally, the persistent mosquitoes left him.

For an hour or so, stopping to rest every ten to fifteen minutes, he moved farther into the jungle until he came into a clearing. There, he came to a trail, which he followed. Soon, he found several deserted villages close to each other. Mick thought they had been deserted due to guerilla activity in the area, making the villages susceptible to dangerous mortar attacks or bombing by Japanese planes.

To his surprise, after he traversed the last abandoned hamlet, just beyond the village, before entering a wooded area, he found Tommy Van Heflin and Sixto Duarte. The three of them were happy to see each other and kept kissing each other on the cheek and hugging and laughing continuously for a long minute.

"Tommy and I were just talking about you a few minutes ago," Duarte said to Mick as he held onto his shoulder. "We were hoping you weren't dead." He grinned, then gave out a short laugh.

"No, I'm very much alive," Mick replied, joining in the laughter. "Hurt, but still alive."

"What's with that wound on your shoulder and your cut hands and legs? How did those come about?"

"Got hit on the shoulder by one of those gun-happy motherfuckers on the whaleboats." He pointed to his right shoulder. "The cuts came from the coral reefs I was unlucky enough to run into as I came onto the shore."

"We came onto land about a half mile away from those reefs," Van Heflin said. "I kept hoping we wouldn't run into any."

"Well, I wasn't so fortunate." He looked from one of them to the other. "The grenade fragments I got on the ship seem to have worked themselves out. I checked my leg a while ago, and they're gone there too. What about you guys? Both of you look unscathed."

"Lucky again. Sixto told me after we ran into each other here he narrowly escaped being killed."

"How so, Sixto? One of the whaleboats?"

"No, I managed to escape those several times. When I came on the beach, a lone Jap with a rifle surprised me. He was watching for prisoners coming to that part of the beach to shoot them. But I ran from him as he continued firing at me. I was fortunate one of his shots didn't hit me."

"Listen, guys," Van Heflin said, "we should head on out another few yards to find a safe place to spend the rest of the night, away from this clearing you just passed, Mick. A native I bumped into about an hour ago told me there are friendly natives in this area and also some guerilla camps have been helping prisoners who managed to make it ashore, especially the wounded like you, Mick."

"You think you can go on a bit farther, Mick?" Duarte asked.

Mick nodded. "Yeah, I can do it, but I need to get some sleep soon."

"We all do." He began to move. "Let's go, Tommy."

Van Heflin didn't answer but joined them in their quest to a safe place to sleep for the night. After walking for another half hour, Mick struggling with his walking stick with the help of both Van Heflin and Duarte, who alternated helping, they came to a secluded area along the slope of a hill. They spent the rest of the night there.

When Puglisi awakened from his sleep atop the floating hatch cover, it was still dark. He was close enough to the coastline to see the glare of bonfires beyond the shore and the cresting waves. He'd never seen the coastline by night, so he had no idea whether those fires were there every night or might be evidence some prisoners had reached shore. Or possibly, they might be guerilla forces, but would they advertise their presence so boldly?

How lucky I am, to have lived through my sleep and not being riddled by bullets from a passing whaleboat. Or maybe the Japanese had given up or thought they'd already killed enough Americans. He hadn't even been aware he had fallen asleep, but now he was glad he had, for he felt rested.

He decided to wait there until dawn. When he finally left the hatch cover, he "thanked" it in his thoughts for having saved his life, and paddled the remaining 100 yards to the shore. As soon as he hobbled out of the beach, in much pain because of his injured leg, and before he entered what appeared to be a jungle area, he ran into a friendly native who was gathering his fishing gear to return home. He explained to Puglisi he could guide him to a camp where guerillas awaited to help the prisoners who had escaped the sinking.

Excited to be so close to the shore, Follett abandoned his flotsam and swam the remaining 100 yards to the beach. As he neared the shore, he saw what appeared to him to be two natives, one holding something looking like a long spear. When he reached the beach, he immediately saw a heavy stick on the sand and picked it up to use as a weapon, in case they weren't friendly.

With his weapon in hand, he called out to the two natives near the tree line, "American Joe, American Joe," remembering back in Manila, he had heard Filipinos referring to American GIs with the name.

"C'mon, American Joe," one of them shouted back. "Come to us. We're friendly Filipino."

Follett kept the stick, just in case, as he walked toward them. "I'm an American prisoner who escaped off the sunken Japanese vessel."

"Yes, Yes, we know," the second native responded. "Where you wanna go? We take you there."

"Hadn't thought about it. As far away from the beach as possible."

"We take you to friend." He turned around and began walking into the jungle. "Follow us," he said, looking straight ahead, not bothering to turn around to Follett.

Follett followed, happy to feel the ground beneath his feet. They continued inland for what Follet thought was a considerable distance, past a few smoldering bonfires. Eventually, they stopped, and another Filipino, probably the "friend" one of the natives referred to, soon appeared.

"I'm here to take you and other Americans to a friendly camp," the newcomer said. "Follow me!"

The sergeant did as he was instructed.

As Dennis Gurley swam to shore, he was still bleeding badly from a gash to the forehead he received from hitting some debris when he dove into the water. As he was swimming the last few yards to shore, he worried about sharks, wondering if they were attracted to blood. He was surprised up until he was swimming the last 100 yards to shore, the thought of sharks hadn't entered his mind. If he hadn't worried before, he wondered, why should he start worrying the last few yards to land.

From the beach, after resting against the trunk of a large tree, he saw a steep cliff and thought it might be a good place to hide until he decided what to do or where to go from here. It was late at night, and he wouldn't mind finding a good place to hide and catch up on some sleep. His body was drained of energy, and he needed to get some shut eye.

It took him an hour or so to get to the cliff. There, he found a small cave, and he decided it'd be a good place to hide. He fell asleep in no time. Several times during the night, he heard Japanese soldiers searching the area, probably for escapees so they could gun them down. He knew they were Japanese soldiers by the sound of their hob-nailed boots.

When he woke up during the night, he thought back to the many hours he had spent on the water, trying ways to get to land. He considered himself extremely fortunate not to have been riddled with bullets while in the water, like many other prisoners in the ocean he saw mutilated by machine gun fire.

Before the sun rose the following day, Gurley realized if he stayed in the cave until daylight, he might be found and shot. The bleeding from the wound on his head had stopped, but he was feeling excruciating pain from two smashed discs in his lower back. Despite the pain, he managed to climb the rest of the cliff from the cave for an hour until he came to a level area where he found a cornfield. To the side of the cornfield, his eyes came upon a Filipino shack built on long stilts. No one was there, and he was so tired he lay down to rest on a woven pallet of straw. He closed his eyes to rest them, and, without intending to, fell into a deep sleep.

When he woke up, a Filipino guerilla stood over him, smiling. He gave Gurley two raw eggs to eat. He hadn't eaten since the morning ration was distributed on the ship before the torpedoes hit, but since then, in trying to find ways to survive during his time in the water, the thought of food hadn't even entered his mind. As he gazed at the two raw eggs in his hand, he realized he was starving and gobbled them, shell and all, without pausing.

When he finished his "breakfast," the guerilla motioned for Gurley to follow him, but Gurley found he could only crawl, the pain in his back being so severe. Getting the message across to the Filipino he couldn't stand up to walk, the Filipino held up his hand, and nodded, indicating he understood.

"You wait here," he said. The man left and in about five minutes, returned. He helped Gurley outside.

There, in front of Gurley, stood a carabao, to which a sled was attached. The friendly Filipino helped him onto the sled. In such a manner, they traveled inland on a road not far from the cornfield for several miles. It turned out to be a bumpy road on the sled, without cushioned wheels or suspension, and caused considerable pain to Gurley's lower back.

They finally came to an area where the Filipinos had set up a small hospital, consisting of bamboo tied together. It was only about the size of a very large room. There were already eight patients in the hospital, being treated for all sorts of ailments, and Gurley was told guerillas were out there finding and gathering more prisoners who made it to shore.

27
THE EVE OF RESCUE

Within minutes after having witnessed the Japanese ritual of dropping what appeared to be pieces of white paper or flowers onto the location where the ship sunk, McKenzie was deep inland. He found a path appearing to lead farther inland, which he decided to follow, hoping he'd come across some friendly natives or possibly guerillas.

Much later, he heard voices approaching. He immediately took cover. Two Filipinos appeared. They were unarmed and seemed to be searching for something or someone from side to side of the path.

McKenzie called out to them, "Hey, Joe!"

The two men immediately ran up to him.

"You're number twenty-three," one of them said to him slowly. "What is your name and rank?"

McKenzie answered, "Staff Sergeant Michael McKenzie."

"Come with us," the other Filipino said.

McKenzie, realizing the two men were searching for survivors, and he was the 23rd one they had found, was relieved to learn he was amongst friends who were ready to help.

The two men took him to an outpost and gave him water and something to eat. After they let him rest for an hour or so, they took him farther inland to a village, where they placed him under the care of a Filipino family, native to the village.

The next day, McKenzie joined other survivors at another location in the same village, from where he and the other survivors were then to be transported by sailboat to another village near the coast on the other side of the peninsula.

At daylight, after sleeping in the cave during the night, Graciano, Carbajal, and the other escapees with them decided to scout the area. Graciano made a G-string from his life jacket to cover himself, for he was naked. On top of a hill in the jungle, they came upon a small field of corn. Hungry, they ate the raw corn right off the husks. They would later pay for their hurried eagerness for they were to suffer from bad cases of diarrhea. As they rested after filling their stomachs with the raw kernels, it began to rain. They folded banana leaves to catch the water to drink. They swallowed enough to satisfy their thirst for the moment.

When they felt rested, the five men continued walking inland along a narrow trail. The prisoner bringing up the rear called their attention to an old lady who was running from behind a tree toward a native house in the distance. Concerned they might be among unfriendly natives, they hid in place. In less than half an hour, three youthful natives appeared a few feet in front of where they hid.

They were yelling, "Hey, Americans, we are your friends. We are Filipino guerillas! Come with us!"

The five men hurriedly scurried out of their hiding place to where the three young men stood. They shook hands with the young guerillas, overjoyed they were among friends.

The three natives took them back up the hill and into the house. Inside, they saw the old woman they had seen running into the house from behind the tree. One of the guerillas ran to a nearby chicken house and returned with eggs. With no hesitation, the five men cracked the shells open and gulped the yolks and egg whites.

The old woman possessed a considerably wrinkled face, with a toothless smile from ear to ear. The three young guerillas were her nephews. She later cooked the five escapees rice, fried corn, and fried bananas, which they ate with much gusto.

Soon after, the five men were taken to a large frame house a few miles away owned by a retired U. S. military man who had remained in the Philippines several years before. The house was now occupied by guerillas and other wounded survivors brought there as they were found after reaching shore.

While there, Graciano volunteered to help care for the wounded survivors. He was assigned the task of pouring hot water on the wounds of all the prisoners, including his own wounds, to prevent infection. For helping with the prisoners, one of the female guerillas who later entered the house offered Graciano a skirt to cover his nakedness, which Graciano accepted. Another guerilla even offered him a "temporary wife," which he graciously refused.

Campos continued on his trek inland, thinking he was lost, when finally, a friendly tribe of Cebuano aborigines discovered him walking aimlessly. They fed him and treated his wounds, and he thanked them. The members of the tribe provided him with a comfortable place to sleep, and the following day they carried him on a bamboo stretcher to a Filipino guerilla outfit nearby. Because he was incapacitated, they placed him with a family of Filipinos to take care of him. Several other American prisoners would soon join him, they explained. From them, he also learned of the original 750 prisoners being carried on the *Shinyo Maru*, only 82 had been accounted for so far.

Midmorning, after Mick, Duarte, and Van Heflin had slept late, not having gone to sleep until three in the morning, Van Heflin, the least injured of the three, went out to scout the area. But, despite the lateness of his having awakened earlier, he soon tired after a short distance and fell asleep under some shrubs beneath a tree. He had barely fallen asleep when he was awakened by a Filipino boy. The youth looked curiously at Van Heflin, then turned and ran off before Van Heflin had a chance to ask him who he was.

Van Heflin, assuming the boy was a friend and they were among friends, returned to Mick and Duarte. He told them about the boy and that they had been discovered. Within minutes, the boy returned with his father.

The father, after glancing from one escapee to the others, broke into a big smile, showing extremely white and straight teeth. He had a strong overbite.

"You're now free," he said, still smiling. "You're among friends. Will take you to them."

"Thank you, thank you," Van Heflin replied. "We'd appreciate your help. We escaped from the Japanese after their ship was sunk."

The man grinned. "I know, I know." He turned and began walking away, his boy trailing him. The three men followed.

The man and his son led them through some thick brush for a little over a mile, to a place where the man and his fellow natives had gathered several prisoners they had found scattered throughout the jungle. None of the three knew any of the prisoners they met there.

After Puglisi tried to keep up with the native fisherman who told him he'd take him to a guerilla camp, he stopped the Filipino and told him he couldn't walk anymore because of his leg, which, he explained, had been shattered on the ship from the explosions.

The native told Puglisi he understood. He set his fishing gear down. "You sit and wait here. Will be back." Without waiting for Puglisi to answer, the man left hurriedly.

In minutes, he returned with a crudely made litter and another man. They made Puglisi comfortable on the litter and carried him to the guerilla camp. He slept there the entire day and a part of the next, when, after awakening, he was taken by cart to a field hospital. There, a Doctor Calo took care of badly wounded prisoners. The next day, Dr. Calo treated Puglisi's leg, cutting out some gangrene with a razor blade.

The following day, Puglisi met a Filipino colonel, whose name Puglisi didn't catch, who poured a large amount of VO whiskey into a coconut shell and offered it to him.

"Here, you drink all of this," the colonel instructed. "You'll need it for the pain from that procedure the doctor did on your leg. They ran out of pain medicine here."

Puglisi drank the strong "dosage" of the fine whiskey, and it knocked him out cold until he awakened the next day. He was awakened by a young Filipino girl, who was trying to feed him chicken soup. He remained in the hospital until the following day, when he was taken with other prisoner patients to a guerilla encampment where they were to rendezvous with other survivors and await rescue.

Graciano, Carbajal, and the other three survivors were moved from the house formerly owned by the retired U. S. military man by sailboat across Sandangan Bay to the village of Sandangan. On the sailboat, they ran into Sergeant McKenzie and enjoyed a small reunion. At Sandangan, they joined other survivors, including Mick, Puglisi, Campos, Follett, Duarte, Van Heflin, and Gurley. The men of the 200th, happy to be together in one place again, rejoiced with another small reunion, drinking home brew one of the natives brought to them. While resting there, the survivors learned although 83 prisoners survived the sinking of the *Shinyo Maru*, one had since died, leaving only 82 survivors to be rescued.

Because the natives of Sandangan couldn't possibly feed and care for the 82 survivors in one place, they were placed in groups of three or four and each group was then assigned to separate families living up and down the seacoast. Because arrangements for the rescue of the survivors would take some planning, the survivors remained living with the separate Filipino families for a week before they were summoned back to Sandangan. Once there, they were informed a native tribe had constructed a bivouac point for them in the mountains away from the village.

Volunteers among the natives and the guerilla forces arranged for the transportation of the survivors to the newly constructed bivouac point only a few miles away, and they all arrived there the following day. There, they met the very primitive natives who built the shelter. They were small in stature and possessed kinky hair. Skimpily clad and wearing bolos hanging from their waists, they chewed beetle nuts. None of them spoke a word of English.

The survivors spent two nights at the bivouac point. The following morning, the senior officer in charge, Colonel Fisher, after breakfast, stood behind a podium and asked the survivors to sit down on the ground of grass in front of the podium. There were no chairs. Those who weren't ambulatory should remain on their litters or wheelchairs, he instructed.

Colonel Fisher gave the survivors a minute or two to get comfortable where they chose to sit.

"Colonel John McGee has joined this group during the night," Fisher continued. "From this moment going forward throughout your rescue operation, he'll be your commanding officer. I want to share with you some interesting facts about him to explain why he's here with us, before I ask him to come out to meet you."

He cleared his throat, then continued. "Colonel McGee was a prisoner at the POW camp at Dapecol, and from there, he was moved to the camp at Lasang. Later, he was one of several prisoners in a Japanese prison ship carrying other prisoners. En route to Japan, like the *Shinyo Maru*, the ship docked in Zamboanga Harbor on June 15 of this year, and the colonel chose that time to escape and jumped overboard.

"Fortunately, he wasn't injured by the many rounds of rifle fire from Japanese soldiers on the ship trying to thwart his escape. He succeeded in swimming away uninjured. This occurred three months before the sinking of the *Shinyo Maru*. After his daring escape, the colonel made his way into the mountains and there, became part of the guerilla forces. When he heard of the survival of those who escaped the sinking of the *Shinyo Maru*, he came out of the mountains to offer his help, and his offer was accepted. And he is here with us today."

At that moment, Colonel McGee walked from behind the bivouac shelter, dressed in military uniform, and went up to the podium. The group of survivors started to get up from where they were seated.

"Please don't stand up," McGee said from behind the podium. "Stay comfortable where you're at, and I promise I won't take long. I'll be very brief." He cleared his throat. "I just want you to know I'm here to offer any help I can be to any of you during your brief stay here.

"I, myself, am not involved in the military process taking place at this moment to get you POWs home where you belong as quickly as possible. But I do know this. I'm told it'll take another week to get you out of here. It's taking a lot of coordination involving several government agencies to accomplish your transportation out of here.

"You don't need me to tell you about the red tape and slowness of governmental and military bureaucracies. And so I ask for your patience. Please enjoy your stay here. A lot of work has gone into making this bivouac point available to you. I'll be glad to answer any of your questions individually after you're dismissed by Colonel Fisher or at any time later. So please don't hesitate letting me know if you have any questions during your stay here. Thank you. I look forward to working with you."

The survivors seated stood up and applauded. There were a few who hollered from joy.

After Colonel Fisher made several announcements, he dismissed the group. Afterward, Sergeant Follett went up to Colonel McGee, who was shaking hands with a few survivors and answering questions.

Follett waited until the colonel was free, then went up to him. He introduced himself and explained he had gone into the jungles after the surrender, along with others, who chose not to surrender but to continue fighting.

"Some of us have now been in touch with the Filipino guerilla forces," Follett explained, "and would rather stay here and continue fighting, instead of being transported back to the States. We'd like to fight with the guerillas."

"I can appreciate your efforts, Sergeant Follett," Colonel McGee replied. "I understand how you feel and applaud you. I, too, would like to stay, but my orders clearly state everyone, including myself, must be rescued off this island."

"There's no exception, Colonel?"

"None whatsoever, I'm afraid, Sergeant. I'm sorry. You must leave with the rest of us in about a week or so."

"Well, I thought I'd give it a try. Thanks for your time, Colonel McGee. And I want to say, thanks for being here for us. You're quite an inspiration, with that daring escape and all." He smiled at the colonel.

The colonel smiled back. "Thanks, Sergeant. I appreciate your support."

The two men shook hands.

28
THE RESCUE AND THE RETURN

After remaining in the bivouac point for a week, the survivors received word they were to be transported to a designated place on the beach just north of Sandangan by evening of the following day. The next day, they were moved out of the bivouac point, the more seriously sick or injured carried by litter or Carabao sleds.

Upon arrival at the beach, Colonel McGee informed them a submarine was expected during the night to take as many of them as there was room for. The survivors drew numbers from 1 to 81 to determine the order of evacuation. Of the 83 survivors, one had died from injuries after his escape. Another survivor, a radioman with unique electronic skills, was given approval to remain, assisting the underground forces as a specialist with their communications. Only 81 survivors were left to be transported back to the United States or elsewhere for needed hospitalization.

Despite his injuries, Mick drew No. 72, which he thought gave him only a small chance of getting on the submarine. He had no idea how many passengers the submarine would be able to carry.

That moonlit evening, the submarine, the *U.S.S. Narwhal,* suddenly surfaced some distance from shore. Two crew members came ashore in a rubberized rowboat. As the boat slid onto the sandy beach, one of the crew stepped onto the beach and inquired how many prisoners were in the group.

"Eighty-one," Colonel McGee replied.

The crewman flashed a light signal to the submarine and received a reply signal.

The crewman turned and smiled. "We'll take every damn one of you!"

The shouts and yells from the survivors were ear shattering.

The other crewman now stepped onto the beach and jammed a staff holding the American flag into the sand. Illuminated by the dim moonlight, the flag waved in the soft breeze.

By the grace of God, Mick thought, these few who survived have finally beaten the Japanese in their struggles against their brutality.

The survivors were carried by native rowboats to the submarine. When all survivors had entered the submarine, they filled every available space.

The *U.S.S. Narwhal* transported the survivors to a military base in New Guinea. The trip took five days. From there, most of them were flown to the 42nd General Hospital in Brisbane, Australia, arriving there in the first week of October 1944. Puglisi and a few of the others seriously injured survivors were dropped off on Windy Island, a small island with a naval hospital capable of treating their serious injuries.

In the third week of October, the survivors boarded the *U.S. Monterey* for the trip to the United States. It was a slow and long trip to Pier 7 on the bay in San Francisco, where they arrived on November 6, coincidentally, the day before President Franklin Delano Roosevelt was elected to his fourth term as president.

From the pier, the POWs were transported by truck to Fort Mason, a U.S. Army post in the city in the northern Marina District alongside San Francisco Bay, where they were to stay until the Army arranged for their transportation elsewhere, depending on their assignments. There, they were told, they would be given a few days to get in touch with their families or enjoy the sights of San Francisco awaiting their next orders.

Most of them opted to contact their families as soon as they could, including Mick. He knew Lilia was staying with her parents when he and she last corresponded by mail. *My God, that was two and a half years ago.* He had her parents' phone number, but he was going to have a problem finding a phone to call her, for all the phones available in the barracks where they were bunking had long lines of soldiers waiting to call home. Instead of having to wait, Mick went out in search of a phone booth somewhere on the post.

It took him a half hour or so, going from building to building at the post before he found a lone phone booth behind the NCO Club. He came prepared with coins, if he needed them, but he called collect, just in case. It was the middle of the afternoon, and he wasn't sure Lilia would be at home. Their child was now two and a half years old, and Lilia would most likely be at work, her mother probably taking care of their child.

He was both nervous and excited as he dialed the operator to place a collect call, and couldn't believe he'd soon be talking to somebody back home. He was hoping it'd be Lilia.

After a few rings, a female voice answered. Mick recognized Lilia's mother's voice. In a shaky, nervous voice, she accepted the call. The instant she heard his voice as he greeted her, she became so nervous and excited she could hardly talk. She also began to cry, pausing several times to apologize for crying and for her nervousness.

But through their excited utterances and the many pauses, they managed to communicate, and he learned Lilia was fine, as was their child, a daughter named Carmen Lilia, and that Lilia was indeed at work at the moment. Through her tears, her mother promised to call Lilia immediately upon hanging up, and either Lilia would call him from her office or come home to place the call. With that understanding, Mick gave her the booth's telephone number and hung up.

Seconds after hanging up, he got even more nervous. He told himself to try staying calm and wait several minutes more, giving Lilia's mother enough time to make the call to Lilia and Lilia enough time to go home to call him or arrange to have her employer pick up the long distance charges.

After to what Mick felt was an eternity, the phone rang, and he picked up the receiver, his hand shaking.

There was no need for hellos. He knew who was on the line.

"Lilia!" he half-shouted into the telephone. That's all he could manage to say.

At the other end, there was no reply. Instead, after a quick moment of silence, Lilia burst into tears. Hearing her cry was too much for Mick to bear, and he, too, began crying audibly into the phone. Together, they were shedding tears of joy, and both knew their words to each other would have to wait until they unleashed their bliss.

Finally, after a long minute, when Mick sensed Lilia was near the end of her crying and had regained some semblance of normalcy, he spoke softly as he wiped away his tears.

"Now that we've both cried our heart out, my darling, please let me hear your lovely voice," he said.

"I-I'm sorry, Mick, but just hearing your voice after all these years just got to me deep down," she said through her sniffles. She had the mouthpiece near enough Mick heard her take a deep breath.

"You needn't apologize, darling. We both broke out crying, not just you."

She let out a short laugh. "I just can't believe this is happening. That you're actually back with us."

"Well, not with you yet, but I know what you mean. Neither can I. It's like a dream, and this isn't really real. Our speaking to each other."

"I feel the same. To me, it's almost uncanny. Unbelievable, even though I prayed this day would come."

"I want to know about your work, but first, tell me about our daughter, Carmen Lilia. Your mother told me her beautiful name."

Lilia laughed. "Oh, Mick, you're going to love her. She's a beautiful, brown-eyed little girl of two and a half now, who I believe resembles her daddy very much. She's full of energy, is extremely talkative in her adorable voice, maybe too much if that's possible, and she's dying to meet you."

"And please tell her daddy's dying to meet *her*! Oh, I can't wait to see her! I love the name you chose, but I'd have been happy with any name you'd have chosen."

"I still can't believe we're talking to each other. Our world here has been spinning ever since we got word from the Army you and the other prisoners were rescued. It's been a long month for us." She paused to clear her throat. "I want to know about you. How are you doing? Are you well?"

He laughed. "I am now that we're talking to one another. I'm mending from some minor injuries, but I'm doing fine, really, Lilia. I'm overjoyed being on U. S. soil." He sighed. "But I want to hear about you. Your job. Are you calling from your office?"

"Yes, I work as a receptionist/secretary for a local attorney. Been here for a year, and I love my work. You'll like my boss, and he's anxious to meet you. To him, you're a hero."

Mick scoffed. "I'm no hero. I was just a prisoner of war and wasn't in any position to be a hero to anyone. I'm just feeling lucky to be alive and that we'll soon be together again. And I'll get to see our little Carmen for the first time. That's what matters to me now."

"Well, my darling, you'll have to accept you're a hero to your entire family. Your parents are so, so proud of you. But it's taken a long time for this moment to come after we heard you were alive and well. When will you get to come home? To your real home, here with us?"

"Not right away, Lilia, I'm afraid. The military is flying most of us to Washington, D C. They need to interrogate us about our imprisonment for a few days."

"I was afraid you were going to say something like that, but I understand. It's disappointing, yes, but I'm just happy you're alive and safe and will be coming home soon. Do you have any idea when you'll be able to come home from DC?"

"Not at the moment, but it'll be at least three or four days. I promise I'll call you again from there the first chance I can get to a telephone."

She didn't want their conversation to end. "Please promise me you'll be careful while you're at the nation's capital and take good care of yourself."

He laughed. "I did a fine job of taking care of myself against the Japanese, so I think I'll be able to take care of myself in front of a few interrogators on our side. I'm not worried about me, I promise you, and you shouldn't worry either."

"But I do." She paused. "And you really are doing well, Mick?"

"Yes, I'm doing fine," he said, trying to sound believable, even though he was lying.

A man almost six feet tall in a one-hundred pound body couldn't be doing well by any stretch of the imagination, by any kind of understanding, he thought, and that'd be a fact he'd never be able to keep from her unless he stayed away from home for another two or three months to gain the weight he lost in confinement. Even then, he couldn't be sure. But it was what it was, he accepted, and he knew he and Lilia and the rest of his family would soon know how to deal with the reality of their situation, which would be something new for them but not for him.

Mick heard Lilia start crying again.

Through her sniffles, she said, "I just can't bear letting you go, now that we're so close to having you with us." There was a moment of silence. "I love you, Mick, with all my heart," she said as she cried.

"I love you with all of my heart too, my angel. You truly are my angel." Tears came to his eyes when he thought of her as his guardian angel. He didn't want to hang up, but he finally said, "I'll call you soon, my love. Goodbye for now."

"Bye, Mick."

They hung up, both relieved their separation from each other for so long would soon be over and they and their daughter would soon be together as a family.

Two days later, most of the group, including Mick, Mannie Campos, Sixto Duarte, Charlie Atkins, Lencho Garcia, Sergeant McKenzie, Sergeant Follett, Dennis Gurley, Rabbit Carbajal, and Pete Graciano were flown to Washington, DC for interrogations by individuals from military and civilian intelligence organizations and agencies.

There, they were questioned over several days in minute detail about their treatment by the Japanese and the conditions they had lived under in the POW camps. During the interrogations, the survivors spoke of the many atrocities committed against them during their imprisonment. Some of them, they were told at the end of the interrogations, might later be sent to the Philippines and elsewhere to testify in war crimes trials.

After five days in the nation's capital, Mick and the other prisoners were given a 90-day furlough to spend with their families. For Mick and other members of the 200th, they would be given the option of fulfilling part of their remaining tour of duty by participating in nationwide tours sponsored by the War Department to speak to civic groups, schools, U. S. Army posts, and other organizations about their experience as prisoners of war.

By no later than December of the year, all of the other rescued prisoners were returned to the United States by ship, including Puglisi and the other prisoners who were treated at the hospital facilities on Windy Island and elsewhere.

29
THE HOMECOMING

Upon returning to Las Cruces, Mick and the other ex-POWs from the community were informed by letter from the city's mayor and other public officials the city and county planned a parade and recognition program to honor them as members of the U.S. Army, as prisoners of war, and their sacrifices in fighting the war against Japan. Of the men in the 200th, only six of them were residents of Las Cruces, and one of them, Andy Gluck, had died trying to escape after the sinking of the *Shinyo Maru*. Aside from Mick, the others were Mannie Campos, Lencho Garcia, Charlie Atkins, and Sixto Duarte. Gluck, too, was to be an honoree at the parade and festivities, *in absentia*.

The parade, which included marching bands from various high schools in the county and El Paso, as well as the bands from New Mexico A & M and Fort Bliss, turned out to be a large event along Main Street, with several decorated floats sponsored by local organizations and civic clubs. At a ceremony banquet held in a banquet hall at the college, the mayor and the state's governor presented the five honorees, as well as the parents of Andy Gluck, with testimonials and certificates, and the honorees were asked to make a few remarks.

All of them, happy to be home with their families, showed their wholehearted appreciation for the loving public gesture and festivities in their honor. And they displayed it during each of their brief comments at the banquet.

But it was obvious to all who attended the banquet or to anyone later who would ask them about their war experiences, that although glad to be back home, the former POWs appeared reluctant to express themselves in detail about their treatment and suffering.

Those horrific events, each of them vowed in their own private world, they would keep to themselves, and if they were ever to tell their real stories to anyone, it would be only to their respective families and loved ones, whom they treasured because of having experienced what they had gone through.

Even then, each in their own way, would eventually bury within themselves much of what they suffered and not tell a living soul for years to come. Each of them, individually, would know in their own heart and in their own mind, when that time would come, if at all.

As for Mick, upon arriving at the train station in El Paso, several weeks before the festivities in Las Cruces, he got his own hero's welcome from his family, his wife, Lilia, his parents, his sister, and several aunts, uncles, and many cousins. Neither Lilia nor Mick's parents could prevent breaking down and crying in front of the crowd when they saw Mick in his 100-pound body. Mick's mother's eyes, especially, appeared soft and wounded.

For Mick, though, the main star of his homecoming at the station had been his daughter, Carmen Lilia, who shined brilliantly in his heart when his eyes came to rest on her innocent, smiling, and lovely face. And her dark brown eyes, just like her mother's.

In the car on the way home, he held Carmen Lilia in his arms all the way from the train depot in El Paso to his parents' house in Las Cruces, where other members of his extended family and many of his and his family's friends gathered at a cookout and celebration of their own to welcome their hero home.

But after the celebrations were over, as would be expected because of his trauma, he went on to suffer for many months and even years from malnutrition and its effects, and from diseases he contracted during his years of imprisonment. Those diseases, such as malaria, would raise their ugly heads from time to time, at night or during the day, no matter, with high fevers, chills, shivers, and other adverse symptoms.

And those symptoms didn't include the sleepless nights or nightmares of his ordeal waking him up at night or from even an afternoon nap, which he would often take because his muscle frailties tired him easily and he needed the rest. Dreadful memories of the Death March, both when he would wake up at night and during the day, would forever visit his mind hauntingly. Most of the time, when he experienced these memories, he'd sit there or walk around, "like a zombie," was the phrase Lilia would use to describe his aloneness and mental and physical separation from the family. Even from his daughter, whom he loved dearly.

Neither Lilia, nor Mick's parents, ever brought up his loss of weight, but he could tell they were saddened by it. He could see their compassion and incredulity in their eyes, and several times in the evenings or at night, he found Lilia in the bedroom, alone, crying to herself. He hadn't approached her then, allowing her the space to grieve. He knew the difference between tears of joy and those of disbelief. And Lilia's, he was certain, weren't tears from her joy of his finally being home.

The tears were from seeing physical evidence of his sufferings from malnutrition, starvation, and deprivation for almost three years. That alone, without focusing on the mental aspects of his illness, carried her to a depth of prolonged sadness from which she wondered if she would ever recover. But she must, she kept telling herself, for not only her sake but for Mick's and for their daughter's sake. *Please, God, help me to remain strong throughout my husband's torment*, she kept praying over and over again in her thoughts and prayers.

Concerned of his loneliness and sadness throughout most of the days at home, Lilia asked Mick's parents to visit with him, first together, and then for each of them to spend time with him alone. His father persuaded him, almost forcibly, to take walks with him around the neighborhood.

Mick would oblige him, but even during the walks he wouldn't open up with his own father. He spoke only of trivial things. The weather, politics, the community. There was no mention of the ongoing war in the Pacific or in Europe. All of them avoided mentioning them.

Even Mick's sister, Elena, who had a busy life with three children of her own, would often visit Lilia and Mick, and she spent much time with her baby brother. She would go up to Mick when saying goodbye to him and Lilia after her visit, and put her arms around him, holding him there as he, too, placed his arms around her. Several times, they'd remain in that embrace for what seemed minutes, each holding each other tightly without a word between them. The scene would always bring tears to Lilia's eyes.

Rarely, when Mick would snap out of his horrific and disturbing memories, he'd be himself again and would listen to Lilia in astonishment as she told him he had been away from them, in another world, when he suffered the effects of his memories. During those times he'd revisit his memories, he explained to her, he recalled every detail, even the smells and the pain he or someone else had undergone. It was, he explained, as if he were reliving, re-enduring, the horrific events he went through.

Often, when these memories haunted him, he chose to be alone, away even from Lilia and Carmen Lilia. On those occasions, which occurred every day during his first two months at home, he'd go out of the house by himself and walk out into the desert toward what was called "A Mountain," a small, rounded mountain near the college campus on top of which the Greek fraternities and sororities at the college had formed a large "A" with large rocks, whitewashing the rocks with gallons of white paint. The "A" stood for "Aggies," the name of the college's sports teams.

Sometimes, instead of walking alone in the desert, he'd walk the countryside to the south of town, farm country, or he'd go off onto the farms and vegetable fields adjoining the foothills of the mesa to the west. On especially cold days, after what seemed hours, he'd walk back home from those excursions facing away from the chill of the winds blowing from the northwest. Often, upon his return from wandering alone for hours, when he'd sit down in a lounging chair in the bedroom, Lilia would pull up a chair next to where he sat without uttering a word, and she'd begin talking to him.

When she'd do that, it was often a one-sided conversation, but she'd continue talking to him, not giving up, often about some experience she had with their daughter or something humorous happening during the day. He'd always smile when she'd speak about Carmen Lilia, but there was no other response.

Once, when she was having one of her one-sided conversations with him, tears welled up in his eyes. It shocked her when she witnessed this rare occurrence. Yet, it was the first time he'd shown a reaction, and she hoped it was a good sign.

"Talk to me, Mick," she said softly to him when she saw the tears, encouraging him. She took a tissue from her pocket and dabbed at his eyes to get rid of the tears, which had begun flowing down his cheeks. "Please say something to me, honey. I beg of you."

That day, she continued with her pleas for several minutes. Finally, he spoke.

"I can't," he said, almost in a whisper she could hardly hear. He said nothing for a long minute, and tears flowed down again. Finally, he whispered, "I just don't know how to express what I feel."

"Well, this is a start! Just do it gradually." Tears began to flow down her face. "I'm here for you, darling. We're all here for you. We're in this together."

He kept staring into somewhere out there in front of him. "I don't know what to say," he finally said softly. New tears appeared. "I need your help, Lilia."

"And I want to help, Mick." Tears of joy appeared on her face for what she believed was a breakthrough. "But you've got to let me. You've got to let all of us get into your head. We understand what you're going through. We love you, and we care for you."

"I know you do. Thank you and bless you for that."

"And you're going to get better. I know you are."

"I hope so, Lilia. I want to."

That conversation marked the beginning of the end. The end of his isolation. Of his heavy depression. Of his grief for what he believed he had lost.

"Your mom and dad and I've talked about what we can do to help, Mick," Lilia explained to Mick one day when he seemed receptive to having a conversation. "All of us agree you'd benefit speaking to a doctor at the VA clinic in El Paso. There's a psychiatrist there, we understand, who's helped a lot of veterans coming back from the war in Europe and the Pacific."

Mick didn't say anything in response, but she could tell he was in deep thought.

"What do you think about doing that, Mick? Getting an appointment with the psychiatrist?"

"You think he could help me?"

It pained her to see the sorrow in his eyes. "He's helped others like you who've come back from the war scarred, like you." She looked into his eyes and realized he was really listening to her. "He called it 'battle fatigue,' I think."

"Who?" He turned to face her. "You *talked* to him?"

She nodded. "Yes, I did, Mick. I called him to explain what you were going through. He called me back, and we talked about your problem."

She noticed a look of disapproval. "I had to do something, Mick. I couldn't bear seeing you like this and not trying to do something about it." She started crying, burying her face in her handkerchief.

She cried for a minute and as she was wiping her eyes and blowing her nose, she felt his hand softly on her shoulder.

"I'm sorry, Lilia," he said. "Please forgive me." He paused, then sighed. "I'm ready to see the doctor. Let's do it. I'm tired of this too. I want to get better."

"Let's do it, for sure," she said, smiling. "And, Mick, you *are* going to get better. I know you are."

"I hope so, Lilia. I want to get better."

Within two weeks, Mick had his first consultation with the psychiatrist. After the first visit, he'd make a trip to El Paso twice a week, first, for individual therapy, then followed by group therapy at the end of the week with other veterans suffering from what the doctor referred to as "battle fatigue," as Lilia had said to him earlier.

In another month or so, Mick became more talkative, more responsive. He began visiting his friends, including the ones from his high school days, both at his home and in other settings. Gradually, he became more sociable and began wanting to see and visit with his parents and cousins more.

After six months of therapy, everyone who knew Mick could see the difference in his behavior. They were all beginning to see the Mick they had known in the past, no longer the lost soul that appeared when he first arrived. He wasn't that man anymore.

He started going to the gym to work out, to build up and strengthen his muscles. And so the change wasn't only mental, it was physical. In half a year, he gained 40 pounds. Since his homecoming, he hadn't felt a stir of lust or even any need or excitement as he simply went through the mechanics of making love to Lilia. But even that had now changed. It proved to be a slow process, but the change in him further encouraged and motivated him to get back his health. And to his family.

After a year, he stopped psychotherapy. He was also close to his normal weight, almost back to what it had been when he entered the army. But his nightmares and flashbacks continued, not as often, but he hadn't gotten rid of them altogether.

In time, after his discharge from active duty, Mick enrolled at New

Mexico A&M as a full-time student, getting some financial support through the G.I. Bill. He had almost two years of course credit when he reenrolled, and in another two-and-one-half years, he received his bachelor's degree in electrical engineering. He had no problem getting a job at White Sands Proving Grounds, White Sands Missile Range's former name, with a private company having contracts with the U. S. Army.

Not long afterward, he and Lilia bought a new home, deciding to stay in Las Cruces, which to them had always been home, even though Mick had gotten several offers from Sandia Labs in Albuquerque and from companies out of state. Soon, Lilia gave birth to a healthy boy, whom they named Michael Joseph, after his father and most likely be known as Mick, Jr.

Even as his nightmares and flashbacks of his captivity and his escape started becoming things of the past, there was one issue Mick would have to work on if he was to become whole again. The one issue was his hatred or aversion toward the Japanese, not only for what they did to him but to his friends—his comrades in arms. Despite his friendship with Captain Hinata Takahashi, of the Royal Japanese Army, he'd been unable to stop despising the Japanese. No matter how hard he tried, he continued to feel hatred for them, regardless of whatever their culture may have accomplished or stood for. He couldn't see them in the image he saw in his friend, Hinata.

Even though there were moments in his past when he had turned to God, had prayed to God, to help in a time of need, he didn't think seeking divine guidance would solve this dilemma for him. To find peace with this issue plaguing him, he'd have to search within himself on his own. But he was at a loss how to do it.

And so, once again, he made a promise to himself he'd continue to work toward finding the answer to his quandary.

EPILOGUE

"Hey, Mick, snap out of it!" Campos said softly, nudging him on the shoulder as they sat on the front row behind the podium at the Frontier Club. "You seem to have been a zillion miles away. We're taking a short break after Sixto Duarte and the others spoke. Pulga's up next, then you."

Mick didn't reply at first. Instead, he shook his head slightly, as if trying to wake himself up from a long nap. "Wow," he finally said softly, "I feel as if I just woke up from a weird dream."

"About what?"

"About everything, Mannie. Everything we went through back then."

"Here, walk with me. The staff officer said the break would be for at least ten minutes. Let's go outside and get some fresh air." Campos headed toward the club's exit.

Mick followed and caught up.

Campos continued. "Everything we went through back then, you said. Like what? Our imprisonment. The Death March? What specifically."

"All of it, Mannie. All of it. Just now, when you nudged me, I was thinking of someone I befriended back in the Philippines."

"Who?"

"My 'godson,'" Mick replied, referring to his friend, Skip Rawlings, from South Carolina. "Skip would be alive today if it hadn't been for me."

"What do you mean?"

They exited the building and walked over to the side, taking in the sun and the fresh air from a breeze blowing across the patio along the front of the club. Others had joined them outside, some milling about the entrance, others having crossed the street to stretch their legs after having sat for an hour or so.

"It should have been me in that work team detail," Mick replied as the two of them sat on a bench.

"Maybe, maybe not," Campos said. "He would have had to survive the sinking."

"Skip would have had as good a chance as any of us."

"I doubt it. He couldn't swim. As well as you thought you knew him, I bet you didn't know that one simple fact, did you?"

"No. How did *you* know he couldn't swim?

"We were in a work detail once. Coming back, the guards let us bathe in a small pond. Skip went into the water to cool off, but he couldn't go beyond the shallow end. He told me then he never learned how to swim." He cleared his throat. "So you see, chances are he would have drowned when the *Shinyo Maru* went down."

"That makes me feel better. But he may have been one of the lucky ones who didn't board the ship."

Maybe, but it wouldn't have mattered."

"What do you mean?"

Just then, the Army staff officer approached the entrance to enter the building. He walked up to Mick and Campos.

"The van's going to be pulling up soon," the officer said. "Our man's arrived. We'll be starting up again when he gets here."

The officer looked up and saw a van approach the entrance. "Well, well, here he is now. I'll go inside and tell everyone and tell them he's here and we'll be ready to start." He walked inside.

"See for yourself, Mick," Campos answered, smiling. He stood up.

Mick, puzzled, stood up as the van stopped at the curb a few feet from where he and Campos stood.

An elderly man, about the same age as Mick, got out of the vehicle. As the man got closer, despite he was now much older, Mick recognized him. It was Skip Rawlings.

Stunned, Mick immediately walked toward him. Before he got a chance to speak, Rawlings spotted him.

"Mick!" Rawlings said with a big grin. "I've been waiting a long time for this." He extended both hands toward Mick.

Mick walked up to him, and the two men embraced.

When they finished hugging each other, Mick turned to Campos. "Skip, you remember Mannie Campos, of course."

Rawlings shook Campos' hand and hugged him. "Sure, I do. Great to see you, Mannie."

"Let's go inside so you can see the other fellows who are here," Campos said.

"By all means, let's do that! Rawlings said, smiling.

The three men started walking into the building. Mick and Rawlings walked shoulder to shoulder.

"All these years, Skip, and I thought you were dead," Mick said to Rawlings, placing his arm around his shoulders.

"And I thought you were too," Rawlings replied. "I was told you didn't survive the sinking of that vessel. Otherwise, I would have tried reaching you sometime during all these years."

"But how? I helped bury you, Skip"

Rawlings laughed. "That wasn't me. An extra team member joined the crew that particular day. Although injured, I managed to escape the massacre. I went into the hills and was taken care of by a Filipino family for a couple of days, before making my way to Corregidor via a small fishing vessel owned by the family's cousin."

"This is amazing, hearing this, Skip. What the hell did you do in Corregidor?"

"I later made my way to an underground Filipino organization back in Manila, and they made arrangements for me to get me off the island. I was later assigned to another unit in the States."

Displaying a wide grin, Mick embraced Rawlings again. "What about your wife?"

The three men arrived at the stage, where the staff officer was instructing the honorees to get to their seats as the program would soon continue.

"Let's take our seats with the others, fellows," Campos said to Mick and Rawlings.

Mick turned to Rawlings. "We can continue our conversation when we get seated, Skip."

Rawlings nodded. He went up to the others on stage and shook their hands, reminding them who he was. He then looked to see where Mick was seated and sat next to him.

"Anyway, Mick, you asked about my wife, Almita," Rawlings said to Mick as he got comfortable in his chair. "After a year or so of red tape, she was able to join me, and we settled in South Carolina, where we've been living ever since."

"Did Almita come with you?

Rawlings looked down and shook his head. "She died last year, Mick, of cancer."

"I'm sorry to hear that, Skip."

"Thanks." A sad look appeared on his face. "We had some wonderful years together and were very happy. I've got three grown children she blessed me with."

"Well, I'm happy about that."

"Hey, Mick, listen. I brought a gift from me to you, all the way back from South Carolina. It's with my luggage in that van that brought me here from the airport in El Paso."

"You owed me no present, Skip." He gave Rawlings a perplexed look. "What is it?"

Rawlings grinned. "It's that drawing you made of Almita and me as a wedding present."

"That was a present to the two of you and for you to keep."

"And I want to return it as a present to you and as a reminder to you of our friendship."

"But how in the world could you possibly have it. You escaped with only a G-string, if you were lucky, and with none of your possessions."

"Almita treasured it so much she kept it in her own, little apartment. When I got in touch with her after I was back in the States, she brought all she owned with her, including the drawing."

"That's amazing. I'll be glad to accept it as a gift from you and Almita."

"I was hoping you would."

Mick and Rawlings had a few more minutes to chat before the program restarted. Rawlings explained he was staying at a bed and breakfast in Las Cruces and expected to fly back home out of El Paso in two days. The two men exchanged phone numbers and arranged to get together later to catch up on each other's life since their separation years ago.

After the staff officer reconvened the program, he introduced Rawlings as a latecomer POW, who would be the last speaker.

"Before Mr. Rawlings' comments, we've got two other speakers to listen to—Jim Puglisi and Mick Duran." He turned to Puglisi. "Mr. Puglisi, you're on." He stepped away from the microphone.

Puglisi began his remarks. He first spoke of his assignments as an artillery gunner across from the Manila Hotel, followed by his mission to protect the bridges at Calumpit so the Americans could get across to Bataan. Lastly, he spoke of Cabcaben Air Field, where he was blown out of his emplacement by the bomb dropped by Photo Joe and hospitalized with a broken back and other injuries.

He ended his remarks with the sinking of the *Shinyo Maru.*

"After the second torpedo hit, there was a third explosion, and the hold was soon engulfed in water. I clearly remember saying to myself, 'so this is how you feel when you're about to die.' I found myself under about 20 feet of water. Swimming, I aimed for the light I could see through the water, and before my lungs burst, I was suddenly in open air, within reach of the ladder. I've often considered some divine presence may have lifted me from down on the keel to the fresh air above.

"After our ordeal, many of the prisoners were sent to our nation's capital for interrogation and debriefing. Others were sent elsewhere. I was one of the ones sent to DC. There, we were questioned about the treatment we received from the Japanese. The military wanted to know the conditions under which we lived while imprisoned and of the atrocities committed against us.

"My life wasn't my own for a long time because I couldn't talk about my experience for 35 years. When I started going to the reunions of the *Shinyo Maru* survivors, I was finally able to talk to my family at length about it. Nightmares and flashbacks? Yes! But I got through those too."

§

When Puglisi sat down, Mick stood up and walked to the microphone. He cleared his throat.

"The effect of my experience in the war has always been hard for me to express to anyone, especially to my family and those close to me.

But it was a gradual process, and it took much strength and patience for my family. And I hope I've shown my gratitude and appreciation to them through the years, but I often wonder if I did enough to even show them that.

"Early on, within three months after my return home, I was asked to participate with other POWs in nationwide tours sponsored by the War Department to speak to civic groups, various military troops, schools, U. S. Army posts, and other organizations about our experiences as prisoners of war.

"For those two months, I was able to speak to others of my imprisonment, but only in such an organized setting, and only in a detached way. I spoke then of events during imprisonment but not of how they affected me personally. There was no emotion in what I said. I just mouthed out facts and events. There was nothing whatsoever said about my feelings. It was almost as if I were relating a story I had read somewhere, with no involvement on my part.

"Other than in this kind of exposure, the memory of what had taken place was locked up inside of me for many years after I had gone on those tours.

"Although I eventually told my parents about my imprisonment, I sometimes wonder if they both died without fully understanding what really happened. They only heard about it in bits and pieces from me over a long period and as I felt more comfortable talking about it. To this day, I'm sorry I didn't tell them the whole story because I owed them so much more.

"I regret now not having told them more about it. I kept thinking at the time, why do they even need to know? Why put them through the torture of hearing about their son being mistreated. To me, it almost felt selfish of me to tell my story to them.

"They suffered, too, and possibly more, for they didn't receive word for over two years whether I was dead or alive. I owed them a lot, and I hope they learned from what I did tell them that in many ways, they kept me alive, because I thought of them every day.

"And to my wife Lilia, who was always there for me, I owed her a great deal, and I want to acknowledge this debt publicly.

"She passed away seven years ago, after our 64 years of marriage. For those years, I felt her presence, if not physically during my years of

272   *A Life Uninvited*

captivity, in spirit. And afterward, when memories of that ordeal haunted me terribly, she was always there, by my side. Together, we gave birth to two beautiful children, my first born, Lilia, who brought me here and is seated in the audience." He lifted his eyes and smiled as he looked at her. "She's the mother of my three grandchildren, two boys and a girl.

"Her brother, our son, Michael Joseph, was born two years after my return from imprisonment, in November of 1946. Tragically, we lost Michael in December of 1969, when he was killed fighting in the Vietnam War. He was only 23 years old when he died, barely one year older than I was when I was captured by the Japanese, or should I say, when we were surrendered to the Japanese.

"How do I feel about the Japanese? To answer this question, I must break it down into two questions. The first, how did I feel about the Japanese when I returned to the United States. The second, how do I feel about the Japanese now? And if the answer is different to those two questions, we must then ask a third question—when or why did the change occur?

"Upon returning to the United States and after being discharged from the military, getting my life back and my work occupied most of my thoughts. Yet, any mention of the Japanese would literally make the hair on the back of my neck stand up.

"That one issue, my hatred, my aversion toward the Japanese, not only for what they did to me but to my friends—my comrades—my buddies in arms—in the Philippines. I just wasn't able to stop despising the Japanese.

"Let me backtrack for a moment. During my imprisonment, I met a Japanese officer, a captain, who I believe was assigned to the prison camps to oversee the treatment of the prisoners by the camp commander. The commander was cruel. Even evil, I think.

"The name of the Japanese officer I met was Hinata Takahashi. One day, I approached him to complain about not being provided with proper tools to do our work. That first conversation with him led to many more we had in the weeks and months to come, even when I was transferred to a different camp.

"I should explain at this juncture he spoke excellent English. He had studied at Stanford University here in the States several years before the war broke out, received his degree, and returned to Japan. He knew our American culture well, having lived amongst us during his university studies. I add this fact to let you know we were able to converse freely, communicate without any language barrier, and get to know each other and learn much about ourselves.

"Despite the brutal treatment by the Japanese sergeants and guards, astonishingly, Hinata and I became close friends. We'd sit and talk about many things. We spoke of the ugliness of war, the misunderstandings between different cultures, and the many issues confronting us in a world sadly setting us apart from one another.

"When he and I said goodbye to each other the last day we spoke, we both hoped we'd see each other again in better times and in better circumstances, yet knowing somehow that would most likely never happen. A few years after the war ended, after I had ridden myself of much of the torment I was experiencing as a result of my imprisonment, I tried to get in touch with my friend, Hinata, several times but without success.

"I still think of him often. Of his kindness, his intelligence, his insight, and his understanding of what I was going through as a prisoner. I knew he wanted to help me but couldn't because of his pledged loyalty to the Emperor of Japan as a Japanese officer. He had a job to do, and no part of it was to befriend a prisoner who was an enemy of his country, even though not of him. And I respected him for such loyalty and his sworn duty as an officer in the Japanese Imperial Army.

"I learned many things as a prisoner, all of us did in our own way, but the one standing out for me is what I learned from my relationship with Hinata, which is that in our world, we must learn to get along with and respect one another, despite the differences in our many cultures.

"Having digressed to tell you of my friendship with Captain Takahashi, let me return to my negative view of the Japanese extending for several years after my return to the States. No matter how hard I tried, I continued to feel this strong hatred toward the Japanese. And this was in spite of my positive feelings toward my friend, Captain Takahashi. I couldn't see the Japanese in the image I saw in Hinata.

"All the other issues of my confinement, the nightmares, the flashbacks, the depression, and the trauma, for the most part, I felt reasonably sure I had either worked out or was still working on.

"But in late 1948, four years after my return, the priest at my church gave a series of sermons on forgiveness. In them, he pointed out that professing to love God and hating others was an 'oxymoron.' This word was new to me. Thinking long and hard about what he said, I finally came to realize, as my pastor preached, scripture brought out I couldn't love God and at the same time, as a professing Christian, hate the Japanese who had mistreated us. I told myself I, too, had to believe in this Christian principle. To me, there was no such thing as being half-Christian. My negative feelings were locked up within me and had to be set free.

"To free my heart of this hatred I had felt for many years, I professed—confessed—my longstanding guilt publicly. I appeared before a group of veterans and admitted I had been wrong—that I was forgiving the Japanese for mistreating me—for mistreating all of us. Doing this one thing finally freed me of the guilt and hatred eating me up inside for more than four years. It opened up my soul, and I felt a great relief from the burden I had carried for so many years. And I finally felt released from the pain of that burden.

"I've often corresponded with a few of the prisoners I befriended in the Philippines. One of them, Sergeant Bob Follett, from Roswell, passed away a few years ago and isn't here with us today, even though, as a survivor of the Bataan Death March and the sinking of the *Shinyo Maru*, he, too, is being honored here today.

"Bob, after the war, finished his university studies, having received a master's in chemical engineering from UNM in Albuquerque. From time to time, he'd keep me posted, by phone or mail, in what he was doing. In 1948, he was approached by a leader of the U. S. textile industry to join him on a mission sponsored by the United States government to help rebuild the textile industry in Japan.

"The war had hurt the industry, even though in 1948, textiles were 55 percent of all Japanese industry. At the time, few Americans knew much about Japan, other than they were our enemy during World War II. He thought that because he had been exposed to the Japanese as a prisoner for almost three years, he was considered somewhat of an expert.

"It took Bob and his wife, who was expecting a child, several weeks to decide whether to accept the invitation to be part of the mission in an unpredictable environment after the horrors of a Japanese prison camp. But he accepted and, within a short time in Japan, he became overlord of the Japanese cotton textile industry, the world's largest.

"He found the job bewildering at first because of its enormity, the lack of knowledge of the language, and a general mistrust of any Japanese individual, mainly because of his experiences as a prisoner of war. But soon, he found some very helpful and insightful Japanese textile people who spoke English, and life got better for him. He began to learn about the true culture and the people of the country for the first time.

"His wife and son soon arrived to join him, and a daughter was born in Japan soon after. All of them found living in Japan extremely pleasurable. Every person they met was wonderful to them and went out of their way to assist them and make them feel comfortable and at home. He never mentioned to anyone he had been a POW, although he supposed some of them already knew.

"After working his government job for one and a half years, because he was well thought of in his field, he was asked to join a prestigious Japanese textile company, which offer he accepted. He spent the next ten years working for the company. During the many years he and his family spent living in Japan, he told me he found the Japanese culture, the country's history, and all of the Japanese people he met, fascinating, and he grew extremely fond of anything Japanese. He even learned to speak Japanese a little.

"Based on his experience, he explained to me, he believed the view he had gained of Japan from the brutal treatment by the Japanese guards in the Philippines was like looking through the wrong end of a telescope. Doing it didn't give you a broad view of things, thus giving you a wrong perspective of a culture's true nature. He laughed when he said to me it took him a lifetime of living in Japan to learn the truth about people of a different country.

"A few years ago, I visited the Trinity Site north of here in Socorro County. I had never been there in all the years since the first atomic bomb explosion took place there. As all of you know, it was this country's success in developing the atomic bomb that made possible the surrender of the Japanese and ending the war in the Pacific.

"During my visit to the site, I saw a group of young Asian men there. They weren't a part of our tour group. I later learned the group were scientists and technicians from Japan who were visiting this facility, White Sands Missile Range, as a part of an exchange program between the United

States and Japan to share in scientific developments in each country. While participating in the program at this facility, the group showed an interest in visiting the Trinity Site, thus explaining their presence the day I, too, was visiting the site.

"The group was there for only about fifteen to twenty minutes, but I saw at one point all of the men took several minutes to bow and chant, as if in prayer and in a show of respect, while standing before the monument erected at "Ground Zero," the precise center of the world's first atomic blast. The blast was a precursor to the two atomic bombs, dropped three days apart some three weeks later, that would annihilate from the face of the earth the cities of Hiroshima and Nagasaki in Japan and most of their citizens.

"I soon learned after my visit to the site that the Hiroshima and Nagasaki bombings have had a profound effect on the people of Japan to this day. Today, the Japanese are strong pacifists. In fact, under Article Nine of the Japanese constitution, the government is prohibited from declaring war, though Japan can maintain a military force for self-defense.

"I had learned, before my visiting the Trinity Site, that for hundreds and even thousands of years, Asian culture has held firm to a strong spiritual discipline in their dealings among themselves and others.

"I wasn't surprised to be moved by this small group of Japanese visitors to our country reflecting on the horrors of war at a place that to them was hallowed ground, knowing the seed giving rise to the bombs dropped at Hiroshima and Nagasaki germinated at this site where they chanted and prayed in reverence.

"I think what I witnessed that day at the Trinity Site is relevant to what I speak to you about my change of feelings toward the Japanese. I've heard it said that with knowledge comes wisdom. What I witnessed at the Trinity Site gave strength to my belief all races and cultures have good and bad aspects of people. The Japanese people are no different. In the Philippines, I got to know the bad under the horrific conditions of war. At the Trinity Site, I got to see the good.

"I think I've answered the question of how I feel about the Japanese. I need say no more, I believe, for you to see clearly the complexity of trying to answer the question I posed with one simple answer.

"Having said what I've said, having bared my soul to you, so to speak,

I must add, in all honesty, that although I've forgiven, I haven't been able to forget. I still have an occasional nightmare. And the flashbacks of reliving the ordeals, they, too, come and go. The handling of that, however, I've turned over to God. I've prayed He give me the strength to deal with *my* issues, *my* problem, without putting blame on anyone else, no matter the past.

"For all the years since my captivity, I've prayed no one ever again, in any culture, in any part of the world, will ever have to see or experience anything resembling in the slightest what we on this stage witnessed and suffered back in Bataan so many years ago."

He turned around to the honorees on stage and smiled at them. "These men up here with me are my buddies, my fellow soldiers, *mi compadres*, with the strongest of bonds between us that no one will ever tear asunder."

§

Mick and his daughter crossed San Augustin Pass, heading back home. The rest of the afternoon had passed with other appearances by the honorees, now numbering 17, with the addition of Skip Rawlings, and Mick was exhausted at the end of the day. So was Lilia, for it had been a long day for her too.

As they passed through the village of Organ, which was just west of the pass, they could see the twinkling lights of Las Cruces, which appeared together with the tiny clusters of miniature buildings below the mesa to the west and the broader western horizon. Despite the coming darkness of the evening, the greenery of the valley and farms surrounding the city was still visible.

What had been a vivid blue sky above earlier in the day had darkened by now, as the sun had set, its rays of light hidden by the large cobalt clouds now filling the western sky, stretching from north to south, after a cloudless morning. In contrast to the darkish blue sky above, the western sky beyond the western horizon had turned a brilliant orange from the late rays of the sun, turning the edges of the cumulus clouds hiding the sunlight a picturesque red, highlighted by a thin, yellow rim bordering the edges.

They travelled in silence for a good while, each one with their own thoughts. Finally, Lilia broke the silence.

"I'm glad you asked me to bring you this time, Dad. I enjoyed coming and meeting some of the ones I didn't already know, including your friend, Skip, who surprised you coming all the way from South Carolina."

Mick smiled. "Yes, my godson. It was so strange, seeing him again. I'm glad you mentioned him. I was beginning to think it was all a dream, my seeing him after all these years."

"And thinking he was dead, no less. He was telling me all about how you two met and about how you helped him become a Catholic."

Mick laughed. "All I did was introduce him to the priest."

"No, according to him, you were quite an inspiration to him, so much so he wanted to share your faith. He thinks highly of you, Dad. As usual, you're being too modest."

"Well, maybe I nudged him along, once I found out he was thinking of converting."

"And to think he's kept the drawing you did of him and his wife back in the Philippines and now is returning to you. That's wild!" She grinned.

"Isn't it?"

"He showed it to me after the program was over, when he went to the van bringing him to Cruces. It's a little rough around the edges, but the sketching still shows well. You've got such a talent, Dad. You should return to doing it. It'll give you something to do."

He frowned. "At my age. I've got plenty to do. What with you and your grown kids. And your aunt Elena's family. All of you keep me busy." He paused and smiled. "And happy. I've got all I need."

"That makes me happy," she said, returning the smile. "He told me you two have plans to visit while he's in Cruces."

"Yeah, he's staying at a bed and breakfast near Mesilla. He took the drawing with him for safekeeping. He'll give it to me there, he said. And he wants me to take him to some Mexican Food restaurants."

"You know a few of those." She laughed. "I'm so happy you'll get to visit some more with him."

"Me too. It'll probably be the last time I see him."

"Maybe not. You can make plans to fly to South Carolina."

He shrugged. "Well, we'll see."

"And your mention today of that Japanese captain you became friends with. What was his name?"

"Hinata Takahashi."

"Yes, Captain Takahashi. The circumstances under which the two of you became friends is a story all its own. A person could write a book about it."

Mick laughed. "I'm too old to be writing a book."

"I didn't mean you should. It was just an expression to point out the importance of something like that."

"Oh, okay. You write the book, then."

They both laughed.

After a long pause, Lilia spoke. "I'm glad I made the trip for another reason, Dad."

He wrinkled his brow. "Oh. What's that?"

"I was deeply moved by what you said. Not only about Captain Takahashi, but overall, the other things you touched on when you spoke to the crowd. You seemed to be in deep thought as you spoke that you may not have noticed I shed some tears as you were speaking. You touched my heart, Dad."

"You've heard me talk about my experiences during the war before."

"Not in the way you expressed yourself today, Dad. You often spoke about it among family with little emotion. I think it has to do with your being afraid to show how deeply affected you were by your experience. It was always as if you were keeping your distance from what you were telling us."

She took a deep breath. "You always gave me the impression before as if you were talking about someone else. Not you. Today, I heard a different Mick Duran telling the story. Your story. Not somebody else's."

He turned to her with a puzzled look. And then he frowned, and suddenly, he appeared saddened.

Neither of them said anything for a moment. They had come to the outskirts of the city, and Lilia slowed down as they approached the north side of Main Street. Their home was on the south part of town, known as Mesilla Park, and so they would have to go through the heart of the city. Lilia stopped at a traffic light.

Mick turned and gave her a deep stare.

"I think I owe you an apology, Lilia."

"Why do you say that. I don't think you need to apologize. I hope you don't think I gave you that impression."

"No, it wasn't anything you said. It's me I'm talking about."

"What do you mean?"

"Just from what little you've said since the pass, you've made me realize no matter how much I've thought all through these years I've managed to finally get beyond all of this, I didn't do a good job with myself and more importantly, with you, my family, of expressing my true feelings. I think I accomplished doing that with your mother, before she died. But I seem to have stopped there, thinking it was what was important. I never included you in, and for that, I'm truly sorry."

The light turned, and Lilia accelerated with the traffic.

"I've never felt excluded, Dad. Nor do I think the others feel they were. I didn't mean to suggest that."

"I know, I know. I'm not saying you did. What I'm trying to say is you've opened my eyes. When you said whenever we talked in the past about my years in imprisonment, I seemed to be telling someone else's story, it opened my eyes to the fact I've been shielding myself. Protecting myself."

"From what?"

"From the truth. I'm too old to get professional help about this, but I'm convinced I need to spend some time thinking about this." He met her stare. "Will you help me try to do this, Lilia?"

"I'll do anything you think might help, Dad. What can I do?"

"Just listen. I want a chance to talk to you and Tomas. And to your children and to your Aunt Elena's children. They're old enough, and we can include them. As much as we've spoken about my years in the war, I've come to the conclusion I've left my family out of my life, so to speak, at least from the war part, by not having deep and honest talks about my experiences and what happened to me. I owe all of you that much." They stopped at another light. "Will you help me do it?"

"Of course, I will, Dad. She smiled at him. "When do we start?"

He grinned. "I believe we've already started. We'll continue with this conversation after Skip and I finish with our visit. I'm looking forward to my working this out, with your help."

"I am, too, Dad. I love you."

"I love you."

Mick reflected on what Lilia had told him on the way home. All these years, he had thought he had come clean, when it came to his family, of being honest about his feelings, not just the events, when he spoke of the war. And now, after listening to his daughter for only a few minutes, he had discovered he had been untruthful to himself and to them.

It had taken Bob Follett a lifetime of living in Japan, he had said, to learn the truth about the Japanese culture. And it had taken Mick Duran a lifetime, to learn something about himself and his family. Obviously, he hadn't done as good a job as he thought he had.

He didn't know how much time he had left to correct things. He owed Lilia and the rest of the family, including his friends, the right to know everything about his war experiences, good or bad, including his being able to speak to them not as if he was relating someone else's story, but his own. And this included explaining his feelings. He owed them that much, and he vowed he'd make every effort in the days to come to do it.

For the first time in his life since his experiences as a prisoner of war in the Pacific, he had trust in himself he'd succeed in those efforts.

Of one thing he was certain. The memory of it all remained, deeply etched both in his heart and soul, yet faintly shrouded by shadows to lessen the pain of being forced to relive past events best forgotten.

AFTERWORD

Following World War II, numerous war crimes trials were held against the Japanese military for atrocities committed during their occupation of the Philippines, particularly concerning the inhumane treatment of Prisoners of War (POWs). These trials aimed to deliver justice for the severe suffering inflicted upon Allied and Filipino POWs and Filipino civilians.

The criminal charges were founded essentially on two premises. First, the allegations against the defendants standing trial that Japanese forces were responsible for widespread abuse, torture, murder, and starvation of POWs in the Philippines, including the Bataan Death March. Second, the death rate for POWs in the Pacific theater (27%) was significantly higher than in Europe (4%), highlighting the severity of the conditions of the POWs under imprisonment by the Japanese.

Prosecutions were held by both an international military tribunal and twos national tribunals. The courts in both venues tried many defendants.

In Tokyo, the International Military Tribunal for the Far East, known as the IMTFE, held trials focusing on high-ranking leaders of the Imperial Japanese Army accused of severe abuse and mistreatment of POWs. In the Philippines, many "Class B" and "Class C" war criminals, including those directly involved in POW abuse and mistreatment, were tried by national tribunals.

These national tribunals and the trials conducted by them consisted of the following two independent courts:

The newly independent Republic of the Philippines conducted 73 trials between 1947 and 1949 against 155 members of the Imperial Japanese Army and Navy.

The United States Army also conducted trials in Manila from 1945 to 1947, prosecuting approximately 200 Japanese military personnel for crimes against United States POWs and Filipino non-combatants.

Here are some of the outcomes on three notable cases:

General Tomoyuki Yamashita, Commander of Japanese forces in the Philippines, was tried in Manila and convicted under the doctrine of "command responsibility" for failing to prevent atrocities committed by his troops, even though there was no direct evidence he ordered them. He was executed in 1946. His case was highly controversial and set a significant precedent in international law regarding a commander's duty to control his subordinates.

Lieutenant General Masaharu Homma, Commander of the invasion of the Philippines and responsible for the Bataan Death March, was also tried in Manila. He accepted moral responsibility as commander but maintained he had no knowledge of the atrocities until after they occurred. He was convicted for the actions of his troops and executed by firing squad in 1946.

Captain Yoshio Tsuneyoshi, otherwise known as "Baggy Pants" in this novel, was tried in Yokohama, Japan, by a military commission appointed by the Eighth Army, United States Army, in a trial held from November 10 through November 21, 1947. He was convicted of numerous charges, one under Specification 3, "permitting and sanctioning atrocities," and sentenced on November 21, 1947 to life imprisonment. On review, the convictions and sentence were upheld by the Staff Advocate's office, stating that "the offenses in Specification 3 alone warrant the sentence adjudged."

In his defense, Captain Tsuneyoshi contended that Camp O'Donnell was never intended to receive 60,000 prisoners and "that when that number was sent, all facilities were overcrowded and inadequate." The defendant further alleged that General Homma, not he, was responsible for the overcrowded conditions.

In reviewing the sentence, the Staff Judge Advocate concluded that "any sentence less than life imprisonment ... would be ineffectual and without benefit to the accused." The reviewing officer further stated that General Homma and two other officers, superiors of the accused, received death sentences, and that "[p]resumably, [the] commission gave due consideration to the theory of 'superior orders' and the higher responsibility for inadequacies in the camp facilities and supplies in sentencing this accused to a lesser punishment."

Overall, the trials conducted by the Republic of the Philippines resulted in the convictions of 138 out of 155 defendants, with 79 receiving death sentences. The United States Army trials in Manila saw a high conviction rate, with 90% of defendants found guilty and 67 executions carried out by American authorities. These trials were crucial for the Philippines in seeking justice and asserting its sovereignty as a newly independent nation.

Two legal precedents evolved from these criminal trials. The first one arose from what was known as the superior orders defense. Japanese defendants often attempted to argue they were simply following superior orders, but this defense was largely unsuccessful. These trials contributed to the understanding of individual accountability in international law, even when acting under orders.

The second precedent arising from the trials evolved from the theory known as command responsibility: The trials, particularly General Yamashita's trial, reinforced the principle of command responsibility, holding commanders accountable for the actions of their subordinates if they failed to prevent or punish war crimes.

The trials left a significant legacy in the development of international criminal law. First, in defining war crimes and establishing principles of individual and command responsibility. Second, although they faced criticism, particularly as "victors' justice," the trials in the Philippines and elsewhere in the Pacific played a vital role in documenting the horrific abuses committed during the war and holding perpetrators accountable. They served as foundational precedents for future international tribunals.

Moving forward to present day, August 15, 2025, marked the 80th anniversary of Japan's unconditional surrender to the Allied Powers in 1945. On that day, Japan paid tribute to more than three million war dead, as concerns grew of rapidly fading memories of the war's tragedy and the bitter lessons from the era of Japanese militarism. In a national ceremony held in Tokyo, 4,500 officials and bereaved families and their descendants observed a moment of silence at noon, the time when Emperor Hirohito's surrender speech began on August 5, 1945, the date of Japan's surrender.

At the same time as this ceremony was taking place, however, just a block away, at the Yasukuni Shrine, dozens of Japanese rightwing politicians and their supporters gathered in prayer. The shrine honors Japan's 2.5 million war dead, including convicted war criminals. Japanese emperors have stopped visiting the Yasukuni Shrine since enshrinement of top war criminals there in 1978. Victims of Japanese aggression in the past, especially China and the two Koreas, view visits to the shrine as a lack of remorse of Japan's wartime past.

At the ceremony commemorating the surrender, Japan's Prime Minister, Shigeru Ishiba, who stayed away from the controversial shrine but sent a religious ornament as a personal gesture instead of praying at the shrine, in his speech vowed to pass his pledge of peace to future generations and called the war a mistake. Yet, he made no mention of Japan's aggression across Asia or expressly apologize.

But he did say, "We will never repeat the tragedy of the war. We will never go the wrong way. Once again, we must deeply keep to our hearts the remorse and lesson from that war."

ABOUT THE AUTHOR

RUDY APODACA, a native of New Mexico, lives with his wife, Nancy, in Austin, Texas. A graduate of New Mexico State University, with a Bachelor of Science degree in mathematics, and of Georgetown University's law school, with a Juris Doctorate degree, he began his career as a trial attorney, practicing for twenty-two years before serving as a judge on the New Mexico Court of Appeals for almost fourteen years, over two as Chief Judge.

He's the author of four previous novels, *The Waxen Image*, *Pursuit*, *A Rare Thing*, and *When the Angels Came*, and many essays, most of which were published as commentaries in daily newspapers, the *Austin American-Statesman*, the *San Antonio Express-News*, and the *Houston Chronicle*.